BELIEVE IN ME

EVA SEYLER

Library of Congress Control Number:
2024923542

Typeset in Cormorant and Quintessential

E-Book ISBN: 979-8-9880877-5-5
Paperback ISBN: 979-8-9880877-6-2
Audiobook ISBN: 979-8-9880877-7-9

To the #MeToo crowd:

I believe in you.

George

*T*here is nothing quite as surreal as becoming a bachelor father at eighteen.

Especially when said bachelor father happens to be in the midst of his second year at a reputable seminary, the faculty of which would be far from impressed to discover one of their star pupils has an apparent morality problem.

It was me, the star pupil and the bachelor father. But I would like one point to be very clear from the start.

I did not have a morality problem.

You, Miss Fizzytwigs, were abandoned on the doorstep of my mother's boarding house one summer morning in 1933. Your birth certificate, tucked into the cardboard box in which you were left, announced you as Hazel Mae, but I can taste words, and Hazel Mae tastes like twigs dipped in shaken-up Coca-Cola.

I'm sorry I can't offer a less pathetic explanation for why I've called you Fizz for the last thirty-odd years.

That birth certificate also listed me as your father, and... I am that.

You asked me for the story, and the only way I can properly tell it to you is to write it out. I think you will understand why this is the better way.

PART ONE

Then she made offers again, and said, If I would be ruled by her, she would make me great and happy, for, said she, I am the Mistress of the World, and men are made happy by me. Then I asked her name, and she told me it was Madam Bubble.

JOHN BUNYAN,
"PILGRIM'S PROGRESS"

George

*L*ouise and I were at an age when anyone over the age of twenty-five felt obligated to enquire about our plans for the future.

That is, they'd ask *me*.

But Louise, who refused to be brushed aside as someone who needn't bother with plans because she was "just a girl", always answered first. She'd launch into a long, articulate exposition about her brand-new commercial pilot's license and how she was teaching her first pupil of, she hoped, many, so she could save up enough to buy her own plane. That goal accomplished, she would get married and have six children (whilst still flying planes).

To this the enquirers invariably responded with an instant of dumbfounded silence, followed by, "Goodness me, however will you manage?"

"I can manage anything," she would reply, coolly. And it was true; she could. Anyone who saw her caring for a zooful of small humans on a Saturday so their frazzled parents could breathe for a few hours, or corralling other energetic small humans in her Sunday school class, would ever doubt her capabilities. Children adored Louise, and she adored them right back. No amount of chaos could faze her. She thrived on chaos the way I thrived on the exact opposite.

Then the enquirers would turn back to me and ask the question again. I'd switch on my polished orator's voice and explain that I was starting seminary studies in January, because I had been working hard to graduate high school early, and they'd look from me to Louise as if thinking, *And how are these two futures going to mesh, exactly?*

People always assumed that, because we were inseparable, we

were an item. We weren't.

My dreams were lofty and a tad vague, to be sure, but one doesn't bother much with practicality when one is sixteen-almost-seventeen.

(Unless one was Louise.)

At any rate, I spoke well and knew it, and had immersed myself in Hebrew study for nearly seven years already. I was sure crowds of thousands would someday gather to hear the Reverend George Graham, famed expositor of Scripture.

"You're awfully full of yourself," was all Louise had to say on the subject. She was not graduating early, because she was quite content to finish high school at the usual time. Her voice had a calculated sweetness in it that, in the earliest days of our friendship, might have earned her a bucket of water over her unsuspecting head.

I suppose I, like many other men, didn't like to admit The Woman Was Right.

Louise had two overarching obsessions. One was her love affair with flight, which began at age ten when we saw a film called *The Air Mail*. After that day, any aviation-related news got clipped from the papers and lovingly pasted into scrapbooks, to be read and re-read. It didn't matter to her that so many of them were about accidents and deaths. She said, "Each one teaches me a new thing not to do."

When Charles Lindbergh crossed the Atlantic in 1927, it sent Louise into a fever of delight and ecstasy. One scrapbook and half of another were specifically devoted to him (and his wife, who flew with him and was therefore even more thrilling to Louise).

Louise even named my dog—*my* dog, mind—Lindbergh.

The second obsession was my uncle Jamie, Dad's twin brother, who was an impossible standard for her future husband to live up to. Obviously she couldn't marry him, and she'd already met, analyzed, and dismissed his five sons from the running as Already Taken, A Literal Fossil, Undependably Volatile, Too Young, and Definitely Too Young.

To be fair, I also loved Uncle Jamie, despite some rather intense theological differences between us. He meant the world to me. But my father was alive and present; Louise's wasn't. So I knew Uncle Jamie met a specific need for her—and she wasn't at all subtle about her determination to marry someone just like him.

The problem was, nobody else could ever be anything close to Uncle Jamie.

There were other things Louise loved, too. Good food. Making impossibly delicate lacy handwork. Pretty clothes. Dancing.

We'd taken ballet lessons intensively for two years, starting in the spring of 1927, with Tabitha Wisniewski, a former principal dancer from Poland. Then I spent several months of 1928 in London courtesy of Uncle Jamie, living at his London flat with my half-sister Beatrice and being put through my paces by an incredibly exacting Russian balletmaster who'd emigrated to London. Afterwards, I came back to Mrs. Tabitha, and Louise and I had done performances in both Salem and Portland with a new company from California.

But when the crash came in 1929, our lessons came to an end. Louise had progressed as far as she cared to with ballet proper (she was adamantly uninterested in pointe), but I was not ready to give it up. There is something about the precision of the art that makes it the kind of challenge I adore.

Fortunately Mrs. Tabitha and her two daughters Olivia and Natalia became the first official boarders at my mother's boarding house. As part of their rent she kept working with me, and Olivia, who had continued to pointe, became my partner for ballet performances. But Louise kept in trim in her own way, and she and I had developed our own brand of what she called "ballet-influenced ballroom dancing".

This was all, of course, frowned upon by the portion of our Presbyterian church family Louise had dubbed the Mrs. Myrtle Morgan Mob. Every church seems to have such a cadre of shrewish, disagreeable old ladies, and Mrs. Morgan (a deacon's wife) was the dominant one at our church. She was scandalized that an aspiring minister and a current Sunday school teacher should condescend to engage in such debauchery as dancing and said so.

Loudly.

And often.

I didn't much mind. I'd have been in her bad books even without the dancing for several reasons. Let me list them.

1. Having heathen parents who didn't attend church.

2. One of these parents being Jewish.

3. Not trying harder to make said Jewish parent Christian instead.

4. Still "stubbornly" identifying as Jewish myself despite my choice to follow Jesus, and doing "all those Jewish things" like the holy days and Shabbat and not eating pig.

5. Being the baby half-brother of the aforementioned successful and therefore surely dissolute English actress Bea Graham. (The entire town knew of her because in 1929 she'd come to California to be in a talkie production of a recent New York stage performance that had been a huge hit, then toured a whole string of theaters along the west coast, including our own Elsinore Theatre. She stayed with us a couple of nights, and her picture had been in the paper.)

Of course, I'd have been thrilled to have my parents go to church with me, but in my family the principal tenet we all followed was mutual respect for one another's beliefs (or lack thereof, in my father's case). In my opinion, personal choice and not coercion was the only way any faith could stick and have meaning.

But I was talking about dancing.

When I wasn't studying and Louise wasn't flying, and Olivia did not require me for a performance somewhere, you could dependably find Louise and me dancing. We had spent most of the summers of 1930 and '31 as street performers in both Salem and Portland. Anywhere there was an open space and a steady stream of passersby became our stage, and we'd come home with a hatful of small change. It added up to quite a lot, always more than covering our train fare. We split the difference into our banks: mine a Mason jar with a chipped rim, hers a sock whose mate had been lost.

Of course our school and other Salem organizations often called on us as well, when planning programs and fundraisers. The attention was flattering, even if neither of us planned to make a career of it, and the stuff we danced to was "not exactly Music", according to Uncle Jamie, who preferred Handel and hymns.

"*I* think he doesn't mind modern music nearly as much as he pretends to mind it," Louise said, dropping on a record of her favorite song from *Show Boat.* "He just likes to razz everyone."

LOUISE

SALEM, OREGON: SEPTEMBER 17, 1931

*T*oday was my birthday, and George and I converged paths on our bicycle rides home—from downtown and the airfield, respectively. George's four-year-old fox terrier Lindbergh barked a greeting at me from his spot in the wire basket fixed to his master's bicycle.

"Happy birthday!" George called.

"My house or yours?" I called back.

"Yours."

I charged off. He raced after me, past his house and down a few blocks, until we swerved around a corner to dump our bikes in the dried-out front garden grass of my place. George scooped up Lindbergh and followed me into the house.

My house was always quiet and cool, unlike the boarding house chaos of George's. I lived alone with my mother, a concert pianist who taught all of the brightest young musicians in Salem.

(Mother was naturally timid; I was not. I'd been working hard finding places for her to give recitals here in Oregon, and occasionally even gigs with the symphony orchestra in Portland, one of which landed her a proper agent. Enid Baxter helped her publish several songs of her own composition and was working on getting her name out there. My mother had once dreamed of traveling the world performing. She should do exactly that, and I believed she would, with Miss Baxter's help.)

We went up to my room, where I kicked off my shoes, tossed my helmet and leather flying coat to a nearby chair, and flopped back onto my bed. Lacing my fingers together under my head, I grinned at George. "Okay, you can show me whatever is in your pocket now."

"How'd you—oh, never mind." He put Lindbergh onto the floor. The dog jumped onto the sunny windowsill to watch squirrels, and George fished out a little box from his pocket and held it out to me.

"It's so tiny!" I squealed, inspecting with delight the perfectly miniature wrappings and bow (he knew how much I loved tiny things) before carefully extracting what was inside so as not to destroy said wrappings or bow.

George said, "It's not the airplane you want, but until you get that one—"

I set the wrappings on my nightstand and flipped up the lid, bouncing as I lifted out a silver chain bracelet with a *Spirit of St. Louis* charm hanging from it. It caught the afternoon light, twinkling like a star. I held out my arm and he sat beside me to fasten it on. A good many links dangled free once he got it fitted around my wrist.

"I can take the extras off," he offered, but I shook my head.

"I like it this way. The dangly bit is just that much more sparkle."

He leant back against my headboard and I sat beside him. He often said my room was a pleasant place, which surprised me, because it was cluttered in comparison with his own. Pinned all over my walls were photographs of aviators, and dancers like the Astaires and the Castles, and fashion plates I saved from magazines. Lindbergh (the real one, not the dog one) was well-represented too, in the form of a bank in the shape of his head, his book *We*, a model of the *Spirit of St. Louis* hanging from my ceiling, and George's own silly drawing of

14

me lying on its wing so I could kiss him on the cheek (Lindbergh, not George). (George doesn't do kissing. I've been waiting for years for him to decide he does.)

As we sat there he slid down until his head was on my pillow, his eyes closed behind the lenses of his round wire-rimmed glasses. I watched him a while, dreaming about putting my hand on his chest and leaning down to kiss him. He was so good-looking, and I wished that my lying here beside him would awaken some sleeping passion in him. But after all these years, I knew there was no point in such wishing, and although nothing hurt more than the George-shaped ache in my heart, I refused to take what he hadn't offered first.

So I said, "It's very appropriate, really, considering the Lindberghs were in the paper today."

I watched his face as he struggled to connect my statement to anything. I wasn't sure he realized I was referring to the bracelet. He didn't open his eyes, even when he finally spoke: a carefully chosen comment. "They're always in the paper."

"Not every day. Anyway, they left Japan for China! It's new news!"

"But they're not flying the *Spirit of St. Louis*," he pointed out.

Ah, so he had connected the dots.

"Doesn't matter, Mr. Literal," I said. "Can't you extrapolate?"

"I'm a minister, not a mathematician," he said.

"Not yet," I reminded him.

"Apprentice ministry counts," he said.

I decided not to engage. I knew he would just remind me he'd applied for a license to preach and he didn't have to be ordained to get started.

So I said, "Anyway, I have news." He waited, still not opening his eyes, and I slipped my arm through his and rested my head on his shoulder. "There's a dance competition on New Year's Eve and I've signed us up for it."

"What night of the week is that?"

"It's not Friday. I checked." He'd become very dedicated to Keeping Shabbat ever since he came back from his ballet stint in London several years ago.

"That's fine then," he said.

"It's sponsored by several businesses and local bigwigs. People are coming from all over to compete. Portland, even. The first prize is $50 and we are going to win it."

"We are, are we?" He opened his eyes at last.

"Yes. Now, what shall it be? Waltz, tango, or foxtrot?"

He considered. "Waltz. Everyone does the foxtrot."

"Not many people do tango."

I was baiting him. He knew it. "Tango might seem a bit... racy."

(George does pick the oddest things to be prudish about.)

I laughed. "Only to you and maybe Mrs. Myrtle Morgan. Anyway, we'll need panache to help us win, which means you need a proper tuxedo."

He groaned. "You seriously expect me to be seen in public in a *penguin suit*?"

"Oh, please," I said. "You wear *tights* without a second thought—how in the world are tights higher on your 'publicly acceptable' list than a tuxedo?"

He ignored the question, his face smugly satisfied as he had a fresh idea. "You don't have anything nearly that formal yourself."

"Oh, but I will. Your mother's agreed to make me a dress. Already spoke to her today before I ran into you. As for you, Director's is having a sale tomorrow. It'll be my treat."

He gave me A Look, and I punched his arm lightly. "Come now, you don't hate shopping *that* much."

He let out a melodramatic sigh. "Happy birthday," he said drily. "A shopping trip is the gift I would rather not have given you."

"Stop grousing," I said. "And now I want to change, so scram."

If George was like ordinary boys, he would have tried to coax me into letting him watch, but he is not like ordinary boys, and immediately left the room to wait downstairs.

Lindbergh stayed with me as I stripped out of my oil-smudged things. For a moment I stood in front of my mirror.

I had a figure, of a sort, but George never seemed to notice it, and I didn't want any other boys to, so I generally stuck to no-nonsense skirts and cardigans which concealed it. But the dress Mrs. Graham

16

had agreed to make me would to be a bold move on my part, to *make* him notice me. I cupped my breasts in my hands—small, but nice enough, I thought. I closed my eyes and imagined it was George's hands holding them, that he was pressed up to my back now, his lips brushing my cheek. It hurt, desire did, and my desire for George was intense.

I'd been in love with him since we were twelve, knew I wanted to marry him, but it was a couple of years before I understood what actual desire felt like. (I suppose the theological word would be lust, but I think of lust as a bad desire, the kind that burns out fast and hurts forever after. What I feel for George is pure and unbreakable and will last until the day I die.)

It was when he came back from England. He left a boy and came back a man. Well, his face was (and is) still very boyish, but he'd gotten much taller and his voice had dropped into a resonant bass that didn't sound like it should come out of that face. He was my same George, but also not. There was an aura of discipline and determination about him, more intense than ever before. It was in the way he moved as much as the way he stood still, and in every word he spoke. He seemed to have settled many of his faith-related dilemmas too, adding to the peaceful resoluteness.

But it was his hands my eyes had locked onto. They'd always been nice hands, but the sight of them made my heart seize up and my face grow hot. I'd wanted them on me, wanted him to whisper lovely words in his new voice while he did things to me with those hands. *Breathe, Louise*, I'd reminded myself as I began to feel light-headed.

I felt light-headed again now. But George's voice from downstairs tore me out of my reverie.

"What's taking you so long?"

Flushing, I tossed on my clean clothes and scooped up Lindbergh, running downstairs with him.

"Your mother promised me a birthday cake," I said. "So let's be off to your place."

"What about *your* mother?" George asked as I deposited his dog into his basket and propped my own bike up against the side of my house.

"She's at a recital with her students. She'll meet us at yours when she's done."

George walked his bike along the sidewalk until we reached his house, and we used the back entrance that led directly into what I'd named the Inner Sanctum—the area only family was allowed in, now that the Grahams had boarders. It consisted of the kitchen, the nook where they took their own meals, and a bed-sitting room where Mr. and Mrs. Graham spent their leisure hours. After the boarders had been served dinner, the Grahams (and often Mother and me, as tonight) settled in for a long evening of our own share of dinner, with a side of chocolate cake, while I reminded everyone that now I was incontestably older and wiser than George was.

"I'll join your lofty, elderly wisdom in three months," he said, helping himself to his third slice of cake. "In the meantime, tell me what ideas you have in mind for this dance."

He didn't need any encouragement from me. George has a melodramatic streak a mile wide, and he is not self-conscious of his dancing or who might see him. Mr. Graham asks him to cut the grass? He piqué battus back and forth until the job's done. Waiting to cross the street coming back from the library? Pirouettes to pass the time. Sweeping the floor for his mother? The broom becomes a stand-in for me. He just never stops.

It's not surprising that Mrs. Myrtle Morgan has such a vendetta against him, since she doesn't understand he can't *not* dance.

GEORGE

SALEM, OREGON: SEPTEMBER 18, 1931

*A*t the store the next day, Louise led me around, making me try on more clothes than all six of my Scottish cousins probably owned combined. Shirts and vests, trousers and jackets, gloves and cufflinks, most of which did not seem actually relevant to the end goal of Dance Outfit. "Am I a doll to you?" I complained. "We came to find me a penguin suit, and we've already found all the pieces of that."

"It's fun to hear you moan. And we've not found all the pieces, because here are the bowties."

"I can't tie those."

"You can't tie any ties. Or shoelaces, helpless man. We'll take one white and one black," she said to the saleslady. "All right, now we are done. Let's go have lunch."

Lunch was a prospect guaranteed to un-grump my mood, and then we went to the high school gymnasium to practice our dances for the upcoming state fair.

During the musical programs at seven to eight o'clock each evening, we'd been slated to dance along with the high school band, and tonight was our final rehearsal with the musicians. It would be the same program every night, which made it easier on us all. We'd picked our favorite routines that would correspond to the band's selections. (Our picture would end up in the paper after one of the performances.)

We got home and had mere minutes to prepare ourselves before Mamma was shouting to us that it was candle-lighting time.

I liked Friday evening dinner. It was comforting and peaceful and a perfect way to slow down and enjoy being together. Mamma didn't keep Shabbat in any meaningful sense herself otherwise; she shopped and worked as usual. Quite honestly I think she did Friday nights for me more than for herself. I took it very seriously, and spent the day in my attic fully absorbed in study or prayer.

I did not, however, object to dancing on Shabbat, as long as we were doing it for fun and not money, and that is what Louise and I did after we finished our dinner.

Dad settled at the table with papers from work. Mamma began the night's dishwashing with the help of Mrs. Pearson, and Louise sat to put on her dancing slippers.

"Do you like dancing in slippers?" Dad asked her, not looking up.

"Love it," she said.

"I wasn't sure if you just did it to be nice to George."

I scowled. My vanity was severely injured by the fact that, no matter how hard I wished it, I'd never been able to get taller than Louise.

"Wonder if you've caught her up yet," Dad said. He came to push

us together, back to back, inspecting us closely from all angles, laying a book across our heads, then calling to Mamma. "Have we a spirit level, Alice?"

Her response was unprintable. Louise giggled uncontrollably, and my eyes rolled up so far into my head it's a wonder they aren't stuck there still. Finally Dad pronounced his verdict. "They're even. What is it, Louise? Five foot six?"

"It is indeed," she said, turning to pat my head as if I was Lindbergh.

Dad sat back in his chair, musing, "It is funny how you've ended up such a shrimp."

"Dad!" I moaned, blushing to the roots of my hair.

"George, stop insulting him!" Mamma's voice came floating over from the kitchen. "He can't help how tall he gets!"

"Or doesn't get," Dad countered softly.

"I heard that!"

"I could grow a moustache," I said. "Maybe then people would take me seriously."

"Can you?" Louise asked skeptically.

Dad laughed again. "Your uncle Jamie was shaving every day by the time he was fifteen."

Mamma's voice from the kitchen again. "Goodness sake, George, you are almost fifty-two and still can't grow a decent beard yourself!"

"Not as if you'd let me!"

"That's beside the point! Leave your son in peace!"

I huffed. If all everyone was going to do was find my unmanliness uproariously funny, I'd go to my room and engage in some light reading. *Expository Thoughts on the Gospel of St Luke*, perhaps.

Louise, who had been winding the gramophone, dropped a record on and took my hand, and I automatically fell into step with her. Dad went to the kitchen to make a nuisance of himself in there.

"I don't know if girls will want to kiss you with a 'stache, George," Louise said.

"As if girls are queueing to kiss me now," I said sarcastically. "I'm a small bespectacled shrimp boy. Anyway, I haven't time for such nonsense, I'm busy." *And no inclination*, I added internally. *Yuck.*

Louise hummed along to the music for a while. "It doesn't matter," she said at last. "I like you just the way you are, small bespectacled shrimp boy."

GEORGE

SALEM, OREGON: DECEMBER 1, 1931

*I*t was pouring rain and growing dark, and Mrs. Pearson had sent me in their car to the airfield to collect Louise and bring her home. We both knew she'd ride her bicycle home if I didn't show up and pre-empt it, and her mother was worried about Louise catching her death.

Nobody was on the field when I arrived and parked near the pilots' clubhouse. The lights were on inside, so I turned up my collar and sloshed my way through the muddy puddles to let myself in.

It was unusually quiet inside, all the pilots huddled together around a central point at one of the tables. Louise, her face on her arms on the table, sobbed her heart out at that central point, and all the men looked somber.

Louise almost never cried, so I hurried over, instantly alarmed. "What happened?" I asked.

Louise looked up, her face a mess. "Keith," was all she could say, and buried her face again.

I looked to the others for an explanation, and Mr. Eyerly, Louise's instructor and boss, gave me a grim look. "We just got a call from the Roseburg airport," he said quietly. "Keith Smith is dead."

"Dead," I repeated. I dropped into a chair and looked at Eyerly. I knew who Keith was, of course. Louise had taken him on as her first student after getting her own license earlier in the year. I'd met him a few times. He was a nice lad.

"He only needed two more hours," another fellow put in. "He'd have had his license as soon as he got back here. Tomorrow, we'd figured, since this rain came in..."

"Tailspin," a third man said. "He went down and the plane crushed him underneath."

Of course Louise would blame herself for the boy's death. I went around the table and shook her gently. "Come on," I said. "Let's get you home." I helped her up and she let me guide her out to the car, where she slumped into the passenger seat. She didn't say a word the entire time I tied her bicycle onto the back and drove us back to her house.

When we entered, Mrs. Pearson looked panicked, no doubt assuming Louise herself had been injured. "She's not hurt," I assured her quickly. Louise dragged her helmet off her head and it dropped with a dull thunk to the hall table. "Come on," I said again, urging her up the stairs toward her bedroom, Mrs. Pearson following behind.

She dropped onto her bed, and Mrs. Pearson gave her a handkerchief. We sat on either side of Louise; Mrs. Pearson stroked her hair and I listened helplessly to her crying, at a loss what to do with this outburst of grief.

"I told him his plane was good to go! I checked it myself!" More sniffs. "They'll blame me for it. He was only sixteen—his poor mother—" She became incoherent again.

LOUISE

Mother held me closely long after George had gone home, until I'd quieted enough for her to offer me tea. I followed her listlessly to the kitchen table and neither of us said anything. I didn't want to talk anyway, so I didn't mind. I liked that Mother didn't chatter to fill silences. Probably it is the Swedish in her.

We drank our tea together and then I went upstairs.

December was usually a happy month, with Hanukkah and Christmas, but all of the anticipation I usually felt for these things had been sucked away by tonight's bad news.

Keith was only a little younger than George and me, and we are too young to die. It wasn't fair. I couldn't imagine my life ending right now, just as I was on the verge of adulthood.

I think I worried George, but when I said I didn't want to talk about Keith anymore, he did what he always does and dropped it, even if he wasn't satisfied that it didn't still need to be talked about.

On the twelfth, I took a long solo flight. I went to Roseburg. I did not go into a tailspin and die crushed under my plane.

GEORGE

SALEM, OREGON: NEW YEAR'S EVE, 1931

*T*he night of the competition, I went to meet Louise at her house so we could be at the Crystal Gardens in plenty of time. Our parents would be along later—mine as observers, Mrs. Pearson as pianist with the ensemble who would be providing music for all the competitors.

When I rang the bell, a formality I didn't usually bother with, Louise opened the door with a dramatic flourish, striking a pose as if she was a fashion model.

I stepped back in startlement. This was my first sight of the dress my mother had promised to make Louise. It was ice-blue and fit her as if it was part of her, drapey and capey and worthy of any Hollywood glamor queen. With her flawless makeup and perfectly finger-waved hair, she looked like a complete stranger—a bit like the portrait of Anna Q. Nilsson on her bedroom wall, in fact. Her earrings and the airplane bracelet caught the hall lights, and her impish eyes glinted. "When you've got your eyes back inside your head, come in and let me do your tie, since I see you're trying to get away without it."

I stepped inside. She closed the door and I fished the tie out of my pocket. She whipped it into a perfect bow in no time, and when she finished, she studied me, hands on my shoulders. "You look fine, Mr. Penguin."

"You look pretty swell too," I said, and meant it.

She shrugged on her coat and looped her arm through mine, and we set off. I felt incredibly lucky—and unworthy—to have a friend like Louise who liked spending her spare hours with me when she could have had her pick of friends from her vast pool of acquaintances. Me, despite my shortness and specs...

"I could grow a great big beard like John Knox," I said, apropos of nothing.

"Don't start off on that again," she said lightly, with a gentle punch to my arm from her satin-gloved fist. "You're fine as you are. Stop worrying about it. Anyway, you have such unfairly perfect skin, you really oughtn't hide it under some dreadful beard…"

I couldn't help laughing.

The Crystal Gardens buzzed with voices and activity. We checked our wraps and found an empty anteroom where we could warm up and run through the routine one last time. Louise had made it extra showy, with several demanding lifts, but as usual, we moved together intuitively. "Nervous?" she asked me, taking my hand to walk into the main hall and wait our turn.

"Only when we aren't dancing. Too busy concentrating when we are."

She squeezed my hand. "We are ready."

Louise had chosen the somewhat incongruous Voices of Spring (Mrs. Pearson had abridged the piece for us, to be within the time requirements), and the dress wasn't the only surprise Louise had for me that night. She'd managed a little sleight-of-hand so tiny paper snowflakes fluttered out of her hands to the floor as we began.

It went swimmingly, we took our bows, and returned to our seats. Louise's skirt swept some of the tiny snowflakes with her, and she bent down to pick them up, tucking them into my jacket pocket.

When the winners were announced, we got called for the first prize of fifty dollars. I was stunned, and Louise fairly vibrated. For everyone's entertainment, I swirled her up off the floor in the same sort of flourish I'd once used to swirl my cape performing the evil fairy in *Sleeping Beauty*.

We walked home in pleased silence, then lingered on her porch, giddy from success, and I impulsively started singing Auld Lang Syne. She giggled and cut me off mid-verse. "Are you going to keep me out here in the cold all night?"

"Are you cold?" I asked.

"Aren't you? It's freezing! Quite literally!"

I hadn't noticed. I stepped close and wrapped my arms around her

28

tightly, finished the song amid the popping of distant firecrackers, and her own arms held me close, and we stood there a long time, perfectly content. Louise whispered against my face, "I'm so glad we won tonight. I'm glad we won together."

Her lips, soft against my skin, startled me. "I'm glad too." I pulled back enough to meet her eyes. "You're swell. The snowflake thing—everyone loved it."

She gazed back at me, expression oddly soft, and for the first time in the six years we'd known each other, it occurred to me that she was incredibly pretty, and for one crazy instant I thought maybe I should kiss her. It was New Year's after all. The feeling perplexed me, since until this moment I'd found the idea of kissing anyone the most disgusting thing imaginable. As quickly I thought, *She'd probably punch me if I kissed her and I couldn't bear that on such a perfect night, just when I finally decided maybe it wouldn't be so bad.* I brushed the backs of my fingers lightly over her cheek instead. She leant into it, eyes closed.

"Come in a while," she said, her voice low. "Get warm before you walk home." She took my hand and pulled me inside, where she hung up my coat and hat and led me to the kitchen. I followed in her blue and shimmering wake and thought to myself how shimmer tasted like whipped cream, which made me oddly sentimental for the chocolate pies Mamma made in summertime.

Louise took two bottles of Coca-Cola out of the icebox. "Hardly champagne," she said, "but it'll do."

"I'm sure champagne is overrated anyway," I said, recalling our stolen sips of whisky at Uncle Jamie's castle—the only alcohol we'd ever tasted. We had not been impressed.

"Maybe," she said, popping off the caps and handing me a bottle. We settled onto the couch in front of the coal stove, still warm with a faint orange glow. The only other light in the room came from the partially open kitchen door. Louise sighed happily and slid down enough to lean her head on my shoulder, cozy and comfortable.

"What are you doing tomorrow?" I asked.

The fingers of her free hand wove themselves with mine, and when she spoke, her voice was soft and low again. "Looking after the

Watkins boys so Mrs. Watkins can clean her house in peace. I'll be done by lunchtime. You?"

Her thumb circled lightly against my palm and I felt a warm, unfamiliar buzzing. Must be my hands coming back to life after being so cold outside. My own voice cracked unaccountably when I answered. "I promised Mamma I'd wash all the inside windows. I guess I'll get everything ready for school Monday, too."

"You could do that Sunday."

"I just want to succeed."

"You will." She handed me her bottle so she could unstrap her shoes and tuck her feet under her. "Shouldn't we toast to something?"

"To school?"

I actually felt her softness drain away as she straightened and huffed. "Something besides school!"

"Well, you tell me, then."

"I'm toasting to... to... to my future beau!"

Her words tipped me off balance. "You've found someone?" I asked. Who in the world had she had time to meet that I wouldn't already know about? Perhaps it was best I hadn't kissed her after all.

"That's for me to know and you to find out." She clinked her bottle to mine with a little more force than necessary and took a rather unladylike swig.

I could tell she was getting into one of her impenetrable moods and, as usual, I had no idea what had set it off.

She silently trickled a tiny stream of Coke through her lips for a long time. "I suppose I should go home," I said.

She kept sipping. "You don't have to go. You could stay."

"It is late." I stood up. "You'll come over tomorrow, then?"

For an instant the moment imprinted itself indelibly on my brain: Louise, leaning slightly forward, eyes turned up to mine. The buzzing in my head began again as, for the second time, I realized how lovely she was.

"Yeah," she said, turning her eyes away, and the spell broke. "I'll be over."

I held out my hand and pulled her to her feet. "Your hands are cold."

"Cold bottle," she said.

I held her hands between mine to warm them. Her face was turned away enough that my nose brushed her hair. As a girl her hair always looked like a haystack. Now it smelled like one. I liked it, this second flash of summertime in the middle of winter. "Do you put something in your hair to make it smell like that?"

"Smell like what?"

"Freshly-mown hay."

"That's my secret," she said, a hint of a smile on her lips.

"You've always been a haystack head." I pulled her closer so I could get another whiff.

"I beg your pardon," she said, eyes glinting. "I haven't been a haystack head for years."

We weren't little kids anymore. The little girl had magically transformed into a woman. Somehow, in just this one evening. My pulse quickened and as I lifted my hand to smooth back some flyaway hairs, I again had the fleeting thought that it might be interesting to kiss her.

I was likely the only boy my age in Oregon who had never particularly cared for the whole chasing-girls-as-pastime thing, who had never kissed a girl or even wanted to. But Louise's cheeks were so flushed, and her eyes so bright, and her mouth mere inches from mine—perhaps I could try it, see what all the fuss was about?

But again I squashed the thought, my nerve failing me. She surely wouldn't appreciate such audacity on my part, even if I wasn't already too terrified to follow through. "You're right," I whispered. "You haven't been." I stepped back. "I should go."

She sighed deeply, but walked me to the door; she handed me my coat and hat and when they were on, she gently pushed me over the threshold.

Maybe I only imagined it, but as I went down the walk, I felt certain I heard the sound of smashing glass coming from somewhere inside.

But it might have only been more firecrackers.

LOUISE

I'd had it all planned out: win the competition, invite George in for a drink, get us situated on the sofa with the dim lighting and my low-cut dress, and he would be so swept off his feet he would take me into his arms and kiss me.

Kiss me senseless, if I was lucky.

I'd dreamed of this night for weeks, how the dress would be my Cinderella magic to wake my sleeping prince. I debated how far I would let him go, and had decided I was game to let him feel me up a little. Just enough that he'd be back for more.

I wondered what they would feel like on me, those beautiful hands of his. Touching my own breasts wasn't terribly interesting, but I knew it would be different if he did it. Knew his lips on mine would be warm. Ever since we'd gotten back to the house, my heart had been in my throat, anticipating... all for nothing.

The moment the door closed behind him, I snatched both Coke bottles and smashed them as hard as I could against the edge of the cast iron sink, pressing my palms to the edge, as if by brute force I could smash the sink too. It took a moment for the tears to follow.

Mother appeared, alarm in her eyes. I turned to flee her scrutiny, but she caught my wrist and stopped my escape. "What happened?"

"He didn't kiss me," I wailed. "I was so sure he would kiss me."

All the joy of the evening had shattered like the bottles and I felt hollow and destitute.

Mother wouldn't encourage me to be the one to initiate a kiss, I knew—unlike Mrs. Graham, who had repeatedly told me that short of knocking him to the nearest flat surface and helping myself to his mouth like a camel at an oasis, it wasn't likely to occur to George I might want that from him. All the same, I knew Mother sympathized with my plight. She wanted George and me together. Everyone wanted us together, it seemed... except George.

It baffled me, because he'd never expressed interest in anyone else. Not even pretty Olivia Wisniewski, who had mooned over him when she was eleven, and even lived in his house as a boarder for the past two years.

"I'm sorry," Mother said softly. I barely heard her over my own (admittedly melodramatic) wailing. I had been on top of the world a few minutes ago, and had plummeted so fast I didn't know what to do with myself. I extricated myself from Mother's arms and began snatching up handfuls of glass bits and throwing them into the bin, my horrified parent trying to pull me away. Only after the sink had been emptied of shards and the little rivulets of red rinsed away did I allow her to bandage me up, and then I fled to my room, where I took off that dress on which I'd pinned so much hope. I threw it into a corner and sobbed into my pillow until I was too tired to cry anymore.

What was wrong with me, anyway?

I couldn't think of anything but how badly I wanted George to hold me and kiss me. I wanted to punch him for being such an oblivious *gentleman*.

The tears gradually cleared my head of both feeling and thought. I didn't sleep much, but by the time morning came, I'd made a decision.

It was time for me to stop mooning about, waiting for George, and get on with some plans of my own that didn't involve him.

But I loved him so much and wanted him so badly that, even though I knew I was making the right decision, it was still the hardest one I'd ever made.

I sat down to write a letter.

GEORGE

SALEM, OREGON: NEW YEAR'S DAY, 1932

I was behind the closed drapes in the communal sitting room, washing the last window, when the most beautiful woman I'd ever seen ascended our front steps. My hand, which had been vigorously scrubbing in my haste to complete this most hated of tasks, came to a standstill; my eyes were riveted on the woman. The sunshine lit her all over as she set down one valise to push the doorbell.

She hadn't seen me, and I resumed my scrubbing, hoping to finish and make my getaway before she did see me. But my escape was foiled by Mamma, who let in the caller and offered her a seat on the couch directly in front of the window where I stood. I peeked through a minute opening in the drapery, waiting, hardly daring to breathe lest I betray myself.

"You must be the lady who 'phoned," Mamma said, seating herself on one end of the couch as she gestured to the lady to take the other end. "Miss Johnson, was it?"

"Do call me Velma! Yes, I saw your notice in the paper about a room available," the lady said. Her voice was low and smooth and powdered-sugary-refined. "I've just come from Pendleton in a rush, to replace a teacher who's been in a most awful automobile accident and won't be back to work for months, if ever. Here are my references—"

Mamma slipped on her reading glasses and scanned the proffered paper.

"This is my first chance to teach in my own field, and I'm so very excited," Miss Johnson went on. "Also I have a month's rent in advance." She took out three crisp ten-dollar bills from her purse and held them out to Mamma, who looked up.

"The room is yours, if you'd like it, Miss Johnson. Would you like to see it before deciding?"

"Oh, I can tell already I'll love it," Miss Johnson said, gesturing at her surroundings. "You have marvelous taste, and it looks perfectly clean and pleasant."

Mamma nodded. "Very well, then. My son will take your bags for you and show you to your room." She stood up and called, "Georgie!"

I emerged, sheepish, from the drapes, silently groaning at Mamma, who perpetually forgot I was no longer three years old. She looked startled that I'd been there all the time, but she only dropped her specs into the pocket of her apron with the money. "I suppose you heard everything, skulking like that. Show Miss Johnson to number four, Georgie." She turned and melted back into the Inner Sanctum, leaving me alone with this film-star-beautiful creature—rosy, raven-haired, slightly exotic-looking—who smiled beatifically up at me.

She was tiny, I realized, now that we stood together. How did someone so small manage a classroom? Perhaps she taught very young children.

She followed me to the hall, where she took off her coat and hat and held them out to me. I took both, unable to tear my eyes away from her. I wanted to pick up a pencil and capture her on paper. *Deep breath, George, don't make an idiot of yourself*, I said mentally. Aloud I said, "You're in number four," indicating the #4 hooks as I hung up her wraps.

She looked up sharply at the sound of my voice, and my face went hot. People who didn't know me were always startled when I spoke, because my voice was awfully deep for someone who still looked like a shrimpy *kid*.

And got called Georgie by his distracted mother.

"How old are you?" she asked.

"Going on eighteen." I neglected to add that I'd be going on eighteen for eleven months to come.

Her eyes said what everyone's said. *You don't look it.* But I let it pass, took up her valise, and launched into my New Boarder Instruction Speech I'd perfected, because Mamma didn't speak to the boarders any more than she absolutely had to.

"That's the communal sitting room we were just in, Miss Johnson. There's a wireless in there if you're musically inclined, and this by the coat rack is the library, if you prefer reading. The dining room is over there, and that door—" I nodded toward it—"is my parents' apartment. Now, if you'll follow me up—"

As we mounted the stairs, I kept going. "You'll meet the other boarders tonight. Dinner at six, cleared away at seven-thirty. Mr. and Mrs. Wagner are in number one. He's a postal clerk and she's a telephone operator. The Misses Robinson have number two. Miss Clara and Miss Faye. Good luck telling them apart, but you'll like them. Everyone does. And they're teachers, too, so you'll have something in common. Mrs. Tabitha and her daughters Natalia and Olivia have number three, and number four is yours."

I opened the door and set the valise inside, but I didn't cross the threshold. I stepped back, watching this wondrous specimen of femininity examine her room. I stood straighter, ridiculously pleased that for once I had a real height advantage over somebody (Mamma doesn't count) and I kept on blethering.

"No lights to be left on when not in the room. Quiet hours are from ten at night to seven in the morning. Breakfast is on from six-thirty to eight. Room 4 has the bathroom from six-thirty to seven in the morning, and eight-thirty to nine at night. The schedule is posted on the door, if you forget. Mamma's very particular about the times being observed—" I had a fleeting, uncomfortable sensation that I was behaving like my endlessly loquacious father, and shut up.

Miss Johnson sat on the bed, bouncing slightly as her eyes took in everything. I stuffed my hands deep into my pockets, knowing I should go, but unready to stop gazing at her. I wasn't even sure she'd been listening to me, but I didn't care.

"What a perfect room," she said. "Pink is my favorite color."

Pink like her cheeks and her pretty mouth and that frock she's wearing...

I experienced the same odd buzzing in my head I'd felt last night with Louise, but it was more insistent now. I took another step back. "Let me know if you need anything," I said, even though I was hardly the person she should be asking.

"Thank you, I shall," she said, her smile making me return it with one of my own. She came to the door and peered around me curiously. "You didn't tell me what those doors are. Closets?"

"That's the linen closet. This one is mine."

"I see." Turning her face up, she said, "I do have a trunk at the station I'll need delivered here."

"I'll arrange it," I said, eager to gain her favor and further dispel, if possible, the illusion that I was "just a kid".

As I was waiting downstairs with the receiver in hand to be connected, Louise came sweeping in, with a dramatic swirl as she hung her own hat and coat on the hook marked LBP. I had to stifle a giggle as the station people got on the line. I solemnly made my request for the delivery of the trunk, but as soon as I'd hung up, I collapsed into laughter.

"New boarder? Do tell!" Louise said, nodding to the coat and hat on Number Four Hook.

"Oh, just another teacher," I said. *The understatement of the century.* I hoped I wasn't blushing. "I'm done with the windows. Come on."

She followed me to the Inner Sanctum and plopped down on a chair in our family's dining nook to rummage in the workbag she'd brought along. I set a plate of cookies between us.

"What's she like?" Louise asked.

"Who?"

"The new boarder."

"She says she likes her room because it's pink."

Louise rolled her eyes. "I hate that room because it's pink."

"We know. How were the Watkins boys?"

"Terrors as usual."

I went to get the book I'd been reading to her, and when I turned back I paused to watch her as she arranged her handwork on the table in front of her. It had become our daily ritual over the summer: I'd read to her for an hour or so whilst she worked on fussy tiny lacy things for her "hopeless chest", and then we danced until dinnertime.

Gone was last night's glamor queen; once again Louise was the secretaryish cardigan and skirt girl I knew far better. There wasn't a hint left of the lithe curves that dress had shown off to great effect.

38

I thought of Miss Johnson upstairs, who couldn't have hidden her curves if she tried. My pulse quickened and I took a few deep breaths to calm myself.

What was wrong with me, anyway? I'd never felt like this before and already I didn't appreciate the way it was complicating my life.

"What's taking you so long?" Louise said, looking up and catching me staring at her. It seemed to startle her.

"I thought I heard glass breaking when I was walking away last night," I said.

Instantly she became prickly. "I'm fine. Now, how much longer do I have to put up with this book you're reading me?"

I slid into the chair beside her and watched her hands, tiny crochet hook flying. There was at least one cut I could see, but I sensed I was treading on dangerous ground and decided not to mention it.

"There are two chapters left. We'll finish it today," I said. I loved reading aloud, alternating grand and deep theological works with the lighter fare and mysteries Louise preferred. It wasn't that she minded my selections, exactly, but Pilgrim's Progress had had Louise's hackles up from the moment Christiana undertakes her journey in the second half of the book.

"Why don't they give the POOR WEAK WOMAN some armor?"

she'd spluttered. "The apostle never said the armor of God was only for men! How come Christian gets armor and does all these brave and glorious deeds and she has to stand by and watch Mr. Greatheart fight all her battles for her?"

I'd blinked at her, not sure how to answer. Louise had no patience for swooning, helpless women, even in allegory. It was one reason she loved *The Prisoner of Zenda*'s Princess Flavia. Princess Flavia had a good strong spine.

"You don't want some fellow to fight your battles for you sometime?" I'd asked.

"Not for me! He could fight them with me!" she'd said staunchly, shaking her tiny steel hook like a reproving finger at me. "And this isn't about husbands and wives, anyway, is it? It's a theological treatise, and it's Biblically inaccurate that even Christian could fight his own battles. It's through the merits of Christ alone that his followers can do any good, for themselves or anyone else."

She'd leveled me with a Look as she spoke; I meekly conceded the point and she'd returned to her energetic crocheting, clearly satisfied at having won that debate.

I started reading, but I felt distracted and muddled in my head and she kept having to poke me to wake me out of whatever brown study I'd fallen into. "What's wrong with you?" she scolded.

"Sorry," I said. "I didn't get enough sleep last night."

"Neither did I, but I'm not aff wi' the faeries every five minutes."

Things improved slightly when we got to the dancing bit of our afternoon. By the time Dad came in from work and Louise gathered her things to go home, I'd forgotten Velma Johnson completely.

Throughout most of the rest of the month, it continued to be easy to forget her. Our paths didn't cross in the mornings because I left early to catch the train up to Portland for my classes, and although our evening bathroom slots were adjacent to one another, that didn't necessarily mean we saw each other. And Louise didn't have a chance to meet her, either.

For a while.

GEORGE

Louise was coming after school so we could Do Things (she hadn't specified what those Things were), and I'd just gotten home from Portland and knew I hardly had time to get ready. I came rushing downstairs, my overcoat on one arm and my umbrella on the other and my tie still undone. I dumped everything on the floor and stood by the hall mirror, one eye watching the window for the blue Buick and the other trying to get the fussy knots to do what they ought to do. (Hopeless. I simply could not master it.) I huffed in frustration.

Miss Johnson appeared in the door of the library, book in hand, and asked softly, "May I help?"

Self-conscious, I submitted to her ministrations, feeling like a small, incapable kid. But only for a moment. Her swift, pretty hands had the tie done up nicely in no time, and her hands lingered an instant too long on my chest before she clasped them behind her back. She didn't look at me as if I was a kid.

Her eyes were blue, but not pale like Louise's. They were like the twilight sky, the deepest blue can go before it becomes black. And they were luminous. Again I longed to take a pencil and try to capture the beauty of those eyes, and so riveted was I by this notion, I was startled when she spoke.

"What did you say, ma'am?" I asked.

She cast down her eyes and laughed. "I was just saying that when I met you—ah, never mind."

"You thought I was a kid. It wouldn't be the first time."

She met my eyes again, sheepish. "Yes. It was your voice that made me realize my mistake. Such a beautiful voice. Miss Clara says you've been involved in theater work?"

"Not the vocal kind. Dance, mostly," I clarified. "But I have studied oration. Dance is swell, but it's not what I'm going to do with my life."

"And what are you planning to do with your life?"

I stooped to retrieve my coat from the floor, but she beat me to it and held it up for me to put my arms into. (Louise never did things like that. She'd tell me, "Put your own coat on! I put *my* own coat on!" My ties were her one concession. It felt nice to be spoiled a little.)

I turned back to Miss Johnson as I did up my buttons. "I'm going to be a minister, ma'am. I started at seminary the first week of this year and I've applied for a license to preach. Dr. Birtchet takes me around with him, too, visiting people and to board meetings and whatnot. He says soon he wants to put me in charge of the Thursday night prayer meetings."

She gave me a swift, penetrating glance that looked like she was trying to decide how this information fit in with the picture she'd formed of me up to now. At last she said, "I'm sure you'll make a marvelous minister."

"I hope so," I said, more earnestly than I meant to.

At that moment, Louise burst in the door and skidded to a halt when she saw Miss Johnson, who stepped back from me, and I realized we'd been standing far too close together for propriety. Blushing, I picked up my umbrella, dropping my hat in the process. Louise stood with her arms crossed, waiting until my involuntary experiments with gravity came to an end, and then I said, "Miss Johnson, this is Louise Pearson."

"Hello," Louise said coolly, offering a limpish hand in greeting.

"Do call me Velma! Where are you two off to?" Miss Johnson's voice had brightened to the tone I imagined she'd use with her students.

"It's a surprise," Louise said. "Come on, George." And she took my hand and pulled me out the door before I could say goodbye to Miss Johnson.

"What was that?" I asked, annoyed, as I slid into the passenger seat of the Buick.

"WHO was that?" she asked, clearly also annoyed.

"The new boarder. The teacher I told you about."

Louise screeched away from the curb and down the wet street. When she came to a stop sign, she said, "You didn't tell me she was a hussy!"

"Louise!" I said, shocked. "That's not fair! You've never even spoken to her."

"I've got eyes, haven't I?" she snapped, stalling the car in her attempt to get going again.

"Maybe you should let me drive, if you're going to be mad," I said.

"I drive best when I'm mad." (She did not, in fact, drive best when she was mad.)

I let out a long breath. "She saved you from having to tie my tie," I offered feebly.

"HA," Louise said. "When you've earned your dog collar, you won't need ties any more. I can't wait."

"Neither can I," I agreed, enthusiastically. "Dumb old ties. Where are we going?"

She didn't answer, and when she shifted gears again, I laid a hand on hers. "Lou, you're not... jealous, are you?"

"Why should I be jealous?" she said.

I sighed. Usually, Louise was the most level-headed and reasonable girl in the world, but every few weeks or so she became an absolute terror. I chalked it up to "even the best of girls have their moments of madness" and never said anything, but also... also it seemed that ever since New Year's Eve, something fundamental had shifted in our easy camaraderie. Louise had been keeping more of her own counsel, busier than usual caring for people's children and fussing around planes at the airfield. I didn't know what to make of it, didn't like it, but it was also true that making time for each other was more challenging, now that we were no longer on the same school schedule.

She was still wearing my bracelet, though, so I knew whatever was bothering her wasn't unsurmountable.

"So, where are we going?" I asked again.

She sighed and softened a bit. "Having our picture taken. Don't squawk, George, it'll make our mothers happy to have a reminder of their young and foolish offspring."

When we arrived at the studio, the photographer and Louise conferred together whilst I wandered uselessly, hands in my pockets, studying the sample photographs on the studio walls: sepia or hand-tinted faces, frozen for eternity behind glass. In each I only saw one face, Miss Johnson's, with those bewitching eyes. I was in love with her eyes, and also inexplicably terrified by the way she looked at me with them. I was jerked out of my musings by the photographer's

voice calling me over. He posed us with one of those silly cardboard cutout moons, and somehow just being there beside Louise made me more relaxed and content.

"Put your arm through hers," the man instructed. I obeyed. "You must look as if you like each other."

That made us laugh and he snapped the picture.

Afterwards, we went to the latest film, *Dr. Jekyll and Mr. Hyde.*

"I saw it last night with Mother," she said. "It was so good, I want you to see it too. Much better than the boring old book."

She was right. It was good. I even had to admit that she was right; it was more interesting than the book. Terrifying, too, and sobering. As we were leaving, her arm through mine so it looked as if we liked each other, she sighed. "That Mr. March is a dreamboat."

I put up the umbrella and we stepped into the street. "As Jekyll or Hyde?"

The old Louise came out as she fondly said, "Idiot. Let's go have dinner."

I still felt a little stunned by the film and I didn't say anything as we walked along, just brooded until we reached one of our favorite haunts: a place owned by Mrs. Rosenberg, one of Mamma's local Jewish acquaintances. Besides the fact that everything was delicious, I liked it because I could always count on the food being safe. No risk of lard or shellfish or cross-contamination, like at the Chinese place Louise sometimes took her mother to because I declined to risk it.

And then we danced at the Crystal Gardens for hours.

Louise dropped me off at my door. It had stopped raining, but the wind had picked up. It was dark, and I had difficulty getting the key into the lock. At last I managed to get inside, where I took off my hat and coat and, by reflex, stepped into the library to turn off a left-on light.

But I stopped in my tracks when I saw Miss Johnson at the bookshelves. She whipped 'round, magazine in hand.

"I didn't mean to startle you," I apologized. My key slipped out of my hand and I stooped to pick it up. "Sorry."

"Nothing to worry about," she said, kindly. "I often have trouble sleeping, so I came looking for something to read. Did you have a nice date?"

I blinked at her. "Date?"

"Wasn't that your sweetheart?"

"Oh. Louise? No."

Miss Johnson came a few steps nearer.

"Louise has been my friend for a very long time. That's all." I could barely get the words out. My heart fluttered like mad at the warmth of her eyes and the cascade of gleaming black hair drifting over her shoulders. I'd never seen anything quite so... well... I didn't know what this feeling was.

Ivy's words from the film we'd just seen played back in my mind. *Come back. You will come back, won't you?*

I forced the image of Ivy tempting Dr. Jekyll out of my head and gripped the brim of my hat more tightly. "What is it you teach?" I said, desperate to find my way back to safer ground. (Fleeing did not occur to me.)

She stepped even closer. "Art. I'm an art teacher at the junior high school."

My interest overrode my desire to appear a cool, confident adult. "What kind of art?"

"Figures, primarily. Some animals and landscapes. Charcoal, pencil, pastel, watercolor. I'm not good with oils. Art history, too. Have you any interest in art?"

"I sketch some," I said.

"You must show me sometime," she said with a gentle smile. She was so close to me—how had that happened? Those eyes of hers were bewitching me again. I couldn't speak, couldn't move, couldn't think of anything but how much I wanted to lean down and touch her pretty mouth with my own, just to see what it was like. I knew it would be improper, even if she wasn't considerably older than I was.

I stepped back and managed a hoarse, "Well, goodnight."

And then I did flee, up to my attic.

I should come in my back entrance from now on, my head said.

I should never use my back entrance again, my heart said.

The moment I'd locked my door I took my long-neglected

sketchbook off the shelf, wiped the dust off with my sleeve, and opened it to the first clean page. Sitting near the light, I sketched the outline of those eyes.

The film Louise and I had just seen played itself over and over in my mind. There had been a sexual element to it which was still making me intensely uncomfortable. When we'd walked out of the theater, I thought how unrelatable to myself was someone who would formulate a potion that allowed him to become a different man with no repressions and no limits. Except he wasn't really a different man.

Dr. Jekyll was desperate to marry Muriel because he was desperate to take a woman to bed with him respectably. Was there, in me somewhere, a Mr. Hyde lurking, ready to pounce on female prey? I had never been interested in girls like other boys my age. Taking girls to bed with me was the furthest thing from anything I'd ever desired.

Come back to me. You will come back, won't you? Come back…

But instead of Ivy's swinging leg, it was Velma Johnson's liquid eyes.

LOUISE
SALEM, OREGON: FEBRUARY 1932

*T*he influenza kept popping around town, and for most of February George was holed up in his attic, obsessively studying and staying un-sick so he wouldn't miss any classes. I left notes for him stuck into the frame of his door, little chatty updates about the real world he was missing out on. I was watching children almost every afternoon and practicing my night flying after dark.

It was ridiculous to be this paranoid of catching influenza. I stood outside his slightly-open door one evening shouting back and forth with him over whether he was keeping up with his dancing (of course he was) and would he do a job with me at a fancy hotel in Portland (he would, but what was it all about?)

"Dance floor entertainment because the leads each broke bones in a freak accident as they left the hotel one night, and the regular substitutes had already planned a tour down the west coast to Los Angeles they couldn't cancel. We'll be the stars until they get back!"

I detailed for him which dances we'd do, ones that would work well with a variety of songs in case there were requests, and reminded him it had been a Very Wise Choice to Buy That Penguin Suit, and there might be more opportunities for us on a bigger stage if we did well.

"But neither of us are planning to make a career of this!" he called down the stairs to me as I was leaving, poking his head out the door at last.

"That's not the point," I called back. "The more money we can make out of it while we're young and beautiful... fifty percent beautiful, anyway... the sooner we can have what we want!"

He rolled his eyes. "Stop selling yourself short, Lou," he said. "The way you talk, you'd think you're an ancient sea hag."

I shrugged and strode off.

Inside, I did feel exactly like an ancient sea hag.

GEORGE

SALEM, OREGON: MARCH 2, 1932

*T*he moment I saw the front page of the newspaper that morning, LINDBERGH BABY IS KIDNAPED, my first thought was irrelevant annoyance that they hadn't used a double P in "kidnapped". Then I realized Louise needed to be warned, so I rushed to the telephone to ring her. As invested in the Lindberghs as she was, not to mention her love for babies, she'd take it hard. When she picked up, I said, "You might not want to look at the paper today."

Of course, being Louise, she heard my recommendation and promptly ignored it. I heard her set the receiver down, open the front door; heard the rattle of unfolding paper, and a strange, strangled squeak.

I hung up and ran out the door, snatching my hat and satchel on the way. When I got to her house, I let myself in to find her sitting against the entry wall, knees to her chest, face obscured by the hands that gripped her hair as if it was all that was keeping her from exploding. She was eerily silent despite the fact that her shoulders shook with sobs. I softly hung the abandoned telephone receiver back in place and sat beside her, unsure what would help.

It was horrible, of course, but I was sure the police had it in hand and would find and reunite the boy with his parents in no time.

Lost in my musings, I was startled when Louise threw her arms around my neck and clung tightly to me. "It's too much," she snuffled, wetly. "I can't bear it. What must poor Mrs. Lindbergh be feeling?"

"I don't know," was all I could say. This new Louise who cried so much was going to take some getting used to. When had it started, the moodiness? Was it before Keith died in that plane crash, or was that what set it off? My mind wandered as she continued to cry, and I wondered where her mother was.

"Hey," I said at last. "Is your mother here? I'm going to be late for my train if I don't go now, but I don't want you to be alone."

Louise shook her head, releasing me. "Go. I'll be fine." But the bleak look on her face as I left haunted me the rest of the day.

LOUISE

I skipped school that day. The next day was George's first time leading prayer meeting, but I didn't go. I just couldn't seem to look at anyone without wanting to burst into tears, and I certainly didn't want to see any babies. I'd have felt compelled to hold them all close and never let go, lest they be snatched by ransom hunters.

Not that Mother let me get away with my seclusion forever. After three days of moping, she came to my room and sat at the foot of my bed. I pretended not to notice, but she didn't go away, and at last she spoke.

"I know you're upset about the Lindbergh baby," she said, gently. "I don't know what to do to make you feel better."

"It's not just the Lindbergh baby," I said, immediately beginning to choke on fresh tears. I scowled, scrubbing at my eyes. I hated this new version of myself that blubbed constantly.

"George?"

I shrugged, still refusing to meet her eyes. Of course George was a big part of it, but since New Year's and my decision to move forward without him, his failure to notice me as a woman had felt somewhat less important. He was up in Portland half the time these days, and I was busy during all my spare hours working for money to fund the venture I'd decided on New Year's to pursue. I hadn't told Mother about that. I hadn't told anyone except the recipient of the letter I'd written.

"Perhaps it's best he's not around as much," Mother said, looking toward the wall where my fashion plates were pinned. "You could be looking for someone else who's actually interested—"

I cut her off. "No," I said. "I don't want anyone else. I'd rather be alone than have someone else."

She sighed and laced her fingers together in her lap. "I'm going to Corvallis next week to work with a few piano students at the university who are preparing for auditions. Miss Baxter arranged it. It won't pay much, but it's something."

I nodded, absentmindedly.

"She also wants me to interview for a teaching position they have coming open. What do you think? Of course, I probably won't get it, but—"

"It never hurts to try."

"You wouldn't be bothered if we had to move?"

"I'll wait to decide about being bothered until I know whether it's something to bother about."

"All right, then." She stood up. "Also, you're going back to school tomorrow. I won't have you moping here anymore."

With that, she left the room, and I hauled myself off the bed. I might as well make the most of my last few hours of moping by doing it in George's attic.

I went up the stairs in the back to his private entrance, knocked and let myself in. He looked up from his table, which was littered with open books and notebooks and pencil shavings. "Hey," he said.

54

I flopped onto his sofa and lounged like all the examples of How Proper Young Ladies Shouldn't Sit, and heaved a huge sigh. "Mother told me I have to go back to school tomorrow because she's tired of me moping, so I came here to make the most of my last few hours."

He smiled crookedly, his pencil poised over his composition book. "Still upset about that baby?"

I nodded, and he went back to writing for a few minutes, but I could tell he was thinking. He paused and turned to me. "You're not personally acquainted with them. The police are doing their best. Tying yourself in knots over this isn't going to help anything."

I scowled, folding my arms tightly against my chest. "Don't you have any emotions at all, George?"

"Sure I do, just—"

I cut him off, my voice dripping with sarcasm. "And the police did SUCH a stellar job when I was kidnapped! What makes you think the ones out there are going to do any better?"

"Well, they did save you in less than twenty-four hours," I said.

"I saved me! Baby Lindbergh can't!" My lips trembled, and my voice rose in agitation. "The police didn't save me. They didn't even find me, wouldn't have found me, if I hadn't gotten to a phone and called to tell them where I was! And it's been longer than twenty-four hours."

"He's a baby. He's too little to be scared," George continued, his tone full of the male urge to Make Illogical Women See Reason.

"BABIES ARE NOT IMMUNE TO FRIGHT." I leapt to my feet and began to pace the floor. "You're such a cold-hearted—" I cut myself off before one of his mother's choice words slipped out.

"She's expecting another one anyway, isn't she? Mrs. Lindbergh?"

I stalked across the floor to depart. He got up and followed me, pressing the point. "Well, isn't she?"

I turned and gave him a look I hoped was positively Antarctic. "I should slap you for that."

"Why not do it, then?"

"Because... because frankly, George, I don't like you enough right now to bother." And I swept the rest of the way down and didn't look back again.

GEORGE

*I*t was good there were a few days between Louise exploding at me and our first hotel engagement in Portland, because an evening of dancing with a woman trying to incinerate me with her eyes wouldn't have been very pleasant, either to us or the hotel guests. She came over to practice Friday afternoon, but she wasn't speaking to me any more than necessary.

"You might cut that tension with an ax, possibly," Dad murmured in the direction of the brief he was working on.

For some reason that made Louise absolutely lose her mind laughing. She broke away from me and flopped herself over Dad's shoulders, limp with hilarity.

I closed my eyes and heaved a long sigh. It was going to be an extremely long week.

Month.

Lifetime?

As she was leaving, she turned to ask me if I was capable of packing my own things or if she needed to come do it for me.

"I'm perfectly capable," I said.

She rattled off a list, only half of which had occurred to me, and I sighed. "Okay," I said, holding my hands up in defeat. "Maybe you'd better write it all down."

We took the train, but we didn't sit together. Louise sat across the aisle, hands idly folded in her lap, watching the lights of the towns pass by out the window. I had brought a book to read, so soon I lost myself in it.

The dancing went well. Louise feigned a cool professionalism that vaporized the instant we were out of the public eye. The train ride home was long, and again she did not sit beside me. I'd finished my book, and became aware that she was neither leaning her head against my shoulder nor putting her arm through mine. She'd done both for so long I'd stopped noticing, and now, without the book to distract me, I felt the absence of the gesture keenly.

She didn't return my wave when we parted, and I sighed. I didn't know how to make it up to her. I still didn't understand what the big deal was.

I let myself in. There was a light left on in the library again, but nobody was there (or in any of the common rooms downstairs), so I switched it off. I made my way to the bathroom. When I came out twenty minutes later, I was surprised to see Miss Johnson's door crack open. "Is that you, George?" she whispered.

"Yes," I whispered back.

"May I speak to you for a minute?"

I hesitated. I didn't want to wake anyone, and I wasn't going to go into her room. I glanced at my door. "Um... sure. Come in here, I guess."

She followed me up my stairs on silent stocking feet. I switched on my lamp and opened my back entrance door to let Lindbergh in for the night. "Have a seat," I said, gesturing to one of the chairs as I hastily stacked my mess of books and papers to give my hands something to do besides be awkward in the presence of those dreamy eyes.

She chose the couch instead, and settled back into it. "I haven't seen you much," she said.

"Seminary is keeping me busy," I said.

"Is it going well?"

"So far, ma'am."

She laughed. "Oh, please do not 'ma'am' me! I hear enough of that all day. "

Unwilling to actually call her by her name, I sat at a safe distance from her and scooped up Lindbergh to pet. Her dark eyes were fixed on me, impenetrable and mysterious and alluring. I couldn't meet them.

"Where did you go tonight?" she asked. "Out with... Louise, is it?"

She nodded toward my copy of the paper moon photograph, which Louise had framed and set on my bookshelf weeks ago.

"We had a job up in Portland tonight. Performing with a hotel orchestra whilst the regulars are out. We have the next two Sundays, too."

"I didn't realize you two were professional dancers."

"Just for now. It's a way to make money. She wants an airplane of her own, and I have to pay my way through seminary somehow. Dad's giving me a little, but most of it's on me."

She crossed the floor and picked up the photo, inspecting it, and nodded. "Well, you make a lovely couple, anyway."

"We're not a couple," I reminded her. Inwardly I added, *At the moment we don't even seem to be friends.*

"Oh, yes. So you said."

There was a pause. Lindbergh jumped off my lap and trotted over to his water bowl. I stood and twisted my hands together behind my back as I faced Miss Johnson. "I'm happy to visit with you, ma'am, but my mother will tan my hide if she finds out I had you here in my room."

She laughed softly. "Well, she won't find out from me, and everyone else is asleep. No harm done."

I was tired and desperately wanted my bed, but she didn't seem in any hurry to leave. She set the photo back down, and cocked her head at a stack of my sketches I'd left there a few weeks ago. Her eyes lit up and she took them in her hands, looking at me. "Are these yours? You still haven't shown me any of your work!"

I watched as she inspected each of my doodles, flushing to the roots of my hair. My sketches were things I guarded closely, with the exception of a very few I made for other people, and having her looking at them without asking felt like someone walking in on me in my skivvies. Of course, I reminded myself, she couldn't know that, and I opened my mouth to ask her to please not look at them without asking, but she spoke first, moving across the floor toward me like a filmy pink spirit, and I lost my powers of speech.

She held out the one I most wanted her not to see, the one where I'd attempted to draw her eyes. "I'm flattered," she said softly. "What made you do it?"

I swallowed and took a step back. "I... I don't know, ma'am. There was just... something I was trying to capture, and I don't think I got it right. Those are the ones I was going to throw in the fire."

She raised her eyebrows.

"I don't like my sketches looked at," I said. "Not without asking, anyway."

"Well, if these are the ones you want to burn, I'm curious what the ones you keep look like."

She set them on the table and folded her arms in such a way that elevated her bosom provocatively. Probably she was not thinking about how it looked; even if she meant anything by it, she couldn't know I didn't get turned on by such gestures. I couldn't help noticing, all the same. I clenched my fists by my sides and studiously focused on a point somewhere beyond her.

"Would you show me the ones you do like?"

I hesitated briefly, then fetched my sketchbook from the drawer of my nightstand and held it out to her. She took it eagerly and opened it to the first page, which was a very rough sketch of Inverlochy Castle where Uncle Jamie lived. I'd done it years ago when we first visited. There were portraits of all my cousins and my sisters, and a whole page of Lindbergh in various poses when he was a puppy. Several pages were all disembodied hands: Mrs. Pearson's at the piano, Mamma's kneading bread, Dad's as he wrote, Louise's crocheting. There were quick doodles of Olivia dancing as well that I'd done because she asked me to draw her a portrait once and I needed the practise. Velma inspected each closely, her expert eye taking in every detail. "Have you ever had any art lessons?" she asked.

"No. It's just something I occasionally play with in my spare time.

Don't have much of that these days."

"Well, you're quite good. I could help you, if you'd like me to."

I sat down in the other chair, her interest distracting me momentarily from my desire for sleep. "I'd like to see some of your art."

"I'll bring some up sometime." She closed my book and got to her feet, holding out her hands to take mine and pull me closer, studying my face as if trying to read something there. "Why *my* eyes, George?"

I wasn't used to being incoherent, but her proximity was flustering me immensely, and I stammered out some nonsense I can't quite remember. I do remember she didn't laugh.

And she stood on her toes to kiss my cheek.

I should have pushed her away, done something—anything—but instead I stood there frozen, her mouth soft against my face, my heart racing from a blend of panic and pleasure.

Let me pause here to clear something up.

I had actively avoided the subject of sex since I was eleven or so and Dad tried to have The Talk with me. I'd covered my ears and refused to listen. I already knew how animals made babies, and the last thing I wanted to think about was how people made them.

So Mamma gave me a book, which was still tucked in the back of my chest of drawers where it had immediately been put, unopened.

Of course I knew, in an impersonal, clinical sort of way, how it worked. Dad was absolutely brazen in his open displays of affection with my mother, delighting in embarrassing her (and me) (mostly me) with wildly inappropriate remarks and saucy double-entendres. Most of the films Louise loved best involved people falling in love and being gooey at some point in the story. I didn't get it. Nor did I understand the appeal of scantily clad women in film and elsewhere.

What I craved was emotional connection, which I'd always had in spades with Louise, and had always found our relationship perfectly satisfying as it was. The intimacy we shared just was, no touching or spit-swapping required.

So when Miss Johnson kissed me, I didn't expect to feel any response at all.

But it was disorienting. The tangle of emotions I'd had regarding this woman since the moment I first saw her rose up suffocatingly around me until I couldn't breathe any more.

As if she sensed I might topple at any moment, she took my hand and guided me to the couch, where she gave me a funny little half-smile and took my glasses off, setting them aside, before kissing me again, on the lips this time.

It wasn't as sloppy as I'd assumed it would be, and I thought, *If I'd known it could be like this, maybe I wouldn't have hesitated on New Year's Eve.* This was long and lingering and sent shivers all through me. I didn't know what to do with my hands or my own mouth, so I continued to do nothing with either, but slowly in response to the kiss I relaxed back into the couch. She smelled spicy, cinnamon and citrus and cloves all in one, delicious.

I don't know how long it went on. It seemed to be both forever and no time at all. But at last she pulled back and smiled enchantingly at me. "You're good at more than just dancing and drawing. Good night, George," she said, and disappeared down the stairs, leaving me utterly baffled by the entire interaction.

I'd been exhausted, but now I was unable to sleep. I lay in bed thinking about the kiss and feeling inexplicably guilty for having let it happen, for having allowed her up in the first place, and also... also oddly *good*, warm and tingly, almost wishing she'd come back and do it some more.

When I did finally drift off, it was to a complicated tangle of dreams that left me unrested.

LOUISE

When I came to meet George Sunday afternoon to walk to the train for that night's work, that little minx of a schoolteacher was just coming back from... somewhere.

"And where are you off to?" she asked brightly.

"Portland," I said, and jerked George along before he could say anything himself. He turned to wave at her, and she blew him a kiss, eyes half-closed, expression flirty.

"What is wrong with you?" I asked, grouchy. (Again.) "She's old. Way older than us. Quit mooning over her!"

"I'm not mooning! All she did was ask where we were going!"

I bored my eyes into him like gimlets, and took note of the fact that he was refusing to meet my gaze.

"You're mooning, all right. Every time you see her you blush and stammer and look at her like Lindbergh expecting a tasty bone."

"I do not!" he objected. "There's nothing between us, so you can shut up."

His sharpness shocked me. He could be obtuse, yes, and we were good at bickering, but he hadn't used that tone to me in... had he ever? I couldn't think of a time. It stung, and I charged ahead a few paces.

"I'm not stupid," he called after me. "Everything is fine."

"Fine," I said, in a loaded time-bomb tone of my own.

I was wearing a pale gold dress, with a very swirly skirt, but much more modest than the New Year's Eve number. I was aware that George kept looking at me, but was equally aware it was analysis, not attraction.

Again I didn't sit beside him on the train, and we didn't speak again the rest of the night except when we had to.

I spent the first several days of the next week in the depths of the Elsinore Theatre, watching all six showings of *Hell Divers*. I didn't ask George to come along, but he invited himself once. I moved over a seat to make the point that he wasn't with me, nor did I share my popcorn. I booed under my breath every time Clark Gable came on screen. "Arrogant, presumptuous bastard. You think you're so entitled, don't you? Please. YOU die this time."

I continued to meet George for an hour each evening to dance, but the tension was still high as the search for the Lindbergh baby dragged on. I cried at the drop of a hat.

I wanted things to be right between us again. I wanted George to understand why he was so wrong about the Lindbergh baby. I wanted him to understand why that schoolteacher was bad news, too.

I wanted him to love me.

George

*T*he baby was dead.

All that time, ever since the night he disappeared, Baby Lindbergh's body had been hidden in a pile of leaves four miles from the Lindbergh house. Louise was once again inconsolable, and wore black to varying degrees for weeks.

I rode my bicycle to the airfield after getting home one afternoon toward the end of May, hoping to speak with her, try to clear up the tension between us however I could. School would soon be out for the summer, and I couldn't stand the idea of spending several more months like we'd spent the last couple.

I arrived to see a plane screaming about in crazy loops and dives. It was like watching *Hell Divers* playing out in real life, and my heart dropped to the ground. Of course this wasn't the first time Louise had done crazy stunts in the air, but it seemed more sinister knowing her recently dark frame of mind.

When she came in to land, I ran over to the plane. She had leant her head back on the seat and had an expression of peaceful exhilaration on her face.

Until she opened her eyes and saw me. "What do *you* want?" she asked, grumpily.

"I want to clear things up," I said. "I don't like us being this way."

"How badly do you want to clear things up?" she asked, a trace of the old bargaining glint in her eyes. I tensed. That glint always meant bad news for me.

"Um... very badly?"

"Badly enough you'll strap yourself into that seat and let me take you up?" She pointed a leather-gloved finger to the seat in front of her.

I hesitated, and she regarded me through narrowed eyes, waiting.

"With or without *Hell Divers* stunts?" I asked, my own eyes narrowing.

The glint in her eyes increased. "With."

I envisioned a fiery death, a death by falling out, a death from heart failure, a death from the eternal shame I'd feel if I was sick in the air.

Louise took off her left glove and examined her nails. "You're not going to die," she said. "The straps will keep you from falling out. Your heart is perfectly fine, you can be sick into the extra helmet if you must, and the tanks aren't full, so if we crash (which we won't), there won't be as much to catch fire."

Some of the mechanics had come up and caught this last bit. "Convince him he won't die if he goes for a ride," she called out to them, nodding toward me.

I scowled, but couldn't very well continue to object with this many witnesses to my cowardice, so I heaved a sigh and gave in. I'd watched her get into planes enough times that I knew what to do, but I wasn't in any hurry. She stood and leaned over me to ensure my straps were properly fastened, whispering, "Nobody falls out of a plane on my watch. Don't fiddle with them and you'll be fine. And whatever you do, *don't touch anything*."

She dropped the extra helmet on my head and buckled it on, and I cringed as far down into my seat as I possibly could. *Peace at any price*, I reminded myself, although I thought this was a desperately unfair price.

The nearest mechanic swung the propeller for Louise, the engine roared to life, and the plane bumped along the ground to the runway, speeding up horrifyingly before the nice, solid earth and then the treetops vanished from view.

I closed my eyes and took a deep breath—not easy with the wind flailing one in the face, I might add. I opened one eye and glanced over the side, immediately regretting it.

Before I could take off the helmet to be sick into, Louise had put the plane into a crazy spinning nosedive. There was no way for me to not see the ground rapidly approaching us.

I might, possibly, have screamed.

Possibly.

She pulled out of the dive perilously close to the ground and climbed again, taking me in a wide, lazy figure eight with the plane nearly sideways for too long. I think I passed out for a minute or two, which was all right by me, because the torture was cut that much shorter. When I lifted my head again, Louise was tapping my shoulder insistently, pointing to the right, hollering "LOOK!" into my ear.

Hesitant, I looked over the edge. The distant ground wasn't quite as dizzying when you weren't heading straight at it. Then I saw the capitol building and realized she was flying us over my house. I wasn't able to pick it out for sure at first, but she dropped down enough that I could see the distinctively weird shape of the flat roof area where we'd often slept on hot summer nights in the past.

And she did that sideways turn thing again and before I knew it we'd come to earth again with a thump.

The engine stopped and I sat there staring ahead of me, unable to move. Louise hopped out, saw my face, and laughed.

"You're still alive!" she cried merrily. "Just like I said! Hop out, goose, I have to put the plane to bed before I leave."

My legs shook all the way to the hangar, and as soon as we got there, I dropped to the ground and focused on breathing myself back to life.

Louise hummed contentedly as she did whatever it is pilots do after landing a plane, and eventually she came and crouched in front of me and said, "Pax?"

"Okay," I said. I gradually got to my feet, testing the steadiness of my legs.

"How was it?" She looped her arm through mine, just like old times.

"Do not ever... *ever*... ask me to do that again."

My stomach still felt unsettled enough at dinner I opted to take a tin of soup to my room to heat on my gas burner later.

But instead of settling to work at my table, I dropped onto my couch, where my mind fleetingly and unaccountably thought of Miss Johnson's eyes. I fell asleep instead of ever opening that tin, and I dreamed Miss Johnson came in, that it didn't matter I always locked my door. That she helped herself to a seat on my couch and grinned at me, eyes sparkling as she snuggled up to me, and I closed my eyes, hoping she'd let me get back to sleeping, but that didn't seem to be on her agenda. She seemed as well-rested as I would later learn two-year-olds are invariably well-rested at five in the morning. "I've been dying for more kisses, George. But I didn't feel it was safe to come up until tonight."

There was more to the dream, which I won't elaborate on. I woke up with a start eventually and checked to be sure my door was actually locked, then heated that tin of soup for breakfast. I went to the drawer for a book Mamma had given me so long ago, and extracted it from the depths. I sat at my table amongst my clutter of papers to read it whilst I slowly ate my soup.

I was surprised to see, in many of the margins, notes in Dad's handwriting. *He'd gone through and made notes for me.*

I didn't leave the table until I'd read the entire book. There was a great deal of space devoted to the allegedly harmful practice I'd done in my sleep. Dad had written in the margins:

> *Your mother was the one who picked this book out for you, but I don't think she read it thoroughly, or else not being a man she doesn't notice some things. Obviously anything can be overdone, but most "self-abuse" talk is utter codswallop, and if anyone should know, it would be me. Do I have "fishy eyes, a weak back, and a lack of vigor"? Never have, never will, and if on occasion you have the urge to do this, it's anything but going to kill you. How do you suppose I got through the war without your mother, and all those years in Turner when she was uninterested in anything but surviving?*

Okay, Dad. That was information I hadn't needed.

There were a load of blank pages at the end, which he'd filled with stuff the book had

> *conveniently left out because apparently only after marriage is one to be initiated into the secret knowledge of sexual intercourse, but no child of mine should think any of this is shameful. Whether you choose to wait until you're married or not is your business, but here's what you should know.*

This was followed by more details than I'd thought possible to give. Not merely the description of the physical act, but how to make sure the girl enjoyed herself as much as I doubtless would. It felt positively indecent, but I soldiered through to the very end, then I pushed the book away with one horrified finger and leant back in my chair to reason things out.

Now I understood my reaction to Louise on New Year's Eve. A physiological response to the mutual excitement of having danced so well. That was all. Okay, and maybe that dress had something to do with it too, in spite of my general immunity to visual attraction. It didn't mean anything, I told myself. And my response to Miss Johnson's kiss had been the same. I knew I didn't love Miss Johnson; in fact, I felt a little scared of her. But the dream (or the reality?) of last night had been undeniably pleasant and, therefore, the response.

I weighed all this against the Biblical injunctions I'd had hammered into me over the years: self-control over all things; flee youthful lusts. Those hadn't been hard for me and I hadn't understood the fuss other boys made over both. Lindbergh jumped onto my lap and I sighed, leaning my head into my hand.

Whether or not Miss Johnson had actually been there last night, personally aiding me in this foray into forbidden territory, didn't matter.

It mustn't happen again.

I was startled by a knock on the door and Louise hollering, "Are you decent?"

Questionable, I thought. "Just a minute." I shoved the book back into hiding in my drawer, tossed the offending clothes out of sight by my bed, and went to unlock the door.

Lindbergh jumped with excitement at the sight of Louise, and she scooped him up and met my eyes over his head. "Your mother wanted me to make sure you were still alive, since the bottomless pit didn't come to breakfast."

"I'm okay," I said. "I brought soup to heat last night and fell asleep over my work, so I had that for breakfast."

She looked over my shoulder at the heap of papers. "Are you going to work for your dad again over the summer?"

"Yes." I sighed hugely. "Starting Monday."

She laughed. "You'll live. So, shall we street perform again this year?"

"I'm game."

"How about today?"

I looked at my table, and she said, "George, school is OUT for the year, you can take a day off!"

"Okay." I glanced at my watch. "It's almost lunchtime. I need to eat first."

She ran her thumb over my cheek, impishly. "And shave. There may not be much there, but it's enough you need to get rid of it."

I rolled my eyes, but we went down the back stairs, set Lindbergh free in the backyard, and entered the inner Sanctum.

Things seemed back to normal. Maybe the plane ride had been worth it after all.

LOUISE

*T*onight at prayer meeting George talked about the seventh Psalm. It was nothing I hadn't already heard, although his time limitations on Thursday night forced him to abridge it from Russian Doorstop Novel to, oh, Magazine Story. (I cannot tell you how many afternoons I've spent listening—okay, *half* listening—to him EXPOUND.) As always, his delivery was perfect and his thoughts clear and organized. At the end, as we were heading to the door to leave, an older lady we all called Grandma Marybelle came hobbling over toward us, leaning heavily on her cane.

She was one of those people who just radiated her love for Jesus in every aspect of her life, and we all adored her. She greeted me and Mother with her customary hug and turned to George.

"Young George, the Lord has asked me to give you a word."

He finished tucking his notes back inside the cover of his Bible and looked up, smiling. "I'm listening."

She hesitated, glancing to see if she would be overheard, then reached out for his hand, speaking in a low voice. "You are a bright young man and you have a clear way of setting out your thoughts. But..." she sighed, clearly not wanting to hurt his feelings. "When you are converted and the Lord takes up residence in your heart, you'll be able to use those talents He's given you so much more effectively."

George blinked at her, his smile still frozen right where it had been when she'd first greeted him. Grandma Marybelle went on. "Now, don't take this the wrong way, George. The Lord told his own disciple Peter about what would happen after he was converted, too, and Peter had already been working for Him a long time. I'm not saying you're not doing good work already. I'm just saying that it will be better after you've personally *experienced* Psalm 7."

She smiled at him, dug around in her bag for a moment, then handed him a small parcel. "My husband was a minister. This was one of his favorite books and he shared it with every aspiring preacher he met.. I think you'll find it helpful." She gave him a hug as well (which he didn't return), and continued on her way out the door, hugging everyone in her path.

George didn't speak until we were almost home. He had looked annoyed at first, but by the time he spoke he seemed more confused than annoyed. Mother went inside and George said, "Is she right?"

I didn't hesitate. "Yes."

"You've never said so."

"I've said you're awfully full of yourself, which is much the same thing, just in less polite terms."

"But I have been converted," he argued. "Why else would I have joined a church and been baptized and all that?"

"I don't think it ever all happens all at once," I said. "It's decisions every day. Learning every day. Wouldn't you say?"

"I guess."

We were silent for a while and I said, "You were rather all about the wrathful judgment and instruments of death aspect. If it was me, what I think about reading that psalm? That there is judgment, but it's fair and involves the deliverance of the righteous from the oppressor."

I'm not sure he heard me, because he said, "I'm used to being criticized for my Jewishness and my use of the Hebrew Scriptures so much, but this is new."

"What's the book?"

He undid the wrapping and angled it so the light from the window could reveal the title. "*Quiet Hints for Growing Preachers.* Well, I suppose that might be helpful."

"I think you should go visit her and talk more about it," I said.

He didn't answer me, and still looked troubled as he pocketed the book and walked away toward home.

GEORGE

I decidedly did not love working for my father, but it was an available job and it was relatively easy, and it did help pay for my schooling and whatever other things I needed. After breakfast that first Monday after school, Louise came to see us off (and be sure I was properly equipped with a tie).

On the way to the office, I watched Dad, who enjoyed the daily parade down the street, beaming at everyone we passed, tipping his hat to ladies, well aware of the effect he had on them.

If anyone had Elinor Glyn's "It", it surely was my father. He still turned heads, even past fifty, even though his hair had gone sandy in the last few years and begun thinning in the back, much to his chagrin. Even if I wanted to be like Dad, I never could be. It wasn't about the specs and the shortness, but something fundamentally different in our natures.

Without my glasses I looked almost exactly like Dad had at my age, but I would never be a charmer, never be a ladykiller with conquests left and right. I would eventually marry, I knew, because it was easier to be a minister if you came with a wife. But whomever she ended up being, I wanted her to be The One and stick with her forever.

Not that there was much point in thinking about it now, since I wasn't going to settle down until I graduated, anyway.

For the moment I was back to the distasteful grindstone of taking notes, answering the telephone when Dad's secretary was busy, and poring over documents until my brain had gone soggy.

"You actually *like* doing this?" I asked Dad that afternoon, returning from an errand I'd run for him. I felt grumpy already and it was only my first day back.

"So much so, I hire other people to do it for me," he said, winking. I cut my eyes at him, but he was still talking. "I wouldn't make a good minister, you know. Or a good earl. I'll leave the former to you and the latter to Jamie and do what I am good at."

"Okay, then," I said, and sank into his vacated chair to sharpen his pencils. Even the part of the work Dad did do himself didn't appeal to me. I watched whilst he and his secretary, a fearsome battleaxe of a woman he had nicknamed Daisy Delight when he'd hired her years ago, conferred about something or other at her desk. She pretended not to be amused by the nickname, but even she couldn't resist him, it seemed. I watched them and I thought, *No wonder Mamma half expected him never to come back to her after the war.* It wasn't that he had any romantic inclinations toward Daisy, but everything about him indicated he could, if he wanted to, bed any woman he set his sights on. It was no secret that he'd been a serial adulterer throughout his first marriage, until he fell in love with Mamma and settled down. He'd never been unfaithful to her. (I knew this because Mamma made no secret of the fact that if he ever was, she would throw him out without ceremony.)

I again thought of my dream of Miss Johnson. My mind had constantly been drifting back to her since. What would it be like to be confident and cool like Dad, to charm her with ease?

But what would be the point?

I was still staring at Dad and Daisy some minutes later, lost in my head, when Dad startled me out of my reverie. I looked at the pencil, which was now only two inches long.

"Och, you thoughtful ones are a' the same," he scolded playfully. "Wouldnae notice a bee stinging you."

"Sorry," I said, determined to pay attention to this next pencil. "Did you ask me something?"

"When you've finished obliterating my pencils," Dad said, "you can *clean the windows and sweep the floor and polish up the handle on the big front door—*"

I threw the two-inch pencil at him, and we both laughed.

74

I was still humming that ridiculous song several hours later when Louise showed up to make a nuisance of herself for the last few minutes of the day.

Ever since Louise's stepbrother had kidnapped her in 1927, she and Dad had developed a rapport I didn't understand, but it was undeniably entertaining to watch them verbally sparring with each other.

"I've been to the grocer for our mothers," she said, as the head of the firm waited for us to get out so he could lock up. "You be your gallant self, Mr. Graham, and take my mother's parcel, won't you?"

He feigned to stumble under its weight and she laughed. "I've finally convinced her to stop trying to cook. It means a great deal of canned soup, but at least when I heat it up, I don't burn it." She took Dad's briefcase, dropped his hat onto his head, and walked along between him and me. "I could have driven, but it's such a lovely day, who wants to be in an old car?"

"I don't mind carrying stuff," I said, taking the other bag. "It's not that far, and Mamma's bags are always lighter." I stuck my nose into the sack. "I see cabbage salad and strawberry shortcake in our future."

"The grocer's boy is delivering the rest of the order. Tomorrow you'll also be having that beef stew with the carrots and potatoes in, and two extra mouths which will happen to show up just as it's being served, because even if Mother doesn't notice what she eats, I get mightily tired of canned soup."

I laughed, because for all Louise's complaining about her mother's inability to cook, the reality was she was little better at it herself. She and I dropped behind Dad, comfortably quiet for a few minutes before my dream again came to my mind and I said, "Sometimes I wish we were kids again. Not all the time. Not the secretive parents part, but—" I tried to figure out what exactly I did mean. "Being an adult is stupidly complicated, that's all."

"We're not adults yet," she reminded me mischievously. "You're the one in such an all-fired hurry to be an adult, not me."

"Didn't say you were," I said, defensively.

"And anyway, I will be an adult before you no matter how you look at it, because I was born first."

I muttered something uncharitable and she laughed. "You need a foxtrot to put you in a better mood. Poor George, stuck in a dusty old office all day with legal papers instead of in his dusty old attic with theological tomes. Let's make an impromptu dance party after dinner. It'll do the boarders good as much as us."

So that's what we did. Mrs. Pearson, uninclined to dance herself, provided the music, and Louise made me dance with the Misses Robinson and Mrs. Tabitha and Olivia and Natalia. I noticed she didn't suggest I dance with Miss Johnson, who had melted out of the room earlier under Louise's withering glares.

It was just as well I didn't have to dance with Miss Johnson. I knew I'd be flustered thinking of the dream.

I finished off by dancing with Louise, because the evening wouldn't have been complete without showing off a little.

"You two are an utter delight," Miss Clara exclaimed to Louise and me as the party broke up. (Or maybe it was Miss Faye.) "You move like... like..."

"Like a well-oiled machine?" I suggested.

"We move," Louise said drily, "like a man and woman dancing. We are not a machine, George. Or at least I'm not. Goodnight."

And she sailed out the door, arm in arm with her mother, into the night.

I went up to my room a little later to find Miss Johnson there waiting for me. She was on my couch with a portfolio in her hand and had pulled the lamp closer so there was more light nearby.

"I was beginning to think of giving up and going to bed," she said, laughter in her voice. "I brought up some art, if you want to see."

The sight of her there set off a flood of confused emotions. I perched on the edge of the couch and took the portfolio from her, afraid to relax too much lest she take that as an invitation to start anything.

I opened it and she scooted forward as well. "I picked all pencil sketches," she said, "since that's what you said you do."

Her style was realistic but stark, with bold lines and deep shadows and a sharp attention to detail. The view from her window; two children playing in front of the Capitol building with their dog;

76

a boy working at an easel; a couple of self-portraits; a few scenes I recognized to be from *Little Women*; and a squirrel on a stump.

"Sometimes I illustrate for magazines," she said. "Not as much now that I'm teaching, but I like to keep my hand in."

"These are beautiful," I said, softly, meaning it.

"I wondered if you'd let me draw you."

"Right now?" I asked, glancing at my watch.

"It wouldn't take long. I can finish it on my own later if I get the sketch down."

"If you like," I said, and her eyes lit up. She pulled out a fresh piece of paper from her bag and a small canvas roll with little pockets for pencils of varying hardnesses, and cocked her head like a bird to observe me.

She got up several times to rearrange the lamp so it lit me to her satisfaction and told me to look at a certain point on the wall over my bookshelf, so I did.

About twenty minutes later she said she had what she needed.

"Am I allowed to see?" I asked, but she snapped the book shut with a glint of mischief in her eyes.

"Not yet. When it's done."

And she gathered everything up and was gone so fast I hardly had time to realize she was leaving.

LOUISE

Mother didn't get the university job. I saw the letter when we got home tonight. They said she was capable but had been led to believe she had the paper to prove it, which she doesn't and another candidate did, and that made me angry. She is being Stoic Scandinavian about it, but I can tell it hurt her deeply. She already feels bad enough for having missed the chance to attend Oberlin Conservatory and acquire the paper that would prove her worth. I wonder what Miss Baxter told the university to mislead them like that. It would have been better not to have had the interview at all. Also, I just know whoever that other candidate was couldn't hold a candle to Mother, paper or not!

My mother sat down at a piano at the age of three and showed such immediate skill that her grandmother gladly spent every last penny she had to get her the best possible teachers. Not many people know that. Nor do they know how she holds scores in her head. How she can immediately identify the pitch of any sound she hears, and whether an instrument is the tiniest bit off-key. She even thinks in verse.

I want so much for Mother to have her dreams come true. Her agent needs to try harder. I'm going to have a talk with her.

Anyway, I decided that now it was summer, it was time to tell Mother of the first stage of my plan.

"I want to quit school," I said to her, after I'd brushed my teeth and was passing her bedroom door on the way to my own room.

She was sitting on the edge of her bed, still dressed, looking contemplative, but when I spoke, she jerked to attention.

"I won't hear of it," she said, without hesitation.

"I want to start working a regular job and move on with my life. I'm done waiting for George."

She bit her lip and considered, then looked at me again. "No," she said. "I gave my consent for the flying lessons, but I will not sit by and watch you drop out of school. You get your diploma and after that you can do as you please. It's only one more year."

I heaved a sigh and went to bed.

The thing with Mother is, I've spent so many years looking out for her and she has, in her turn, been unexpectedly tolerant of my flying (of which she didn't approve and probably deep down still doesn't). It is very, very hard for me to do things I know will hurt her, because she's already been hurt so much by life. And I do worry about leaving her alone, with nobody to make sure she remembers to, say, eat occasionally.

I asked her once why she'd never looked for another husband, and she said she'd been approached a couple of times by widowed men from church (this surprised me, as I would have thought I'd notice anyone the slightest bit lovestruck with her) but she'd vowed that as long as I was under her roof she was never risking my safety around stepfathers again (once was enough) and refused all offers.

"I don't need a man," she'd said staunchly. "I need my daughter to be safe, and anyway I have my piano."

I flopped onto my bed and made a few quick calculations in my head, then decided I would do what Mother asked.

I thought of the reply to my letter that I'd fished out of our mail without her seeing and hoped the offer would still be there next summer.

This summer, I was going to make the most of every day so when the time came, I could be gone quickly. I took a pencil and scratched out a reminder to myself.

"Speak to Mr. Eyerly re: air mail delivery."

GEORGE

*T*he summer drifted by, and I had no more disturbingly lucid dreams of Miss Johnson, but I did have the actual Miss Johnson in my room many times. She always came when it was very late, sometimes as I was getting ready for bed, and kept me up talking for hours. She said she suffered from insomnia.

I wanted her to stop and not to stop, because whilst I longed to get plenty of sleep, she got me drawing for her and taught me things I didn't know, technique that had never occurred to me, and my art did improve.

One night she said she wanted to show me how to make better use of perspective, and I watched, fascinated, as her hand and the ruler guided the pencil to create a web of outlines and guidelines, explaining all the while the rules for what she was doing, until the form of her picture began to emerge on the page. Her face was all concentration and, unlike me, she seemed completely unbothered by my watching. I could never draw worth beans if people were watching me. As she worked she explained about other things as well, such as positive space and composition, but I hardly heard her.

It was a garden scene, with a little girl sitting on a bench built around the trunk of an ancient tree, surrounded by rose hedges and other flowers. A path led away to an open wrought-iron gate in the background. The little girl on the bench wore an old-fashioned frock and held a sketchbook and pencil and was looking directly at me with an adoring smile when she handed it over.

"It's you, isn't it?" I asked her. There was something *living* in this drawing that had pulled me right into it. I could almost smell the roses and hear the oak leaves rustling overhead and the laughter of the little girl, felt the pull of that gate to see what was beyond it.

"The last truly happy moment of my life." Her face had become sad; her always-haunting eyes refused to meet mine.

"Why?"

"There was a photograph of this moment, you see. It's why I know how I looked just then. My mother's priest liked to photograph me, and later he gave her a copy of this one. I had to look at it every day, sitting on the sideboard, for the next ten years and remember."

"Remember what?"

She tucked her pencils back into their pockets, not meeting my gaze. "He took the picture and then asked me if I wanted to play a game with him at his house. Of course I did. We'd play tag or hide and seek many afternoons. And also he always had my favorite candies. He'd slip them to me after confession and after mass. My mother didn't allow me to have much candy so it was our little secret."

I waited. She folded her hands on the table and continued.

"At the rectory it was very quiet. Usually the old woman who did his housekeeping was banging about somewhere, but she wasn't around that day, and the curate wasn't either. I asked him for a peppermint and he said he had a whole bag full waiting for me as a prize after the game. 'Can we play hide and seek?' I asked, and he said he had a better idea.

"I trusted him, George. I liked that he hugged me a lot and let me sit on his lap for stories. Nobody else did those things. Well, his game was a ruse, of course. What he did to me was... well, I'll let you fill in the blanks. Afterwards I ran home and told my mother. She said I mustn't accuse a man of God of such a wicked thing. She never called a doctor to look at me, or looked herself. She refused to believe me and said I was lying to get attention or cause trouble for the father."

I stared in silence until she realized I had no idea what blanks I was supposed to fill in. "He raped me, George," she said, bluntly.

My heart raced with horror. "People do that? To little girls?"

Her face was stony. "You're such a child, George. Yes, they do. And they get away with it, usually."

I laid my hand on hers and she raised it to her lips and kissed it, holding it tightly. "It wasn't just that once, either. So many, many times. He said God had told him to teach me how to help him feel better."

I had no words and just sat there in silence for a long time, holding her hand. "Then after about two years he lost interest and some other pretty little girl caught his eye. He didn't want gangly ten-year-olds."

"I'm so sorry," I said, my eyes filling. Hers were dry, which mystified me. I asked, "Doesn't it make you want to cry?"

"I ran out of tears years ago." She sighed and briefly leant her head against my shoulder as if telling the story had worn her out. "Anyway, nobody wants me now. One man thought he did until he found out about the priest. I was just trying to be honest with him. That was the end of that. Men only want an untouched maiden." Her voice was bitter. "So I changed my name and ran away from home and went to college to become an art teacher instead."

"It wasn't your fault," I said.

"He was so beautiful," she said, as if she hadn't heard me. "How could someone so beautiful be so rotten inside? I was so sure he really cared about me. Nobody else loved me, not then, not now."

"God loves you."

She laughed. "No, he doesn't. He didn't stop that man."

"That wasn't God's fault. We have free will."

"*My* free will wasn't consulted. No, George, I don't believe in God anymore. Don't try to change my mind."

"But you do deserve to be loved," I insisted.

She kissed my hand again, then dropped it as she got up and tied her canvas roll of pencils closed.

At the door, I opened my mouth to try once more to comfort her, but she pressed her fingertips to my mouth and shook her head. "Forget I ever said anything about it, George."

And she left, not just for the night, but for an entire week, visiting friends in Pendleton. I found that, haunted by her story, I missed her company and wanted to prove to her that she was worthy of love. I decided that must be why she wanted to kiss me so much. She was sad and needed comfort, and who was I to refuse her a little of that?

Louise more or less abandoned me that summer as well, which was part of why I didn't try harder to get rid of the only other person interested in spending time with me. Louise had begun flying air mail and was hardly ever home, so I had nobody to dance with or see pictures with.

Louise sent postcards, when she could, but it wasn't the same.

So Miss Johnson it had to be.

My mind was flustered and confused from lack of sleep, to the point even my father was noticing it at work and being unusually sharp with me.

One Friday night, I fell asleep at my table upstairs and was startled awake by soft hands squeezing my shoulders.

It was Miss Johnson, of course.

"Did you miss me?" she asked, her eyes bright.

I tried to play it cool, but the truth was I was very pleased to see her. "I did, rather."

"I've finished your portrait at last. I'm sorry it took so long." She unrolled the scrolled paper in her hand and pinned down the two edges with her fingers to keep it flat so I could inspect it. She leant in closer so her cheek was pressed against mine. "I'm so afraid you won't like it."

I studied the drawing in silence for a very long time. She'd portrayed me in profile. It was unmistakably her style, which I was coming to believe I could recognize anywhere, but it also had an element of softness that didn't usually figure into her work. There was something of the religious in it, with the lamp angled so as to create an almost-halo behind my head.

"Is this how you see me?" I asked.

"It's how you looked. If you hate it, don't say so."

"I don't hate it. I just wasn't expecting something so... saintly?"

She removed her fingers from the page, letting it roll itself closed, and helped herself to a seat in my lap, resting her forehead against mine, her hand against my face. "You are a saint. You've been kinder to me than anyone else has bothered to be."

I shrugged slightly, uncomfortable with the praise.

"I know I'm a lot older than you," she went on earnestly, "but sometimes I feel like I stopped growing up that day when I was eight, that I'm still that little girl trapped inside a woman's body. And you are so lovely and kind and … oh, I don't know. I feel like you could make me right with the world again, if you could only love me a little. You do love me, don't you?"

"As a friend, yes," I said, cautiously.

"I don't ask for anything more than that," she whispered, and then she kissed me.

There was something desperate about it, and when she paused for a moment at last, she said, "I met someone I knew while I was gone. Someone from before I ran away. I think he recognized me. It scared me. I don't want anyone to know where I've gone." She pressed my hands to her breasts. "I need comfort, George."

"What kind of comfort?"

"Make me forget."

I took my hands away, a little panicked. "I don't want—"

"I'm not asking you to take me to bed with you. Just a little touching."

I looked away, my fingers nervously tracing the corner of the nearest book cover to hand, lost and confused.

So she took me over to my couch and demonstrated exactly what she expected of me, and I, in a moment of weakness, did what she asked.

When I'd finally satisfied her, I looked at my hand as if it was some alien thing that couldn't possibly have been controlled by my brain, and some of my sense returned to me. She lay back in the cushions, eyes closed and blissfully limp. She didn't see me wipe my fingers off on my handkerchief as I scooted backwards as far as I could without leaving the couch.

"Don't run away," she said, not moving. I couldn't speak, and when she at last opened her eyes, she laughed, a merry rippling sound. "You should see your face!"

She slid down to her knees on the floor in front of me. "All right, you deserve a little of the same as a token of my gratitude."

"What—" I began hoarsely, but she pressed a finger to my lips and got into my trousers with an efficiency that should have alarmed me.

"You mustn't," I said.

"It's not a sin if we're both dressed and only using our hands."

I thought of Dad's commentary in my little book, indicating his general agreement with this philosophy, but what she was doing to me drove any sort of reason out of my head completely. I sat there, lumplike, awash with feelings I didn't know what to do with, until she'd finished with me and I felt like the world had stopped spinning and that I could sleep forever.

I must have dozed off, because the next thing I knew, she'd gone, and I was alone with Lindbergh. I sneaked down to the bathroom to clean up, and made sure my door was locked when I came back.

Then I went to bed, but I didn't sleep. I was too busy brooding over what had happened, afraid of a reprise, hating that it had felt so nice.

Miss Johnson wasn't to be so easily put off, however. Only a few nights later, I happened to meet her as Lindbergh and I were on our evening stroll, and she went along beside me, seeming to be in love with life and the world.

I wasn't happy to have her there, and I interrupted her monologue, "Where will this stop, ma'am?"

"What do you mean?"

"What happened the other night." I almost choked on the words. "Next time you'll want something else. You're toying with me and my virtue and I don't like it."

She tried to take my arm, but I shook her off and lowered my voice. "I don't want you in my room any more, Miss Johnson. I don't want you touching me or asking me to touch you."

"Who are you saving yourself for?" she asked, a hint of scorn in her voice.

"That isn't the point. The point is it's not you."

"You like kissing me. Or else you're very good at pretending."

I flushed. It was true, I did. But I evaded responding to that. "I can't marry you. You know that. A minister's wife needs to at least believe in God! And I don't want to be... intimate... with anyone but the person I marry."

She stopped walking and looked up at me.

I stuffed my hands deep in my pockets, fixing my eyes on hers. "Listen," I said, my heart in my throat. "I liked what you did to me the other night. That's all the more reason not to have it happen again. I am choosing to exercise some self-control. I messed up and that's all there is to it. So... please... stop coming to my room. I need you to let me be."

I ran the rest of the way home, Lindbergh at my heels.

Louise

The air mail flights were marvelous. Mr. Eyerly arranged everything, and I went to Seattle by train to collect the plane I'd be using and make my first run of deliveries. The man in charge there seemed surprised to see I was a girl, but I finally convinced him that I was, in fact, a licensed aviatrix and a flight instructor, with many hours logged of both night and day flying. I got to make stops all the way down the coast to San Diego and back again, and I was busy all the time, so I hardly ever made it home. But I sent postcards.

Mother and George wrote to me, too, in Seattle, so I could collect their letters whenever I came back there. George's were unusually restrained. Ordinarily full of grand thoughts and plans, now his letters mostly just told me what he was doing every day, which was going to work and coming home to study. It struck me as odd, and I wondered what was going on inside his mysterious head that was too big even for his powers of expression.

Until I made it home for a quick visit one weekend, and then I knew.

It was that schoolteacher.

I wasn't sure what precisely was going on, but *something* was, and the first opportunity I had I took George aside and demanded to know. He shrugged and said everything was fine and nothing was going on.

He was lying, which was also uncharacteristic of the George I knew, and my worry deepened. I could see he wasn't happy, yet I also saw how his eyes followed that woman around the room any time she was nearby. It was like he couldn't help himself. I saw her, resplendent with curves and exotic beauty, and thought, *I can never compete with that. If that's what attracts him, I can never compete.* I wished fiercely for the millionth time that I wasn't such a boring bean pole.

After George went up to his attic, I caught Mr. Graham by himself for a minute when he came out to have a smoke on the porch and asked him, "Aren't you going to do anything about George and that schoolteacher?"

He didn't answer right away, just stared through his smoke out across the yard.

I went on. "He won't talk to me, but something's not right. I know it. Surely you've noticed."

He tapped some ash into a flower pot on the railing. "I haven't wanted to worry Alice, and Miss Johnson hasn't broken any rules I know of. We can't exactly throw out a boarder without good reason, and anyway this house is her business to run and I don't interfere unless she asks me to."

"He's your son," I objected. "What's more important, him or the income?"

He took another drag, sighed, and nodded. "I'll keep an eye," he promised.

I stepped back from the railing, but didn't leave, my fingertips still resting on it. "Am I ugly, Mr. Graham?"

He looked at me as if shocked. "Absolutely not," he said. "Whatever makes you think that?"

"Because he's never once looked at me the way he looks at her."

He put his arm around me and hugged me to his side, kissing the top of my head. "Then he's a fool. But who ever really knows what's going on in that head of his, Louise? You're both young. There's time. It's not as if there's anything actually going on between them."

I wanted his words to reassure me, but I wasn't sure he was right. "You don't think they're having secret midnight rendezvous at the park?"

He laughed. "That boy might be suffering from a case of puppy love, but she's got better things to do with her time."

I looked up at him. He dropped the butt of his cigarette into the pot and met my gaze. "I'll keep an eye. I promise. But I don't think you need to worry about a thing."

But I knew George's father too well to believe he really thought that.

GEORGE

School began again, and Miss Johnson was otherwise occupied at last. But she did come up one time, on a Saturday night, to apologize for her behavior the last time and promise it would never happen again, that she was content to let it just be kissing. She'd gotten carried away in her loneliness, that was all. And I, like the fool I was, let her in. She kept her word, though, and I convinced myself it was all right now.

One evening I was studying when I heard a step on my stairs. My heart leapt to my throat and dropped to my toes as it always did when Miss Johnson was nearby. But it was early for a visit from her.

No, it was only Dad. He wandered in, hands in his pockets, wearing his lawyer poker face that, at home, always means he's terribly ill at ease but isn't about to let you know as much.

"Hi, Dad," I said, watching him furtively whilst pretending to study.

"All alone?" he asked, casually. Too casually.

"Of course," I said, instantly defensive. "Why wouldn't I be?" And then I could have kicked myself, because I'd just fallen for my own father's infamous disarmament tactics.

Dad ran his fingers idly along the back of my other chair, flexed them, and sat down. "Does she spend much time here, George?"

The impulses to protect myself with a lie and pour out my confusion to my father instantly went to war.

"I would like to invoke my fifth amendment rights," I said at last, quietly.

Dad sighed. "There's something about her," he said, his tone still unnaturally casual, "that says desperation and danger."

"Nobody else thinks so," I muttered. Not true, of course. Louise certainly thought so. Her latest dire warnings still rang in my head. *You're too good for the likes of her.*

"Nobody else in this house has been around as much as me," he reminded me with a rueful smile, drumming his fingers lightly on the tabletop. "Not that I'm proud of it, mind, but it's a rare woman I can't read like an open book."

I still wouldn't meet his eyes, which I knew were fixed on me. He cleared his throat and waited, obviously expecting me to offer defense or argument, anything but this stony silence. He didn't know the stony silence hid a desperate wish to know exactly what he'd read in Miss Johnson.

"I won't interfere," he said at last, "but I wanted to—to be sure you were—"

"I'm fine, Dad," I interrupted, and it sounded sharp and utterly unlike me, and I think it startled me as much as him. Although he will take on a stranger quite fearlessly, personal confrontation within our family makes Dad back off like a cornered mouse, and he backed down now, lifting his hands to indicate surrender.

"Okay," he said. He waited a minute as if hoping I'd relent, but I didn't, so he said goodnight softly and left, closing the door behind him.

I stared at the door for a long time, my studies forgotten. How had he known? What had betrayed me, and did anyone else also know Miss Johnson came to my room?

If Louise knew, I'd have heard about it. If Mamma knew, she also wouldn't have hesitated to give me a tongue-lashing (after throwing Miss Johnson unceremoniously to the street), so I doubted either of them knew.

Kicking out a paying boarder was not something Dad or Mamma would want to do for no good reason, and I was pretty sure Dad wouldn't tell on me unless it became absolutely necessary.

The thought occurred to me then that it was too late and the damage had already been done. Miss Johnson had taken away something from me I would never get back, and I didn't want to contemplate that too deeply. I just needed to make sure she took nothing more.

Easier said than done. The truth was, Miss Johnson had become a sort of addiction for me, something I didn't want but couldn't say no to. For all my bravado on that walk back in August, when it came down to it, I could never follow through.

Which is why, one night in October, she was in my room again and we were sitting at my table drinking tea. I told her about Dad's and Louise's warnings, and she reached for my hand and squeezed it. "Well, I'm not here to make trouble for you, George. Wouldn't dream of it."

I looked at her, not feeling any easier in my mind.

"Kissing isn't a sin," she said. "And I promised I wouldn't ask you to do anything else!"

I took my glasses off, not to kiss her, but to press my hand over my eyes. I was getting a headache and desperately wanted to relieve my exhaustion by climbing into bed and falling asleep.

She rested her chin on one hand and ran the fingertips of her other hand up and down my arm. "You do look so like your father with your glasses off," she said, dreamily. "Well, a younger version, anyway. He's gorgeous."

"Can't help being nearsighted," I said, inwardly wishing that if she found Dad so attractive, she'd pursue him instead. Then Mamma would take care of this entire problem by kicking her out.

She scooted her chair closer to me. "Well, we'll have to sit closer so you can see me properly."

Her tone was layered with meaning I was too tired to decipher, and attracted and repelled me all at once. The attraction won out, however, and the next thing I knew I was kissing her, and then she was astride my lap and I was dazzled by the softness of her legs under my hands, and I remembered the relief she'd brought to me that other night and knew I was teetering dangerously close to letting her do it again.

She whispered, "I think you would be absolutely marvelous in bed, George."

The words startled me and I blinked and shook my head to clear the cobwebs, and I pushed her off of me, panicked. "I can't," I said, hoarsely, frustrated at my delayed resistance. I buried my face in my hands and took several deep breaths. "It's wrong. I won't be like my father."

She was on her knees, framing my face in her hands. "It's normal. Natural." Her voice was oddly hypnotic. "You were made to do this."

I pushed her away again, perhaps too roughly. "You need to go. Go and not come up here any more. Ever. I mean it." Babyish tears threatened what little composure I had left.

She gave me a hurt look, but she left.

I locked the door after her, threw myself onto my bed where Lindbergh had been curled up asleep for ages already, and I wept bitterly, for the first time realizing I was in chains I couldn't break on my own, and the chains were of my own making. I should have listened to Louise and Dad. I had to put Miss Johnson out of my mind, out of my sight, out of my heart.

I was so tired.

In the cool, rational light of morning, I wondered (as I often did) how much of what happened last night had, in fact, happened and how much might have been a dream and whether it had really been so bad.

But I had to stop rationalizing it all away. Dream or not, I was still lusting after a woman I barely knew. I didn't even know her birthday, let alone anything concrete about her family or background or where she grew up. She herself had admitted the name she used now was not her real one. I only knew the now of her, and, as Louise was constantly reminding me, Miss Johnson was too old for me.

As I prepared the lesson for that Thursday's prayer meeting, I became acutely aware that I was the least fit person in my congregation to deliver it. I soldiered through, but my shame was intense, and I knew I couldn't hide anything from God. It was his opinion that ultimately mattered to me. My allowing Velma Johnson into my life had fogged any vision I had of what God's will for me actually was.

Miss Johnson again avoided me, and I avoided the communal parts of the house as often as I possibly could. I think Dad knew something had shifted, but he didn't ask, and Louise had gotten somewhat moody again since school began, without elaborating to me why. It possibly had to do with losing the argument with her mother about skipping out on finishing her last year of high school when she could have been working and earning money instead. We still danced, Louise and me, but my heart wasn't in it, and I was distracted, and we weren't reading together or talking like we used to.

One night, a couple of weeks before Thanksgiving, there was a knock on my door. I'd been expecting Louise, so I'd left it unlocked and called out "Come in!" from my room where I'd been putting away the latest batch of my clean laundry before Lindbergh could fur it. I heard my outside door open, but when I poked my head around my bedroom doorframe I was alarmed to see it was Velma standing there, her face full of penitence.

"I'm here to make it up to you," she said, taking a box of Lyons' Tea from her bag. "I bought it on the way home tonight. I know it's your favorite. Shall we make peace?"

She took off her hat and coat, draping them over a chair back. She was wearing an ivory and pink floral dress that clung in all the right places. I averted my eyes, knowing I should say no, but also... maybe she was in earnest and I didn't want to withhold forgiveness from someone genuinely sorry.

"Okay," I said, and turned back to my task so I didn't have to look at her.

She hummed softly as she lit up my gas burner and got the tea things from the shelf, and I thought it was a bit alarming that she'd come so early. What if Louise showed up whilst Miss Johnson was still here?

"I'm expecting Louise," I informed her, still not looking at her as I came out of my room to sit on an empty corner of my bookshelf.

"Well, I shan't stay long," she assured me, moving toward me with a cup in each hand. I mutely took the one she held out to me, my breath catching in my throat in spite of myself. She was so beautiful.

She raised her cup. "To us, George," she said.

I didn't raise mine. "Us, as in how?" I watched her suspiciously.

"As fellow artists pledging friendship eternal."

I still sat there like a lump, so she clinked her cup against mine and took a sip.

At last I sighed and began to drink my own. It was strong tea, with cinnamon added to it, and I drank it quickly, thinking the sooner I finished it, the sooner she would leave.

She refilled my cup, and I thought, *I will drink the entire rest of the pot if that will make her leave sooner.* Miss Johnson didn't have a second cup herself, just watched me with an unreadable expression in her eyes.

When I'd finished, she took my cup and set it aside, folding her arms and leaning against my bedroom doorframe, as if she was waiting for me to speak.

98

"It's rather warm in here, don't you think?" I said, huskily.

"Feels all right to me."

I stood up, intending to open a window, but I seemed to have lost the ability to balance myself. I fell back onto the shelf-seat and put a hand to my head attempting to still the dizziness my movement had caused.

She came over to me, gave me her hands, helped me to my feet. Her dress was falling off her shoulders, and I squeezed my eyes shut against the spinning act my head was doing, against her. I tried to get some deep breaths, but that didn't seem to help.

She pushed me up against the wall, and with a little shake, that dress of hers came the rest of the way off, sliding like a floral waterfall to her feet, and I stared stupidly at her. I'd never seen a naked woman before—not a real one, at any rate. She wasn't marble or paint. She was a living, breathing woman, and she had me under her thumb.

An enchantress.

I am mistress of the world, and men are made happy by me.

My hands had become passive and wouldn't respond to my mental commands to push her away. She pressed them against her bare breasts.

I closed my eyes, refusing to look. WIth a shudder all Louise's words and Dad's warnings flooded into my mind, and my own failed attempts to keep Velma at bay.

My hands dropped away from her the moment she let go of them. I desperately wanted to lie down and sleep, anything that would shut her out and clear my head of her spell. She unbuttoned my shirt slowly and deliberately as she went on.

"Men are all the same, really. You all only want one thing."

You started it, I wanted to say, but her touch against my bare shoulders was like an electric shock as she slid my shirt off.

She made appreciative noises about the muscles in my arms that were betraying me when I most needed them, and I found my voice. "No," I whispered, my voice choked. "We're not all the same. I don't—I don't want this..."

"Yes, you do," she countered, caressing my traitorous parts that responded to her in spite of my desperate wish that she would go away and spare me this. "You've wanted me since you first laid eyes on me. You've lusted after me. You're just too damned stubborn to let yourself be a man about it."

Again I thought she had driven me to it. It was only her eyes I had loved at first, and now I hated the sight of them. "Velma," I said, my voice an unmanly whimper. "Go away. Don't—don't do this to me."

She gave me that smile again. "Potiphar's wife wasn't as clever as I am." She pulled at my wrists, and I stumbled away from the wall toward her, my head spinning more wildly than ever. I felt unnaturally hot and too distressingly weak to resist her. She dragged me along until she could topple me onto my bed.

"I'm desperate," she said. "I've wanted you since the minute I first saw you, and since you won't give in—well. I tried to make you initiate. Since you won't... well."

I couldn't speak; I could scarcely breathe, she was pressing my chest so hard with her hands.

"It's not fair that you get everything I never got," she said, her voice breaking. "Parents who adore you. Who'd die to protect you. I need you to understand what it's like to be hurt."

She has gone mad, I thought.

"My angel preacher boy," she murmured, the words cutting like a knife, as her lips brushed my skin. "Fallen angel, in a minute. You'll be mine forever now, even if you never see me again. Because I will live in your head until the day you die. You will never make love to anyone without remembering *I had you first*."

I tried one last time to push her away, but my arms felt like jelly and my mind had begun to fog over. I don't remember much after that.

The next thing I knew, the morning light was streaming through my window and woke me like an ice pick driving between my eyes, and I was curled into a ball under a blanket.

A woman's silhouette rose up, reaching for the drapes, and I cried out, "No! No, go away!" and turned my face into my pillow to hide the light and my springing tears.

The drapes fell, cloaking the room in a comforting dimness.

"I know you're not wearing your glasses, but surely your eyes aren't that bad! Who did you think I was?"

It was Mamma's voice, and like a small boy I sat up and reached for her, and she came to me, her face intensely concerned. Mamma doesn't much like being touched, but she didn't pull away as I clung to her and cried inconsolably into her shoulder for a long time.

"I've been trying to rouse you for ages. I don't remember you ever sleeping so deeply! What's going on?"

I wanted to tell her what happened, but I couldn't get past, "She said—"

"Who is 'she'?" Mamma asked, after my third or fourth attempt. I could feel her worry like a tangible thing. I didn't typically cry in front of my mother, let alone hang onto her like a lone rock in a stormy Pacific Ocean.

"Velma. Miss Johnson," I finally managed after a long sobbing stammer.

Mamma tensed. "Do you want to tell me this or would you rather I fetch your father?"

"Don't leave me," I begged, still clinging. My head was splitting, and the idea of being left alone filled me with horror.

Mamma helped me lie back down and laid one cool hand over my forehead like a blessing. "What did she do to you?" Her voice was thin.

I shook my head. I couldn't tell my mother that.

"Well," she said at last, drily, "you needn't be prudish. I can draw my own conclusions. Aside from the fact your dog got left outside last night, my sense of smell is in good working order, plus you're not usually inclined to sleep in your birthday suit on top of your covers."

"*Mamma*," I moaned in shame. I hadn't needed to know that's how she found me.

"I'm not accusing you," she said, still stroking my head. "I once engaged in an ill-advised drunken liaison myself. We all do stupid things. We can move on. I find it difficult to believe you instigated something like this, however."

I groaned. "I didn't, and I didn't want any drunken liaisons, and anyway I didn't drink anything but two cups of tea."

Mamma's hand immediately went still. "Tea that you made?"

"No, she made it. I was folding my laundry in here."

She rushed out to the other room and I heard her fussing with the teacups and rummaging around. She returned with a bottle in her hand, which she upturned and let a few drops fall into her hand so she could taste it. I watched through one cracked-open eye.

"Your father would be able to say for sure, but I'm guessing this was vodka." Her lips pressed tightly together. "You wouldn't have tasted or smelled it in the tea, and once she got you buzzed she'd have loaded the second cup with almost nothing else, knowing you'd never notice." She set the bottle down. "For all I know, she could have added something else to the mix, too. I'm calling your father. This is serious."

I didn't have the energy to try and stop her. I closed my eyes and wished I could go back to sleep. I did sleep for a while, because when I next opened my eyes, the light had shifted in the room, and my head hurt a great deal less, although it still throbbed when I sat up. Lindbergh had been let in, too, and he snuggled up to me, chin on his paws, looking at me with devotedly doggy concern.

I eased myself to my feet with a groan and made my way to my chest of drawers and pulled out clean clothes. I dressed, slowly, my fingers stubbornly clumsy over the buttons. I found a pair of socks and crept out slowly toward my front room. I saw yesterday's clothes, still lying where Miss Johnson had left them, and I shied away from them as if they were lethal poison. I dropped miserably into the corner of my couch, leaning my head back into the cushion and closing my eyes, forgetting I'd intended to put on the socks still in my hand.

It was only then I realized Dad was there, too, on one of my wooden chairs. I didn't see him, but he spoke. "Son, your mother told me what she knows about last night. Can you tell me the rest?"

I didn't stir or open my eyes. "Does this have to be now?" I asked, weakly.

"Well, that depends," Dad said. "After she phoned me, your mother went to have it out with Miss Johnson, but she didn't turn up at school today, without any explanation. Came back to find her room all in a mess. Only the essentials seem to be gone, so I'm guessing she's skipped town. Leaving behind a stack of rather filthy books in her room that your mother's currently feeding into the fire downstairs, I might add."

I made a disgruntled noise.

"She also found these." Dad came to sit beside me and held out several sketches, all of them recognizable as me and Velma in a variety of compromising situations. I turned my face away. "None of *that* ever happened."

He set them face down between us. "Your mother told me about the tea. I agree, it was vodka," he went on. "And I'm gathering there was some sex involved in whatever happened here?"

"Dad," I said, my throat constricting. "I don't want to remember."

I felt a light touch on my hand, and I flinched away as though his fingers were fire. He withdrew them and regarded me solemnly. "Did she force herself on you, George? Is that why she had to drug you, because otherwise she couldn't overpower you?"

I blinked at him, tears burning in my eyes. I looked at the socks in my hand. "Yes," I said, almost too quietly to be heard.

Dad's face twitched and he pressed one finger to his mouth. "Why, George? Why would she?"

I told him. "She kept saying she was sorry and wouldn't tempt me again," I finished. "I was stupid enough to fall for it. She was lonely and hurting. Things happened to her when she was little. I pitied her. I was trying to be her friend, and sometimes we did have lovely times just drawing together."

Dad rubbed his forehead with his hand. "Do you want to press charges? Because it's going to be hard to find her at this point, and proving anything outside of what was in that teacup will be your word against hers, but I will do anything I can for you. You know that."

I squeezed my eyes shut. *My angel preacher boy. Fallen angel, in a minute.* Her words flooded back into my mind and I shrank even further into my couch. "No!" I said sharply, and more loudly than I'd intended. I couldn't bear having to tell a court what she'd said, what she'd done, how *stupid* I had been. I couldn't bear reliving it. And Louise would have a heyday saying "I told you so."

Louise. "You haven't said anything to anyone?" I asked, panicked. "I mean about me—this—"

"Not without your say-so," Dad said. "Your mother is furious, but she'll keep quiet, too, if that's what you want."

"Please," I begged pathetically. "Don't tell anyone. If Louise has to find out, I want it to be from me, not anybody else."

Dad held out his hand to me again, and this time I put mine in his and he squeezed it. "I should have stepped in sooner. I knew something wasn't right... I wanted to give you space to make your own decisions." When I didn't answer, he stood up. "I'll get you some coffee."

Lindbergh jumped up to lick the tears off my cheeks.

Later that night, when I was putting away some books from my table, a piece of paper fell to the floor. It was the sketch of little Velma in the rectory garden, from that long-ago art lesson. At the bottom she had written:

> *This keep in remembrance of me.*
> *I loved you, angel preacher boy, the only way I knew how.*

LOUISE

I was all set to go over to George's as planned when the telephone rang. It was Mr. Eyerly, from the airfield, asking me to make a quick night run to Roseburg for one of the other lads whose car had refused to start and he couldn't make it in time. I scribbled an explanatory note to George, left it stuck into his doorframe, and hurried off to the airfield. He would be busy studying anyway, and he always worried if he knew I was night flying, so it was easier on both of us for me to not knock.

I made my flight there and back and fell into bed for the few remaining hours until morning, when I dragged my unwilling behind to school. When I came home, Mother was sitting at the piano, not playing. She looked up when I ungracefully flopped onto the sofa, and said, "That art teacher who was boarding at the Grahams' has disappeared."

My eyes popped open. "What?"

"Alice says she left in the night."

"Well, good riddance. Maybe now George can stop being a dope over her."

Mother sighed. "You noticed that, too?"

"Of course I did."

"I don't think he's been very happy for quite a long time," she said. Her fingers soundlessly traced the edges of the piano keys.

"Maybe he murdered her and buried her in the basement like Dr. Crippen," I said, in jest. Mother gave me a disapproving look.

"Sometimes people mistake things when they're young," she said, quietly. "Maybe he's confused about what it actually means to love someone."

"Well, if he could channel even *half* of the energy he wasted pining after her into paying attention to me, we'd be married yesterday," I said. "I should go see him."

"I'd let him be tonight," she said, reaching out a hand as if she could stop me. I shrugged and went to have a bath.

GEORGE

SALEM, OREGON: DECEMBER 1932

After that first day, I shut up like a clam about what happened, to everyone. The boarders and Louise and Mrs. Pearson all knew something had happened—Velma Johnson's departure was precipitous, after all. But Louise seemed to assume it was just me moping that my crush had left. She'd long ago stopped bothering to lecture me, but I knew Louise must be thinking about her now. Her and me. Wondering what we might have been to each other.

I felt painfully alone. I pulled away from everyone, including Louise, too ashamed to face what had happened. I didn't want to relive it, so I stuffed it all and tried to pretend everything was normal. But the memories came to haunt me in darkness and dreams. If I hadn't been almost eighteen, I'd have been tempted to crawl into my parents' bed, to know I wasn't alone, the way I'd done when I was very little.

Early in December, Louise came to my room, where I was curled on my couch with Lindbergh, as if impersonating a hedgehog would protect me from facing facts. She stood there with her arms folded: not angry, just assessing.

It had been a long time since we'd been alone together, and the distance that had expanded around us over the last many months seemed uncrossable. I looked at her with a sense of hollow desperation.

"Are you getting any sleep, George? You're pale as a ghostie and turning into a regular twig."

"Hello to you, too," I said, trying for the old levity, but I didn't meet her eyes, only hauled myself to my feet and paced, my hands deep in my pockets. She followed me, laying a hand on my arm, and I paused. The ever-present airplane bracelet caught a sparkle from my lamp, and for some reason the sight of it pushed me over the edge. Louise cared about me, and I had been such a terrible friend for such a long time. I sank to the floor and started to cry.

Louise was a safe person to cry with. She joined me on the floor, cradling me in her arms, stroking my hair, whispering, "Rest, George. Rest. Be quiet."

I don't know how long we sat there, but eventually I cried myself out. Louise handed me one of her man-sized handkerchiefs.

"Is this something to do with... with *her?*"

I blew my nose. "I can't tell you."

She raised her eyebrows slightly in that "seriously, George" expression I knew so well. I dropped my gaze away from her scrutiny and blew my nose some more.

"Talk to me, George. Please just tell me. Whatever it is. I can help."

I shook my head, and she sighed, clearly disappointed at my refusal.

"Your mother sent me to fetch you," Louise said, after it became obvious I wasn't going to be volunteering any further information. "Dinner's on. You've hid out long enough and we need to practice dancing. Also, you've a letter from Uncle Jamie."

I didn't want to go downstairs. I didn't eat much dinner, my heart was not in the dancing, and my mood was still heavy when I finally escaped up to my room several hours later, to read the letter I'd stuffed unopened into my pocket.

I'd written a couple half-hearted letters to Uncle Jamie in the past month, paragraphs of nothing, and for some reason I found myself dreading the contents of this one. What if he'd found me out? With shaking hands, I unfolded the paper.

My dear George,

Your latest letters concern me deeply. They do not seem a bit like you. Where is the George who loves to share his latest theological discoveries and grand dreams? What has happened to so utterly change you? Please remember you can always tell me what is in your heart, and I will never share anything with others that you wish to remain private.

My feelings of loneliness and defeat intensified, and I fetched paper and my fountain pen and scribbled a note back.

Dear Uncle Jamie,

Something has happened, and I don't know how to write about it, but the shame is eating me away. Mamma and Dad know, but I don't want to talk about it with them. Mamma is too angry, and Dad wants to solve the unsolvable problem. I just don't know who I am, or what I am, anymore. I wish I was dead. George

I shoved the letter into an envelope, addressed and stamped it, and took it downstairs. The house was silent and sleeping aside from my own stocking feet and Lindbergh's nails clicking softly after me. I bundled up in the coat and hat hanging on my peg, slipped into my shoes, and stepped out into the cold December mist with my dog.

I dropped the letter in a mail collection box a few blocks from our house and walked on down the quiet street. Finding no relief in mere movement, I returned to my own back steps, sank onto the topmost one, and sobbed.

In the cold solitude, I realized several things all at once. My ambitions had been foolish and self-serving. My sole motivation for my career choice had to do with my confidence in my own abilities and the thrill I got from my audiences' flattery. Now I allowed myself to think about it, I wasn't sure I'd ever had the true spirit of Christ in my heart.

Grandma Marybelle's words of months ago came back to me with a slam. She had been right. I'd thought I was a mature adult and understood so much, but now I knew I was anything but, and I couldn't follow a calling to the ministry with that sort of self-reliance, not if I wanted to be honest about the work.

I buried my face in my knees and, with one hand on Lindbergh's head to anchor me to reality, I started talking to God in a way I hadn't in a very long time.

I can't get rid of this guilt and I want to be free. I was wrong, what I let go on for so long. I should have told someone and trusted the consequences to you. Should have talked to you, at least, and I didn't. You said if anyone comes to you, you won't cast them out, so... I'm here. Help me believe you forgive me, so I can forgive myself, and change me to what you want me to be instead of just what I want.

The night was quiet, the mist otherworldly, and I looked at the sky, as if I expected an audible answer. *I've been awful. I need absolution, assurance, anything you can give to help me know you still love me. If I should even continue at seminary. Am I too wicked to be a minister now? Have I gone beyond pardon?*

I rested my head on my arm against the top step, becoming drowsy as my teeth chattered and my limbs no longer wished to function because of the cold. I kept praying for a long time, Lindbergh standing guard beside me as if he knew this was a moment requiring nobody interrupt me.

And then something odd happened.

I had my eyes closed, huddled there on the steps, but I felt a sensation as of a blanket being draped over me, and even though my eyes were shut, I could see it was made of light: gentle, golden light, warm and reassuring, as if God himself was wrapping me up and taking me in his arms to soothe and rock his troubled child. Every tense muscle in my exhausted body relaxed.

I didn't know yet if I could still be a minister, but I was warm, and God loved me. That was all that mattered just now.

I do not remember going into my attic, but when I woke in the morning I was snuggled into my bed, and hot embers glowed in my coal stove.

Both Christmas and Hanukkah presents were the furthest thing from my mind that year, and I foolishly waited until the twenty-third to do my shopping. I'd almost asked Louise to come with me, but she'd been busy helping Olivia prepare to leave on some ballet adventure after New Year's, so I set out alone without asking her.

I bought rosewater for Mamma. Pretty lace-edged handkerchiefs for Mrs. Pearson, because she always carried them. Hideous pink and purple argyle socks for Dad.

For Louise, I had more difficulty. I wandered aimlessly, out of my element in this sea of possibilities. I considered earrings, but I'd already given her a bracelet and I was afraid more jewelry might look like groveling.

I ended up at the bookstore, which was comforting to me, being there in its familiar walls, smelling the delightful booky smell. Louise was not a great reader, but her analytical brain did enjoy mysteries, so I asked the salesman what the latest mysteries were. (It was not a genre I kept up with.) Maybe she'd let me read it to her. It had been nearly a year since we'd last done that.

"Well, we have one copy of *Have His Carcase* left," he said, taking it down to show me.

I didn't even crack it open. Louise liked Sayers' books.

"I'll take it." I took a moment to inscribe the inside before letting him wrap it for me, and I added it to the pile beside me in the passenger seat of the Buick.

Louise should be here, I thought, holding the parcels and ribbing me good-naturedly about how much dithering I did, and how only Uncle Jamie could possibly be more at sea when it came to gifts.

And that's when the lightning bolt hit me, dazzling me with the obvious. I sat there with my mouth open like a frozen fish, trying to take it in.

I was the one Louise wanted. *I* was the Uncle Jamie substitute she'd been waiting for.

And waiting.

And waiting more.

Because I was too stupid to see what was right in front of me.

I leant my head on the driving wheel and let the tidal wave wash over me. The way her insults were always somehow so sweet. Her patient tying of my ties, despite complaining like fury. The times she'd stood up for me when I wasn't sticking up for myself. The way she liked to nestle into me in a way that was cozy, but not in the least bit inappropriate.

I like you just the way you are, small bespectacled shrimp boy.

Get warm before you walk home.

Shouldn't we toast to something?

She'd *wanted* me to kiss her that night. She wouldn't have punched me. The dress, the Cokes, the toast, it was all a shameless bid for my attention, and it had *almost* worked.

If I had kissed her, if I'd opened the door for her to tell me her feelings, there would never have been any Velma Johnson. I'd have been too busy planning a future with the girl who'd been bickering with me for seven years, dreaming of continuing to bicker with her for the next seventy-seven, to bother with some seductive art teacher with a predatory bent. I would have been safe.

I started the car with a warmth in my heart I hadn't felt in ages, breathless from the headiness of realizing I was loved, and not just as a friend, by a girl I loved back, in my own way. I could go home right now, take Louise in my arms, tell her I'd finally figured it out. Maybe it wasn't too late.

Then, like ice water, the thought: *I'd have to tell her what really happened with Miss Johnson.*

I wasn't ready to do that. It was too raw to discuss.

And also, if I was going to be honest with myself, the idea of touching or kissing Louise romantically terrified me. She would want that, and I didn't think I could deliver. It had been hard to explain to Miss Johnson how I didn't feel attracted to people that way, and I felt so broken by her, I knew it would be even harder to connect now. Louise deserved someone who could make love to her with abandon and like doing it. Before Velma, I hadn't cared to try; with Velma I had learned it wasn't so bad; after Velma, I didn't know if I could ever like it again.

I sat there with the engine idling, trying to imagine it. Taking Louise aside, away from everyone's eyes on us, and pulling her into my arms and kissing her. She'd be warm and responsive. She'd like it. She'd want more. And that was where my mind dropped its shutters with a slam. The "more" was Velma Johnson's hands all over me and a complete lack of control. I wasn't ready to face that again, not even with Louise.

I drove home morosely. It was the first night of Hanukkah, and Louise and her mother would be over. Mrs. Tabitha, Olivia, and Natalia usually joined us, but this year they were going to spend the evening with other friends.

I piled my gifts onto Mamma's bed, then went to my room to get ready for the evening. As I passed the photo of Louise and me on that silly paper moon, arms linked so we looked like we liked each other, I picked it up and studied it. I remembered that day as clearly as if it was yesterday: dinner and dancing and *Dr. Jekyll and Mr. Hyde.*

Remembered the way Louise had cradled me in her arms the other day as Muriel had in the film with the agonized Dr. Jekyll. *Rest. Be quiet. Rest.*

How had she held it in for so long? How had I never noticed?

Maybe I hadn't wanted to notice, because to notice would mean facing facts about myself I preferred to leave undealt with.

How could I, the child of parents who so enthusiastically and rather loudly enjoyed each other, have turned out so unlike them?

Surely it wasn't normal for me to be this way.

In contrast to my subdued melancholy, Louise was in a particularly effervescent mood when she burst into the Inner Sanctum with her mother, bearing their own gifts.

Mamma took their coats and laid them on the bed, and the celebrations began in earnest once Dad arrived home bearing a ridiculously large sack of Hershey's kisses, which had to stand in for gelt because there wasn't proper gelt to be had in Salem.

"Mother's got a new job!" were Louise's first words. "Well, for the next six weeks, anyway!"

"What is it?" Mamma asked, and Mrs. Pearson explained that she'd been contracted to play live from a radio station in Portland three times a week in the early afternoons for an hour. It wasn't the best time of day, but it was a place to start, to be heard. She was to play a mix of current and classical pieces, and her agent was letting her stay at her place for the duration so she didn't have to constantly come up and down.

"What about your students?" Mamma asked.

"I've told them we'll resume when I return," Mrs. Pearson said.

Mamma beamed, and Louise hugged her mother fiercely, and we all went to the window to watch Mamma light the first candle.

I adored Hanukkah because it was so *happy*. Even today, in my despair, the atmosphere of celebration went a long way toward lightening my mood. We all spun the dreidel with the competitive intensity of small children. Mrs. Pearson won the lion's share of the Hershey's kisses, and we all stuffed ourselves with delicious food. Mamma took up a sufganiyot at one point, turned to Dad, and said something to the effect of, "Is raspberry still your favorite?"

"You know it is," he said, and she smashed it against his mouth and started to dart away, but he caught her wrist and pulled her back in for a melodramatic kiss that left jam and icing sugar all over Mamma's mouth. "Guess we have to lick each other clean now," he said, far too loudly.

"NOT IN FRONT OF MY VIRGIN EYES," Louise yelled, feigning shock, and the two of them went around the corner to do whatever it was they had in mind.

After they emerged, with disturbingly little evidence of the smashed doughnut remaining on either of their faces, we began to hand gifts around.

Louise had knitted me a red and gold scarf exactly as long as I was tall, with a smaller matching one. "For Lindbergh, if you can convince him to wear it," she said. "I had leftover wool."

"It's so... bright," I said, secretly loving it very much.

"Not as bright as your father's ties," she retorted, "and anyway your boring old wardrobe needs a bit of dash." Turning to Dad, she said, "I went questing for the most hideous necktie in town, and I do believe I found it." She tossed him a parcel, which he caught with a grin, and for a moment the room became loud with groans from Mamma and me, whoops of delight from Dad, and uproarious giggling from Louise. It was indeed the most hideous strip of painted silk ever, but he immediately swapped it with the one he was wearing and sported it proudly the rest of the night. Mamma scolded Louise for encouraging him in his nonsense.

I put on the scarf and discovered to my delight that, when wrapped in it, nobody could tell whether I was wearing a tie or not. I said this aloud, and everybody laughed again. Lindbergh tolerated his scarf long enough for Dad to take a photograph of us, but afterwards I tucked it into the corner of a drawer and forgot about it.

Throughout the evening, I watched Louise with new eyes, and when the night ended and I went to bed, that icy bucket of despair poured over me again. I was alone, so intensely alone, walled in by my demons, and I couldn't breathe and everything was closing in black around me.

Lindbergh must have gone to get Dad, because an indeterminate amount of time later I became aware Dad was beside me on my bed, whispering to me to breathe, stroking my hair, his hand warm and gentle like that blanket of light from God.

I couldn't turn back time to last New Year's Eve and fix the mess I'd made. I couldn't explain to Dad what was wrong. I could only lie there, nestling as close to him as I could get, because I thought if I stopped feeling him there I would no longer exist. I would drown.

Louise

Well, *something* is up with George.

He seemed more himself tonight. Not much, but a little. But he kept watching me, and I felt like he had things he wanted to say, but didn't know how to. I guess when you go as long as we have without having our usual time together, it gets harder to know how or what to say. I know I have trouble these days. There's so much I'd *like* to tell him, but it's hard to bridge that gap.

Anyway, it was good to see him smile about the scarf, and inside the front of the book he gave me, he wrote: *To the best friend anyone could ever ask for. Maybe we can read this one together like we used to. Merry Chrismukkah from George.* I imagined him saying the words and it made me happy. Sometimes I wished I could eat his voice with a spoon.

I sat at my desk and ran my fingers over his familiar backhand and thought about his quirky habit of using his composition books from back to front—not, he said, because it was the Hebrew way, but because when you're left-handed, nothing is designed for you and you have to make things work as best you can.

I loved that he was left-handed, like Uncle Jamie.

tPeople of Uncle Jamie's social status usually have very formal dining arrangements, with the man at the head of the table and the wife at the foot, but Aunt Estelle sits to his right because, she says, they can hold hands under the table while they eat. They are not like most people of their class. I've seen they can behave, when guests are present, but when it's just family, the table was the goofiest exhibit of bedlam I've ever seen. Uncle Jamie pretends to be put out, but we all know he loves it as much as anyone.

I dreamed often of having the same seating arrangement in the home I'd make with George someday, except I'd hold hands with him on top of the table during our meals, not underneath.

I looked at the wall where I'd hung his silly drawing of me kissing Charles Lindbergh and felt warm inside remembering the obvious pleasure it had given him to make it for me.

I thought of the glances George kept surreptitiously giving me all evening. There was something puppylike in that look, shy and a little lonely. For some reason it made my heart ache, and I went to bed wishing I could hold him close and comfort away whatever was troubling him.

GEORGE

SALEM, OREGON: JANUARY 1933

I shouldn't have been surprised when Uncle Jamie showed up at our house the second Saturday afternoon in January. I expect he'd planned to set out the minute he received my pathetic letter.

Good old Uncle Jamie.

We'd been in the communal sitting room on opposite ends of the couch (Louise had all but moved in whilst her mother was in Portland) and I was reading Louise her new book, when the doorbell rang. Louise got up to answer it, and the *shriek* she emitted made the rest of us run out to see who was murdering her.

It was just Uncle Jamie, and Dad and Louise took turns hugging him for a straight five minutes. I hung back, self-conscious, knowing full well I'd be grilled at some point in the near future.

I was so anxious about the confrontation I knew was coming, I could hardly eat, and the hollow ache in my heart grew larger. It was hard to sit beside Louise as I always had and yet have our formerly intimate friendship be hanging on such a fragile thread. It had been hard to read to her. I hoped it would get easier, that the cloud between us would clear away.

I was jerked out of my mealtime woolgathering by Louise poking me and saying, "Well, I'm glad you're here, Uncle Jamie, because if anyone can sort out this bundle of joy next to me, it'll be you."

I knew she was trying for levity, but it was salt in my wounds, and I bit my lip, mumbling words that were supposed to be excusing myself from the table, and escaped up to my attic.

Maybe if I let myself cry, I'd feel better. But try as I would, I couldn't get any tears out. I lay my cheek against the table. It was hard and uncomfortable, but the pain felt like penance, so I didn't move.

It wasn't long before Uncle Jamie made his way upstairs and came to sit on the other wooden chair beside mine. He laid a light hand on my shoulder and said, "All right, laddie, out with it. You're like a ghost of yourself. What has happened to you?"

His voice was so kind. I didn't lift my head, but his presence triggered something and the tears started. He stroked my hair and waited, patiently.

"Velma Johnson," I said at last, my voice flat.

"The teacher who boarded here." His steady eyes were fixed on me. I could feel them.

When I finally managed to speak, my voice was uncomfortably loud in my own ears. "She said she wanted what I wouldn't give her. There was a priest who did horrible things to her when she was little." My voice caught, and then I did lift my head and saw the look on his face, and all the words tumbled out in a rush. Every detail, stumbling in embarrassment. "I never had alcohol before," I said, when I'd finished my tale of woe, gulping down a sob. "Well, not counting the sips of whisky Louise and I sneaked at the castle when we came for Susan's wedding. Anyway, it didn't take much before I was completely at her mercy. Dad thinks she put something else in too, maybe morphine."

Uncle Jamie put his arms around me, hugging me close, and I let a few tears slip out, and it felt freeing somehow, cleansing, to let them come. "I don't want it to be true, Uncle Jamie. But I was so stupid, I should have seen—"

"You were innocent, George. That's not bad. The bad thing is an older person taking advantage of that innocence. This is not your fault. It is entirely hers."

"But I've lost my reputation," I said. "I can't be a minister. Even if nobody else knows, I'll know. God will know! I'll never be able to forget it!"

"Shh," he said into my hair. "It's still a fresh wound, but it will heal, I promise you. You've committed no sin. There's nothing to forgive yourself for. Not one single thing. You give this to God, and He will heal you. What other people think doesn't matter. What matters is your confidence that nothing stands between you and your Savior."

I trembled quietly in his arms. "But isn't my not stopping her a sin?"

"She *plied you with alcohol!*" he exploded. "You didn't have control. You're not a criminal. Not in the laws of the land, not in the eyes of God." His own voice caught, and he held me more tightly. "Oh, George, why are the predators *so damned good* at finding the purest people to destroy?"

For a long time, neither of us spoke again. I was so tired; the heavy burden had been on me for so long. He helped me to my feet and over to my bed, where he dropped to one knee and, as I had once long ago done for him, he took off my shoes and set them aside, covered me with my quilts as if I were a small boy again, and kissed the top of my head.

"Can you get back up again all right?" I asked him, sleepily.

"Aye, I'll manage," he said.

But I didn't see how he managed, because I was asleep in seconds.

In the morning, the whistle of my teakettle woke me. I sat up slowly, slightly cramped from Lindbergh having slept on my chest for who knew how long. He looked very pleased with himself, but tumbled off when I stretched and sat up, stumbling my way past Uncle Jamie, who was the cause of the teakettle screaming. When I came back up from my wash, I got into my church clothes and came to my table looking and feeling much more myself than I had in weeks.

Uncle Jamie was like that for me. He had a way of putting things into perspective in a way nobody else could do for me. He smiled at me, a rare gift from my usually staid and somber uncle, and he brought me a cup of tea.

I had refused to drink any tea since That Night, and I felt cold all over when he set it before me. I stared at it for a minute and looked back up at him.

"There's only tea in it," he said, as if reading my mind, and gave my shoulder a gentle squeeze as he went downstairs, leaving me alone with that tea.

I could dump it. He wouldn't know. Except he probably would, because Uncle Jamie knows things.

It's all right. It's safe tea. And I took a deep breath and lifted the cup to my lips and drank.

There was no vodka, no cinnamon, no anything else. Only tea, strong and black and proper.

I could do this.

I carried my cup with me to the door to let Lindbergh out to the garden to do his morning business. I was still standing in the open door when Uncle Jamie came back upstairs. I sensed he was about to ask me something deep, and I decided to divert him before he got started.

"You didn't bring your dogs," I said, watching Lindbergh far below.

"I've gotten well enough in the last few years that I'm not as dependent on them as I used to be. Pain is real, but it is possible to overcome it."

"What happened to you?" I asked, feeling reckless and bold. I had told him my darkest secret. I wanted him to tell me his.

He was quiet for such a long time, I thought he wouldn't answer. "I watched somebody I loved explode before my eyes in France." He said it matter-of-factly, but I knew deep in his sensitive heart it was far more than a mere fact. "Forgiving myself for it took years. It was preventable; that was the worst part. But like you, I wasn't rational. I'd been falling apart for months." He paused. "You'll find a reason to keep going, George. Give it time. You let your guard down, like we all do sometimes, and the devil got to you. Now take God's hand and don't let it go again. He'll see you through."

I drained the last of the tea and tapped the cup with my fingers.

"Does Louise know?" Uncle Jamie asked me next.

"No."

"Why?"

"It's too personal."

"I thought you two shared everything."

"Not that kind of thing. Anyway, it's a little... complicated for us lately. This past year has put up some sort of distance between us. I don't like it, but there it is."

He fixed me with a Look, and I hesitated before I went ahead with what I was thinking. "I'm not attracted to girls. But I'm not interested in boys either, so I don't suppose I'm deviant. I don't..." I trailed off. "I felt perfectly satisfied with how Louise and I were. Just being together. It made me feel good and confident and whole. But I know she wants more and I'm not sure I can give her that, and even if I wanted to, I'd be constantly thinking of Velma and how broken she's left me."

I couldn't interpret his expression as he dropped into the nearest chair. "You can perform, but you don't want to, is that it?"

"I guess. I mean..." I huffed and pressed my fingertips into my forehead. "I love Louise and she deserves a man who is enthusiastic about giving her the physical love I don't want to."

He kept staring at me, and at last he said, "You need to give yourself time. Of course right now you're still working out this mess with Velma, but that doesn't mean you will never develop that kind of attraction to Louise. You did say you kissed Velma and liked it."

There was another long silence before he went on. "Are you really telling me you feel no attraction? Because I have watched the two of you dance and argue and exist side by side all these years and there has seldom been anything more like an old married couple than you two."

I laughed bleakly. "If there is, I feel nothing. At least... nothing sexual. Just wholeness. She's the other half of me."

He gave me a skeptical look, but he didn't say anything more.

LOUISE

George walked ahead of us to church, leaving me and Uncle Jamie to have a few minutes' private conversation.

"What's going on with him?" I asked.

"That's for him to tell you," he said, exactly as I knew he would. I sighed.

"That schoolteacher was bad news," I said. "I am surprised Mrs. Graham never saw that."

"Perhaps she did," Uncle Jamie said. "Perhaps not." Then he abruptly switched topic so quickly I was taken aback. "Do you remember the first Sunday you and I went to church together?"

It was a stupid question. The day was burned into my brain forever, and he knew it. He went on, "Have you ever told George what happened that day?"

"No," came my instant and indignant response. "Nobody knows except you and Mother. It's not something you just... tell!"

"I only wondered," he said, mildly. His face never betrays anything, and I got suspicious.

"You haven't said anything to him?"

"I never betray confidences, young lady."

I slipped my arm through his and beamed at him in grateful adoration as we ascended the steps, where George had stopped to wait for us before we all went in together.

GEORGE

*A*fter church, I told the rest to eat without me and took Lindbergh for a walk instead. Louise started to get up as if she intended to go with me, but I saw Uncle Jamie shake his head ever so slightly at her, and she sighed and sat back down again.

I walked with Lindbergh until we'd reached a particular stand of oak trees in a place called Bush's pasture. They reminded me of my childhood haunts in Turner, and of the first time Uncle Jamie had talked with me about God and prayer. I often walked here for my morning talks with God, but I hadn't been in over a month. Aside from that night on my steps, I hadn't prayed or studied my Bible or anything. I was unsure of so many things: not so much whether God could still love me, but whether I actually had a calling to be a minister.

I sat on a rock and looked at the steely sky. "Uncle Jamie said I was not too great a sinner," I said aloud. "I still want to do this work, if you really called me to it, and I want to be rid of this burden of guilt. Louise was right when she said nobody can help himself out of his sins. Through the merits of Christ alone." I talked for ages, spilling it all out with nobody but God and Lindbergh to hear, until the peace I craved finally settled back into my heart, along with a deeper conviction than ever that God did want me to keep on with my studies at seminary.

When I finally got back to the house, I was very tired, but calm. Louise came out to meet me on the back porch as I was about to go up my stairs to my attic, as if she'd been watching for me. She took my hands and studied my face, her own face etched with worry.

"I'm going to be all right," I said, quietly.

"Is there anything I can do?"

I shook my head. "Just keep being you," I said. "I've unloaded it all on God."

Unexpectedly, she threw her arms around me and gave me a ferocious hug. Usually when she hugged me, I never quite knew what to do with my hands, and for a moment I hesitated. Then she sniffled, and I said, "Hey, it's all right. It's really all right." And I put my arms around her and held her close. It felt right, and a tear trickled out of my own eye thinking how much more she deserved than me.

"About Miss Johnson," I heard myself whispering. "I'm sorry. You were right. But I don't want to talk about her again."

"Okay," she whispered back. "We won't." She still clung to me as if she, too, knew this was a moment not likely to be repeated and she wanted to treasure it, but at last she pulled back, looking all wet in the eyes. "I saved you some dinner."

"I'm not that hungry," I said, but she was already dragging me inside for it.

"You're a wee ghostie, lad," she said, in perfect imitation of Uncle Jamie. "Now eat before the wind blows you straight into the ocean."

So I ate, to please her, and then I did go to my attic for a few hours of solitary contemplation of the book Grandma Marybelle had given me so long ago and which I'd not yet read. When I'd finished, I went down to find my parents, Uncle Jamie, Mrs. Pearson, and Louise still sitting there.

"What is it?" Dad asked, and I held up the book.

"Listen to this." And I read:

> *Preachers as a rule are not simple enough. They imagine that deep thought and big words must go together. Let them read the first chapter of John's Gospel. No profounder piece of composition was ever written, and most of it is in monosyllables. "All of your sermons should be of the simplest," said Martin Luther to a growing preacher, and all successful preachers have acted on that advice. Bookish words which have not been domesticated in the speech of the average member of the congregation ought to be avoided. The great words are nearly all short words, God and man, heaven*

and home, wife and child, life and love, faith and hope, joy and grief, pain and death, all these and a hundred like them drop easily from the tongue. The words which lovers know and which mothers speak in soothing and instructing little children, and which fathers whisper in the chamber of death and sob beside the grave, and which all men use in carrying on the life and business of the world, are all simple words, and these are the words which should be most frequent on the preacher's lips. These words are stained through and through with the heart experiences of many generations. They carry with them a light and fragrance which fill all the room in which they are spoken.

Louise made faces that indicated she was biting back commentary, but Mrs. Pearson smiled warmly, and I felt that everyone understood without my needing to explain.

"That's just one bit," I said. "It's as if this entire book was written for me in all my uppity pomposity. Wait. That has four syllables."

"Try pride," Louise murmured. "Well, good for the book."

The next day I went to visit Grandma Marybelle, who had been too poorly to attend church for a long time, and we had a very long talk about the book, and we both shed a few tears. I didn't tell her the whole story, just some hints, but she seemed to understand. She prayed for me, and I for her, and I left feeling light and hopeful.

A few days later, she died.

LOUISE

SALEM, OREGON: JANUARY 1933

*T*onight George had prayer meeting again, for the first time in a while, and when he got up to speak, he opened up his Bible to the seventh Psalm.

"I know," he said, "that I've already once spoken on this psalm, but I don't believe I really understood it last time, so I hope you'll allow me to share some different thoughts."

And immediately I knew something had changed. Everything about his bearing and presentation was infused with such a sense of personal investment I had to remember to close my mouth after it fell open. Mother and I looked at each other and I could tell she was as surprised as I was. Gone was all the talk of wrath and arrows of judgment. Instead my friend stood there allowing his raw, beating heart to be exposed to potential criticism by the words he spoke. This time he lingered on the parts that talked about "if I have sinned"— because, he said, "I *have* sinned," and how God is able to make us righteous and defend us against sin and the wicked.

George is much more of a naturally weepy person than I am, but usually he has it well reined-in when he speaks. Tonight, several times, that composure cracked.

I just wish Grandma Marybelle had been there to see it.

GEORGE

*O*ne more thing about the first two-thirds of that year.

I would often look at Louise and question everything. Had I been wrong in believing she was interested in being more than friends? It made me feel strange all over thinking about it.

Because I knew once the subject was broached, we could never go back to how we were before, and I loved what we had too much to risk it, now that life was almost back to how they had been before Velma.

I say almost, because there was something different and unspoken. She seemed softer, less prone to teasing me, and she was completely focused on getting through the school year so she could be off on her Grand Adventure that she refused to tell me or anybody any details about.

But school ended, she graduated, and she didn't leave Salem.

I hoped perhaps she'd changed her mind and was going to stay.

I still didn't want to tell her the truth about Velma Johnson.

And now you have the backstory, Fizz. I expect you can guess what's coming next. You do know how the story ends, after all, even if you weren't clear how it began.

PART TWO

I am no bird, and no net ensnares me: I am a free human being with an independent will.

CHARLOTTE BRONTË,
"JANE EYRE"

GEORGE

SALEM, OREGON: AUGUST 12, 1933

I came in for breakfast after my morning walk to find Mamma and Dad in a mutual flap over the tiniest human I'd ever seen in my life. Dad had it close against his chest under his bathrobe, and it was screaming louder than I'd imagined such a small thing could scream. Mamma was frantically trying to warm some milk and find something to use as a blanket and a diaper all at the same time.

"What in the world?" I said, and Dad tried to explain over the ruckus.

"We heard a loud bang and a car screeching off, and then another noise... thought it was a cat, so I came out to investigate, and this baby was in a cardboard box on the doorstep."

"What kind of vile person abandons an infant like that?" Mamma spluttered. She'd finally succeeded in warming the milk. She didn't have a bottle, but she found a clean rag and got the baby to suck milk off it, which brought fits of quiet to the room at last. "And why our door? I should call Louise. If anyone can calm this baby, it'll be her..."

Not being particularly enamored of babies myself, I didn't give a hoot about the noisemaker, although I mentally assented to the idea that Louise should be summoned. But I forgot all of that when I glanced at the cardboard box as I passed and saw an envelope, which I lifted out, and then I knew why our door. A wave of nausea washed over me as I saw words scrawled across the front in handwriting I knew all too well. Cruel, heartless words. *I tried multiple ways to get rid of this, but it just wouldn't die. It's your problem now, angel preacher boy.*

I hit my head on the corner of the table passing out, which led to another flap, but I didn't have to hear it because I was out cold for a good half a minute. When I opened my eyes, Dad was propping me against him. He'd opened the envelope to look at what was inside. His mouth was pressed into a thin line, and he mutely held it up to Mamma.

She took one look and threw it to the ground, her eyes flashing, her mouth twisted as if she couldn't decide whether to cry or scream.

"What is it?" I asked weakly.

Dad reached for the paper and held it up so I could read it for myself. I squinted at it, uncomprehending, for some minutes. It was a birth certificate. This baby's, presumably, but why was that so angering?

"Only four days old," Mamma spat out. "That heartless bitch—"

Then I saw the words. *Full name of child: Hazel Mae Graham. Sex: Female. Date of birth: August 8, 1933. Legitimate: No.*

I covered my eyes with my hand and realized the table corner had knocked my glasses off. No wonder I couldn't focus. "Dad..." I said.

He helped me to my feet and over to their bed, where I collapsed and closed my eyes whilst Dad read me the rest, his voice unsteady. The child's mother? Velma Johnson, age twenty-nine, occupation: none. The father? George Graham, age eighteen, occupation: seminary student.

I was so angry I swiped the paper out of Dad's hand. It landed near the foot of the bed, and I turned over to hide my face in his pillow. I didn't cry. I was furious. Humiliated, too, but mostly furious. *Legitimate: No. Father: George Graham, seminary student.*

The baby was you, of course.

Mamma came in and said to Dad, "I need you to fetch me things from town. This child has nothing."

Dad snatched a pen and paper, and took a list at Mamma's dictation—in shorthand, because he used to be a secretary and still uses shorthand lavishly—and then he got shaved and dressed in a hurry.

He brought my glasses over before he left, and I put them on and sat up glumly as the world came into focus, propped Dad's pillow behind my back, and folded my arms across my chest. The initial fury was fading, and I felt like a sagging post-Hallowe'en pumpkin. Velma had carved out my soul and replaced it with this... this damning piece of paper and the noisy thing Mamma was still trying to soothe in the kitchen.

I took the paper again gingerly, re-reading it, my head pounding with the anxiety welling up in me. On the day you were born, perhaps at the very time, Louise and I had been sitting at the Elsinore, watching *International House*. It seemed vapid in retrospect. *I will never be able to escape this. Every time I look at this baby I will remember what its mother did to me. Everyone will assume I was immoral.*

But there was something else, too. This wasn't just about me. *Legitimate: No.*

Not only was I branded for the rest of my life, you were too. *Legitimate: No.*

It was so brutally, calculatedly unfair.

And then Louise walked in.

My heart thudded to the floor at the sound of her cheery voice in the kitchen. Now she would know. She would know what had been done. I could no longer hide it.

"Hallo, Mrs. Graham!" she called brightly. "Well, what have we here?"

"Special doorstep delivery," Mamma said crisply. "More like doorstep abandonment. Damn that woman."

Louise's face went all soft like it does any time she sees an upset child, and after a minute of cooing and petting, the screaming silenced and Louise beamed at Mamma, who looked relieved. Then Louise glanced toward me. I think she hadn't seen me yet. My hand crept toward the birth certificate, but she was too quick and I not subtle enough. She snatched it up with her free hand and read it.

I didn't want to see her reaction, but I also couldn't not look. All the color drained from her face as she glanced from the certificate to you in her arms to me.

"You—you *slept* with her?" Louise said. Her voice trembled and the look of devastation in her eyes cut me straight through. She

dropped the paper as if it had burned her fingers and stepped back, her eyes brimming with tears, her hand to her mouth.

"Louise," I said, "I—" I reached for her. She shook her head and backed away further. Her entire face contorted, desperately trying not to cry, but she lost control, pushed you back at Mamma and fled from the house. The back door slammed behind her, and the wailing

140

immediately began again.

I got off the bed to run after her, but Mamma caught my arm and pushed me back to the bed. "Let the girl cry in peace," she said. "You're going nowhere until we've had a family council."

But the moment Mamma disappeared upstairs with you to search for smallish blankets, about half an hour later, I darted out of the house, running like fury to the Pearsons' house. I bounded up the steps and let myself in. "Louise!" I hollered, frantic.

The house was too silent. I called again, anguish eating at my insides. Mrs. Pearson—timid, fluttery Mrs. Pearson—half-staggered out of the kitchen toward me and hid her face in my shoulder, crying. Mechanically I put my arms around her to comfort her, but how could I comfort her when I had no hope of my own, when I needed comfort myself?

"She's gone," Mrs. Pearson whispered through tears. "She wouldn't say where or why or anything. She just threw things in a bag and ran out the door saying she'd write to me later." She looked up at me. Her eyes were full of pain and anguish, too. Her voice had the old brittleness in it that had almost completely gone away in the last couple of years. "What *happened*, George?"

I shook my head and gently extracted myself from her arms and went into Louise's room. It was in disarray: drawers half-open with clothes hanging out, gaps on her bookshelf where her navigation and flight books were missing, aviatrix photographs torn off their pins on the wall.

It was what remained that was unbearably significant. Our paper moon photo, my silly drawing of Charles Lindbergh and the "Spirit of St. Louise"… anything I had ever given her, or made for her, remained in place like silent, accusing fingers. Something shriveled within me. The room without Louise was a diamond whose sparkle was missing. Too silent. She had actually gone.

I sank to her bed and stared vacantly into space, numb and cold inside. I don't know how long I sat there, but at last I rose to my feet and moved toward the door. My eyes caught a glimpse of sparkle on the carpet. I bent and found the chain of the bracelet I'd given her, the one she'd never taken off since I'd fastened it on her wrist on that long-ago birthday. I took it up in my hand. It was broken, and the *Spirit of St. Louis* charm was missing. I put the chain in my pocket and crawled around on the floor until I found the charm in the far corner. She must have hurled it as hard as she could as she stalked out. I held it in my palm, biting my lip, and leant back against the wall. I deserved this, I knew I did, but if only she'd given me a chance to talk to her—

You've had nine months to talk to her, my conscience pointed out. *You're an idiot, George. You've lost her for good now.*

I sat there so long, Mrs. Pearson came in to see if I was all right. She saw the charm in my open palm and burst into tears.

"What did you *do?*" she wailed.

I couldn't speak.

Back at my house, Mamma had words for me about running off when she'd told me to stay put, but her words bounced off me as if I was wearing armor.

By this time, the rest of the household knew a baby had been left on the steps, and Mrs. Tabitha was involved, running between the Inner Sanctum and the rest of the house with questions and answers. Had Miss Johnson deliberately chosen a Saturday to dump you off, to humiliate me, knowing everybody would be home?

When Dad arrived back, the three of us, with you noisily suckling at a freshly-sterilized bottle in Mamma's arms, sat together. Mamma and Dad rained questions down on me, but I stared stupidly past them, the Louise-shaped emptiness inside me hurting so deeply I couldn't process anything else. *We're not adults yet. You're the one in such a hurry to be an adult.*

Never had I felt less adult than I did at this particular moment, faced with being a parent.

"She's gone," I said, finally, interrupting whatever my parents were saying, and I looked at them, both gone suddenly silent.

"What?" Mamma asked, disoriented at the sudden derailment of her train of thought.

"Louise. She's gone." I hoped I didn't sound like I was about to cry.

They both stared at me hard and I said it again. "She's gone." I took the broken bracelet out of my pocket and held it out for them to see, then got up and went to my attic.

A little while later, Dad knocked on my door and let himself in. I was lying on my bed, Lindbergh at my side and the broken bracelet still clutched in my hand. He sat on the edge of the bed and sighed, taking my free hand in his. "I'm sorry, son. This is a lot to pile on you all at once, I know."

I didn't say anything, and Dad waited, quiet for once. I was touched at the effort it must have required for him to hold his tongue, and at last I said, "What if people at school find out?"

"They don't have to. They've no reason to ask, and unless they ask, you've no reason to tell." Then he added, "What are you going to do about it?"

"About what?"

"The baby."

I hadn't thought that far. It didn't seem real. Surely I would go to sleep and wake up to find it had all been a nightmare. "What should I do?"

"I can't make that decision for you, son. Personally I wish you'd keep her, but..." he trailed off.

After another long silence, I said, "Dad?"

"Hmm?"

"If I'd kissed Louise after that dance competition we won, none of this would have happened."

He looked surprised. "You thought of kissing her?"

I nodded, miserably. "I didn't because I was sure she'd be mad and I didn't want to ruin a perfectly nice evening. And I was..." I hesitated. "Afraid of turning into you if I let myself go once."

He rubbed his forehead with the heel of his hand, a crooked smile on his face. "Ah, George lad. You don't just 'turn into' anything. You just grow into what you were born to be. You do realize she's been crazy about you since forever, do you not?"

"I... yes, well, it finally hit me at Christmas last year."

"Why the hell didn't you tell her then?" Dad's voice rose just slightly.

"I'd have had to tell her what happened with Velma. It seemed too hard. I could barely think about it without panicking, let alone tell anyone."

"You could have written it out."

I could have. I hadn't thought of that. "But also I felt I wasn't... worthy of her anymore. That she deserves someone who isn't... tainted."

Dad rolled his eyes heavenward as if praying for patience. "George, if anyone can beat out your Uncle Jamie for crippling self-doubt, it's you."

I turned my head aside a bit away from him. He reached out and stroked my hair. "She never said a word," I said. "Never once hinted that's what she wanted from me."

"Some girls are very patient about waiting for the man of their dreams to make the first move. She's been dealt some hard blows in her life, too, George. I don't know all the details, but I do know she refused to be the initiator of romance between you two."

"How do you know that?"

"She told your mother, years and years ago. She's been playing her cards close to her chest ever since."

Man of someone's dreams, me?

I like you just how you are, small bespectacled shrimp boy.

I sat up and propped my pillow behind me. "What am I going to do, Dad?"

"Take care of your child, for starters. If you keep her, which, as I said, I hope you will."

Not an answer calculated to ease my anxiety. "I haven't any idea how," I said.

"Mamma will teach you. Every baby deserves love, son. This one will need it more than most, I suspect."

"Legitimate: No," I mused aloud, and shuddered. Velma had actively tried to miscarry you, perhaps even tried to get someone else to abort you for her. But you hadn't had any of it. You were there to stay, tenacious and determined and needy. When I looked at your round pink face, I wondered, would I always hear the words, *It's your problem now, angel preacher boy?*

"What if it grows up to look like her?" I asked. "*Be* like her?"

144

Dad sighed. "Can't help you there," he said. "All I can tell you is, any baby is its own person, and loving her and protecting her will go a long way to making sure she doesn't end up like her mother. Mamma will care for her during the day. You can have her at night. You won't have to give up school." He paused and added, "As for the illegitimacy, don't forget technically so were you."

"But I had your name and nobody knew you and Mamma weren't married," I countered. "It's not the same."

"She has your name," Dad said.

I heard footsteps and Mamma came in and laid you on my lap. "She's dry and fed," Mamma said. "And I gave her a bath. She's got an awful rash. I don't think that woman washed or changed her properly once."

I'd never held a baby in my life and I didn't know what to do with my awkward arms. Mamma went on, "I've called the doctor to come have a look at her. I'll send him up when he comes. Shortly, I hope. Tonight I'll stay here with you and show you how to care for her."

I looked up at her, and Dad said, "Alice, have you considered he might not want to keep the baby?"

Mamma looked at him as if he had two heads, and I felt dazed. Everything was happening so fast. Was I to be given no more say in what I wanted to do with you than its mother had given me in your existence?

But then she seemed to realize she'd been operating on an assumption, and she looked at me with a new and searching expression. "I'm sorry, Georgie, I didn't mean—"

"I have to have time," I said. "I can't think straight right now. Could you all just... go away for a little while so I can try to figure things out?"

Dad took you out of my lap, and he took my speechless mother by the arm and guided her away, leaving me alone until Lindbergh came out from under my bed to sit beside me.

LOUISE

*T*he bus rattled and bumped down the highway, but I hardly noticed. I was far too absorbed in my misery.

All this time, I'd thought George was so jealous of preserving his virtue that he wouldn't even get close to me, but he'd given it up for Velma Johnson? I could not fathom it, could not. He was a dark horse, but even so, I'd been sure of my ability to read him. He'd had a crush on her, that had been obvious, but last Christmas he said it was over and he was sorry, so I supposed that was the end of it.

If he was going to sleep with someone, *why not me?* I was desperate for him to have me.

Through my stinging tears, I emptied the contents of my knapsack onto the empty seat beside me and sorted through it, folding the clothes, stacking the books, repacking it all and stuffing it under the seat in front of me where I could keep an eye on it.

The miles went by, and my fury increased that George could go nine months acting as if no life-altering event had ever happened. I can guarantee that if it had been me, I'd have been so over the moon I'd have had to tell somebody. I supposed it was possible he was embarrassed to admit he'd done it because it's out of character and the last thing anyone would expect. STILL.

Writing to Uncle Jamie, that's what I'd do. Writing to Uncle Jamie was always a good way to sort out tangled thoughts.

GEORGE

Mrs. Pearson came to my attic an hour later. She knocked on my bedroom door frame and poked her head around timidly, and I sat up and motioned to the chair Dad had vacated. She sat down, and she didn't say anything for while.

"Why did you do it, George?" she asked.

"I didn't. Hasn't Mamma told you the whole sordid story?" I didn't bother to mask the sarcasm.

"No, she sent me here to hear it from you."

I sank back into my pillow and heaved a sigh. "A spiked drink. That's what happened. It was the only way she could get what she wanted because otherwise I'd have been able to keep her off me." I was surprised the words came out so easily.

"Oh!" Mrs. Pearson, taken aback, straightened a little and looked distressed.

"I'd have told Louise that, if she hadn't run off. I didn't know any more about this baby than anyone else until today. I'm sure she thinks I betrayed her. I couldn't tell her. I didn't know how."

Mrs. Pearson continued to be silent, and I didn't say anything else either for a while.

"I don't know what to do," I said softly after minutes had ticked by. "If I was a girl, I'd have been sent away to 'relatives', give the baby up for adoption, and come home with nobody any the wiser, or at least everyone would pretend they weren't. If she stays home and keeps the baby, she's ostracized forever. What happens when it's the boy who gets saddled with the illegitimate baby? There's no script for that."

"I don't know," Mrs. Pearson said. "But I promise you will never know the half of what a girl like that experiences. You're a man. People will make excuses for you. You might have to face some sort of disciplinary measures at church, perhaps, but the world at large isn't going to bat an eye. They'll consider you a heroic figure for taking responsibility and doing what they would frown on a girl doing."

I looked at her, surprised at the keenness of the insight. I didn't know Mrs. Pearson had thoughts like that, any thoughts that couldn't be arranged on staves and played out on the piano.

She gave me a half-smile. "I know, you're surprised I have anything in here but fluff and music." She pointed to her head, and I felt myself flushing. "It may seem like that, but it's not true."

I got off my bed and went to the door to let Lindbergh out, then came back and stood with my hands in my pockets, and the two of us locked eyes for a few minutes.

"I know what it's like," she said, with deliberation, "to be a woman stuck between a rock and a hard place. Imagine, if you will, conceiving the child of a man who is a monster, and having to choose between being socially acceptable and... not being socially acceptable."

I gaped at her.

"You can fill in the gaps," she said, with a crispness that reminded me of my own mother. "I almost died. But I have never once regretted my choice."

"Do you think I should give Hazel to someone else?"

"I said I never regretted *my* choice. You have to decide whether you would regret yours."

She stood up, her hands clasped at her waist, and stepped closer to me. "And I won't tell you what to do, but I will make a suggestion. Give it a couple of weeks. Pray about it. She's here now, after all, and can't be callously disposed of, so make your decision on what would be best for *her*. And if you don't want to keep her yourself, please consider carefully to whom you entrust her. It could be that Miss Johnson knew the baby would be better off here than with her. With a better chance of growing up safe and happy."

"Would you take her?" I asked. "Theoretically."

"Ask me that after you've had a few weeks to think it over."

And then she was gone.

I went downstairs. Dad was holding you and dozing in his arm-chair, and I pulled Mamma aside and whispered, "Did you know Mrs. Pearson had an—" I hesitated even to say the word, but Mamma understood.

"Of course I knew," she said. "She came to me for help because her Christian friends wouldn't have done a damn thing but be plati-tudinous."

I folded my arms and leant back against the counter. Mamma glanced up at me. "You're surprised."

"Well, yes. She's the last person I'd have expected to—" Again I hesitated.

"Oh, grow up, George! You've fathered a child and you know about these things. Abortion isn't a bad word."

"It is to some people," I said quietly. (I had yet to reconcile the Christian and Jewish views on the topic in my own mind.)

"Well, not to me, and not in my house." She turned the pot she was scrubbing upside down to drain on the counter and dried her hands on her apron. "So, are you keeping the baby or are you not?"

I looked toward where it was quietly sleeping in my father's arm. "I think I'm going to give myself a little time to decide," I said at last.

She nodded. "All right. I'll be in your attic tonight with her."

After dinner, she did just that. We ended up making a bed of blankets on the floor of the sitting room area of my attic, in front of my coal stove, letting you lie there without a diaper. It was messy, but Mamma and the doctor both said keeping your rashy bottom dry was important if we wanted it to get better. You fussed and wanted milk constantly, even if you proceeded to throw it right back up again.

Mamma didn't cut me any slack whatsoever. She brought up a jug of water and a small saucepan and showed me how to mix the formula Dad had fetched. "There are half a dozen bottles and nipples here. You'll have to use a clean one every time, so whenever she's asleep, come wash them and give them a bath in boiling water. A great nui-sance, I know, but you'll have to get used to it. And here's a container of flannel rags. Keep some water in with them all the time so they're damp and you can wipe her off more easily."

The instructions seemed to be never-ending, and I was astonished that women were expected to just *know* all these things.

The fact that the next day was Sunday was so far from any of our minds, it was not until four in the afternoon that we remembered.

We'd been in my attic all day, Mamma and Dad and me and you and Mrs. Pearson, all finding we needed one another very much and seeing new sides to each other that previously I, at least, had never noticed.

The hitherto unknown gentle and adoring way of my father with a baby.

The emotional intensity of shy Mrs. Pearson.

The unleashed fury of my mother toward anyone who could do such a dastardly thing to a helpless infant on top of what she'd already done to me, her son!

The fact that Louise had two older half-sisters and a baby brother who all died when the entire family got the influenza back in 1918.

"Louise never told me about them," I said.

"She hasn't told you a lot of things," Mrs. Pearson said, her voice sharp. "And anyway I can hardly bear to think of them myself!"

But the real bomb was Mamma dropping the fact that she'd lost another baby after Dad joined her in America. "It was a girl. She was born too soon." And she and Mrs. Pearson sat side by side on the couch, having a good cry.

"Women are very sensitive about their babies," Dad whispered. "Well, most women are," he amended, when I gestured helplessly toward you. "Your mother was heartbroken she didn't get a chance to have more. But she was already forty-one then, and I didn't think she should risk it another time..." He trailed off. "That white rose bush she propagates and carries with us everywhere... it's from the rose bush your sister was buried under."

Dazed from sleeplessness, I stared at him, but scattered bits of mental information clicked together at his words. "The scars on Mamma's wrists," I said, and he nodded.

"It's why I always keep my razor locked up. I don't think she'll ever do it again, but I won't make it easy for her."

Mrs. Tabitha, who was stepping up for kitchen duty for the time being, brought us lunch, which we only took scattered notice of. We took turns walking the unhappy you and attempting to sleep and wash bottles in shifts. The doctor showed up again around two o'clock and expressed concern again about the rash and how much weight you'd lost from the birth weight listed on your certificate.

A little after four, dutiful deacon's wife Mrs. Myrtle Morgan herself knocked on the door of my attic, then opened it and walked in without waiting for an answer. "That Polish woman said you were out," she started to say, "but I had to find out what kept you all from church this morning—"

Mrs. Pearson jumped up from her chair and shrieked, "Louise! Sunday school!" instead of greeting the unwelcome visitor properly, and collapsed again with her face in her hands. It suddenly occurred to me Louise hadn't been there to teach her children's class that morning. Nor had I been there to lead the singing like I was supposed to do the second Sunday of every month. And neither of those absences could have gone unnoticed—not a chance. I already felt shell-shocked enough from barely sleeping the last twenty-four hours, on top of this sudden fatherhood. What else had I forgotten? I stared up at my church's most notorious meddler, whose eyes were not on me but on the squawking thing I held.

"Well!" she said, indignantly. "What is this?"

Dad took Mrs. Myrtle Morgan firmly by an arm and conferred with her in very Scottish-sounding undertones. I was trying to get you to nurse at your bottle instead of shriek (hopeless), and walking up and down like an automaton with you bundled to my chest because only then would you be quiet.

Mrs. Morgan clutched at her pearls. "Well! I wouldn't expect anything else from a young man who DANCES!"

And she flounced away.

Dad followed her down the stairs, and fifteen minutes later he reappeared, sent out the womenfolk, and took you from me.

"Go lie down," he said to me, and I gratefully obeyed. When I woke again, Dad was still there, sitting on the floor with his chin in his hands, singing you a silly little song as he watched over you, lying on a blanket in nothing but your skin.

"Hallo, son," he said, when he noticed me. "Better?"

I nodded, mutely.

"When old Mrs. Battleaxe left, I telephoned your minister," he said. "Explained everything to him before she has time to get to him. He wants you to come call on him as soon as you can, so the two of you can decide how to proceed."

"How am I going to manage?" I asked. "Louise is the child charmer, not me. I don't know what to do with this—" I gestured to you. "I'm already exhausted. I don't know how I can possibly keep up once school starts."

"It will come," Dad promised. "Your sisters had a nanny, but I admit I am rather a sap for babies. Surprised everyone, except Maggie, who assumed I was hanging about the nursery to carry on a flirtation with the nanny (which I wasn't, by the way, she wasn't my type) and the result was the girls liked me and gave me a reason to come home. If it wasn't for them, I rarely would have, I'm sure." He bent over Hazel again and lightly touched her scrunchy nose with a fingertip, grinning. "She's a bit of a monkeyface right now, but they all are to start out. You wait a week or two, and you will see how sweet she'll get."

I made a skeptical noise. "And if I still decide I don't want to keep her?"

"Then you'll become the biological father of an adopted sister, because I for one am not about to let her go very far away. You may not be sure if you love her, but I am sure *I* do."

I let out a hollow laugh, and he reached up to the table where Mamma had left a clean stack of diapers waiting. "I guess you've aired long enough, lassie. Your gran will be sure to ask me." I watched him deftly folding and pinning, wondering if I, who still couldn't manage shoelaces and ties at eighteen, could ever master this art.

"I've been through your ties whilst you were sleeping," Dad said, as if reading my mind. "Tied them all for you. All you'll have to do is put them over your head and draw them up tight. Funny how Louise never thought of that solution, isn't it?" He winked at me.

It took me a few minutes to parse what he meant.

She'd never minded tying my ties at all. She did it because she wanted to.

The doctor came every day until your weight gain caught up to his expectations and the rash cleared. You weren't as scrawny, and your skin no longer looked red and patchy. I'd even gotten used to holding you by the end of the first week, and oddly, I found it comforting. You were so warm for such a tiny thing, and helpless, and as much a victim as I was. We'd both been misused by a heartless woman who cared about nobody but herself.

And I began to find that, when I looked into your round pink face, what I heard was not "I'm your problem now, angel preacher boy." What I heard was, "I will love you forever if only you will love me."

One week after you appeared on the doorstep, Dad and I went to the Portland hospital where you had been born. At first I protested, saying I'd rather go by myself if we had to go at all, but Dad had an agenda.

"If they have anything relevant to say, we're getting depositions," he explained. "We want every bit of ammunition we can get, on the off chance Velma shows up again and demands to have her child back. Courts usually rule in favor of the mother, and if we have witnesses that she was disinterested or hostile, it's points for us, since you can't definitely prove she raped you and all we have is the note she left in the box—you still have it, I hope?"

None of this would have occurred to me, of course. "Mamma stuck it somewhere. Ask her."

We spoke with the physician who'd attended at the birth. He was a kind fellow, and pleased to hear you were thriving, but unfortunately had no information about Velma. "Never saw her before she showed up to deliver," he said. "I assumed she was a vagrant, since she said she had no address, and she showed no interest whatsoever in the baby. Told the nurse to come up with a name for the birth certificate."

"Could we speak to that nurse?" Dad asked.

She was found and brought in and was happy to talk to us for a few minutes. "She was a mean one," the nurse said sadly. "She wouldn't touch the baby after she was born. Wouldn't even look at her. It was heartbreaking! She told me to think of a name when the birth certificate got filled in, so I used my mother's name and my aunt's name, and put down Hazel Mae. If I'd known there was a father involved, I'd have told her she ought to let you name it—"

"Oh, it's better this way," Dad broke in with a grin. I rolled my eyes. Hazel Mae was not a name I would have chosen, but Louise did always say I was terrible at naming things, so Dad was probably right.

The nurse went on. "She up and left when nobody was watching, before we even discharged her. Not sure how she managed that, without anyone seeing! We were dreadfully worried what she might do to the baby. I'm glad she's safely with you."

I said, "I'm perfectly all right if neither of us ever see that woman again. I never knew she was having a baby. She never told me. Having it dropped on my doorstep was as much a shock to me as anyone."

The nurse gave me a curious look. "She's quite a lot older than you, isn't she?"

"I don't want to remember what she did to me," I snapped, then lifted a hand. "Sorry. It's... a lot."

I felt vaguely disquieted as I rode the train back home. Mamma was waiting to hear all the details, and when we finished relating them, she looked at you, asleep in her arms. "Your mother is a no-account whore, Hazel. A no-account whore." She looked at me. "Are you eating with us tonight?"

"I have to finish my little speech for tomorrow, so I'll just have some soup in my room," I said, and retreated to my attic, where I laid you into the wicker laundry basket I'd lined with blankets as a temporary bed and heated a tin of soup. By the time it was ready, you were fussing again, so I laid you on my lap as I ate it, scanning the pages of my "little speech", occasionally pausing to edit. Dr. Birtchet, our minister, had given me permission to have a public word before the sermon tomorrow, even though we both knew it could create an uproar, not having run it by the elders and deacons first. But he believed me when I told him what had happened and said he was willing to take the risk if I was.

After all, it was more likely that I, the young and audacious upstart who DANCED, and not he, the respected reverend doctor, who would get the worst of it.

156

You fell asleep on my knees whilst I rewrote the final draft into a tidy, legible copy, and read it through aloud one last time.

"If Louise was here," I said in your general direction, "she'd be listening and telling me how to make it better, but you're all I have now, baby girl." I leant down and put my face close to yours, stroked your cheeks with my thumbs.

You opened your dark eyes, looked straight into mine, and smiled at me.

Nobody will ever convince me babies don't mean to smile before they're six weeks old.

My heart melted right into your tiny hand and it hasn't hardened since.

LOUISE
SAN DIEGO, CALIFORNIA: AUGUST 1933

When I arrived in San Diego, there was nobody to meet me, because I hadn't had time to contact the person to whom I'd been referred, so my first move was to find a telephone directory. I found the YWCA where I could rent a room by the night and settled in.

The next morning I telephoned the man in charge of the air mail at the San Diego end and was quickly given that job back. I'd been dependable and never had any accidents on my previous run, and he was happy to hire me again.

The difference was that instead of going all the way to Seattle, I would fly only as far as Medford, and then turn south again, leaving a northern pilot to take care of that end. I didn't want to risk having to land in Salem and being seen by my mates at the airfield, even though I knew I could count on them to keep mum.

And now I would be taking passengers, too.

GEORGE

*I*n the morning I put on my black suit and a somber silver-grey tie and handed you over to Mamma before you had time or audacity to puke on me. I declined breakfast and walked to church in a roundabout way, praying the entire time that God would grant me a spirit of love and not vindictiveness. I knew I was about to step on toes and make people uncomfortable, and that people like Mrs. Myrtle Morgan would doubtless wave me off as an upstart, but Jesus himself didn't mince words when the occasion called for it, and it was not for myself I would be pleading today. It was for you.

Your smile of the previous night flashed into my mind and made me warm inside as I mounted the steps of the church and met Dr. Birtchet in his office. I was there early, as planned, so I could be sprung upon an unsuspecting congregation.

And I waited. I waited through Sunday school and the hymns and prayers. I had no stage fright, but I did have a knot of another kind of dread in my gut.

When I stepped up to the pulpit, it was not with any sense of thrill or naive excitement at a chance to orate. That had all vanished last December. Rather I had a heart full of determination and more personal investment in my topic than ever before. I leant forward, my hands gripping either side of the desk, scanning my audience. The congregation seemed to be holding its breath. Some appeared openly hostile to my presence behind the desk. Most faces appeared carefully blank. Some eyes remained fixed on laps. A few of the deacons glared at me, poised on the edges of their seats as if prepared to eject me forcibly at an instant's notice.

I found Mrs. Pearson, sitting near the organ, and she gave me a tiny smile. It settled me, and I flipped my notes face up and began to read.

"'When Jesus had lifted up himself, and saw none but the woman, he said unto her, Woman, where are those thine accusers? hath no man condemned thee? She said, No man, Lord. And Jesus said unto her, Neither do I condemn thee: go, and sin no more.'

"The apostle John, in relating this story to us, never denies that a sin was committed; nor does the Lord Jesus, else he would have no need to say 'sin no more'. What we see is that the Lord Jesus knows the truth of the entire matter, that in order for the woman to have sinned, first a man sinned by seducing her. A man either caused that she should be tempted and fall, or he forced himself upon her against her will. Does our Lord excuse the man more than the woman? I say no. For he wrote on the ground the sins of every man present, and

162

in shame they all turned and left, leaving the woman alone with the Saviour, who alone can cure sin. We all have sinned and come short of the glory of God.

"There are also instances in the Scriptures where a woman is the temptress and destroyer, as in the example of Delilah, who for money seduced men.

"We are always quick to assume in every situation who the guilty party is, but we need to remember we are mortal and have not the omniscience of the Lord, who searches the heart and who alone can know the innocence or guilt of each party. It is an arrogant injustice against our brothers and sisters for us to be so unfair as to assume guilt of one or another—an injustice not only in the eyes of man, but in the eyes of God. Was David permitted to escape the consequences of his sin when he helped himself to Bathsheba, another man's wife? He was not, and sorrow pierced his heart and life from that fateful day until he took his last breath. But remember that judgment came from God, and not man.

"God would have us treat all sins and sinners as equal, preferring neither the man nor the woman above the other, but to make a calm and thorough investigation into the case and, by the wisdom of the Holy Ghost, to discern the truth and do justice to both parties. We should not fear to call sin by its rightful name, but woe to those of us who abuse our duty to our church family to have respect of persons, to give favor to the man over the woman, simply because we are men.

"Let us not forget the words of the Apostle Paul, that in Christ there is neither male nor female, and no preference should be given to one over the other in spiritual matters. We are all born to sin; we all require the saving blood of the Lord Jesus. We will none of us escape judgment. Let us guard against hasty conclusions, against prejudice, against the pride of perceived moral superiority one over another, and remember the words of John Bradford. There but for the grace of God goes Deacon Smithers, go Mr. and Mrs. Morgan, go Dr. and Mrs. Birtchet. There but for the grace of God goes George Graham." I paused, meeting the eyes of those I had named, attempting to meet other eyes which refused to meet mine. The tension in the room was so thick I could taste it, and I took a deep breath. One more paragraph. I could get through this. Then come what may.

"I urge you to consider carefully in your hearts your own thoughts and conduct toward the one you perceive to be in sin: me. And I urge you to consider the illegitimate child you all know of by now. My illegitimate child. She did not ask to be born. She did not ask for the desertion her mother inflicted on her, any more than I asked for the abuse to which her mother subjected me. My child is worthy of the love of Christ and the church as much as any one of you. I know that my presence here in the desk this morning is an offense to many of you, but I am asking no favors for myself. Do with me as you will. 'But whoso shall offend one of these little ones,' that she be excluded from knowing the love of the Saviour because of your coldness of heart, 'it were better for him that a millstone were hanged about his neck, and that he were drowned in the depths of the sea.'"

And I took my pages, walked down the center aisle to the door and out into the sunshine, and went home.

When I arrived there, Dad and Mamma looked at me questioningly, and I sank into Dad's chair, exhausted. I tossed my speech to Dad, who took the pages in hand.

"Did you get tarred and feathered?" Mamma asked.

"I didn't stay long enough to find out," I said. "I don't think they knew what hit them."

"You don't look like you know what hit you," Mamma said. She handed me a cup of tea, which I accepted gratefully.

"I don't, quite." The tea settled me almost immediately. "I expect we shall have callers today. The bravest ones will come in person and the rest will use the telephone."

Dad handed my papers to Mamma, with a wink at me. "That's telling them, son. Nothing to lose, so lay it all out. My son, arbiter for social justice in the name of Jesus. About damn time, too, I'd say."

Mamma laughed out loud when she got to the end, not unkindly. It was a laugh tokening approval.

"This sounds," Dad added, "as if you've decided to keep her."

I smiled, not meeting his eyes as I bent over the bed where you were lying, calm for the moment, and let your tiny hand grip my finger. "I think, deep down, I always knew I was never going to let her

164

go, but I guess now I'm stuck with her."

As I was speaking, Mrs. Pearson let herself in, flushed and a bit flustered. She sat at the table, fanning herself with the magazine closest to hand, and Mamma poured her tea as well and pushed the cup toward her.

"Well!" said Mrs. Pearson.

"What do you say, Mrs. P?" I asked. "Will the deacons be coming round to put me in the stocks?"

"I'd like to see them try," she said. "Do let me hold her, George."

I handed you to her, and Mrs. Pearson cuddled you, relapsing into silence.

Shortly after I knew the service would be ending, the front bell rang, and Dad went to answer it. In a moment, he was back.

"It's the MacMillans," he said.

I raised my eyebrows, retrieved you from Mrs. Pearson, and went out to meet them.

"We've just stopped in on our way home to tell you how brave you were today, and you and your baby have our full support. Mrs. Pearson was quite animated in her defense of you, too."

I looked at him, confused.

"I suppose she wouldn't ever tell you herself. Well, as soon as you were gone, she stood up and said out loud and clear 'that darling boy won't say a word in his own defense, so I'm going to!' That you're the nicest boy she's ever known, that it wasn't your fault what happened, only it wasn't her place to say why, but she lost her daughter over this kerfuffle and wasn't about to lose you, too, and if we didn't all do our Christian duty by you and your baby, she'd go rejoin the Lutherans."

"Wow," I said, unable to think of any more intelligent response. Mrs. Pearson had never spoken up "loud and clear" at any point in my memory about anything. "That's... impressive."

"Anyway, our daughter may still have things you might find useful. I'm going to ask her this very day."

I thanked them and they stood to go, but as I was showing them out, more people arrived. It kept up all afternoon: people bringing me words of affirmation and support, wanting to meet you.

I did make careful mental note of roughly sixty percent who did not show up or telephone, so I could keep you well clear of them.

"I still can't help but feel it would be the exact opposite if I was a girl," I complained to Dad that evening.

"You're probably right," he agreed. "But no reforms happen overnight, son. You have to keep planting what's right into people's heads, and hope the seeds take root."

I wrote to Uncle Jamie about you, of course. Not right away. I was too overwhelmed and sleep-deprived at first to do any letter-writing. But two weeks after you came, I penned him a quick note telling him the news, and my sadness over Louise's departure, and confessing I'd been in love with her all along and too stupid to realize it until it was too late.

It was Aunt Estelle who answered, with a postcard.

George darling, somebody's leg is flaring up and he's a bit ferocious. He wrote you the MOST ridiculous letter, which I have "lost" and will make him rewrite in a few days when he's come to his senses. We love you and DO send us a picture of your little one. Aunt E.

P.S. Because I know you will ask, the gist of the letter could be summed up in this: don't be so wrapped up in your own head that you don't interact with other people like a minister ought to. A fine one to be dispensing THAT advice!! All right, he has improved in the last few years, I'll grant him that. What he means to say is that he hopes your ministry will come from the heart, not just your head. P.P.S. GO FIND LOUISE, IT ISN'T TOO LATE!!

Dad walked in after rapping on my door that evening. He had you all bundled up for bed, and he was beaming, but when he saw my face, the smile left his. He opened his mouth to question me, but I cut him off.

"How oblivious to everything would you say I am?" I shoved the letter at Dad.

He sat in the other chair, took up the letter with his free hand. For a moment there was no sound but your snoring as he read it, then he laid it on the table again. "He's not entirely wrong, but he is having a rough time. Did you know I can always tell? I get twinges." He tapped the date at the top of the postcard. "That day they were off the charts. They always coincide with him suffering. Doesn't matter if I'm thousands of miles away."

I sat there, surprised at this odd turn in the conversation. "I didn't know that," I said at last.

"Has Jamie ever told you what happened to him in the war?"

My curiosity was instantly piqued. Dad didn't often tell old family stories, unless they were his own, and even those were rare.

"He was vague when I asked him," I said, and Dad leaned back, making his sit-tight-and-have-a-listen noises as he shifted you to his shoulder and kissed the top of your silken wee head.

"Jamie was like a turtle," he began. "Our father was so terrible to him, I can't say I blame him. His way of protecting himself was to live inside his head. He didn't notice things. Well, I've never been sure if he really didn't notice them, or if he just turned a blind eye. Either way, it kept him from having to confront the ugliness in his life, and there was so much ugliness, and he hated confrontation. In our family, confronting our father always led to Jamie getting a beating, on top of the many he got just for existing. Jamie didn't have friends, not real friends, outside of an old man at Eton who was the only good father figure Jamie ever had. But he died in our last year there. Tore Jamie to pieces, losing him." Dad sighed before continuing..

"I was popular and Father liked me. I got attention, I was well-socialized, but trying to get Jamie out of his music and into other people's lives was virtually impossible. He was scared and hurting inside, and he drowned his sorrows in music the way some men use drink, to survive. Nobody was more shocked than I was when he started courting Estelle, and even then he was so afraid I would try to steal her from him, he threatened to banish me from the castle." Dad laughed softly. "That was one reason I married your sisters' mother, trying to reassure him I wouldn't interfere with his girl, and we all know what a fabulous success that was." He tucked the blanket in closer around Hazel and kissed her head again.

"So he married Estelle, and he was actually happy for the first

time in his life. But he was still very much trapped inside that shell
of his, with no desire to get out. Estelle tried, but mostly he let her in
rather than come out himself, if that makes sense."

I nodded.

"The war came, I fell in love with your mother, joined the army—
here's an example of how oblivious Jamie was. Anybody with eyes
could have guessed my orderly was underage. Everyone said Willie
was nineteen with a wink and nod, but Jamie? It never occurred to
him to be suspicious. Willie was only just fifteen when he joined up.
Jamie saw him every day and never once questioned whether he was
the age his papers said he was. Then there was the girl."

Dad went silent for a while, as if reluctant to resurrect this
memory. "Aveline. She was thirteen years old and some German
fellow had just raped her when Jamie found her in an old barn. He
took her back to billets and cared for her as tenderly as if she was
his own child. She changed his entire life and outlook. She was very
like him—artistic, sensitive—except for the fact that she didn't miss
anything. There was nothing she couldn't ferret out or infer, nothing
she wouldn't notice. She knew Willie was only sixteen. When Jamie
found them together in a hayloft later on and Aveline accidentally
let his real age slip, Jamie came to me and gave me a royal ticking off
for not having told him. I said it was obvious to everyone except him.
Jamie was becoming increasingly irrational by that time. We could all
tell he was losing his grip on reality. The war was a terrible place for
him. Anyway, Aveline shouldn't have been with him the day she died,
a few days after the hayloft incident, and he never stopped blaming
himself for her death. She should have been sent off to Estelle long
before, but he kept finding excuses to keep her with him."

"How did she die?" I asked, not sure if I wanted to hear the answer.

"She stepped on a mine." Dad's words were matter-of-fact, as if
he was summing up a case, and for an instant he sounded just like
Uncle Jamie had when I'd asked him what happened to him. "She'd
just pushed Jamie to safety in a trench after he got shot in the foot. He
was a disaster for years after. We all worried he'd never be right in the
head again. But one thing came out of it for the good of all. He realized
how much he was missing out on. His own children were growing up

right under his nose, and he didn't even know them. Since then he goes out of his way not only to pay attention and notice things, but to make sure you know he's paying attention and noticing."

I stared at Dad. It was all a lot to take in, and Dad didn't say any more for a while. He stood up, put you into my arms. I took you mechanically and didn't look up until several minutes had gone by and Dad still stood there, hands in his pockets, amusement on his face.

I looked at him, bemused. "What's funny?"

"You." He ruffled my hair fondly, as if I was still five years old. "O son of mine, you are so like him, I just want to slap some sense into you, if it would help, but it wouldn't. Anyway, he's right, George. Get ahead now, start paying attention now. It's not too late." He started to leave, then turned his head, eyes alight as if he'd had a revelation. "You know what the name Aveline means? Hazelnut."

And then he was gone.

I stood and took you to the bedroom to lay you in your wee basket, but at the last minute I changed my mind, and I lay you on my own bed next to me. I tossed my pillow to the floor so you wouldn't suffocate against it and climbed under the covers, tracing your tiny face with my fingertip. You were not at fault for anything. You hadn't asked to be born, but you did need someone to love you. To notice you. You would teach me to pay attention, because your survival would depend on being lovingly noticed and attended to, and I would do the best I could to make sure nobody ever hurt you.

That was the night I first thought about what your name tasted like, whispered "Miss Fizzytwigs" into your hair, and never again called you anything but Fizz.

How helpless an infant is, I thought. I held you close to me, tiny and warm, and fell deeply asleep for two hours until you woke, demanding a bottle and a change.

LOUISE

CALIFORNIA: SEPTEMBER-DECEMBER 1933

*U*ncle Jamie sent me some money when he heard I'd left home, and I bought a used motorbike with it. Getting around on my own was marvelous! I made friends with all the fellows at the airfield, and instructed them they were not to tell any strange men that they knew me. Fortunately they were all very quick to agree to it.

I wouldn't stay long in San Diego, though. Mr. Eyerly put in a word for me at Plover Field in Santa Monica, where they needed a flight instructor, as did my air mail boss in San Diego, although he wasn't happy about losing me. I went there and they liked me and started in December, after the instructor I replaced moved on.

I made enquiries about some cheap rooms, too. Things were fine. I could survive perfectly well without George, thank you very much.

I did miss Mother, though. I wondered what she was doing. I wrote to her to let her know I was fine and had work, but until I could get a post office box, she wouldn't be able to write back. Santa Monica and all of the other cities down there were bigger than Salem, so I banked on that as a way for her and everyone else to not easily find me, even if they knew the city I was in.

GEORGE

SALEM, OREGON: SEPTEMBER 1933

Dear Uncle Jamie,

Dad told me you were right. He also told me what happened to you in the war, a little more explicitly than you told it. I hope you don't mind. About the girl you found. Anyway, he says I ought to mind what you say. It is true Fizz is not easily ignored.

I've tried to think through it all, calm and rational. It's soon going to be a year since that night, and it's still hard to be detached. Impossible, really. But here's what I've come to so far: Velma was violated, repeatedly. She was eight when it started happening—younger than Louise and I were when we became friends. I honestly can't fathom the atrocity of that. Supposing Louise's stepfather had done such things to her? She would have fought, yes, but what can a small girl do against a strong adult man in the end? Nothing. And he—that priest—repeated his offense time after time, perverting not only the way an adult and child should relate to one another, but her picture of God himself. It makes me shudder.

Nothing excuses what she did to me, but I am coming to understand why she became what she did, and I find myself weeping for her. For the small girl who lost her innocence at the hands of someone whom she should have been able to trust unconditionally, who grew up confused and lonely and grasping for strands of happiness that forever eluded her. For small Velma Johnson I weep bitterly, and for the choices she made to prey on others rather than to break the chains of evil.

Louise never spoke of Sam without a shadow passing over her face. His cruelty broke something in her, but she's also developed a steely resolve, an intense sense of self-advocacy, and deep sympathy for anyone in trouble. She can be prickly, but only to protect herself. I know the real Louise is anything but prickly. Inside is a girl bursting with love and a brain that goes into raptures when tested on wind speed calculations and a heart that lights up like sunshine over anything beautiful.

I understand why Velma didn't want to be left with the baby. Mamma is angry because it was designed to humiliate me, and she's probably right. But we all know the stigma attached to unmarried mothers. She didn't do what she did intending to have a baby. It was an unintended consequence, and she did humiliate me, but it also was self-preservation.

I'm still not used to Louise being gone. I keep thinking I'll see her around, expect her to come walking into the house, or get up to go see her and tell her things, only to realize I can't. It is painful. Sometimes I take Fizz over to Mrs. Pearson's house to keep her company, because I think she is feeling the loss even more than I am. But she's been gone more than usual, too. I guess her agent must be keeping her busy with engagements.

Meanwhile I live in a constant state of anxiety lest the seminary find out. Dad says what they don't know won't hurt them. The majority of the elders and deacons stripped me of all my church duties and demanded that Dr. Birtchet tell seminary, which he promised to take care of, but I don't think that means actually contacting them. He's on my side, at least. Still, it's not impossible that someone else will take it upon themselves to be the talebearer.

I accept it. I miss teaching, but this does leave me more time for study and my family.

What's left of it.

It's almost Yom Kippur and the person whose forgiveness I most crave is lost to me. I pray that, wherever she is, she has forgiven me.

George

LOUISE
SANTA MONICA, CALIFORNIA: DECEMBER 1933

Dear Uncle Jamie,

I've got a room! Well, a couch, actually. I'm sharing with another young lady who advertised for a roommate. We have a tiny kitchen, she has the bedroom, and I have the couch. It's a bit of a dump. There are eight apartments in the building, not counting the landlady's rooms, and all of the occupants are women. The landlady, Mrs. Slater, is terrifying and prone to showing up at all hours to make sure none of the girls have gentlemen in their rooms and complaining if anything is less than spotless. But it's a roof over my head and it's cheap, and that is all I require at the minute.

My roommate's name is Shirley Corwin, and it turns out she is also a dancer! She works at one of those dime-a-dance places as a taxi dancer four nights a week. She's not as trained as I am, of course, but does fine for a place like that. During the day she works as a waitress, and always has such interesting stories about both jobs.

Anyway, her dancing gave me the idea of looking for a dancing job of my own, but at the risk of sounding snobbish, I don't want to settle for a place like where Shirley works. I went to the library and made a list of all the upper-crust hotels within fifteen miles and have written to all of them to ask if they need a trained professional dancer for floor shows. I haven't heard back from any of them yet, but hope springs eternal.

Louise

GEORGE

After you came into my life, and Louise went out of it, I took the gramophone upstairs. Dad and Mamma never used it anyway, and my silent attic required sound. (Well, mostly silent. You had a lot of opinions, which you voiced very loudly, but you know what I mean.)

After I'd dragged that upstairs, I piled all the records into a box and took them up, too, followed by the shelf which had housed them. When I'd gotten it all arranged, I laid you on a soft blanket with a rattle and the teddy someone had knitted for you, both of which you ignored, because what I was doing was so much more interesting.

I wound the gramophone and set a record on it. It was bizarre to hear this music to which I had waltzed countless times with Louise and not be dancing myself.

My daily exercises were such a force of habit by now I couldn't feel I'd properly begun my day without them, but my feet itched to properly dance. I glanced at you, and because nobody was around to see, I scooped you up and cuddled you close, dancing with you instead. You were a very small partner, and rather unimpressed, but you were better than nobody.

When I wasn't dancing with you, I talked to you, because there was nobody else to talk to, and because I didn't know how to talk to children I just pretended you were another adult instead. You seemed to fuss less when I was talking to you, anyway. I read to you and sang to you and practiced sermons to you, and eventually you grew to love the dancing, grinning over the music and giggling when I spun you around.

So, for your four-month-birthday I stopped at the music store on my way home from the day's classes to buy a record. The clerk knew me well, and lit up at the sight of me. I hadn't been in for months.

"Where have you and Louise been?" he asked. "I haven't seen either of you for so long, I—"

I cut him off. "I don't know where she is."

"Oh." He looked curiously at me, as if hoping I'd elaborate. I didn't.

"I need a dance tune," I said. "A present for someone. Can you recommend me something brand-new she'll love?"

"A new girl?" His face brightened with the idea of intrigue. "I've got one left of the latest song everyone's buying. Would you like to hear it?"

"No, I'll just take it," I said, paying him and hurrying away before he could try to ferret out any more information. I didn't even look at it properly until after dinner, when I took it and you upstairs. I warmed you a bottle over my gas burner whilst I dropped on the new record and picked you up. It was a foxtrot, but the words stopped me dead in my tracks only a few steps in.

You were getting drowsy and hardly noticed. The bottle was ready and I popped it into your mouth, my ears riveted to the words of the song.

It's a Barnum and Bailey world,
Just as phoney as it can be,
But it wouldn't be make-believe
If you believed in me.

It brought to mind that other song from *Show Boat* Louise adored.

Might as well make believe I love you
For, to tell the truth, I do.

Unbidden, tears sprang to my eyes. I imagined dancing to this new tune with Louise, imagined her warm in my arms, her movements mirroring mine. I bowed my head to press my lips to your hair, dampening your fuzz with my tears. I tucked you snugly into bed and went back to play the song again.

It punched me right where I hadn't been prepared for an attack, and it hurt so much I couldn't stop listening to it. I paced the room, listening over and over again. I took out the broken bracelet from my desk drawer where I'd stashed it and kissed it.

"Louise," I whispered. "Why couldn't you believe in me?"

I knew the answer, but I still had to voice the question. I sat on my couch. How perfect it would be for the three of us to be here, together, like we ought to be.

Except I didn't know if Louise's love for babies could extend as far as this baby.

The months went by, during which we all enjoyed your rapidly developing personality. Mamma had bought a book to write down everything about you, and spoke only Yiddish to you, saying you had time enough to catch up on English later.

Your eyes had gone fully brown by the time you were six months old, and I cannot lie that it was a relief you had my eyes and not your mother's. You learned to say Da and reach out your arms for me when I came home in the evenings, after spending all day at school thinking of you.

You were occasionally gleeful (pulling my glasses off my face when I was anywhere within reach was the funniest thing in the world to you) and always loud unless strangers were about. You did not approve of green beans nor the cutting of teeth. You did approve of being held. I learned to live life one-handed so I could pacify you, clingy koala child.

Mamma said I was spoiling you, but I noticed she too was quite ready to hold you rather than let you cry. And Dad, of course, hardly wanted to be separated from you anytime he was home.

Mrs. Pearson also loved you immensely. One night shortly before Christmas she came up to my attic to see me and have a few minutes hugging you before she went home to bed, and she surprised me again.

"George," she said. "I still believe you and Louise will still end up together against all the odds."

I laughed. "Well, you have more faith than I do."

"What I mean is—" she hesitated, then looked at me. "I want Hazel to think of me as her other grandmother from the start. Not wait until the two of you work out whatever it is Louise needs you to work out."

I studied her curiously. "And if we never do work it out and Fizz is calling you grandma, won't that be odd?"

"Perhaps." She sighed. "Well, have her use my name. And while we're at it, it's high time you stopped 'Mrs. Pearson'-ing me. You're grown up now. I want you to call me Lydia too."

"If that's what you want, then I will," I said. The idea felt odd, but I tried it. "Lydia." Her name was cool and silky rosewater, quite pleasant.

She handed you back to me reluctantly and said, "I'm going to be in Portland again for a couple of weeks, so I won't see you again until after the New Year. Merry Christmas, George." And she kissed my cheek and vanished, leaving me a little stunned.

PART THREE

*Because one is growing into manhood, outgrowing one's old ideals;
they are being shattered into fragments, into dust; if there is no
other life one must build one up from the fragments.*

FYODOR DOSTOEVSKY,
"WHITE NIGHTS"

LOUISE
SANTA MONICA, CALIFORNIA: FEBRUARY 1934

Dear Uncle Jamie,

I finally heard from my mother! It was short, a postcard. I have written to her several times, but only just got my post office box, so she could reply. It stung. I'd have thought she'd write a little more than what she did. This is what she said.

Dear Louise,

I am glad you are well and that I can write to you. Things are going on as usual here. You don't want to hear about George, so nothing to tell on that front. His parents are well and said to send their regards when I told them I had heard from you.

I just got back from an exhausting whirlwind engagement in Seattle, so I will keep this short. But I wanted you to know I love you and wish you would come home.

Mother

I suppose she's annoyed with me and thinks I deserted her. I guess I sort of did. But I couldn't stay and face Traitorous George every day. I don't even want to think about him and Mother is right, I don't want to hear about him either.

I wonder what he did with the baby. Maybe his mother is caring for it. I'm positive he won't want anything to do with it. I always assumed we'd get married and have babies, but... is he even capable of being fatherly?? Maybe it's better we're not together. My babies will need a father who will care for them. Distancing oneself is good! I can see clearly now we would never have worked!

I'm glad Mother is getting engagements further afield. Seattle is still not that fabulous in my opinion, but maybe her agent can find her something here in California next. I will ask her to look into it. What she really needs is to get noticed out east.

Anyway, I finally heard back from one of the hotels I wrote to. It's called Casa Del Sol and it's right on the beach and rich people come there in droves. I went and auditioned with one of their dancers and they hired me on the spot. I started two weeks ago and I will work there two nights a week to start with, Saturday and Sunday nights. My usual partner's name is Winslow Peel, and he's all right, but not as good as George. There I go again. As a person I don't like Winslow much, not because he tries anything on with me, but something just feels off about him. There is another couple, too—Joyce Kinsley and Gordon Parrish, and sometimes we swap partners depending who's available at any given time, or if someone is sick. We usually do one or two performances during the evening, and dance with the guests in between. Rather like Have His Carcase, now I think of it!

And I've got a few students at the airfield, too. There are some who are mortally offended that a mere GIRL thinks she can teach them, but usually they quickly reconsider their opinion when I take them for their first flight and pull some Hell Divers stunts on them and still land them safely. It's great fun to give them a little scare.

But I am all right! Give my love to the family!

Louise

GEORGE

I hadn't made any close friends at seminary in the last three years, which was partly because I was not good at making friends and partly because getting too close to anyone would involve your existence becoming known.

Fortunately, since most of my classmates lived in Portland, it was impossible to do much together. So I remained polite but aloof and nobody seemed bothered.

That day in March began like any other Friday, except that a first-year student approached me between classes to ask me if I'd take time to have lunch with him, because he'd heard I was Jewish and had questions about my perspectives on several things, for an essay he'd been assigned. I agreed to meet him, and we had a long discussion outside in the cool spring sunshine, me doing far more talking than eating and he scribbling notes as fast as he possibly could. I couldn't help but wonder if he'd even be able to decipher them later.

We were interrupted by a breathless messenger. "I've been looking for you everywhere, Graham!" he said. "Your mother telephoned the dean's office and he sent me to find you. She needs to speak with you urgently."

Mamma would only disturb me here in an emergency. Something terrible must have happened. I snatched up my things and ran, forgetting to take my leave of the lad I'd just been speaking to.

Once in the office, I picked up the telephone and tapped my foot impatiently whilst the operator connected me with home, and Mamma answered.

Mamma was seldom hysterical, but she certainly was now. "George, you have to come home. Hazel is sick. The doctor's been in and it's scarlet fever. She's so sick. I'm scared she's going to die on my watch and I'll never forgive myself. Please, please come home right away!"

I recalled my own childhood, how paralyzed with fear Mamma had gotten when I'd had scarlet fever or flu or anything else. I'd always thought she was overreacting, but now for the first time I understood. A tight squeezing around my middle, that was the fear. Because a child is irreplaceable.

I forced calm into my voice. "I have one more class, Mamma," I said. "Could I come after that?" She just sobbed, and I went on, "If she's quarantined and I come home, I'll have to stay home."

"Do you think I don't know that, George?"

The sickly squeezing tightened more. I knew there was really only one choice, and I made it. "Okay. Let me have a word with the dean. I'll come home on the next train I can catch."

"Please hurry," she begged.

"Yes, Mamma," I promised, my own voice unsteady.

I set the receiver down, swallowed, and slowly turned to face the dean, who was regarding me with mild curiosity and concern.

"Someone is ill at home?" he asked.

And I forced myself to utter the two words I'd so studiously avoided saying for the last two years.

"My daughter, sir. She's dangerously ill with scarlet fever and I have to go home at once. I won't be able to come back until the quarantine lifts."

He fixed me with a gaze that tried to see through me, as if he was about to test me. "Can't her mother care for her?" he asked.

"Her mother is—" I paused. "No, sir, she has no mother. Only me."

He eyed my left hand pointedly.

"No, I'm not married, sir."

"But you have a daughter."

Tell him she was left on the doorstep and you took her in. It wouldn't be a lie, something whispered in my head.

I took a deep breath. "Yes, sir, I do."

186

"I think you need to explain yourself, Graham," he said, leaning back in his chair as if prepared for a long inquisition. "You know we have a high moral standard to uphold, both at this institution and, after leaving it, in our professions as ministers of the Gospel."

"I realize that, sir, but I don't have time to explain it all now. My daughter has no one to care for her when I am gone except my mother, who runs a boarding house and has to be careful of infection."

He didn't look satisfied, but he sighed and reluctantly gave in. "Very well, then. But I will expect a full explanation, in writing, as soon as possible."

By the time I arrived home, the quarantine signs were already up: one on the inside door of the stairs leading to my attic, and the other on the outside door of the back stairs. The doctor had said as long as you remained there, the rest of the house could continue as usual, since it was completely closed off.

Lindbergh followed me in the back entrance and Mamma was there, pacing the room with you in her arms. I took her into mine.

Your poor body flamed with heat, your limbs dangled listless and limp, and your lips were parted in your flushed face. I kissed your hot, damp head, and put my free arm around Mamma, who collapsed sobbing into me.

"It's going to be okay, Mamma," I whispered, mechanically, although I couldn't be sure.

"Tabitha is going to take over the downstairs work for me. I have to stay up here since I've been with Hazel all day. Natalia hasn't had it, so she's going to Olivia's. The other boarders are all out until this evening, fortunately, and she's telephoning them to let them know they can stay with Lydia if they're not comfortable coming back here during the quarantine."

"Has Dad had it? Have you?"

"I have. He doesn't remember. He's staying at Lydia's, though, just in case."

Scarlet fever hadn't ended well for Beth March, and the dread tightened inside me. I hugged you closer and told Mamma to go rest on my bed.

Mrs. Tabitha delivered a big bottle of Clorox and a bundle of Mamma's clothes to the door with a note saying she'd bring up a pail of water every day for washing, leave our meals at the regular times, and empty the chamberpot we'd be obliged to use. (I guess it was good we still had one from our old days at The Dump, tucked away in a pile of old junk in the shed out back.) It was a nuisance, but we soon settled into a routine of shifts of resting and caring for you. Lindbergh was always near you, too, sensing you were in some sort of danger.

I admit, though, that even when it wasn't my turn to look after you, I couldn't tear myself away from your side. Tending you during those weeks, several things that had previously been murky crystallized into clarity for me.

I'd intellectually accepted you were my child. I even loved you. But now the emotional part of me that always came to life far too late to do any good kicked in, too. You were my daughter. I was your father. You were worth more to me than my reputation.

Reputation was gnawing at me, nonetheless. I couldn't shake the ominous feeling the dean's parting words had given me.

But most of all, faced with the possible loss of you, I finally understood Louise's distress over the Lindberghs' baby, and I wished I could go back in time and slap that self-absorbed George in the face repeatedly, as well as fall on my face at Louise's feet and beg her forgiveness.

The doctor came every afternoon. Mamma had collapsed on my bed into an exhausted sleep during one visit, and he asked me how I was holding up.

"I think I'll be asked to leave seminary," I said, despondently. I'm not sure why I told him that.

"Oh?" He shook his thermometer and took your temperature.

"Because I'm not married, yet have a child. What kind of example is that as a minister?"

"I thought she was left on your doorstep."

"She was. But I am her father. That's why she was left here."

"I see." There was a long pause as he continued to assess you, but eventually he spoke again. "Sounds to me like you should find a wife posthaste. Whatever happened to Louise?"

"She was mad at me about the implications of Hazel's existence and left."

"Ah." He tucked his things back into his bag, gave my shoulder a squeeze, and took his leave after giving me a few instructions.

You lay on my couch, still hot and not fully aware of your surroundings. I kissed you, brushed your fair hair off your face, and walked over to the window to look out.

I wanted Louise *so much* right then. I wanted her to come in with her brisk efficiency and imperturbable positivity and just... sit on the couch beside me and fuss with my ties or any of the other silly things she used to do. She used to weave her long fingers into my hair and scratch my head like I was a puppy, usually accompanied by a lecture on whatever she had on her mind that day. I missed that more than I could express.

I'd been such a fool to have missed out on the love she'd wanted to give me.

In a few days, the crisis had passed, to my great relief. But the quarantine still stretched out before us for a couple more weeks, and during that time it became evident you had completely lost hearing in your right ear.

"At least it's not both," the doctor said. "Poor thing, though."

Now that my mind was relieved from the fear my child was going to die, I wrote to the dean. I laid out for him the entire story, told him he was welcome to contact Dr. Birtchet as a reference, and Dad asked to add a postscript when I dropped it down from the stairs to him so he could read it. He took a pencil from his pocket and wrote something, then read it to me.

My son has never been in trouble of any kind outside of this incident, which he can hardly be blamed for. It wasn't his fault that woman drugged him. George works hard and has been a dutiful and loving father, even though it would have been in his own better interest to deny she was his and place her elsewhere. That's more than I would have done at his age. Sincerely yours, George W C Graham.

189

"I feel like I'm on trial," I said, leaning over the railing and meeting Dad's eyes.

"Well, here's hoping they'll be as fair as Dr. Birtchet and most of your church folks have been to you. I have to say I'm surprised you've made it this long without anyone there having caught wind of Hazel."

There was a pause. "Do you mind dropping it in the mail for me?"

"I'll do that."

I wanted more than anything to go hug my father just then. I missed him.

But I was stuck with only you and Mamma for company, which was mostly all right. One night after you were asleep, she and I sat on the couch together, her hands folded idly, looking rather as if she was about to descend into one of her spells of mere existence, and I decided to try to engage her out of it.

"Mamma," I said. "Am I ever going to be allowed to know about your parents?"

She frowned, not opening her eyes. "Why do you want to know about them?" She said "them" as if she was referring to something nasty on her shoe.

"Because they're part of me, and you've never even told me their names."

I knew their names because I'd wangled them out of my father years earlier, but Mamma didn't know that.

She sighed deeply. "They were furious at me for my affair with your father."

"I gathered that much."

"They'd have been happy if I had an abortion, probably. But I'd wanted a child for years and didn't know if I'd ever have another chance, and anyway I adored your father and couldn't have been more pleased to have his child, despite losing everything else over it. Even not knowing for sure if I could trust him to come back to me after the war, I couldn't bear the thought of not having you. And your father was pleased, despite the scandal ripping his girls away from him. Anyway, I decided that I'd put up with my father's controlling attitude for thirty-five years too many and when they walked out of my house that day the ties were all cut. I don't miss them. I feel nothing for them. I don't care where they are or what they're doing."

"Were you the only child?" I knew the answer to this, too, but I wanted to hear it from her.

"No. And before you ask, I don't care about my brothers, either. They were just like my father. Judgmental as hell. And my mother never dared to stick up for me. I guess that's why I'm so attached to Hazel. Her mother might be a whore, but Hazel's not to blame for that."

"Her mother," I pointed out, "was a broken and hurting woman."

Mamma waved that away. "Look, I don't hesitate to call myself a whore in regards to how you came to exist. That Johnson woman didn't love you. Look at you. You're getting all jittery remembering what she did. You know I'm right."

I decided not to engage on that point. "What were their names?" I asked.

She gave me a Look she usually reserved for my father when he was being an idiot, and employed the use of all my names in a tone that brooked no argument. "George Lucian James Graham, it is enough for me to cope with that your voice is just like my father's. I can live with it because you're my son and you don't have a Russian accent. But I will not bring their names into this house. Now go to bed before I have to send you out for a switch."

I held in my laughter until I'd closed my bedroom door and climbed under my covers. Mamma had never switched me in my life and she wasn't about to now, either.

"Nathan and Elke Shapiro," I whispered defiantly into the darkness, then fell into contemplation about these grandparents I didn't really know.

I had met them. When I was thirteen and Uncle Jamie paid for me to study with that Russian balletmaster in London, I looked for them. It wasn't hard to visit all the various London synagogues until I found the right one. Anytime anyone asked for my name, instead of giving my father's name, I said I was a Shapiro. It was one of those almost comically stereotypical Jewish surnames, after all, even if it hadn't been my mother's name once. Each time I had to be introduced to any other Shapiros in attendance, and that's how I found my Shapiros.

Elke was there alone that day. She said she would take me home and introduce me to her husband, if I liked. I walked along with her and as we waited at a street corner for a break in the traffic, I said, "Do you know who I am?"

She cocked her head at me and seemed to really look at me for the first time. "Should I?"

"I'm Alice's son."

She went very pale and glanced around nervously, as if expecting someone to come along and strike her down just for having heard this information. She gripped my arm and asked, "Is she well?" Then, "Oh, my husband will be so angry with me now, if I bring you home and he finds out who you are..."

"I won't come in," I said. "I just wanted to see you for myself. And for you to see me."

She took my hand and we crossed the street, and when we arrived at a house she said, "Wait here," and went up the steps and inside.

A few minutes later she returned with a little parcel. "I'm sorry I can't ask you in," she said, again with that nervous twitchiness. "Take this. And... be well, George. I'm sorry..."

She disappeared back inside, and I went back to Uncle Jamie's place to open the parcel. It was an autograph book. Olivia Wisniewski and her sister Natalia both had autograph books, which they'd asked Louise and me to write in. In Mamma's, there were Yiddish inscriptions by relatives and English ones by schoolmates. My Yiddish was still shaky at that point, but I got the gist of most of them.

It unsettled me, thinking of all these people who had written these verses and notes to Mamma, lost to time, because I could never ask her about them. Bertha, Gertrude, Ruth, Rebekah, Cecily, Sarah, and so many others.

But tucked in at the end of the album were three photographs. One was Mamma with her brothers when she was nine or ten. One was her at perhaps sixteen, holding a rose in one hand and a ribbon in the other, looking shy and proud of having won some sort of award. The last one was Mamma standing with her two younger brothers in front of the front door. She looked like she was trying not to cry.

Again I wished I could know more about the circumstances behind each photo, but without breaking my promise to Dad, I never could.

When I got home, I showed Dad the album and the photographs the first chance I got.

"I didn't tell them where I lived or what my actual name is," I said. "Elke was terrified when I told her who I was, though."

Dad had looked at the photographs for a long time, getting a glimpse of a version of Mamma he'd not had the privilege of knowing, and there was a soft look in his eyes.

I received a brief response from the dean, who said my letter and situation were under review and they would let me know their decision soon.

"Soon" being a rather relative term to theological types, I shouldn't have been surprised I didn't get a response for two more weeks.

The letter came on the Thursday evening before the quarantine lifted. Dad had left it on the step and was waiting below to hear what it said. Mamma came close, worry on her face.

My heart leapt to my throat and my fingers trembled as I slit it open.

Dear Mr. Graham,

We have discussed your case, and although we personally believe you to be innocent of any indecency, the reputation of the school must be maintained. Considering the injunction to avoid all appearance of evil, we do not believe we can allow you to remain without setting a negative precedent for further lowering of standards in future.

We are not expelling you, but we are requesting you quietly withdraw from the program. We would ask you also to prayerfully consider whether your calling is, in fact, to the ministry at all.

Sincerely, etc.

I didn't say anything. It didn't sink in immediately. I stood there numbly staring at nothing.

"Toss it down, son," Dad called, and I let it flutter to the grass below. He stooped to pick it up and read it aloud so Mamma could hear.

I'm not sure which of them was more outraged.

"Appearances!" Dad spluttered. "Appearances more important than justice! An appearance of goodness can be a false front, too, don't they know?"

"He would have been done in December," Mamma said. "To cut him off now!"

I looked up wearily. "Let it go," I said.

"I don't want to let this go," Mamma said. "You've worked so hard for this. It's not fair."

You came trotting out to see what the fuss was about and stuck your face between the bars of the railing. "Gran-Da!" you yelled, your face beaming. Mamma scooped you up so you wouldn't run down the stairs. (You'd bounced back quickly after your illness, and was keen to expend all the extra energy you'd accumulated.) Dad waved and smiled at you despite his irritation at the school's letter.

Then I said, "Fizz is all that matters now. If the school doesn't want me because of her, I don't want the school. I'll—I'll find some other way or place to finish, somehow."

There was a pause, then Dad shrugged. "If that's what you want, so be it. You can come back to work for me in the meantime."

LOUISE
SANTA MONICA, CALIFORNIA: APRIL 1935

Dear Uncle Jamie,

Winslow was fired last week. It turns out he was soliciting favors from guests, which we are not allowed to do, and he didn't seem much bothered by whether the guest was male or female as long as he got some money out of it. I didn't know men did things like that with other men, which Shirley laughed at me about. Sometimes I feel like there is so much I don't know and I want to seem sophisticated and all that but then something like this happens and I realize I'm not sophisticated at all.

Anyway with Winslow gone we were down to Joyce and me and Gordon, but our boss put out an urgent request for new talent, and this afternoon Joyce and I had to go meet two potential dancers.

Bob Merrill was capable but nothing to write home about. The second one introduced himself as Carlomagno Fernando Javier Joaquín Antonio Vallejos ("but you can call me Carlo"). He is swoonworthy. Joyce and I didn't even need to dance with him to know he would be a hit with the hotel guests. Frankly he could have stepped on toes and nobody would have minded. But it turns out he's an excellent dancer, much better than Winslow and heaps better than Bob. He must be over six feet tall, and he's got black wavy hair and mischievous eyes. Boss says I'll be the one to get him most of the time, since Joyce and Gordon really do best with each other.

After the audition, I asked him if he'd like to have a late lunch with me, and he agreed, so we found a local diner and I got his life story. He's from Argentina, of Italian extraction on his mother's side, and he came here last year to try to get into pictures. His last name is pronounced va-shay-hos, not va-yay-hos, because they speak a different sort of Spanish there than the Mexican kind. He speaks decent English, considering he hasn't been here a terribly long time. When I told him I was a pilot, he asked if I would take him flying sometime. He's always wanted to ride in a plane. I said of course, I'd be glad to.

He's living at the YMCA right now, because he's got no money. He has a day job at a restaurant, serving, and he promised me we'd have lunch there sometime soon, but it doesn't pay much. He also auditions for parts at Hollywood studios often, and sometimes he gets hired as an extra, but so far he hasn't gotten any speaking parts. He is sure it's because his English isn't good enough.

"I'll help you with your English if you teach me Spanish," I said, and we had a deal.

I liked him immediately.

Also, I remembered that there was a dance school somewhere in the area (it was the one that came to Salem and did Sleeping Beauty with kids in most of the roles, when George got to play the evil fairy with a startling amount of relish) and it turns out it's not far from me, so I went to ask if there was anything I could do for them, and they hired me to come in two days a week to work with choreography!

And also I am tired! I guess I'll sleep when I'm dead!

Louise

George

SALEM, OREGON: APRIL 1935

Quarantine lifted just in time for Easter Sunday. Passover had begun a few days before, and Mamma had to leave the de-leavening to Mrs. Tabitha—possibly the only time she hadn't either done the task herself or assisted in some way in all her fifty-seven years. It made her a little twitchy.

But we made a treasure hunt so you could find the ten plagues of Egypt hidden around the attic, and Mrs. T left us everything we needed on the doorstep for Mamma and you and me to have our own Seder. You, four months away from being two, were old enough and verbal enough to participate. It gave me a little thrill to watch your bright eyes as I prompted you for the first time through the four questions you'd someday recite without a hitch.

I was glad to bid farewell to the inescapable scent of Clorox, and you, freed from your "prison", tore all over the house like a liberated monkey, making a very charming nuisance of yourself. The Misses Robinson were so happy to see you again and gave you an enormous chocolate egg.

You were able to go to the Easter service with me, too. Even Dad came along, which surprised me to no end. He hadn't set foot in church since your baptism, the previous Easter. You hid your face in his shoulder a while, having been so long away from large crowds of people, but soon you began to recognize some of your favorites among the teen-aged girls who all coveted a chance to cuddle you, and by the end you was bouncing with excitement to see what loot you might charm out of them that day. (A peppermint, a smaller chocolate egg,

and a red pencil, if you're curious.)

The Monday after Easter, I went back to work for Dad, with a great sigh of resignation, but also knowing I had to do *something*.

On Thursday after dinner he sent me back to the office for several files he'd forgotten to bring home with him. I took you along with me, to expend some of your energy before bedtime.

You took ages on your little legs and were constantly sidetracked by the squirrels skittering among the roots of the trees on the Capitol grounds. They delighted you so much, I didn't stop you from chasing them and squealing joyfully, but I did call after you. "You'll scare them away, Fizz!"

Finally I persuaded you that we could stop and visit the squirrels again on our way home, and I swung you up to my shoulders for the rest of the walk to the office. It took me several minutes to locate the specific thing Dad needed, especially because you had climbed onto Daisy Delight's desk and were sitting perilously close to the edge disassembling a fountain pen. I managed to rescue the pen and your dress from disaster just in time and redirected your attention elsewhere.

As I locked up, you tugged at my jacket. "Da!" you said, pointing.

I glanced in the direction of your finger and sucked in a breath. The capitol dome was pouring out smoke. For an instant I stood frozen, then unlocked the door again and went for the telephone.

The fire department told me they'd already been notified, and I locked the door for the third time that day, stuffed Dad's document into my inner jacket pocket, scooped you up, and set off at a near run.

Back on the capitol grounds, a crowd had gathered on the grass. One lady had situated herself quite comfortably, as if she was at a picnic and this was any old bonfire. Others hovered close to companions looking worried. Everything seemed oddly quiet; passing cars slowed, and conversations were held in whispers.

You clung to me, also silent, but trembling, sensing something was amiss, that this building shouldn't be smoking like a bad chimney. You whimpered and clung to my ears like you always did when you felt insecure and distressed.

"It's okay, Fizz," I said into your good ear. "The firemen are on their way. See, there's a truck already here, and more coming in. They're going to put water on the fire and make it go away. You'll see." But I noticed the newest trucks were marked Portland, and my heart sank. This wasn't looking good.

It was growing chilly, and I knew I should get you home to bed, but something kept me rooted to the spot. The smoke was growing thicker and I wished the firemen would hurry up. Surely they could get it extinguished in time to save the building and its precious contents, couldn't they?

"George!"

I whipped round and saw Mamma pushing her way through the crowd toward me. "George, I thought I'd never find you! We saw the smoke and I was so worried—" Her eyes rose to the smoking dome and in the fading light her face looked deathly pale.

I reached inside my jacket for the papers Dad wanted. "Here," I said. "Take these to Dad and put Fizz to B-E-D, will you?"

She nodded and gave me a tight, unexpected hug. "Come, Hazel," Mamma said, and you went without protest until you realized I wasn't coming too.

"DA!" you screamed, and tried to wriggle out of Mamma's grasp, but Mamma held on tight.

"Go with Gran, Fizz!" I had to shout to be heard.

And flames began to shoot out of the dome. I stepped further into the crowd of onlookers, and your wailing faded into the collective gasps of horror and other screams from some of the women in the crowd.

I knew there had been a fund intended for building a vault to protect state records several years ago, but the governor had shot down the idea as needless expense and the vault had never been built. Now all of those records were going up in smoke and flame before my eyes. I heard occasional smashes of glass from inside the building, and the dome became engulfed in a rainbow torch of flame.

Any thoughts I'd had of finding a way to help rescue valuables left me. No sane person would enter that inferno now.

I watched until the dome, weary of resistance, leaned and sank into the open arms of the building below it, feeding the fire with a whoosh of fresh air.

Smoke and tears pricked at my eyes at the sight of the destruction of this beautiful piece of our history.

I didn't stay long after the dome fell. I knew you would be upset that I had, from your perspective, deserted you when you were scared. I felt guilty for having stayed to gawp uselessly instead of putting you first.

When I arrived home, the sidewalk in front of our house was full of our boarders and many of our neighbors. Dad stepped aside from the group. "Your mother watched out here for a minute, but Hazel wouldn't stop screaming, so they went inside."

I made a Scottish noise of self-reproach. "Should have just brought her home myself. Poor lass."

You glared at me when I entered the Inner Sanctum, your face streaked with tears and snot. I went to the sink to wet my handkerchief. The water trickled feebly, but eventually it got damp enough to clean up your face. I bent toward you to wipe it clean, but you reached out a little hand and slapped me.

"Bad Da," you said.

It didn't hurt, and your baby rage made me want to laugh in spite of myself, but I managed to keep a straight face.

"Do *not* hit, Fizz," I said, sternly. "Not acceptable. Now let me wash your face."

You squirmed, making it as difficult as possible for me to succeed, but eventually, between Mamma holding your head in place and my persistence, I got your face clean. Then I held out my arms to you. "Bedtime, Fizz. Let's go upstairs."

I took you up and settled you into bed, but the moment I turned to go, you started wailing. I went back to you, crouched, and said, "I'm just going to let Lindbergh in, Fizz. I'm not going away."

"Hold you, Da," you said, and reached for me.

We looked unblinking at each other for a moment, then I said, "I will hold you if you do not hit me again."

You snuffled out from under your covers and into my arms, and after letting in Lindbergh for the night, I walked you up and down the attic floor, steering clear of the window where I could see the unnatural glow of the fire against the smoky night air, singing softly to you until at last you went limp and heavy with sleep.

Only then did I stand at the window and watch the blaze. My remaining hope was that the firemen could successfully keep it from spreading to nearby buildings and houses. Eventually I sat on my couch, settling you more comfortably, and soon I too fell asleep.

In the morning I woke when you slid off my lap and started demanding breakfast. I unfolded myself, stiff and sleepy, and escorted you down to Mamma, washing my face at the kitchen sink. The water pressure was back to normal. A glance at my watch told me I'd missed my morning bathroom slot, and I sighed.

"Can I borrow your shaving stuff, Dad?" I called. "Otherwise you're getting a sloppy assistant today."

"Go ahead," he said, and I went to their bedroom, where he was putting on his tie, and gestured with a nod to the dressing table. "Water's there. Still hot. Help yourself."

Mercifully he refrained from any comments whilst I fussed over my face. I'd used his straight razor several times, but not often enough it no longer made me nervous. When I finished, I hurried upstairs to change into fresh clothes and brought down a clean dress for you.

By then Mamma had installed you at the table with a plate of scrambled eggs and buttered toast, banana slices, and a cup of milk, which you were consuming in your typical leisurely fashion. Mamma handed me a plate too and I slid into the chair beside you. Dad joined us, the document I brought last night in one hand and the newspaper in the other. He unfurled the latter and read us the account of the fire. You stared at him as he read, and went quiet and still. I saw a look of raw fear creeping into your face. Mamma noticed it too and laid a hand on Dad's arm. "Stop, George," she said in a low voice, indicating you with the slightest nod of her head. Dad looked and immediately turned the pages of the paper to something else. But you had climbed onto my lap and entwined your arms around my neck like a parasitic vine.

I kissed the top of your tangled hair and whispered, "It's all right, Fizz. Nothing's going to hurt you."

There was more screaming when I left for work with Dad, and I turned back to try reassuring you I would always come back to you, but it didn't stop you crying, so Mamma pushed me out the door and said to scram and she'd settle you.

I felt like a heel walking away, though. If only I'd taken you home myself last night and then gone back to look at the fire. Perhaps you'd thought I was going into the fire. I didn't know how much a child your age understood, but you seemed sharp. I'd probably scarred you for life. I sighed.

As if reading my mind (how did he *do* that?), Dad said, "Do you remember when you were a year and a half old, George?"

"No," I admitted, after a moment.

"She'll be fine," he said, putting an arm around my shoulder and giving me a swift side hug as we went along.

I still wasn't convinced that some tiny part of your brain wouldn't file this nightmare away for later, but I didn't say any more about it.

The smoking shell of the capitol as we passed it gave Dad pause, and again he put his arm over my shoulder and said, "Imagine, son, if this entire town looked like that, and you'll have some understanding of what so many of the towns of France and Belgium looked like, during and after the Great War."

I glanced at him. His face was serious, with a look of sorrow and regret in his eyes. I wondered if he was thinking of the price Uncle Jamie and thousands of others had paid for being in that war, and of the thousands more who didn't survive it, and was about to ask him when he said, "Another war is coming, George. It's inevitable, with what's happening over in Germany right now, even if most people don't want to think about it. It might be ten years or more, but it will come. I'll be too old for it, but you and your sisters and cousins won't be, and *that* scares the hell out of me."

LOUISE

SANTA MONICA, CALIFORNIA: FEBRUARY 9, 1935

I tore open the telegram my dance studio boss handed me, my hands shaking.

It was from my mother.

> *MEET ME AT HOTEL ROOSEVELT MORNING 10TH.*
> *HAVE IMPORTANT NEWS. NOT ABOUT GEORGE.*

I crunched it up in my hands, trembling all over. I knew the place. It was one of the fancy hotels I'd written to asking for dancing work. What in the world was Mother doing at the Hotel Roosevelt?

But the next morning, I rode my motorbike to the hotel, which took the better part of an hour. I was glad I'd left as early as I had. At the desk I asked for my mother, and they called up to her room.

"She'll be down momentarily," the front desk lady said. She gestured me to a seat, but I didn't sit. I watched the elevator doors, clenching and unclenching my fists in anxiety, until it opened and Mother appeared.

I almost didn't recognize her. She had color in her cheeks, sparkle in her eyes, her hair was waved, and she looked like she was actually remembering to eat sometimes. It was a shock to see my mother was, in fact, incredibly beautiful. She ran to me with arms outstretched and took me into a tight hug, which also shocked me. I'm afraid I stiffened a bit. She took my hands and guided me to a nearby bench, where we sat, and I immediately noticed she was wearing a ring: a light green pear-shaped stone with diamonds, on her left hand. I glanced up at her, my heart seizing up inexplicably. Who had given my mother a ring?

She followed my eyes and seemed to read my mind. "That's what I need to talk to you about. I got married last week."

"You WHAT?"

"You heard me the first time," Mother said briskly, but her cheeks flushed pinker with an underlying excitement.

"Just out of the blue, like that, not a word to me?"

"You don't exactly tell me what you're doing, do you?" Mother's voice was sharper than usual, and she sighed. "No, I met him a year ago. It's not sudden."

"Who is it?" I felt drained of all energy, and it came out expressionless. Not sudden? Compared to waiting for George, a year was nothing.

"Konstantin Zafirov."

I frowned slightly, knowing the name but struggling to place it. Then it clicked. "*The* Konstantin Zafirov? The conductor?"

Mother nodded, and I stared, lost for words. "How—"

"An act of God through some bad oysters."

I stood up and stuffed my hands into my trousers pockets. "Look, I—I can't stay to hear the whole story now. It took me almost an hour to get here and it'll take me as long to get back to the airfield, and I have a student at ten, and this afternoon I'll be at the dance school. If you want to talk more, you'll need to come to my hotel tonight at seven. Casa Del Sol on the Santa Monica beach. I'll arrange it all. Just tell them you're my mother at the door."

And I left, because I knew I was about to cry.

I held in my tears until I was off on my motorbike, and by the time I reached the airfield, I'd gotten myself back under control, but the first thing I did when arriving there was to tell Tom, "My mother has shown up. She telegrammed the dance school yesterday. She's married."

Carlo and I arrived at the Casa Del Sol at a quarter to seven, and the two of us stood out of sight until we saw my mother and her man come in. She was in a dark green velvet evening gown, gems which matched her ring sparkling in her ears and at her throat, but even they couldn't top the sparkle in her eyes. The man on whose arm she hung wasn't much taller than she was, sturdily built with somewhat unruly greying hair, and he was completely absorbed in adoring her. He looked like the sort of man who delighted in giving hugs and would be good at it, too. *Well, let him try*, I thought, porcupinely. They were shown to the table and Carlo tapped my shoulder.

"We are on in five minutes," he whispered, and beamed at me with an adoration similar to the adoration the man with my mother had displayed.

The band played our cue. I plastered on my professional face and Carlo and I glided out onto the floor. I studiously avoided meeting anyone's eyes during the dance, but especially Mother's, because I knew I would lose my concentration if I did. When the dance ended, we bowed, and I took Carlo by the hand, bringing him over to the table.

"Mother," I said, "this is my partner, Carlo Vallejos. Carlo, this is my mother Lydia and the man she just told me about, Konstantin Zafirov. He's a conductor."

Carlo bowed and smiled and shook their hands, and I slid into the empty chair and waved him off. "Go back to work now, Carlo, I'm busy."

"Your wish is my command," he said, giving me a doleful expression. "Enjoy your dinner, all of you." And he left.

"He is working tonight," I said, to keep things casual. "I requested the night off in return for making it up tomorrow."

"What is it you do, exactly?" Mother asked.

"We dance for the guests a few times during the evening, and dance with the guests in between."

There was an uncomfortable silence for a moment as I took a sip from my Coke. Then I laced my fingers together on top of the table and fixed Mother with a stare. "How did you know where to send the telegram? How do I know you're not going to run home from here and tell George everything you're finding out about me?"

"I don't snitch," Mother said, looking offended. "Don't be

bullheaded and foolish. As for how I knew where you worked, I supposed there could not be that many dance studios here, so I wrote to the library in Santa Monica and asked. Then I—"

I waved my hand. "Okay, I get the idea."

Mother leant forward and her voice was low and unusually stern. "I have come all this way because I love you and miss you, and the least you can do is give me a few hours of your time without fussing at me, don't you think?"

I glanced at Mr. Zafirov, who was silently sitting back with his arms folded, not interfering. He was the unknown in this new equation, but it clearly he knew when he oughtn't butt into a situation. I gave him some grudging respect for that, and changed the subject. "So how long has this been going on? The two of you?"

"We met in Seattle, a year ago, when I had that concert there. We hit it off right away. His wife died years ago and he has a daughter a little younger than you. Mira. I've been out to see them twice in Philadelphia and do concerts and a recording, and in September he asked me to marry him. I agreed, but said I wasn't ready quite yet. Well, he showed up at my house on his way to San Francisco, and I suggested we go ahead with it. It seemed like the right time. He's a good man and we are going to be very happy."

"We already are." Mr. Zafirov had a nice voice, not as deep as George's, but almost, with just the barest hint of foreign accent.

"What are you?" I asked, forgetting momentarily to be annoyed with him for stealing my mother without telling me first.

"You mean where I come from?"

I nodded, and he said, "I'm Macedonian. I don't know if you're familiar with Balkan geography and history, but I was born in a town called Kriva Palanka. It's in what's now Yugoslavia and used to be Serbia and has also been part of the Ottoman Empire. My family emigrated when I was eleven, in 1903. My native language is Macedonian, which is similar to Serbian and Bulgarian, but I can also speak Russian—my first wife was Russian—and a little Greek, and I get by in French, though I don't consider myself fluent."

The waiter brought us our food then, so for a moment we were all distracted. Mr. Zafirov eventually looked up from his plate to ask,

"Do you dance here often?"

I stabbed at my chicken. "Yes. Saturday and Sunday nights always, and often Wednesdays and Fridays too. I was scheduled to work tonight, but I convinced Joyce to step in for me for the rest of the evening and I'll take her shift tomorrow night."

"Is it a safe job?" Mother asked. "That friend of yours is dancing with guests. Do you have to do that too?"

"It's part of the job," I said flatly. "Yes, it's respectable. The boss looks after us girls, but also Carlo won't let anyone bother me. He can be a bit of a nuisance, but he's useful. He's from Argentina. Wants to get into pictures. Everyone wants to get into pictures."

"So you work here, and the airfield, and the dance school?" Mother looked incredulous.

"How else do you think I'll manage to get my plane? It's not like I have anything else to do." I knew I sounded bitter, and Mother laid a hand on my arm.

"You are so thin and pale," she said. "Are you taking care of yourself? I worry all the time about you. You never tell me anything! I hardly know if I ought to believe you're really as safe and well as you say."

"I'm fine." Mother pressed her lips together at my words, her expression demanding the truth, so I admitted, "Seeing you makes me feel things. I don't want to feel things, Mother. I'm alone in this big city fighting my way toward what I want and I don't... it's hard to see even my mother has had better luck than me." I threw my fork to the table and hid my face in my hands, and Mother put her arm around me and spoke soothingly.

"Perhaps I should have told you," she said. "I wanted to tell you, but it was—well, it's hard to pour out one's heart to a blank wall."

I slumped back in my chair, knowing she was right. I had been an extremely neglectful daughter. For a moment I stared at nothing in particular, then turned to Mr. Zafirov. "So what am I to call you?" I asked.

"Whatever you're comfortable with. My daughter calls me Tato, which is the Macedonian equivalent of 'daddy'. The rest of my family calls me Kosta. Your mother still forgets I have a name half the time and calls me Mr. Zafirov."

That got a choked laugh out of me, because it was so spot on for my mother, and I started to cry. Mother handed me a clean handkerchief from her purse—one of her beautifully pointless lacy ones. "It's too much," I said through my tears. "Everything is too much. Ugh, Mother, why can't you get handkerchiefs that are useful?" I dropped the already drenched thing onto the table in front of me.

"George gives them to me the way you give his father appalling ties," she said. "You should come home with me. I'll still be in Salem for a few months. Mr. Zaf—Kosta—is off to Europe on a tour and it could just be us for a little while. Come home."

"No," I said. "Not as long as George is around. And don't tell me I need to hear him out, because I will get up and leave."

Mother sighed and put her arms around me. "Will you please let us come to your place for a while tonight? It's doubtless quieter there and you don't have to worry about crying in front of us."

I hesitated, but when I glanced at Mr. Zafirov, he looked genuinely enthused about the idea. I hated that I was liking him in spite of myself, but there was something in the man I couldn't help warming to.

So after we finished eating, we got a taxi to my apartment.

"My daughter is eager to meet you," Mr. Zafirov said, as we settled into chairs—him in Shirley's tatty armchair, Mother and me on the couch. And he proceeded to tell me the entire story of how his daughter survived the automobile crash that killed his first wife and son, how Mira now was in a wheelchair because she has so much nerve damage she can't trust the feeling in her legs and it was safer and more comfortable for her.

"And you leave her alone?" I asked.

"Oh, never. I have a large immediate family, and she has a nurse companion who is with her six days a week. On Margaret's days off, one of my sisters or sisters-in-law, or my mother, comes to stay with her. She's very active, Mira is. She started and runs a youth orchestra, helps at church, and does beautiful needlework that she stocks up all year long and sells at our yearly church fair."

"What kind of church is it?" I asked.

"We are Orthodox Christians."

I didn't know what he meant, and for a good half an hour he explained. I turned to Mother in bewilderment. "So are you going to be Orthodox too?"

"I haven't decided," she said. "Kosta knows and he's all right with it. But we will have an Orthodox wedding."

"Marriage blessing," he corrected, and she smiled.

"Yes. And we would love if you could be there."

I contemplated this. "Well, the people I'll be ordering my plane from are somewhere in Pennsylvania, but it's going to be several months at least before I have enough."

"Well, you tell us when you have an idea," Mother said. "It won't be until the autumn."

Then they told me the story of how they met and fell in love, interrupting each other in a way that should have been adorable, but instead rubbed my heart more and more raw. At eleven o'clock Shirley came in, earlier than usual, and my visitors took that as their cue to leave.

Mr. Zafirov did a thorough search of his coat pockets at the door, hunting for something, which he found at last. "I just remembered. I have a few tickets to the concert. I'll give you two. You and your friend can come. It's Saturday." He held them out to me.

"What time is it?" I asked. "We have to work that night."

"There are two. One at two o'clock and one at seven-thirty. You can make the earlier one, I hope."

I took them.

But I didn't go to bed. As soon as they had gone, I went to Carlo's place, where I waited on the front steps until he got back from the hotel.

"What are you doing here, *mi vida?*" he asked, sitting beside me.

"I want," I said, "for you to kiss me into oblivion."

He cocked his head at me in some bafflement. "What?" he asked.

"You heard me."

Then the pieces fell together and he said, "Ah, I see. You are jealous of your mother's happiness."

"I'm not!" I protested. "You're always wanting to kiss me. Well, do it. Touch me. Do whatever you want to me."

He looked at the sky, smiling. "Do not tempt me too much," he said.

"I'm not tempting you. I'm telling you."

He took my hand, brushing his lips over the backs of my fingers. "And I do not want you to offer yourself in haste because you're angry. I would be taking advantage."

My entire body was screaming inside, desperate for the relief I knew I could only get if I went all the way, right now, this minute, and I could have slapped him for being so honorable. The man was always trying to feel me up, for heaven's sake!

Which is why I knew what I was asking for would be amazing right now.

"Louise," he said, softening the S in my name in that incredibly sexy accent. "First of all, we would not be alone because my roommate is in tonight, and second of all, I'm going to take you home." He raised me to my feet, and I, furious, stalked down the steps ahead of him.

He caught me up and took my arm, but I shook it off and refused to talk to him. I got on my motorbike and tore away before he could climb on behind like he usually did.

Shirley had gone to bed by the time I got back. I didn't undress. I flopped onto my couch, turned my back to the room, and put my pillow over my head so nobody would hear me cry.

Of course, in the morning, I knew Carlo was right, and that I should be thankful, but I still felt morose and grumpy just the same.

On Saturday, Carlo collected me in a car borrowed from a friend, and we drove to the concert. Mother met us at the door, beaming, and Carlo gave each of us an arm as she guided us to where we'd sit—a very good seat, indeed. I didn't want to know how much such seats would have cost.

"Is he well-off?" I whispered to Mother.

"Enough to live comfortably," she whispered back. "Not rich, by any means. Fame doesn't equal riches, but I don't care about money."

It was Tchaikovsky's fifth symphony, with which I was not familiar, but I was entranced by it, and fascinated by the way this man... my

new stepfather, I realized, with a little discomfort because I associated the word with drunken brutes... handled his work. He threw his entire self into it, his hands and face beautifully expressive, coaxing sounds out of the orchestra that were devastating to my emotions. I was in tears and didn't even know it until Carlo handed me a handkerchief.

When we left, Carlo returned the car to his friend and, at the door of his flat, he pulled me into his arms, kissing the top of my head, and I leant into the embrace.

"I'm sorry about the other night," he said. "I mean that I made you angry."

"You were right," I said stuffily. "And thank you for being a gentleman."

"For once, at least," he said, with a smile in his voice. His hands slid down my silky dress to my behind.

"We're out in the *street*, Carlo!" I hissed, but I couldn't help laughing.

"Not exactly," he murmured. "We are in the door of my building."

I turned my face up to him and then he kissed me.

For a very long time. I melted back against the stone doorframe, mind fizzing like shaken-up Coke. It should have been awkward and weird, but it wasn't, perhaps because this man knew what he was doing.

"Take me upstairs," I breathed, when he came up for air. I thought if he let me go, I would plummet, but he didn't let me go.

He also didn't take me upstairs.

"If I took you upstairs," he said, his voice low, "we would both regret it in the morning. You because you're not in love with me, and me because I am very much in love with you."

"Damn you, Carlo," I moaned, clinging to his lapels for dear life. "Damn..."

"Damn that man," he whispered into my neck. "For always standing between us."

That made me stop cold, and for a moment I felt lost.

Because for the first time in a long time, the mention of George didn't make me angry.

It made me sad.

Crushingly, horrendously sad.

I stepped back, uncertain about everything in my life once again.

"I'll see you at the hotel," I said, and I hurried away as quickly as I could manage.

*G*EORGE

SALEM, OREGON: MAY 1935

I came home from work to find a letter waiting for me from Scotland, but it was addressed in Aunt Estelle's handwriting, not Uncle Jamie's. That wasn't terribly unusual in itself; she often addressed his mail for him because she liked to be near him. But it was an unusually thick letter, and I turned it over several times, wondering, before deciding to save it for later and tucking it into my pocket.

You were overjoyed to see me safely home and demanded your usual daily quota of pirouettes, jumps, and tosses in the air that terrified my mother and delighted you.

"I know what I'm doing," I kept saying. "I am not going to drop her! If I could do this with Louise, I can certainly do it with a person just a fraction of her size!"

(To be fair, it does throw one's center of gravity a bit to do jumps whilst holding a small child, but I declined to mention that part.)

After dinner and putting you to bed, I sat at my table and opened my letter. Aunt Estelle's handwriting inside, too. I hoped nothing was amiss with Uncle Jamie.

George darling,

I have had enough of this nonsense!! You know your uncle and his Silent-As-The-Grave policy about confidences, which has its place, of course, but this is getting absolutely ridiculous and therefore I have pilfered these letters from the rather considerable stack he thinks I don't know where he's hidden. I figure he won't notice if a few are missing any more than he knows I read them all when he's away.

Your uncle has known all along where Louise is, and I'm not talking about the post office box she uses to write to her mother because she's afraid Lydia will let something slip to you if she gives her her actual address.

I looked up in surprise, trying to take that in, an unexpected fluttering in my heart.

I can guarantee you Jamie has never told Louise anything about you, either, or what you're up to, since she left. And because you two so obviously need to be together, I am choosing to intervene this way since I cannot physically bang your heads together and shout JUST KISS at you. However, to avoid the full wrath of my lord and master when he inevitably discovers my subterfuge, I won't give you either her proper address or her post office box. I think you'll be able to connect enough dots from these three selections to give you an idea where to start your search.

Lovingly and VERY IMPATIENT FOR A WEDDING INVITATION, your Aunt Estelle

I set the letter aside with a trembling hand and picked up the three letters her letter had been folded around. They were written on plain copybook paper, torn untidily out and folded with a complete lack of precision. Typical Louise. I unfolded the one marked "#1" and my heart stopped short at the sight of Louise's familiar loopy, energetic handwriting with its usual quota of misspellings. I squeezed my eyes shut, suddenly hit by a wave of loneliness I hadn't allowed myself to feel for months.

August 12, 1933
Dear Uncle Jamie,

I'm so mad at that George, I want to shake him until his brains either click into place or fall out. How can someone be SO SMART and yet be SO OBLIVIOUS to the girl who's been wild about him for years?? I've waited and waited for him to make his move, but I might as well not exist as anything but someone to tie his blasted ties for him.

I'm not being petty in saying all that. The last straw has been laid on this camel's back, and I'm writing this on a bus south to San Diego. I left in such a hurry I didn't bring anything but a few clothes and a few books and my sock full of savings. I didn't have time to get that reference letter out of my desk, but I hope I'll get along without it. I guess if not I can find a place for Mother to mail it on to me. I had to rush, you see, to get away because I knew George would be coming after me trying to smooth things over with TALK but talk isn't enough for me any more.

He has a CHILD, Uncle Jamie, an actual CHILD. Its mother is that awful Velma Johnson he was sickeningly besotted with last year. She left in such a hurry, and now I know why she was so keen to be gone. So EXOTIC and so BEAUTIFUL and EVERYTHING I AM NOT. I knew she was trouble. No wonder he was mopey after she left. Did you know? It just occurred to me perhaps he told you, and if so I am a bit jealous, although not surprised, because over the past year it feels like more and more we are on either side of a wall that we stand at and talk to each other over the top of. Everything is different now, even though we spent as much time together as we could.

Yes, that wasn't wrong. I cringed inside. I'd been keeping distance because I didn't want to taint her with my secrets and shame.

George thinks I'm in love with the idea of someone like you, and I am, but he has no idea how much like you he is. He's so much more like you than his father (THANK GOD, I love him, but

GOODNESS WHAT NONSENSE) *that he really could be your son instead. Like Thomas. Not noticing anything. Well, you notice things, but I expect it's because you've had a lot more years to train yourself to pay attention, and Thomas and George don't seem to realize they SHOULD be noticing anything outside of their silly fossils and books. George is so focused on his Calling to the Ministry, he doesn't have any space in that head or heart of his left for me. He might as well be a Roman Catholic priest at this rate.*

Why, Uncle Jamie?? Almost a year gone by, and not once did he ever even HINT at me that he'd actually slept with her. I feel so betrayed, even though I suppose I have no right to, as we "weren't together". Still! He could have told me! Could have opened his heart to me. I'd have been mad, but at least it would have been honest, and we'd have found a way to work through it, because I think he WAS sorry about it afterwards. But he's such an idiot!!!!! Why are men so stupid? Were you ever that stupid? I'm not sure I want an answer to that question.

I've been saving myself for him all this time, never letting anyone else even kiss me, and now I feel like it wasn't worth it. Like I want to go sleep with someone else out of spite, just to hurt him. Only he probably wouldn't even care. And anyway nobody wants me. I'm not curvy and jaw-droppingly gorgeous and in demand. Just a boring old ugly scarecrow whom nobody wants, just like Sam always said.

I know this letter is all over the place, but you'll have to forgive me. I just can't stop crying.

Louise

PS. I won't do anything foolish, I promise. I'm just telling you how angry I am. And please please PLEASE don't ever say anything to George about me, where I'm going, or what I'm doing. He doesn't deserve to know anything about me any more.

I set the letter down, tears in my eyes, took up the letter marked "#2" and opened it with some trepidation.

December 22, 1933
Dear Uncle Jamie,

My new address is on the envelope, since I know I can trust you, but I also have a post office box—box 313, here in Santa Monica. That's the address I've given Mother, because who knows if, on the off chance George might run across one of my letters she might carelessly leave lying around, he might try to write to me.

My job is flight instruction here, but at the moment I'm mostly hanging about being a nuisance and fixing engines and maintaining the planes and proving my worth to the fellows here, because you know, GIRLS. Who wants to learn to fly from a GIRL. I do have a few students, though, including the ones the previous instructor hadn't finished with. I'm still waiting to hear back from those hotels I applied to dance at. What WOULD good old Mrs. Myrtle Morgan have to say about that. O the degeneracy of us young people. (Don't worry, it will be a perfectly safe job if I get it.)

I'm staying too busy to think much about George, but I would be lying if I said he isn't on my mind whenever I have a quiet minute. I keep seeing things and my first thought is, "I must tell George," only to remember I can't. I'm still angry, but the truth is I still love him so much and always have. I don't see how he couldn't ever have guessed that. Maybe I assumed too much and he just didn't ever feel the same way about me.

A large part of it stems from the fact that, of all the women he might have chosen to fall for, it had to be HER. I'd have been far more understanding if it had been, say, Olivia or Natalia—after all, they're Jewish too. But VELMA JOHNSON? How did she so successfully fool everyone else in that house into thinking she was so trustworthy and delightful?

I should be happy. I'm here doing what I've longed for years to do, and I'm doing it well and managing to put aside money every week, and yet I'm as sad as if my best friend has died, because it feels like the George I thought I knew is dead. I wonder if he is happy. My heart flinches a little thinking of that poor baby of his. My heart went out to her that morning she first came, before I knew who she was, and sometimes I feel I did the wrong thing in running away if only because she needed looking after properly. It's not her fault her mother stole George from me, after all. I guess someone will take care of her, though. Mrs. Graham would see to that.

And look at me rambling on still about George when I'm mad at him and moving on with my life.

I love you and tell Aunt Estelle I'll answer her letter soon.

Louise

I set that letter down and reached for the third and last one. My heart hitched to see it was a very recent one indeed.

March 2, 1935
Dear Uncle Jamie,

Ah yes, of course I get a lecture for indulging in another rant about George in my last letter. I've been a good girl and held it back for a very long time, as you know, but the feelings aren't going away so why bother.

You say I could be like Ruth with Boaz and demand he do right by me, but I've never wanted that. In this one thing, I'm still convinced he needs to make the first move. If I'm the one who has to propose to HIM before he realizes what's up, then he'll never have me. He's always been too quick to agree to whatever I suggest, you see. Marriage is something too serious for that.

It all doesn't change the fact that, a year and a half on, I STILL LOVE HIM SO MUCH AND I CAN'T STOP LOVING HIM NO MATTER HOW UTTERLY MADDENING HE IS. Was. Probably always will be.

I dreamed for so long of the future I took for granted we'd have together. I thought we'd drift into adulthood and marriage as naturally as anything. But I guess nothing is certain in life. I thought dancing might wake him up. There's a lot of trust and intimacy in dancing, and what kind of boy doesn't find it even a LITTLE exciting to get to touch a girl?

222

I had noticed her, in a way. I'd been aware her body was changing, that it was different from mine, and there was an intriguing mystery there. But I respected her dignity (and also her fists) too much to waste time daydreaming about it, largely because the idea of kissing had always been so disgusting to me right up until the moment Velma Johnson showed me it could be otherwise. As Louise's dance partner, I'd touched her in places I wouldn't touch other girls, yes, but there had never been anything sexual in it for me. It was just part of the hard work that dancing is.

I'm never going to be the only one for him, and it bothers me. Maybe it shouldn't but it does. So much is expected of girls, whereas almost the opposite is expected of boys. Have relations with several girls before marriage? "Well, boys must be boys! Sowing their wild oats!" But I genuinely thought George wasn't that sort.

(Oh, Louise, if only you knew how much it pains me that you'll never be the only one for me.)

I suppose it's my pride at fault here. I don't want to admit I might have been wrong to run away. I don't want to appear to be groveling at his feet for forgiveness when it is he who committed the wrong. Don't want to give up the safety of what has become my new life. Honestly, I love my life, but... sometimes I am so terribly lonely. Carlo would like to change that, I know.
I was thinking how something did change in George after Miss Johnson left, and for the better. I wish I knew what it was. He went from being a pompous ass to thoroughly humbled and genuine, overnight! Knowing now they'd been carrying on, perhaps it was because he realized he wasn't infallible after all? Still, why couldn't he have told me? Nine months is a LONG time to keep a secret like that.
I remember after she left, the first time he got up to lead the Thursday prayer meeting, how solemn and earnest and humble he suddenly was, and how lovely his hands were, gripping the side of the desk like he meant business, and I felt all melty inside, wishing I

could be the desk. It was startling. Why am I telling you this?

I glanced at my hands. They weren't anything so remarkable: just the same long-fingered Graham hands Dad and Uncle Jamie and most of my cousins and half of my sisters had. The hands were as much a Graham trait as the left-handedness that pervaded the family, and I was rather pleased to have both, by whatever freak of happenstance. But it hadn't occurred to me there might be anything particularly attractive about them, let alone that Louise would have liked me to touch her with them. I blushed hot at the mere idea and turned back to the letter.

The reason all this came swooshing back into my heart so suddenly is, Mother turned up recently with a man and informed me they'd just been married. I was shocked beyond words. I asked her why she never told me about him before and she said writing letters to me is like talking to a blank wall and why bother. But the sight of her so obviously happy and in love broke me open. If even she can manage to find love, at over forty? If George showed up here someday, oh... I don't know what I'd do. Why think about what will never happen? And I AM still mad at him.

You can burn this if you want, like the rubbish it is. I'll probably regret having written it at all the minute I drop it in the box to send, so I'd better do that now before I have time to think better of it.

Love, Louise.

I sat there for some time, stunned, staring at the letters as if afraid they were an illusion and might vaporize.

I glanced over them again.

I didn't have time to get my reference letter out of my desk.

Mother turned up recently with a man and informed me they'd just been married.

I hadn't had a clue Lydia was seeing anyone. I felt as shocked as Louise must have been.

But more importantly...

Carlo would like to change that, I know.

Who the hell was Carlo?

I rushed downstairs and poked my head into the Inner Sanctum. "Mamma!"

"What, Georgie?" came her voice from somewhere I couldn't see.

"Did you know Lydia got married?"

"Of course I did."

"Why did nobody tell me?"

"If you haven't noticed she's been blindingly happy for the past year and constantly flitting off to Philadelphia, that's on you. Is that all you came here to ask?"

"No," I said, kicking myself for, again, not noticing something so important. "I'm running out for a minute. Can you keep an ear out for Fizz?"

She appeared in her dressing gown. "It's awfully late," she said. She looked very tired.

"I'll sit with her," said Dad. "You go on to bed, Alice."

"Thanks," I said, and slammed the door accidentally in my haste to be on my way.

I let myself into the Pearsons' house and called out, softly, "Lydia? Are you here?"

She emerged from the living room. The wireless was on, but she went to shut it off as soon as she saw me.

"I'm sorry to trouble you," I said, "but what is this about you having gotten married?"

She went pink and I saw at once that she was, in fact, very much in love with somebody.

"Oh," she said, clasping her hands in front of her with a girlish delight. "It... happened quite unexpectedly. I met him in February—not this year, last year—when I was in Seattle. It's a long story. He's a conductor. He came out west to do concerts in San Francisco and Los Angeles and stopped in here to see me. We'd been engaged for a few months, but I decided I was tired of waiting and suggested a civil ceremony so I went with him and we got married in San Francisco.

That was in February. He had a European tour already scheduled, so he left for that and I came back here. He got home today, to Philadelphia. He sent me a telegram to let me know."

She was so pleased, it was impossible to not be happy for her. Of all the people I knew, she was the most deserving of happiness after her hard life thus far.

"Come here," she said, beckoning, and took me up to her room, where she had a photograph on her nightstand that she picked up to show me. "That's him and his daughter, Mira. She's nineteen. She reminds me so much of Louise. She was in a bad accident when she was eleven; that's why she has the scarring on her face and she's in a wheelchair. I adore her."

"What's his name?" I asked, handing the photograph back.

"Konstantin Zafirov. We should have met at Oberlin. He was there when I was supposed to have gone."

As she took the photograph, I noticed the ring on her hand, and sighed deeply that I hadn't before. "I'm glad you're happy," I said, and meant it. "Fizz and I will miss you when you're gone, though."

"Oh, I'm going to miss all of you, too!" she said. "So much. You'll have to come visit."

There was a pause, and then I asked, "Aunt Estelle sent me some letters Louise sent Uncle Jamie, because she says she's tired of the nonsense and wants me to find her."

"Oh!" She put a hand to her mouth. "I'm sure he's heard a lot more from her than I have." There was a hint of unhappiness in her tone for the first time since I'd come in. I decided not to engage on that point.

"Well, it's my fault she ran away to begin with and, I suppose, for not trying harder to get her back." I sat down on the edge of the bed and sighed, and she sat beside me, and we were quiet a while.

"You two are lost souls, apart from each other," she said, finally. "I want my daughter back. For her to do more than send me vague letters reassuring me she's alive and well but never telling me anything much. I want her with you."

"So you don't know anything about this Carlo fellow?"

"She dances with him. I met him, when we were there. He's very much in love with her, but I don't think she loves him. I could be

226

wrong. Sometimes it's hard to tell with her."

She'd been good enough at hiding it with me, I thought, but I didn't say it. "Do you mind if I look in her desk? There was apparently a reference letter she left behind in her rush to be gone. Aunt Estelle told me to take whatever clues I could get from the letters she sent, and that's one of the only ones I really have to work with."

She got up and I followed her to Louise's room, which hadn't changed since she left. It felt wrong to sit in her chair digging through her things, but I did it anyway. Lydia took one drawer and I took the other, and after a moment of sorting through the mess, she cried, "This might be it!"

She bent closer to me so I could see better as she unfolded the letter, and exclaimed, "It's from Amelia Earhart herself!"

It was a cordial, typewritten reply to some enquiry Louise had apparently sent her at one point. It was dated May 1932, and gave the names of several pilots to whom Louise might apply, were she to come to the Los Angeles area. In the bottom margin, in Louise's handwriting, were the words: *Wrote Harris June 11, rec'd answer July 30, have promise of work if I can come down this fall. Will Mother let me drop out of school? No replies from Sanders or Green.*

"*That's* why she was so keen to drop out of school," Lydia said softly, and looked out across the room, face contemplative. "She was already thinking of leaving, then. Before Hazel."

I sat back. "Because I didn't know she was in love with me and she was tired of waiting," I said, equally softly.

We put everything back and I walked home, the Earhart letter inside my jacket pocket. Dad was fast asleep on my couch when I got in. I didn't wake him.

The next day, I spent most of my time in my room deep in thought, perusing the letters over and over again, trying to form a plan as well as wrap my head around the idea that Lydia was married and going to leave. You had gone to the Inner Sanctum, and after lunch I ventured down to see how you were doing, no closer than before to a solution to my problems.

Dad was lounging on the bed with a book, slightly untidy, and Mamma was cooing over you, just coming awake from a nap. There was something calculated about their casualness that clearly indicated they'd been interrupted in some shenanigan or other.

I sat on the floor and held out my arms to you, who wriggled out of Mamma's arms and ran into mine. You were snuggly for about seven seconds before toddling across the floor to the box where your alphabet blocks were kept, then pushed the box back toward me, dumping it out noisily.

"She's kind of cute," I said to nobody in particular.

Dad laughed. "Very." He glanced at me over the top of his book. "You all right, George? You seem in a mood."

"He's always in a mood," Mamma said from the other room.

"Thanks," I said drily.

The letters were heavy on my mind. Louise might, even now, be consorting with her heroine of the air. Might be on a date with Carlo, whoever he actually was. I scowled, then let my mind drift back to those declarations of love and desire Louise had penned and wished desperately that I hadn't been so stupid that she had to confess them to someone else instead of keeping them for my eyes only.

Mamma left her bowl of bread dough to rise and sat down with

handwork, and I built a tower for you with the blocks. Mamma began speaking, not looking up from her work. "The seminary isn't going to take you back, and you loathe working for your father. Having you mope about with your nose in books is getting rather tiresome, Georgie."

You swept down the tower dramatically and clapped her hands, waiting expectantly for me to build her another one.

"He's never *not* had his nose in books," Dad said.

"He didn't used to *mope*," Mamma said.

This time I built two towers, side by side. "And your point?" I asked, after you had slammed the towers down with great delight.

"My point is," said Mamma, "you're never going to be yourself again without Louise."

I looked up. Was everyone conspiring together without my knowledge?

Dad regarded me with fondness. "She's right, you know. You ought to go find her and kiss her like you mean it."

Mamma shot Dad a Look. "Maybe talk to her first."

"What about Fizz?" I asked, exchanging a suspicious look with you as I built up another tower.

"Take her with you."

You held up a block. "Da," she said. "What's this?"

"D for diaspora. Or dichotomy. Or Da."

You held up the other. "F," I said. "F for facetiae and Fizz."

You picked up a third from the pile. It was L. I bit my lip, but said softly, "That's L." L for Louise. I couldn't say it out loud.

"L for love," Dad said. He was still looking at me, and something in his eyes made me long to be small again like you so I could climb onto his lap and be held.

"Why did you all never tell me Louise was in love with me?" I asked.

Mamma answered readily. "She said, and I quote, 'I tell George go and he goes, or do this and he does it, and I want him to think of it on his own.'"

"And your mother said she'd divorce me if I said anything," Dad added.

You climbed off my lap and started making a long line of blocks stretching from my feet in a haphazard line toward the chair where Mamma sat. *Velma came along and ruined everything, I thought. I wouldn't do it again. I wouldn't want to repeat it, but I wouldn't have Fizz otherwise, and I cannot imagine a life without Fizz in it anymore. I suppose we just have to make the best of our consequences.*

"Aunt Estelle sent me three of the letters Louise wrote Uncle Jamie. That's what was in the envelope yesterday," I volunteered after a long silence, glancing at my parents, who both looked a bit startled.

"And?" asked Dad.

"I... don't want to repeat all she said," I said, blushing and ducking my head away.

Dad grinned. "I always thought Louise was ready to jump you at the slightest hint of invitation. I was becoming concerned that you didn't seem to catch on."

"Not every man in the world has your insatiable need for sex, George," Mamma murmured.

"Not every woman in the world has yours," he said back. "Well, maybe that one laird's wife who—"

"We were talking about our son," she said severely, cutting him off.

"So we were." He was not one bit chastened.

"I've got a little saved up," I went on, deciding to pretend I hadn't heard any of that. "I was thinking of seeing if I could find an old milk truck or something I could live in on the road. If we still had Sirius, I know where I could get an old surrey, but..."

"A truck will be faster," Dad said. "Whereabouts are you heading?"

"She's somewhere in the Santa Monica area. That's all I could gather from the letters. No address or definite place names besides that."

"You could go by train," Dad said.

"I want to be independent. Have a place to sleep even if I can't get a room anywhere. And being on my own timetable would be better for Fizz, don't you think?"

"And what do you plan to do with Hazel whilst you are working, assuming you can find work at all?" Mamma asked.

"I don't know," I said, honestly. "But if God wants me to go, and I think he does, I can leave those details to him."

"I'll buy you whatever vehicle you want," Dad said. "It would be my pleasure to contribute to any cause that gets you where you belong."

"Thanks," I said, shy at the supportiveness.

Everything fell into place then in a way that made me surer than ever I was making the right choice. We found a temperamental old milk truck for cheap. I painted over its fading picture of a girl and her cow with white paint and had windows put into the sides for air. Mamma made clever canvas covers for them that could be rolled up when we stopped and would keep out the dust when we drove. We bolted a cot to the floor for me, with a mattress underneath for you to pull out at night, and bolted crates with latchable doors into the opposite corner to store food and clothes in. Dad showed me how to make a camp stove from a coffee can in the manner of the Scottish Travellers he'd known as a boy. There was a lockbox for the depositions about you and whatever money I didn't want to carry on me that could be hidden easily behind a secret panel in one of the crate cupboards.

Once it was ready to live in, there came the difficult choices of what to take and what to leave behind. A few changes of clothes, of course, new straw hats that Lydia had given us. Soap and towels and toothbrushes and a comb. A washbasin and two sets of tin plates and cups and utensils, and a pan to cook in. A knife and a wooden spoon and mixing bowl, and food and water dishes for Lindbergh. My bicycle could be strapped in place, too.

It was the books that were the most difficult. My Bible and a hymnal were obvious, but in the end the only other book I brought along for myself was *The Prisoner of Zenda*, purely for the strong association with Louise. I'd read it to her at least five times. I also added in a few of your favorites.

And I allowed myself one completely frivolous item: the gramophone and a dozen of the records from our collection. They fit, wrapped in extra blankets, under my cot.

I was pleased with the arrangement. Self-sufficiency had always appealed to me. Lindbergh would make a fine guard dog, and you would be a handful no matter what method of travel we chose.

The only thing that left me uneasy was it being a motorized vehicle. "I won't know what to do if it breaks down," I said glumly, to Dad, as we looked it all over one last time the night before my departure. "Wouldn't have that trouble with a horse."

We'd marked out my planned route in red pencil on a map, and now we stood there looking at the silent truck, sitting and waiting to fulfill its task. Dad laid his arm over my shoulders. "Aye, right, I miss Sirius too. But you'll be all right. Just remember you'll need to get new tires when you get to Los Angeles. These ones should last long enough to get you there."

I nodded. He'd drilled me in how to change and patch tires over the last several weeks. I was familiar with this on a smaller scale, having done both with my bicycle, but it was far more unnerving on a large truck.

We went back inside, where Mamma and Lydia were having tea. You were in bed already, and we sat for several hours, knowing it was the last time we'd all be together for a yet-uncertain length of time. I'd traveled to Scotland and London in the past, but there'd always been a set return date. I didn't like uncertainty.

GEORGE

SALEM, OREGON: JUNE 23, 1935

*B*efore the sun was up the next morning, I dressed and shaved and opened my desk to take out the silver bracelet Louise had broken. I'd had it repaired, and it was going to come along with us. I buttoned it into my shirt pocket, gathered up a few last-minute things, and swept my attic with one final glance of sentimentality before closing the door to it for the last time.

I gave Lindbergh his breakfast, Mamma gave me mine, and we packed yours into a lunch pail for later. Mamma was unusually emotional, which I could tell because she had been up for who knew how long cooking an astonishing assortment of all my favorite treats to send us off with. I myself felt weirdly weepy. Right before it was time to go, I carried you outside, wrapped in a blanket. My sweet baby. You were too little to realize how drastically your life was about to change.

Lydia took her in her arms and you snuggled into her to sleep some more. She would be coming with us as far as Junction City, wanting to visit Louise's father's grave once before catching a train to Philadelphia and her new life with her new husband. Her belongings were loaded into the back already, and I was glad I didn't have to start my journey completely alone. Dad handed me his camera and extra film; Mamma brought out a bunch of roses big enough to decorate a dozen graves and a small paper sack which she laid on the floor at Lydia's feet.

I hugged my parents and started up the truck. Lindbergh hopped onto a cushion on the seat between me and Lydia and curled up, and I drove down the street. As I turned the corner, I caught one final glimpse of Mamma and Dad, arms around each other, waving bravely, and then I couldn't see them any more, and I choked up, feeling extremely not brave, until Lydia's hand touched my arm and squeezed it lightly.

"It will be as hard for them as for you," she said, her voice gentle. "You're their life."

I tried to muster up a smile for her, but I'm not sure I succeeded. By the time I'd made it to Highway 99, though, I'd collected myself. It was an odd way to trek across creation, this was—my entire life and possessions now limited to what my truck could hold. But as I glanced at my dog and my daughter, I thought, *Everything I need most is right here beside me. And, at least for a few more hours, I have Lydia.*

When we arrived in Junction City, I made sure the tank was full of gas so we wouldn't have to stop again for a long time. This was the town where Louise had been born and spent the first ten years of her life. Lydia directed me to a road where we could see the house in which she used to live, and then to the graveyard.

You began to stir and left Lydia's arms for mine, your face sleepy and unimpressed. I let you sit on my lap and snuggle, as you liked to do when you woke up, until your little brain was ready to face the day. So the three of us sat and waited, and then Lydia led us to the family plot, her arms full of the roses and I carrying the little paper sack as we wound our way among the stones.

It was peaceful here. I'd always enjoyed cemeteries, finding them a good place to be quiet and think. I'd first spoken to Louise in the one across from my house in Turner, and now I was here to meet her father—or as close as I'd get to meeting him this side of eternity, anyway.

The plot was outlined with a tidy border of river rocks, the grass overgrown and weedy. I thought, *There are far too many stones in this plot.* I crouched down and looked closely at the one at the edge.

MARTHA PEARSON, 1884-1913

BABY PEARSON

THEY SHALL DWELL IN THE HOUSE OF THE LORD FOR EVER.

234

I hadn't realized the first wife had died in childbirth. For some reason tears pricked at my eyes for this woman I'd never known, a woman who'd had to die so Louise could exist.

Next was a smaller stone, a simple square of polished granite listing just a tiny bit to the right. Three names.

MARTHA, 1910-1918.
VIOLET, 1912-1918.
DANNY, 1917-1918.

I sat in front of that one and the tears did escape my eyes then. You, who had wandered off to talk to a carved lamb on another headstone came back to me and butted your way into my arms.

"Too many dead babies," I said to her, hoarsely. "They might have been your aunts and uncle. They didn't have a chance to grow up. The Lindbergh baby didn't have a chance to grow up. And I'm just now actually realizing what all of that means."

"Dead?" she repeated.

"It's like going to sleep, but for a long time, and if you love Jesus the next thing you'll know you're waking up to see him coming to take you to heaven."

"Oh." You framed my face with your tiny hands and put your face so close to mine she went cross-eyed. "Fizz dead?"

"No, of course not." I hugged her. "Fizz is very much alive."

"Go now?"

"When Lydia is ready."

I struggled to my feet and stepped over to the last stone. On one half it read:

LOUIS INGMAR PEARSON, 1882-1925.
BELOVED HUSBAND AND FATHER.

On the other half it read:

LYDIA PATRICIA PEARSON, 1892- (date of death still blank)

Underneath, spanning the width of the stone, there were the words:

Come away to the skies, my beloved, arise …
And with singing to Zion return.

"You're going to be buried here?" I asked her, and she nodded. Her face was wet and flushed.

"I know, usually the honor would go to the first wife, but... when he died and Martha already had her own stone, I took it upon myself to make the decision. I'm sure it made the family angry, but I couldn't care less."

"What about Konstantin?"

"I can't be buried with him if I don't convert, and he already has a stone like this with Maria's name on half. We discussed it already. We'll be dead. We won't care where our mortal husks get put."

How odd, I thought, that a woman who came as a mail-order bride to marry a man she'd never seen, could have formed so strong a bond with said man, and he with her, that this was the arrangement she'd seen fit to make for their final resting place.

Or perhaps... perhaps there was a bit of spite in the woman, and this was her way of telling the Pearson clan exactly where they could go. I'd begun to understand there were depths to Louise's mother I would never plumb.

Lydia handed me the little paper sack then, and I opened it to find six of the pretty little rocks Mamma keeps in a jar for moments like this, and my heart squeezed. I already missed her so much.

I knelt at your side and held out the stones in the palm of my hand. "These are for memory, Fizz," I said. "Flowers will rot away eventually like bodies do, but stones are forever. Memory is forever, and a blessing."

"Forever," you singsonged breathily. "Go now?"

"First we leave the stones," I said. I took your hand and led you to Martha and the baby's grave. "Two go here," I said, and handed you two, which you set on the ledge. "And three here."

You arranged the children's stones along the top of that headstone.

236

"And the last one goes here," I said, pointing to Lou Pearson's half of the remaining marker.

"Okay," you said.

"You take as long as you need," I said softly to Lydia. "I'll go back to the truck and give Fizz her breakfast."

She nodded gratefully, and you slowly consumed your breakfast from the tin pail: buttered toast and apple slices and fried egg, one slow bite at a time. I watched Lydia,  who visited the stones in the same order you and I had, and I saw her crossing herself and bowing three times as she laid flowers at each one. I'd never seen her do that before, and it piqued my curiosity.

She lingered over the last one, and bent to kiss it, before rising to her feet and coming back to us.

"I've never seen you cross yourself," I said to her as we sat there waiting for you to finish eating.

"It's something Kosta and Mira have taught me," she said. "Mira taught me a prayer when we visited the grave of her mother and brother: 'Grant remission of sins, Lord, to all our fathers, brothers, and sisters who have departed before us in faith and the hope of the Resurrection, and make their memory eternal.' You bow and say it three times."

I considered this, and she went on, "I know you probably think it's not right—"

I held up a hand. "What I think isn't what should matter. It's what God thinks, and that's between you and him to work out."

She smiled gratefully at me. "That's much nicer than the reaction I got from Louise," she said, and I couldn't help but laugh. "She is so like her father. Unswervingly Protestant. I mean, technically I am too, having been raised Lutheran, but..." She shrugged slightly. "The moment Louise got me alone, she had many words to say about my joining myself to a man of a faith like that."

"Did they get on well?"

"They did. She seemed reluctant to admit he'd won her over, but he has, I'm sure of it. The thing with Kosta is, everyone loves him. He's just... warm, you know? And it attracts people. But she was not happy about the difference of faith. Your mother wasn't happy at first, either. She heard his name and assumed he was Russian, and you know what she thinks of Russian Orthodox."

I did know. Rants about the pogroms that had driven out my ancestors and slaughtered many of my relatives had peppered family conversations for years. "I was sure to ask him," Lydia hastened to add, "if he had anything against Jews. Because I would have broken it off if he did. Fortunately he doesn't." She turned my wrist so she could see my watch. "I guess we'd better get to the station."

Once there, we unloaded her trunk and valises and sat on a bench to await the arrival of the train.

"When I got off the train from Minnesota twenty-three years ago," Lydia said thoughtfully, "I never dreamed what was ahead of me. And much of it was hard and sad. But Lou often reminded me of the Scripture verse, 'I will never leave you nor forsake you', because his family would have loved for him to leave and forsake me, and he said he never would, and even if he did, Jesus never would. He was right. And now I have a husband who adores me and whose family welcomed me right in and I've never felt so sure of anything, or so much as if I belong, as I do with him. And them." She looked at me. "I am going to miss you, George! But I hope soon you'll manage to get Louise to come around and we'll get a wedding invitation. I'd invite you to our church wedding, but I don't know yet when it will be."

"I understand," I said. "And I probably couldn't make it all the way to Pennsylvania. Louise is the one who should be there, anyway, and I doubt she'd come if I was going to."

Soon after that the train pulled in, Lydia's trunk was loaded on, and there were final hugs and kisses and waves as it pulled away, and

238

then it was out of sight, and I was really alone with you, and the fact hit me like a bomb.

Hand in hand with you, we walked back to the truck, and I started it up, and we continued south.

About fifteen minutes later, you had finished the remains of your breakfast except for one bite of egg you'd dropped for Lindbergh. "Out," you said, clashing the lid on the lunch pail repeatedly.

"Can't get out right now, Fizz," I said. "We have a long, long way to drive still today."

"Why?" You tried to stand up on the seat, and I caught you around the waist with one arm so you wouldn't fall.

I wanted to say, "We're going to find you a mother." But instead I said, "We're going on an adventure, Fizz."

"Why?"

"Because your father is an idiot and needs to fix what he messed up."

"Why?" It was your newest favorite word, and I sighed.

It was going to be a very long drive.

You kept up a steady stream of questions for some time, then fell asleep on the long-suffering pillow of Lindbergh.

When we reached Roseburg, we stopped to make sandwiches and I let Lindbergh and you run around a little before continuing south. Forever anxious about running out of gas, I also filled up again.

You were astonishingly good at being where you oughtn't within seconds of your parent turning his back. I was used to having extra eyes on you besides only mine (we all know how oblivious I am). Fortunately Lindbergh was astonishingly good at staying near you, but the constant distraction of playing the Where-Is-Fizz-Now game was rather exhausting. I was glad to get back on the road where you could be contained.

We made another gas stop in Medford, and continued on to Yreka, where I had planned to stop for the night. Shortly after crossing the border into California, you decided you were done with this traveling nonsense and kept up a steady howling for the last hour and a half.

There's not a lot between Ashland and Yreka, and I felt far from comfortable parking for the night directly by a highway, so I soldiered on despite your misery making me miserable, trying to reason with you as best I could.

In Yreka we found a place to park among some trees near a creek. I was exhausted from the howling child, but managed to get through my exercise regimen anyway—in between having to shout at you repeatedly to stay away from the water.

For supper we had cold beans straight out of the tin because I was too tired to make a pan dirty that I'd have to wash. I decided, in order to keep tabs on the child, I'd have to involve you in everything I did. We fetched a pailful of the creek water so Lindbergh could have a drink, then got you ready for bed. You helped open the windows, pulled out your own mattress and bounced on it, and crawled in circles over the entire truck for fifteen minutes before you were ready to have me read one of your books. We said our prayers, and finally you went to sleep, Lindbergh at your feet, watchful as usual.

I lay on my cot, awake for a long time. The fresh air drifted through the windows, pleasantly cool after the warmth of the day.

A pang of loneliness washed over me as I realized how far south I was—further south than I'd ever been, and I shed a tear or two thinking I might not see Salem again for a long time, perhaps ever. I had no idea what awaited me in Santa Monica or where my life would take me from there.

I turned to my side, hugging my pillow, wishing it was Louise instead, as darkness fell and sleep at last overcame me.

In the morning I woke up early enough to have a quick wash by the creek and begin cooking our breakfast on the little stove before you woke up. You climbed down, dragging your beloved knitted baby blanket Mrs. Pearson had made behind her. You wanted to sit on my lap and were grumpy when I said you had to wait a minute. "Here, have a pancake," I said, flipping one out onto your tin plate and drizzling syrup over it. You waited until I cut it into bite sized pieces, however, before starting to eat it, slowly, stickily, with your fingers, still grizzling about not being able to be on my lap.

After a few minutes, I doused the fire and let you climb onto my lap to cuddle, slicing bits of apple with a small knife and taking turns eating the slices. By the time we finished the apple, you were ready to be Daytime Fizz and got off me to play with Lindbergh and get grass stains all over your dress.

We stayed there all day. I gave you your first swimming lesson (mostly you just wanted to splash around) until we were no longer in shade, since I burnt to a crisp in the sun, so we spread out a blanket on the grass in the shade and lay down. You soon drifted off to sleep. I rolled onto my stomach to watch you sleeping and thought how marvelous you were. We'd looked through all the old family photographs together a few nights before leaving, and it was uncanny how much like Dad you looked. Side by side in toddler photos, you could have been twins.

I was interrupted out of my reverie by footsteps. I looked up. A lanky, unshaven man with a rifle slung over his shoulder peering at us from a great height. Lindbergh pricked his ears and stood at attention, cautious but not unfriendly.

"Who're you?" the man asked. He spoke softly, presumably in deference to the sleeping you. I told him.

"Well, you're on my land."

"Oh, I didn't know. I'll leave as soon as she wakes up. Very sorry."

"That your little sister? You got parents about?"

"Oh. I... am the parent, actually."

He raised his eyebrows, obviously skeptical.

"I was giving her a bit of rest," I explained. "We drove seven hours yesterday and it's the first time she's spent so long traveling, you see."

He scratched his head contemplatively and spat off to one side. "Any chance you might want to help with haying for a week?"

"Wouldn't say no," I said.

"Just 'til my son gets back on his feet. Crushed his ankle so bad he had to go all the way to Ashland to get it fixed up. He's fresh back from getting the cast off and he's not supposed to do a lot of heavy work."

So, when you woke up, we went to his house and parked by his barn, and I learned how to harvest hay. The farmer, surprised at my strength relative to my size, asked if I'd done this before.

"No," I said, and gave him the usual explanation. "I'm a ballet dancer. We're stronger than you think."

He couldn't afford to pay me much, but what he did give me I was grateful for, as well as for the reprieve from travel that pleased you very much. You got to stay in the farmhouse playing with the farmer's grandchildren, who were a little older than you were.

LOUISE

SANTA MONICA, CALIFORNIA: JUNE 23, 1935

I got a letter from Uncle Jamie yesterday, in which he apologized profusely because he'd just found out Aunt Estelle had pilfered several of my letters and SENT THEM TO GEORGE. He says she was tired of "this nonsense" and she had never made any promises to keep her mouth shut, so interference it was.

I was too shocked to know what I thought of that at first. He said they haven't ever *had* such a fuss at each other before as this has caused, and he hopes I will forgive him for not keeping the letters hidden better and Aunt Estelle for playing at matchmaker, despite the fact that she refuses to be sorry and won't tell which ones she sent except that she picked ones with "the scantest of clues"—to let George attempt to be Sherlock Holmes, I suppose.

Today, though, Carlo and I went to the beach together, and it distracted me for a bit. After we'd been in the water for a bit we settled under the big umbrella. He stretched out to take a nap and I, absorbed in knitting and watching the children shrieking happily on the beach, had almost forgotten he was there. My hands stilled as I watched one particular little girl, not quite two, dashing headlong toward the encroaching wave of water while an older sister ran after her, and I thought of George's child.

She'd be about this one's size by now. I wondered if she was all right, and whether George loved her. I was thankful for my sunglasses, so nobody could see the tears springing unbidden to my eyes. Time was ticking away. I was already half past twenty, and I had no prospect of children of my own any time soon, and it *hurt*.

But I couldn't hold back the tears for long. They flowed silently as my hands stilled in my lap.

The idea that George now probably knew all kinds of embarrassing thoughts I'd had about him was painful. I cursed myself for all the nonsense I'd told Uncle Jamie over the last couple of years and wondered if he knew yet what George had done with the information. I would ask, whenever I got over this funk enough to write back. I also made a mental note to tell my airfield friends again that they weren't ever to say they knew me or my whereabouts. I wasn't about to make it easy for George to find me, if he did get any sweepingly grand ideas about seeking me out to lay out all his excuses again.

"What is it, *mi vida?*" Carlo had sat up and was peering into my face with concern. His arm slipped around me, drawing me into his side, and the gesture pushed my tears from silent to not-so-silent.

He held me, rocking me gently, and I thought, *It should be George holding me, and that should be our child shrieking with delight as she runs at waves. Ours. Not his and someone else's.* I hated him for falling for Velma Johnson, and I hated myself for hating him.

"You are thinking of that man again," he said, with a sigh. "And here I was going to propose to you again tonight."

I dug in my bag for a handkerchief and blew my nose and tried to speak casually. I wasn't about to admit to him I was hankering after having babies. "Why can't I forget him, Carlo?"

"Because you are still in love with him," he said.

"I am not."

He laughed. "There is something else, too, yes?"

So I told him about Aunt Estelle, and he listened, and I was annoyed at him for seeming to find it amusing.

I took off my sunglasses and glared at him, gorgeous and golden-brown in the June sun. "I'm trying to forget him, in case you don't remember that," I said snappishly.

"How about you let me kiss you some more, then?"

I remembered how good it had felt when I'd let him kiss me months ago, and how hard I'd had to work at resisting the urge to try it again. And I thought, *The only way I can forget George is to replace him.* So I said, "Okay."

He looked surprised. "Okay as in... I can kiss you?"

I nodded, suddenly overcome by fluttering terror. Kissing Carlo once was an impulse. Kissing him a second time was deliberate betrayal.

But George betrayed me, I reminded myself, and this is only a kiss.

The surprise had been replaced by sparkle, and Carlo pulled me onto the blanket beside him and turned to face me. He was so much bigger than me. So much bigger than George. Then immediately I was angry with myself for yet again letting one dead to me continue to haunt me.

Carlo's mouth was warm and for several minutes I was lost to everything else. My mind was absorbed in feeling, in thinking that George was missing out on so much by not wanting to do this with me.

The idea made me more aggressive, and Carlo drew back. He didn't let go of me, but there was a hint of resignation in his eyes. "You are not kissing me, are you?" he asked. He flopped back onto his back again and laid an arm over his eyes. "I cannot kiss you to oblivion if you keep thinking about how much more you would rather be kissing him."

I sat up and began stuffing all of my things into my bag.

"You are not leaving?" he said.

"I am," I said. "I was already furious at Aunt Estelle and now I'm furious at you, so I am going to drown my sorrows in a long hot bath before I have to be on my feet all night tonight."

"Look, I do not mean to offend you," he said, pleadingly, reaching to catch my hand.

"Well, you have. I'll try to be over it by evening."

And I stalked away across the sand.

I wasn't over it by evening, and I regret to say neither was he.

GEORGE
CALIFORNIA: JUNE 28, 1935

*I*t was a good thing, it turned out, that I'd had work for a week, because on our way to Chico the van broke down, and it covered the expense.

We weren't far out of Redding when it sputtered out, so I piggybacked you for a mile to find help. Eventually I located a man who knew a man with a neighbor who was a mechanic, and he drove us back to the van to figure out the issue.

Spark plugs, it turned out.

Louise wouldn't have needed to walk to town to diagnose that.

I gave the man cash to buy the replacements, plus extra for his time, and after a while he came back and showed me how to put them in. By that time, I didn't feel like going anywhere. I just found a parking place in Redding for the night.

It was Friday, anyway, so I figured it was as well we spend the Sabbath here as anywhere. Mamma had given me the candlesticks we'd always used, the ones she'd been given upon her marriage to her first husband, and a box of candles. You and I lit them and said the usual prayers as the sun went down, and then you and Lindbergh played fetch with sticks.

On Sunday we drove to Yuba City. Right outside town, there was a group of campers, so we joined them. I did our washing (you had wet the blankets) and fixed up a clothesline between the van and tree to dry them. I went ahead and did our clothes, too, since I was already at it.

There was one family with older children, as well as several single men. Lindbergh dutifully followed you around, and I visited with the adults as I worked. When they found out I was a lay minister, they asked if I'd have a service of sorts with them since it was Sunday. I gladly agreed, and when I finished the washing, those interested gathered together for an hour to pray and sing and I shared some thoughts on the 139th Psalm.

As evening came on, someone built a fire, and several more vagrants drifted in. One of them seemed a little tipsy, and I grew uneasy about having you out of my sight, so I fetched you to come get supper at our van.

For a while things were all right, but the tipsy man had seen you and soon wandered over. Lindbergh went alert, ears back. You immediately hid behind me.

"Hey, pretty girl," he slurred out. I glanced over at the main group around the campfire, hoping someone would notice and come to my aid. He was a big man, but he was drunk. I was confident I could take him on, if only I didn't have to also worry about you.

"Who are you?" I asked, voice blank of expression. I picked you up, and you hid your face in my shoulder. I stepped away from the man, only to find that I'd backed myself into the side of the van, letting him get far too close for comfort.

He didn't answer; I started mentally running through my options, but before I decided how to proceed, he reached out and touched your hair. He smelled foul, and you swatted at him, glaring.

That made him laugh. "Feisty one, ain't ya? Come on, give old Uncle Boyd some sugar, huh?"

Lindbergh snarled and leapt for the man's hand, biting him before I could grab the dog's collar and stop him.

He'd never bitten anyone before. I hurried to put you into the cab of the van. Lindbergh jumped in beside you whilst the man straightened and cursed, and I took him by the collar and hissed, "You keep your filthy hands off my daughter."

He laughed. "Shrimp," he said. "I'll have you for lunch and her for dessert."

Oh, will you, I thought, and before he knew what was happening,

I'd knocked him down and pinned his arms behind him with a grip that he hadn't expected. Another man came up, having noticed what was going on by now, a Black man. He seemed to hesitate on the edge of things, but he had stationed himself firmly in front of the van door to keep the drunk from getting to you.

"He's trying to get at my child," I said to the Black man, straining with everything I had to keep the drunk pinned.

The Black man urgently beckoned to two others by the fire, and they came over just as Uncle Boyd was breaking free of my grasp. "Get out," one of them said, and he socked the creep in the jaw and hauled him out of the camp.

For a moment the two of them punched ferociously at each other, until they'd finally driven out "Uncle Boyd". The white men said they'd make sure someone kept watch all night. "We got kids too," one of them said. "You all go on to bed."

The Black man still hovered near the van door, looking anxious. "Thanks," I said. "For calling those fellows over."

"I'd have hit him myself, but they'd have lynched me," he said, shaking the hand I extended. "If that man comes back, he might still. Blame me for getting him beat up."

"Stay here," I said. "They'll have to get past me first."

He stared at me in disbelief. "You serious?"

"Of course. You can be inside and Fizz and I can stay outside."

"My stuff's over there," he said, pointing to a ragged blue bundle propped up against one of the trees, and I went to fetch it for him.

"Shucks," he said, when I came back. "You're a lifesaver. I'm Cosmo Styles, by the way." He held out his hand.

"George Graham," I replied, shaking it. "This is Hazel, but I call her Fizz, and my dog is Lindbergh. Where are you headed?"

"South," he said. "Don't know how far you're going, but if you're game, I'd be glad to share what I got if you take me as far south as you go."

"Santa Monica is where I'm headed," I said. "You're welcome to ride along. I'd be glad of the company."

His mouth dropped open. "Well, that's just south of where I'm going! San Fernando for me."

"Excellent," I said. "I have to warn you, though, I'm going slow. Fizz doesn't much like traveling, so we stop a lot."

"That's okay," he said. "I'm in no rush. I went out to Tuskegee Institute two years ago, ran out of money and had to quit, and I've been hitching my way back for the last few months. I stop and work whenever I can find someone who'll have me. Gotta look out for yourself when you're my color."

I considered that. It was not something I'd ever thought about. "There aren't any Black folks where I come from," I admitted. "In fact, you're the first one I've ever spoken to."

"Where are you from, then?"

"Oregon. There were laws to keep your people out. Technically they're repealed, but I'm afraid a change of law doesn't mean a change of heart for the population at large." I sighed. "But people of all colors and persuasions are welcome to my little home as long as they aren't perverted drunks trying to get my small child to kiss them."

He grinned. "I got sisters and I love kids. Nobody's gonna hurt your little one when I'm around."

I nodded approvingly, and we sat in easy silence for a bit. "Well," he said, after a pause, "I'm beat. Mind if I turn in?"

"Go ahead," I said. "It's high time for Fizz to be heading to bed anyway."

Cosmo was snoring softly within seconds of rolling out his bedroll. Lindbergh and you settled together onto our own blankets just outside the door, and after story and prayers, I settled down myself and lay awake, full of new thoughts and wonder.

I was glad to leave that place. In fact, I got up before you were awake and drove on, to put as much distance between "Uncle Boyd" and us as possible.

Cosmo joined us later in the front seat with a mandolin which he absentmindedly strummed and plucked as I drove. There was an instant, easy bond between us that surprised me, who didn't make friends easily, and within an hour we were well on our way to learning one another's life stories. I told him how it was that I was Jewish and a Christian, and he told me his story.

250

"My mother came west after the race riots in Tulsa in 1921," he said. "It's better here, although there are still parts of town we avoid. I was little, but I still remember it. I don't think anyone will ever forget it."

"What happened?" I asked, ashamed to admit I'd never heard of it.

"White mobs came and attacked us. Destroyed more than thirty city blocks—our businesses and homes. Fires all over the place. My father died, burnt alive. You know what white folks do

after lynchings and stuff? They take photos of the dead Blacks and make postcards out of them to send around. A picture of my father's body was one they used."

"That's horrific," I said, incapable of comprehending the inhumanity of it.

Cosmo went on. "A lot of us left afterwards. It was a nightmare. I don't want to tell the worst things with—" he beckoned toward Hazel with his head. "But it was hell. And they've pretty much hushed it up and pretend it never happened. My uncle and aunt and their kids stayed behind because their home survived. They told us about the postcard."

I shook my head, aghast.

"And I thought Jews had it bad," I said, contemplatively.

He fiddled with the tuning pegs on his mandolin. "You personally, you don't have a Jewish name. You don't even look Jewish. Nobody's ever going to refuse you service or attack you on sight. I gotta watch my back all the time. No hiding what I am."

I considered this for a while. "I might understand just a little," I said. I told him the story of my London grandparents, and finished, "So I decided, on my way home, I'd tell people my last name was

Shapiro, because I was curious how people would react. Some didn't care. Some refused me service or acknowledgment. But everyone immediately knew what I was, and I could quickly see where I stood with them. My life isn't ever at risk, though. I guess that's the difference."

"It might be, someday," Cosmo said. "I've got a bad feeling about stuff happening over in Germany. That Hitler fellow..."

I nodded. "It's very worrying. I'm glad to not live there, but I'm troubled for those who do."

"What do you think of me?" Cosmo asked after another long silence. "Since you said you've never talked to any Black folks before."

"Well," I said. "In books, it seems like authors want to make you out as unintelligent. You talk just like me. The books have it wrong."

He laughed. "Oh, we do talk a bit like that, among ourselves."

"That sounds like how I talk differently with my parents than with the wider world. Or my Uncle Jamie's family. They all drop their posh accents at home and revel in being Scottish."

LOUISE

SANTA MONICA, CALIFORNIA: JUNE 30, 1935

*W*e were at the park, Carlo and me, seeking shady spots to escape the warmth of the day, but so many people had had the same idea, it took a while to find a place of our own.

He took sandwiches out of his knapsack and handed me mine. I unwrapped it and took a bite, but he hesitated.

I glanced at him. "What? Is it time for our periodic marriage proposal?"

He laughed but there was a slight tension in it. "Louise, I have to know why you still love that man."

"I don't."

"You say that. You do not act it."

I pretended to be fixated on inspecting the lettuce in my sandwich, but he kept talking.

"You have good life here, *mi vida*. You fly and do all you say you always want to do. But you are not happy, even though you get to dance with me. It is that man, yes?"

He wouldn't ever say George's name, and it always reminded me uncomfortably of my own routine dismissal of Velma Johnson as "that schoolteacher". "What makes you think I'm not happy?"

"Well, you do not marry me."

"Maybe I don't need a man to be happy," I countered.

"You need kissing to be happy. I am good at kissing. He was not."

"He might have been very good at it."

"But not with you."

I huffed, dropping my sandwich half-eaten into my lap and

turning my best annoyed expression his way. Darn it, this man read me better than I wanted to admit.

"You are porcupine. You would rather puff out all your prickles than let anyone get close enough to win your heart. Because that man you want, he did not want you. I want you."

"Want me or love me?" I asked.

"Why not both?

I took up my sandwich again and had another bite. "The last time we went out together like this, we got mad at each other and I left. Imagine if we lived together. We would be at each other's throats all the time. No, thank you. I adore you, you're a marvelous dancer, you should be in pictures, and you do kiss beautifully, but I will never be able to live with you. You really ought to take that ring back instead of waving it under my nose all the time."

That made him laugh in spite of everything, and we managed to not end the outing furious at each other.

GEORGE

ELK GROVE, CALIFORNIA: JUNE 30, 1935

*W*e stopped in Elk Grove next. I found a Presbyterian church and asked the minister, Reverend Coates, if I could park by the church for a few days, and he gladly permitted it. His wife insisted we join them for dinner, and that we all come in and have hot baths.

While you were splashing about in yours, I started shaving. It had been quite a few days and, on closer examination, I thought I had the beginnings of a decent moustache and decided to leave it. Being mistaken for your big brother and the previous night's run-in with "Uncle Boyd"... well, I guess I wanted to start looking as grown-up as I possibly could.

"What do you think, Fizz?" I asked, turning to you for inspection.

"Potato," you said, not looking, occupied with making a pile of bubbles on top of the water. It was your newest favorite word and your favorite food. You played with potatoes like dolls.

I gave Lindbergh a scrubbing, too.

Mrs. Coates was incredibly talkative and made the three of us a delicious lunch, and before we knew it, she was insisting we take the extra rooms for the night and have a break from van life. Cosmo sang and played his mandolin as she was preparing dinner, which delighted you. You had warmed to Cosmo immediately. That night, sitting inside four walls around a radio for the first time in what seemed forever, I felt at ease and peaceful. I closed my eyes and listened whilst you drifted to dreamland in my arms.

GEORGE

When we reached Bakersfield, my wallet had gotten very empty, and Cosmo agreed we should make a longer stop and find work to replenish the cash supply. I sent a telegram to my parents, asking them to forward any mail to this post office for me to collect.

When their parcel arrived, it was like Christmas. I'd sent postcards regularly along the way, ones I'd bought ahead of time, to my parents, my sisters, Lydia, and Uncle Jamie, but this was the first time I'd been able to get replies since leaving home. There was a new book and dress for you, and letters from Lydia ("Louise will be so surprised!") and Uncle Jamie ("I cannot believe my wife would resort to such underhanded perfidy!") and Mamma and Dad ("there is nobody to eat the leftovers now!")

Dear Mamma and Dad,

Thanks heaps for the parcel and the books (and my old ones!) for Fizz. I frequently think if we have to read The Story About Ping *just ONCE more, I will lose my mind. I can read all three of the ones we brought along with my eyes shut by now, but that is her favorite. Tonight she picked* The Tale of Two Bad Mice *from the new stack, which she loved. Perhaps a bit too much. Oh dear.*

And the dress is perfect. Brown to hide the dirt, of which she is getting into plenty.

We've acquired two new members to our little traveling family. First, there's Cosmo Styles, a Black man who helped me save Fizz from a drunken creep who wouldn't quit bothering her. He's my age and we have hit it off very well. He found us a job at a local farm, harvesting lemons. It will keep us busy for several months if we need it to, and there's an almond operation nearby we can move on to afterwards.

Second, last night as I was stirring our soup pot, I heard her loudly calling, "POTATO, DA, POTATO." I kept stirring and figured she was just playing with one again. But she was insistent, so Cosmo went to investigate, and the next thing I knew she was running ahead of him toward me with her arms held out full length, and in her hands a tiny fuzzy ball of fur. "LOOK, DA."

For a moment I was terrified she'd picked up some rabid animal, but it was only a kitten. "My po-TAY-to," she said happily, over and over.

I was not impressed, of course, with the idea of another mouth to feed, because I knew there wasn't a chance she'd let that cat out of her sights now she'd found it. I asked her where it came from, hoping maybe it already had a home, but as far as I can discover, it just wandered in. None of the other farm workers had seen it before. (We all live in a haphazard group near the farm, in tents or shacks or cars.)

Anyway, I had to teach her how to hold the kitten properly, but here's the interesting bit. Potato seemed instantly connected with Fizz. She tolerates Cosmo and me, but she's as watchful of Fizz as Lindbergh is, and she's already made it clear to Lindbergh that she is queen, to his annoyance. But Fizz sleeps better with Potato at her side and seems calmer overall. I decided it was a fair tradeoff.

One of the Mexican migrant workers, Lupe Vasquez, showed me how to wrap a long cloth to hold Fizz on my back whilst I'm working. It's a marvelous solution during her naptime, but she doesn't want to be there all day, of course. Fortunately this little community of farm workers is very close-knit; many of us have children, so there are usually older children available to keep an eye on them when we're working. Lupe has three herself. Mostly she works here in Bakersfield, hopping from farm to farm as the crops come ready, and moving as needed to others nearby. She doesn't speak much English, but we manage all right. Love, George

At the end of five weeks' work, Cosmo and I had each managed to save forty-five dollars, and we decided it was about time to push on. But we stayed long enough for you to celebrate your second birthday with our new friends. Lupe scraped up enough to make a little cake just for you, and Lupe's children strung pretty glass beads on a string to tie around your neck. It was a glorious day, but bittersweet, since we were sad to leave our friends.

LOUISE
SANTA MONICA, CALIFORNIA: JULY 28, 1935

Carlo asked me to come up to his room after we finished our shift at the hotel that night. He sent me ahead of him while he knocked at his landlady's door to find out if any studios had left him messages since he'd gone out.

Her response was a tired, "No, Mr. Valley-joes."

I gathered it was a request he made of her often.

Then he followed me up. I was curious what sort of room he had, not ever having made it past his front steps before.

Also, I was edgy. Being alone in his rooms with this extremely attractive man was not like being alone with George, who could be depended upon to leave my virtue intact regardless how much I might wish otherwise.

Carlo had played the game well, pushing his boundaries and seeing how far I would let him go. He only kissed me on the lips if I asked him to, but his hands roved, and he often kissed my cheek or shoulder, or my fingers. He would gladly have me... *if* I could fully put George in a box and throw away the key.

I settled onto the couch and he asked me if I'd have a drink. At my shocked silence he laughed and said, "Prohibition is over, you know."

"It's not the legality of it that bothers me."

Carlo poured himself some concoction and sat beside me, lifting my face so I could look into his worshipful eyes. The smell of the drink brought back uneasy memories. "What does bother you?"

"My stepfather used to do terrible things when he was drunk. I... associate the smell with him."

He immediately got up and poured it down the sink, then returned to me. "In that case, I don't need it."

I let myself relax a little, eyes scanning the room. There was a bedroom through the door, with two narrow beds crowded in, and this sitting room, and a tiny excuse of a kitchen. It was exactly the type of room George would have thrived in. Darn it all, why did everything make my brain circle back to George?

Carlo's hand, holding mine, was warm and brown and strong, and when he brushed his lips down the side of my face to my neck, I startled in surprise at the jolt it gave me. He laughed softly and did it again.

"I do not know the English words to tell you how I feel right now. I want you, *mi vida*. Forever."

"There's a difference between wanting and loving," I whispered. "If it was just about wanting, this would be absolutely mutual."

"When I get into pictures, you'll never lack anything again. This—" he waved his hand about dismissively. "This will go. We will have a mansion and a pool and you can have all the planes you want."

I laughed. "You're so cocky, Carlo. Why are you so sure of this whole pictures thing?"

He stretched out his hands in a gesture of incredulity. "Look at me! The women will be begging for my autographs and falling at my feet. You will be jealous all the time!"

"That sounds exhausting," I said. "You don't need me as part of that. Why do you think I'd want to spend my life like that?"

He slid his hand under the hem of my skirt a little, testing the waters, and leant in close. "Because you have worked hard all your life and deserve some ease and you will welcome it. You want babies, and we would make such pretty ones. Also, I am a very good lover, if you give me a chance."

The fingers crept higher until one reached the clip of my garters and snapped it open.

Oh, I was tempted. So very tempted. He was electric, and we were alone and had never had such a perfect opportunity.

Why not? I thought for a moment. *Why not let him? George didn't keep himself for me.*

But sleeping with someone to spite George, even if that someone was Carlo Vallejos, was something I couldn't stoop to, in the end.

I put my hand on his and pushed it out from under my skirt.

"You may kiss me," I said. "But nothing else. If you brought me here for more than that, I'll leave now, if that's all right."

But my voice was unsteady. The power of desire was having its effects. *Gosh, he was gorgeous.*

He whispered into my neck. "Why do you still love him, after all this time?"

And instead of denying it, as I usually did, I said, quietly, "I really don't know."

He drew back and sighed melodramatically, muttering something in Spanish before looking at me with a not entirely pleasant expression. "I do not like the competition, Louise."

"I'm not the one making a competition out of this. I'm here to enjoy a nice snog, preferably without you reminding me of George every thirty seconds."

"You think of him every twenty-five!"

It was my turn to sigh melodramatically. He wasn't wrong, but I wasn't about to admit that aloud.

"All right, then, I'll go home," I said, and got to my feet, reaching for my purse.

GEORGE

SAN FERNANDO, CALIFORNIA: AUGUST 11, 1935

The van came to a stop in front of a row of sleeping houses. We'd arrived in San Fernando at last. It was dark, and late, because Cosmo had fallen asleep and I'd gotten lost and, though I'd eventually succeeded in waking him, it had taken a while for him to figure out where we were and direct me.

"Boy, oh, boy is Mama gonna be surprised to see me!" Cosmo rubbed his hands together with delight and bounded toward the door. I hung back, holding you, who were hugging Potato.

A light came on, the front door opened, and the woman let out a "Hallelujah, it's Cosmo!" before pulling him into a tight, long hug.

"Hey, Mama, I brought my friends I wrote you about," he said when she finally let him go. "George, come on!"

Lindbergh followed me up the sidewalk, and we were warmly greeted as well. "Call me Della," she said, grasping my hand. "Cosmo, your little sister broke her leg last week! She's gonna be so glad you're home!"

"How she do that?" he asked.

"She can tell you," Della replied. "Now y'all must be hungry. Come on in."

Soon she was feeding us toast with butter and jam, fried eggs and sardines, and a cup of milk for Hazel, who was too sleepy to bother much with it, so I drank it for her. Then she took us to meet Belinda, her broken-legged daughter.

"Belinda! Look who here! Your brother made it home!"

Belinda opened her eyes, confused for a moment, before breaking into a grin and reaching out her arms for a hug. Cosmo introduced us. "Belinda's fourteen," he said. "There's June Bug, over there, she's seventeen, and nothin's gonna wake her up before she's ready."

In a moment, two more siblings had come running up and tackled Cosmo. They tussled for a moment before he dragged them over. "And these are my brothers. Denver, he's fifteen, and Nigel, he's nineteen. This here's my new friend George. He's twenty like me, and his little girl Hazel just turned two. Gramps lives here too, but he's deaf as the sidewalk and ain't gonna hear us until morning."

"Okay, you lot, shoo off to bed, we got church in a few hours!" Della said above the noise, and off they all scurried.

Cosmo took you and me to the room he shared with his brothers. "Y'all get off that bed, Denver," he said, swatting the general rump area of the lump under the quilt. "Let George and his baby have that and come on down with me."

I couldn't sleep. Even after the boys settled, I lay awake, curious about this lively household, and thinking of Louise. You snored at my side, arm flopped across my neck, while Lindbergh laid across my feet and Potato took up half my pillow. I thought of all Cosmo had told me about the horrors they had all endured fourteen years ago, when he was so little. One night after you were asleep he had gone into more detail. How, as he and Nigel and June had been trying to get home from their grandparent's house through the chaos, one pregnant woman was strung up and cut open and her baby stomped to death on the ground as she dangled above.

"I was so worried about my mama," he said, tears choking his voice. "She was carrying Belinda then."

I wanted to be sick. How could human beings be so cruel to other human beings, just because their skin was a different hue?

When morning light began to creep over the horizon, I extracted myself carefully from the bed and stepped over the sleeping Cosmo and Nigel and headed to the bathroom.

As I came out, I heard a whisper from the girls' open bedroom door.

"Hey! George! It's me, Belinda!"

I peeked in and she said, "I can't sleep. My leg hurts. You ever break a leg? Come here and sit on the chair."

I sat, and I said, "Not a leg, but I did break an arm once when I was twelve. It's worst the first few days for sure."

"This is the fourth day," she said forlornly. "How'd you break yours?"

"Got hit by a car. Cracked some ribs, too. I guess I was lucky that's as hurt as I got. What happened to you?"

She grinned sheepishly. "I was on the roof trying to get my cat out of the attic vent and when I was coming down the ladder it tipped over and I smashed on the sidewalk."

I winced. "Climb the roof a lot?"

"Just to get the cat. She gets stuck up there, see. I keep telling Mama to have someone come close it off. Maybe now she will."

"I hope so. What's your cat's name?"

Belinda reached for the curled-up kitty and plopped it on her lap. "Muffin. Because she's toasty golden and fluffy like a muffin. Your baby has a cat, too. What's its name?"

"Potato," I said.

"Funny name for a cat."

I laughed softly. "It's her favorite word."

"Where's your wife? Ain't you got one?"

"I don't—" I began, but June stirred in the corner, so I put my finger to my lips. Belinda grinned, and I tiptoed out before her sister woke and felt alarmed at a stranger in her room.

In the boys' room, Cosmo was sitting up and yawning. "You coming to church with us this morning?" he asked.

"Sure," I said.

So a few hours later, after stiff competition for the use of the bathroom between June and her brothers once they'd let me use it, the neighborhood's only two white people were escorted to church by three tall, strapping lads and their sister. Della stayed behind to look after Belinda.

As a guest of the Styles bunch, I was heartily welcomed, and quite taken aback by the exuberance of Black worship and preaching.

Afterwards, the Styleses introduced me to Reverend and Mrs. Hays, who asked you and me to come have dinner with them the next evening. We walked home to a lunch of fried chicken (not fried in lard, Della assured me with a grin).

Cosmo carried Belinda down so she could eat with the rest of us, and you quickly warmed to her, although Muffin and Potato were not exactly pleased with each other's existence.

The next evening, Reverend Hays and his wife Hannah invited me to park the van by their house, and the day after that I was offered part-time work cleaning the office of the Black newspaper, the *California Eagle*. After a few weeks there, I found the commonality I'd felt with Cosmo extended to Black folks as a whole. I loved them, and being among them woke me up to an entirely new facet of America that was ugly and frightening. Here in California things weren't as bad as elsewhere, but there were still places in the city they wouldn't venture, for their own safety. So many of my new friends had stories of brutality their family members had experienced. Even if it wasn't as drastic as what had happened to Cosmo's father, it was still wrong, to have to live with that reality of discrimination and aggression. That they could never assume any white person was a safe white person. It made me furious.

After a few weeks had passed, I took you to Della and ventured to go to the elementary school where the kids of this neighborhood attended and asked if they needed any assistant teachers. They took me on a trial basis. I'd never taught before, but I figured this was as good a way as any to learn the art of it. I was as out of place as a gorilla at the south pole, but once the kids got used to me, it actually worked out well, and I became unexpectedly fond of many of them.

One evening after you were asleep, I flipped open my notebook. I hadn't had time to write in a while, and the last heading I'd jotted down was: *Sunday Sacredness: Inherently Antisemitic? Early Christianity Seeking to Distance Itself From Its Jewish Roots.*

I sighed. It was something I felt strongly about, but in light of the things I was learning every day here, I decided it could wait, and I penned a different heading. *Would Jesus Accept Jim Crow?*

GEORGE

SAN FERNANDO, CALIFORNIA: SEPTEMBER 1935

I didn't have time to look for Louise those first couple of weeks; I was too busy getting settled. But the first opportunity I got, I drove to the Santa Monica library to search their telephone directory for all the numbers of local airfields, not just in Santa Monica but in the greater Los Angeles area. But from every one I called, I got only evasive unhelpfulness. "Who wants to know?" one fellow said, and promptly hung up.

Either people were extremely unfriendly down here, or Louise had set up some sort of protection alliance for herself on every airfield in southern California.

I suspected the latter.

So I got a map and marked all the locations with a precision that would have pleased Louise.

I resolved to start visiting them that very next week, but then I got sick. I rarely did get sick, but whatever this was knocked me completely flat. Hannah Hays found me delirious in the van after catching you wandering around unattended, and made both of us come inside the parsonage until I got well, which ended up being almost two weeks, and I still felt like a limp rag afterwards. Nobody else caught it, and I never did know what it was.

Everyone was good to me and Hazel, however. Reverend and Hannah Hays refused any payment, so I always put as generous an amount as I could spare into the collection plate each week. I went back to work and within a few weeks was mostly recovered. I also had acquired a few extra jobs tutoring a few of the local children after school who struggled with reading, as well as high schoolers who were hoping to get into universities and worried about passing their exams.

But when I went to the airfields, there was no Louise at any of them, and nobody would even tell me if they knew her. I looked again at the library, scouring the newspapers on the off chance that there might be an item about her.

Nothing.

I studied again the letters Aunt Estelle had sent me. Dancer at a posh hotel? Well, I couldn't very well go hunting there. I'd never afford to get in one, let alone the dozen or so I'd need to visit in hopes of chancing on her.

I was also reminded anew of the mysterious Carlo, whoever he was, and my sense of urgency increased.

LOUISE
PENNSYLVANIA: OCTOBER 16-23, 1935

I arrived in Bradford on a Wednesday afternoon, after a long, dull train journey. It should have been more exciting to get to travel that far, but it wasn't. There's so much sadness across this country. So many people struggling, so much want, so much dirt. It made me feel foolish and silly, spending my hard-earned money on a plane when so many people just need a square meal.

But also... I needed to earn my own square meals however I could.

I went straight to the airfield after I got in, and was shown to my plane: my very own Taylor J-2 Cub. It gleamed in the late afternoon sun, painted blue, as I had requested. I took her for a brief test flight and spent the rest of the evening lettering her registration number (NC-7821) and her name. Asterope, I called her, after one of the Pleiades, as I'd dreamed about long ago when I was twelve. There were six other Pleiades I could have chosen, of course, but Asterope was the one I'd always loved the sound of most.

I'd already paid half down, but now I handed over the precious remaining $735, latched my bags into the baggage compartment, and flew to Philadelphia for my mother's wedding.

When I landed, I put Asterope to bed and headed out to find my mother, whom I soon found waiting amongst several parked cars.

I expected Konstantin would be with her, but he wasn't. After giving me a hug, Mother climbed into the driver's seat of a tan roadster and started it, driving us away quite capably. She saw my shock and laughed.

"I am not a helpless mouse anymore."

She seemed vibrant and, as it had in February, it sent a pang through my heart, seeing the light in Mother's eyes, her new confidence, and the serenity that came with knowing you'd found your place in the world.

"I must warn you," she said. "Mira is a bit off her best today. The weather is changing and she always has more pain around this time of year. You mustn't mind her too much if she seems grumpy."

She parked the car in a garage with many others, and I followed half a step behind as she led me into the lobby of the Drake Hotel. The doorman said, "Good afternoon, Mrs. Zafirov!" and tipped his hat. The elevator man said, "Good afternoon, Mrs. Zafirov!" and didn't have to ask which floor she needed. On the seventeenth floor, he let us out, and Mother led me down the hall to the door, which she unlocked and held open for me to step in.

Cello and viola music floated out to my ears, and an unfamiliar spicy scent hung in the air. (Incense, I learned later.) I hesitated as Mother closed the door behind me and dropped her keys into a beautiful enameled bowl on the table by the door. "Home, darling!" she called, and the music stopped. Konstantin appeared, a bow in one hand. He kissed Mother and held out his free hand to me.

"Do come in. Mira is perishing with impatience." He lowered his voice. "She's having one of her bad days, so don't take it personally if she gets feisty."

"Mother told me," I said. I took a deep breath and looked from him to Mother. "I'd... like to go in alone, if you don't mind."

Konstantin waved me on, moving to stand beside Mother, his arm about her waist. I straightened and went into the next room. I was more frightened of meeting this new stepsister of mine than I'd ever been behind the controls of a plane. Just as I reached the gorgeous rug marking the boundary between hall and living room, I stopped.

The girl in the wheelchair hadn't heard my approach; she was putting her viola back into its case while a cat wound itself around her legs. A second cat was basking tummy-up in the sunny window, and a third one scampered off into hiding when it caught sight of me.

It was a curious room, with its velvet draperies, and in one corner a votive burned on a small shelf beneath peculiar pictures of Mary and Jesus on either side of a cross. There were other pictures, too, of haloed people I didn't recognize. I looked away when I heard the click of the latches on the viola case, back at the girl. Our eyes met.

Her gleaming, wavy brown hair, in braids elaborately pinned up, framed a pale face with soft golden-brown eyes. The scarring on the left side of her face from the accident was pink and slightly raised, but she was so beautiful. I couldn't help but wonder what she made of me, my hair flattened unbecomingly from my flying helmet, and my face smudged, and my flying clothes boyish in comparison to the soft, drapey frock she was wearing, brown with a twining scarlet floral pattern.

"Sit down," Mira said, nodding at the chair next to where a cello was propped against the sofa. I sat, and she went on. "I'm Mira. Obviously. Are we to be the sort of sisters who can't stand one another, or the nicer kind?"

"I don't know," I said, quietly. The cat that had been circling Mira's

legs jumped onto her lap, and her pretty hands stroked the cat as she leaned back, briefly stiffening and squeezing her eyes shut as if some pain had stabbed her. I could hear the cat's purring from where I sat.

When the pain passed and Mira let out a long breath of relief, she said, "I want to show you something, now that I finally have the chance to."

She wheeled her chair across the room to a bookshelf next to the icon corner and selected a small framed photograph from amongst a veritable mob of them, then came back to me and set it on my knee. "That's the latest photograph Lydia has. From right before she left to come here."

With trembling hands I held it closer to my face. It was my George, his hair slightly mussed as if he was outside in a breeze. His face was relaxed, with the hint of a smile, and in his arms he hugged the baby that had driven me away.

Only she wasn't a baby; she was too big to be called a baby here. Her fair hair stood out all around her face and she glared at the camera with dark eyes just like her father's.

That's how much time had passed.

While I'd been working like a maniac to forget, that tiny, scrunchy infant I'd thrust back at Mrs. Graham had become this little girl with a personality.

I forgot momentarily to be angry. "He kept her," I heard myself whisper, and glanced at Mira. "He... kept her?"

She nodded. "From what I hear, he is a dutiful and loving father, and when it came to choosing between her and seminary, he chose her. They made him leave when they found out."

I couldn't find words to express how much that thought hurt me. Seminary had been George's obsession, and he'd been kicked out?

Then I remembered my grudge and thrust the photograph back at Mira, turning my face away. I couldn't bear to meet her eyes. "Guess he would want to take her baby if he can't have *her*."

Mira leant in and took my hands, holding them in hers.

"Louise," she said. "He loves you. He was just afraid to tell you what happened. Lydia wanted to, but you won't listen, so I'm going to sit right here and hold your hands until you hear it. That woman put something in his tea one night. That's how she got what she wanted. It wasn't what *he* wanted."

Her words knocked me off-kilter and I tried to pull my hands away, but her grip was astonishingly strong. "What?"

That's when I did start crying. Remembering what my stepfather Sam had once threatened to do to me. I'd never told George about that, because even after all these years it still seemed that, somehow, speaking of it would make it real.

This was not at all how I'd envisioned our meeting going. I had assumed we'd talk, stiltedly, about ourselves and our parents and my journey across the country. I never imagined she would plough right in with *this*.

She waited patiently until I had collected myself, gently put the photograph back on my lap, and then, as if the previous conversation had never happened, she said, "Have you ever been to an Orthodox church service before?"

"No," I said, disoriented by the topic switch.

"We're done talking about George," she said, seeing it. "I've said what I've wanted to say for the last year and a half and now it's on you to do something about it. So we are going to discuss the marriage service." She looked at the door. "Tato! Lydia! We're ready for you."

Maybe she was, but I wasn't sure I was. It didn't appear I had much choice, however. Our respective parents came in. Konstantin bent down to kiss the top of Mira's head, and my heart wrenched at the obvious tenderness between them. He glanced at me as if he wished to do the same to me, but wasn't sure if I'd accept it.

For the moment, I wasn't ready to accept it. He sat on the couch, and Mother nestled up to him, tucking her legs underneath her.

"We need to prepare Louise for the service," Mira said. "She's never been to an Orthodox church before. I thought not, but I had to check."

"*I* think," Mother said pointedly, "Louise might like a chance to pull herself together and change out of her flying clothes before you begin drilling her, Mira."

I threw Mother a grateful look and fled the room. She followed me to show me the bathroom and whispered, "Was it very terrible?"

"She talked about George." I looked down and realized I was still holding the photograph.

Mother smiled, and I couldn't tell if there was sympathy or amusement in her face. "Well, someone had to, and there is nobody quite like Mira for butting in where she might not be welcome. A little like someone else I know."

"Did you tell her about him hoping she'd do that?" I asked.

Mother gave me a cryptic shrug. I held out the photograph to her, but she closed my fingers around it and pushed it back at me. "You keep it. You know where that photograph was taken?"

"No."

"In the cemetery in Junction City. George took me there to visit

your father's grave, and I caught the train from there to come here. He sent me a copy later when he had the roll of film printed." She lifted my chin so I had to meet her eyes. "George loves you, Louise, more than you can possibly know. Now go wash up."

She brought me my suitcase, and I locked myself into the

bathroom, ran myself a bath, and took as long as I possibly could manage before emerging again. At least I was in a properly feminine dress now, and my hair looked tidy.

Konstantin was in the little kitchen with Mother, and they stepped around each other as if it was some sort of dance, occasionally leaning in for kisses, sharing smiles. Mira was at the dining room table with a book in front of her. I stood with my hands behind my back, between the kitchen door and the dining room table, uncertain what to do with myself. She caught my eye and mimed gagging as she beckoned toward our parents.

Before I could respond, Mother appeared with a stack of bowls and bread plates from the cupboard.

"Oh! You're out," she said, handing them to me. "Here, set the table."

I was glad to have something to do, so I laid the dishes, then came back for the silverware and napkins and glasses. Konstantin came out with a tureen of soup and Mother followed with a tray of sliced bread, a butter dish, and a platter of roasted potatoes. It smelled amazing and I realized I was starving.

Konstantin sat at the head, Mother to his right, Mira on his left, and I took the remaining chair at the foot. There was an empty chair beside Mira, and I asked who it was for.

"Elijah?" I asked, facetiously.

Mother laughed, but neither Mira nor her father understood the joke.

"That's Margaret's chair. My nurse-companion. It's her day off today. You'll meet her tomorrow."

Konstantin and Mira and my mother all bowed their heads, so I did, too. I watched the three of them cross themselves, and Konstantin said, "Christ our God, bless the food and drink of your servants, for you are holy always, now and forever and to the ages of ages. Amen."

They all crossed themselves again and Konstantin served us the soup. "This," he said, "is rice and meatball soup. I hope you like it. It's one of the things we ate at least once a week all the time we were growing up."

It was delicious, as was the crusty bread lavishly spread with butter, and the roasted potatoes, which Konstantin stirred in with his soup.

"Tato is incapable of not having potatoes at least once a day," Mira said with a laugh, helping herself to some and passing me the dish. "You don't have to put them in the soup, though."

Even Mother ate a generous helping, and I thought, *No wonder she has color and a figure now.* It's not much fun eating when your food is boring and you burn it all the time.

"Your mother wasn't joking when she said she couldn't cook," Konstantin went on. "Fortunately for all of us, I spent much of my childhood in the kitchen getting my mother's culinary secrets out of her."

Mira didn't say anything more about the wedding service (had her father had told her to back off?) because instead she began talking about her cats and asking me questions about the plane I'd come to collect.

"Will you take me flying?" she asked. "And before you ask, yes, I could get into a plane. I get into cars and other vehicles. Just need a hand sometimes."

"I could, if you'd really like to," I said.

"I would really like to."

After a brief lull in the conversation, Konstantin spoke. "Tomorrow night we'll be going to my parents' house and having dinner with them. All my brothers and sisters and their families will come too. They are all eager to meet you."

"Maybe you should tell me what to expect," I said, already anxious at the idea of being the lone Protestant amongst this horde of new relatives who were... something so different and unfamiliar. I wondered briefly what George would think of Mother marrying someone of a faith like this.

"Well, it will be Friday, which is a strict fast day," he said. "Which means no meat, dairy, fish, eggs, oil, or alcohol. I have three older sisters and one younger brother, with eleven children so far amongst them all. Matushka Slavka, my eldest sister, is married to Father Andrei, and four of the children are theirs. Vasilia and Liliana each have two. I have Mira, and my brother Zoran has three."

Later that night, after Mira had fallen asleep, I came out for a glass of water. The light in the dining room was still on, with music scattered all over the table. I leant to look at it. A symphony, another one by Tchaikovsky, not the one I'd heard him conduct in February. I picked it up and squinted at it, then set it down again and turned to the sideboard. It was positively overflowing with papers, mostly music, but as I riffled through one stack, a letter fell out to the floor. I picked it up. The date was from February of 1934. Right after Mother and Konstantin met, I remembered. It said:

Dear Mrs. Pearson,

    Do not apologize for the kiss! It surprised me, but surprises are good more often than not. The kiss was a very good surprise, and I am constantly thinking about it and wishing you were close by, as I would rather like you to do it again.

I quickly stuffed it back where it came from. Even my nosy streak didn't want to keep reading whatever *that* was. But I was astonished Mother would have already kissed him so early on in their acquaintance.

The thing that struck me the most, however, was the liberal misspellings. Even I, whose spelling had always been pathetic, saw at once that this man's gift was not in the realm of literary genius.

I was startled by footsteps behind me and turned to see Konstantin emerging from the bedroom with a pencil sharpener in hand. He had a pair of half-moon specs pushed on top of his head, and his top two shirt buttons were undone. "I can't stand a dull pencil," he said with a crooked smile. "Didn't want to wake Lydia, though, so it took a bit to find it in the dark."

He sat in the chair in front of the music, picked up his pencil, and began sharpening it. "Can't sleep?" he asked, not looking up.

"No. Too much to think about."

"Sit with me?" He gestured to the chair next to him. I hesitated, but decided I'd better not be rude, and sat. I drew my glass of water close and took a sip, cocking my head to read what he was writing now, above a measure on the clarinet line. *Remind Blackstone this shud be solful as if dreming of larg stak, not plod like ancient donky.*

"Your spelling is worse than mine," I said.

He laughed, self-conscious, flushing. "I know. I almost didn't write to your mother for the shame of it. Then I decided a woman who was that shy and still managed to kiss me after knowing me for mere hours would probably forgive my abominable mangling of the English language." He sat back in contemplation. "Macedonian doesn't have as many phonetic variations as English. It's easier to spell. English makes no sense. I gave up trying years ago."

"I concur," I said, "although French is even worse. I discovered that in ballet class."

He grinned at me. "French *is* in a league of its own."

"Weren't you still little when you came over, though? I thought it was easy for children to learn new languages."

"Eleven. See, the trouble is, speaking it came easily enough. But reading and writing... some of our Cyrillic letters are the same as the Latin ones, but they have different sounds, and I'd already learned to read and write Macedonian years before coming here." He flipped over one of his sheets of music and wrote a string of letters and tapped each one as he explained that the sounds they make in Macedonian are completely different from what an English speaker might guess. "My American teachers constantly scolded me for mixing up my letters. My sisters didn't ever seem to have any trouble, so I got scolded at home too. After a couple of years I finally stopped having to think so hard about the new sounds of those particular letters, but even then, I spelled things how they sounded. Still do. Speaking English is one thing; writing and reading it completely another. Mira has the opposite problem. She's fluent in her mother's Russian, my Macedonian, and English, but because Russian and Macedonian alphabets are just a little different from each other, she mixes them together sometimes if she tries to write one or the other."

"Did you want to come to America?"

"I didn't exactly have much choice." Again he smiled, and it was so bright and genuine I grumbled inwardly yet again at how *likable* this man was. "I wasn't happy about it. We were poor and everything was in upheaval and I had a music teacher I liked and was heartbroken to leave behind. Things were better here. We were still poor, but at least there wasn't a constant threat of war. But the officer at Ellis Island put my name as Constantine with a C (and an E at the end). I legally changed it back eventually. Stubborn, I suppose, but that first day I looked at our papers and up to my parents and said if they ever called me 'Sondztantineh' I would hop on the next boat back if I had to stow away. I liked it how it was! It was bad enough they dropped the ending off our last name. We had been Zafirovskis before."

I had to join him laughing at that. "I mix up letters, too," I said. "And I don't even have the excuse of English as a second language. It's like they... just don't want to stay on one line. My eyes are always seeing words and letters from the lines above and below and getting them all confused."

He regarded me curiously. "Fortunately intelligence isn't defined by only one thing. That would be dull. We can all fill in the gaps for each other, wouldn't you agree?"

He was right. I thought of how I did George's arithmetic for him and he fixed my essays and read to me, and...

"George would simply eat up that little language lesson you just gave me," I said, softly, and suddenly I wanted to cry.

Konstantin didn't lecture me about George. He gave me a look with nothing but kindness in it, and that didn't help. I could tell he was inviting me to talk if I wanted, that he'd listen.

Instead I choked out some pathetic excuse and fled to shed quiet tears into my pillow before worrying myself to sleep over the forthcoming Family Dinner.

The dinner turned out to be fine. As usual, I befriended the children first, and once I knew them, I felt less anxious about the adults. Father Andrei, with his beard, reminded me of the preconceived mental image I'd made up for Rabbi Zylberman back in my childhood before I met him. This man looked far more like that stereotype than the rabbi had himself. Again, before and after the meal, there was the crossing themselves and the prayers just as Konstantin had said them the previous night. Again we had soup, but this time there was no oil or meat in it.

Or so I thought, until I dipped into it and a small shrimp appeared on my spoon.

I leant over to Mira, who was beside me, and whispered, "I thought this was a no meat day."

"Things with no backbones don't count," she whispered back. "So we can have shrimp or calamari, say. It's a special occasion, so Baba splurged."

This sounded bizarre to me. I had spent so many years mostly eating kosher because of Mrs. Graham and George that I still generally didn't eat shellfish or pork. I didn't have any personal religious objection to eating shrimp, so I ate the soup, but it still felt odd.

"Now you must all sing for Louise," Mira said, when a rare silence fell. "Sing her the great doxology. Even her Protestant sensibilities can't object to that."

As the resident priest had presided over the prayers before and after dinner, everyone looked automatically to the resident conductor for a cue now.

Konstantin sang out: "Glory to Thee, Who hast shown us the light!" And his sisters and brother and several of the children spontaneously turned toward the icons on the east wall, joining him in a sort of chanting music, in perfect four-part harmony. It was gorgeous and gave me chills. I gaped; and Mira was right. There was nothing objectionable at all in the words. On the contrary, they were very beautiful. "All of us sing in the church choir," she said, when they finished. "Not always all at the same time. But aren't they marvelous? All my uncles and aunts are singing tomorrow."

I nodded, still speechless.

Back at the Drake late that night, we had prayers—or I should say, everyone else did, and I observed. Then we went to bed.

The previous night I'd had Margaret's bed, but this time Mira and I had to share because Margaret was back. I didn't particularly object. She said she had to be on the outside so Margaret could help her out in the night if needed, so I settled into the wall side. Once she'd gotten herself situated and Margaret switched the light out, we all lay there in the quiet dark.

"Mother says your legs hurt more this time of year," I said to Mira.

"Not my legs. I don't have much feeling in them. More my back. It'll adjust." But she didn't want to talk about her aches. "So, our parents being so twittery over each other. Doesn't it make you positively ill?"

I made a noncommittal noise instead of answering, thinking again that Mother and Konstantin were tame in comparison to George's parents.

Mira sighed. "When I asked the Theotokos to find a new wife for Tato, I didn't know he was going to start behaving like a constantly tipsy raccoon! I'm telling you, from the minute he told me of her until now, every other word out of his mouth has been 'Lydia this' and 'Lydia that' and sitting down every five minutes to write her letters or postcards. And playing *Liebestraum!* I started hearing it even when he wasn't playing it! And then he goes and marries her in some bland and characterless civil ceremony instead of waiting like a reasonable man for a church wedding! It was her idea, they say, and they were both unbothered by my scolding. What's the hurry, anyway? Since when do people their age need to romance each other like they're teen-aged goons? You know what he said? 'It is better to marry than to burn!' As if quoting Saint Paul at me makes it somehow okay!"

So then I did tell her about George's parents. "Although, they are more predatory than gooey. Mother and your father will settle down. Probably. Eventually. But they're not that old, not really."

In the morning, everyone was busy from the first moment. Mira and I brought Mother into the room we were sharing to help her get ready. Margaret brought out the dress from the closet. It was a deep purple silk, flowy and elegant.

"Like Saint Lydia of Philippi, the seller of purple," Mira said, beaming and clasping her hands. "Oh, Lydia, you're so beautiful."

I fastened the buttons up the back, and Mother sat at the dressing table to arrange her hair. When she'd finished, she put on her stockings and shoes, and Mira handed her a package, her face radiating excitement.

Mother opened it and, inside, was a scarf of the same silk as her dress, but exquisitely embroidered with gold thread, a pattern of birds at either end and a geometric border all around. Mother looked up with tears in her eyes. "Mira, it's too much!"

"Nothing is too much for you," Mira said, and kissed her cheek. "Let me tie it on for you."

Mother did, and I watched Mira carefully arrange the scarf on Mother's head, pinning it strategically so it wouldn't slide off.

"Now I must see to Tato," she said, and wheeled out, leaving Margaret and me to finish attending to Mother, who was looking at her reflection with eyes softened by tears. At her throat she wore the cross pendant Mira had given her.

Mother opened her earring box and considered, looking at me. "I wore Mormor's pearls when I married your father," she said. "Should I wear them again?"

I took the box and considered the options, glancing at her dress, and finally I said, "You ought to wear the peridot ones that match your ring." I took them out and handed them to her, and she beamed and put them into her ears.

"You could have Mormor's pearls today," Mother said, but I shook my head.

"These are fine," I said, indicating the little gold hoops I usually wore, and I took out my own dress and spent a few minutes putting on a little lipstick and settling my best hat onto my head while Margaret and Mira tied on their own headscarves. Again I had that sensation of displacement, of being an outsider in someone else's culture, far more strongly than I'd ever felt with Mrs. Graham and George's Jewishness.

Margaret and I came out ahead of Mother. Konstantin had emerged and looked as nervous as a schoolboy, but incredibly sharp, and his hair was unusually tidy.

"Are you ready?" Mother asked from inside the room, and we all said, "Yes."

She peeked around the door, and then stepped out. I watched Konstantin's face and saw tears in his eyes. They stepped toward each other and he leant in to kiss her, lightly. Hand in hand, they followed the rest of us out of the room and to the car, which had been brought around to the front. Mother and Konstantin got in, and I got into the back seat. Vasilia and her husband pulled up as well, and Margaret and Mira got into that vehicle, after which Mira's chair was folded and tucked in beside me.

When we parked, two of her uncles carried Mira up the front steps, while Margaret followed with the chair. At the top, Mira and chair were reunited, and we entered the church behind Konstantin and Mother. Many people were already there, and we waited while Konstantin and Mother lit candles and kissed icons. Mira and Margaret followed behind and did the same; I stood back and watched, regretting that I had not allowed Mira to prepare me for what to expect, even if I declined to participate in any crossing and bowing myself.

The priest came out and, shortly after, the ceremony began. Mira beckoned me to come stand beside her, close to the front of things,

on Mother's side, so I could see clearly.

On either side of the church stood Zafirovs, chanting hymns and responses. I can only describe the sound as lush. Still, I was bewildered the entire time and never entirely sure what I was supposed to do. There was nothing I could find to correspond to any wedding I'd ever attended before: there was no exchanging of vows, but rather a blessing of their rings, a crowning, and something with sharing a cup, with readings and chanting in between.

The handmaid of God Lydia is betrothed to the servant of God Konstantin. ... The servant of God Konstantin is crowned unto the handmaiden of God Lydia.

I was touched, more than anything, by the tender way Konstantin kept his arm lightly around Mother's waist at every possible opportunity, as if he had to keep reassuring himself she was there. This was a man who had known his own cup of sorrow, and did not want to let this chance at happiness escape him. And at the end, when they kissed, it was so sweet I almost couldn't stand it. It was chaste and appropriate, unlike Mr. and Mrs. Graham might have been, but it made me ache with longing for George in a way none of his parents' demonstrativeness ever had.

After it was over, everyone shared a meal that Slavka had organized, along with cake, and many people came to meet me and introduce themselves and congratulate me, as if my gaining Konstantin Zafirov as a stepfather was as exciting as the blessing of the marriage. Clearly he was very loved by a lot of people.

The celebrations went on for hours and carried over into the Zafirovs' apartment. At some point Konstantin and Mother vanished, presumably to enjoy their new status as blessedly married instead of just legally. I could picture her blushing and protesting because the house was full of people, and him saying that was precisely the reason they should steal away, because nobody would hear a thing.

I myself hid in Mira's dim bedroom for a while. I took the small picture of George and his baby out of my purse and held it, not looking at it, thinking about all Mira had said and Mother confirmed. About the panic and hurt George must have experienced at the hands of that awful woman. He hadn't wanted to talk of it any more than

I'd ever wanted to discuss the depths of Sam's depravity. Perhaps he didn't even know how. For all his vast intelligence, the topics of sex, kissing, and romance were ones he studiously avoided.

And Uncle Jamie knew, I was sure. Knew and hadn't breathed a word, as surely as he never would have told George any of my secrets.

The door opened, and Mira rolled in. "What are you hiding in here for?" she asked.

"I just wanted to be quiet for a bit."

Mira closed the door behind her and switched on the lamp by Margaret's bed, allowing her to see I was holding the photograph.

"What are you thinking about?" she asked.

I shrugged, and she shifted in her chair, looking a little uncertain for the first time since I'd arrived.

"I don't think we've gotten off to the best of starts," she said. "I know you're angry with me for what I said when you first came."

"Everyone is conspiring against me," I said, tossing the picture aside in a huff. "Of course it's irritating."

She ran one finger up and down the armrest of her chair for a minute before speaking again. "What if it's not that people are conspiring?"

"What do you mean?"

She clasped her fidgeting hands together and fixed her eyes on the cross above her bed. "I discovered shortly after my mother died that when I prayed for things, they happened. Or sometimes I have dreams... For example, one night a voice woke me up saying 'Tell him to go.' So I called for Tato and he came and I said, 'You're supposed to go.' And he said, 'What on earth are you talking about?' and I said, 'You tell me.' And he admitted he'd been asked to go to Seattle to conduct and he didn't want to, because what in the world would Seattle have to offer him? And he was going to write to decline. That voice is why he went. That's where he met Lydia. That's why you're here now."

I didn't meet her eyes. She went on. "Lydia asked me to pray that you and George would get back together, so I did, and the next I heard he'd got it into his head to go looking for you—"

"Who?"

"George, of course. And clearly he hasn't found you yet, which means what's holding things up must be you. Because you are hiding from him, aren't you?"

I wouldn't tell her about all the airmen I'd told never to let strangers get to me at the phone or airfield, or the times I'd called reporters to rant at them for putting my name in the paper.

"How would he even know where to look?" I said, determined to argue the point.

"I prayed about that too. He'll know somehow. I don't worry over the details."

I couldn't decide if Mira's perception of the power of her own prayers was valid or merely audacious.

"Anyway, I want you to like me, and I'm sorry."

I looked at her with skepticism, and she amended. "Well, not for what I said, just for how I said it. Now, make things even by telling me off for something."

I considered. What *did* really bother me? Was it the houseful of joyful relatives who all adored Mira and each other, providing her with an experience I'd never had but had desperately longed for?

I scooted myself back against the wall and slumped there. "I don't have anything to tell you off for, Mira. I'm stubborn and bitter and jealous." My voice caught a little and I scowled.

"It's okay to cry," she said. "I won't laugh."

"I want—I've always wanted—what you have in spades. Your family, I mean. Instead I got one who loathed Mother and me and it's always been just her and me against the world since my father died. I wanted to get married and start having a big family so my children would never have to know what that sort of loneliness is like. I know you lost your mother and brother, and that's awful, but you still have all the aunts and uncles and grandparents to love you through your loss. But George wasn't making a move, and I felt... well, worthless." Mira didn't say anything, so I went on. "Do you know what it's like to feel like nobody loves you?"

"Not in that way," she said. "I do have a wonderful family. People outside the family are... another story." She paused, as if wanting my approval to continue, and I nodded.

"I don't mind this chair, and my family doesn't mind this chair, but do you have any idea what this chair makes *most* people think? That I'm stupid. They talk to Tato instead of me as if I'm too idiotic to understand. Nobody cares that I can speak three languages fluently, run a youth orchestra, am a good musician and needleworker and all the other things I do. They see the chair and they think, A great big girl like that in a chair, why, she cannot possibly be intelligent! But I get to come home to where I'm safe and loved, so I get by." Her own eyes brimmed. "I want you to be part of my family. They will love you if you let them."

"Even if I'm Protestant?"

"Even so."

I sighed, and she reached for my hand. "Come kneel here with me," she said softly. She crossed herself as she began to say a prayer. Part of it sounded like something she had memorized, but then she said, "Let my family be Louise's family and let us be truly sisters."

After we'd all finally gone to bed, I lay awake for some time, listening to Mira breathing. She was warm and, in her sleep, had snuggled in against my arm. In spite of everything, I found myself enjoying the closeness, thinking of my own dead sisters and wondering if I'd ever cuddled up to them the way Mira was to me now. It made me realize how much I'd missed out on all these years, and thought perhaps Mira was right about one thing. People did want to love me, and I was resistant. I was still too stubborn to admit it to her or anyone else out loud yet, though. Was it true George would find me because of this girl's prayers?

You could go find him, my inner voice reminded me.

I stroked Mira's hair, soft like silk. No, I wouldn't find him. I'd wait and watch to see if Mira's intercessions worked.

I kissed the top of her head, and only after that did I manage to drift off to sleep.

The next morning we went to church, a long and unusual experience. Konstantin and Mira were in the choir that morning, but Mother stood with me. She participated in the service as fully as anyone else there, occasionally leaning in to explain to me what was happening, except for taking communion, because she wasn't Orthodox and therefore not allowed. But there was a light in her face I'd never seen before, and I couldn't decide if it was something to do with the service or the way she and Konstantin kept catching each other's gaze.

I decided Mira was right. They were nauseating.

They didn't eat breakfast on Sunday mornings, and I was starving, but trying to keep up with the service distracted me somewhat. Afterwards we went home and had lunch.

Mother gave Mira a hand as she transferred from her wheelchair to the couch so she could put her feet up. Mira got out her needlework, and Mother and Konstantin played together. He was a fine cellist, and I could have listened to them forever, if they'd been playing straight through. But no, as true musicians always do, they kept stopping and replaying the same phrases over and over.

I was used to that, and also used to tuning it out.

A Steinway, though. Mother must be in heaven. I felt a twinge; what had happened to the piano Daddy gave her? I'd ask later. I knew she was renting out our house in Salem; maybe it was still there.

Margaret had gone to spend the afternoon with a friend, since Konstantin and Mother were both home to help Mira if she needed anything, so it really was just us. I sat quietly for far longer than I usually would have, taking in the room, the icons, the repeated bars of music. I saw Mother and Konstantin's wedding crowns had been placed, along with their wedding candles, on a shelf in the icon corner.

"What are the crowns and candles there for?" I asked, and Mira turned to glance at them, although I doubt she needed to.

"It's tradition to have them there, or hung on the wall above the bed. It was Mama and Tato's crowns and candles there, up until February. I have those ones in my room now, safe in a box. It's nice to have the shelf filled again."

"What are the other pictures? I recognize Mary and Jesus, but not the rest."

The music stopped as Konstantin looked up, eyes crinkled in amusement. "A dangerous question. Mira is a walking encyclopedia of saints. Better settle in."

290

Mira dropped her needlework into her lap and rolled her eyes at her father, then shifted so she could look at the icons, crossing herself. "I can be brief. They're our patron saints. Tato, of course, is Constantine, and mine is Sophia the mother of orphans. My second name is Sofia. There's Nicholas of Myra for my brother Nikola, and Mary of Egypt for my mother Maria. Cecilia of Rome is Margaret's. I also put up Lydia of Philippi for your mother." She grinned. "Do you have another name besides Louise?"

"Just Berglund. Mother's maiden name."

"Hmm. Well, you don't have to share a name with your patron saint. People who convert as adults choose their own, after all. When Margaret converted, she chose Saint Cecilia."

"I won't be converting."

Unfazed, she went on. "And of course George the Trophy-Bearer, of dragon fame, though there are..." She counted on her fingers. "Six or seven other Saint Georges too. Lydia, what's George's daughter's name?"

"Hazel Mae."

"Ah, well, nothing there."

"Did he pick her name?" I asked Mother. George's capacity for naming things was often limited to whatever he'd most recently eaten.

"No."

"Did... she?"

"No. The attending nurse did. Velma wanted nothing to do with it. She tried to get rid of the baby beforehand and failed, if the note she left in the box can be believed."

I felt sick. "How awful," I said, softly. "That poor child."

"Enough of sad things!" Mira said, and turned to me. "So will you take me flying? You leave on Wednesday?"

"Yes, very early. We could do it either tomorrow or Tuesday."

"Tomorrow," she said.

The next day Mother drove Mira and me to the airfield, and with some difficulty we managed to help Mira into the plane. She strapped herself in, beaming, and I briefed her on what to expect and what not to do.

"We won't be able to hear each other," I said, "but if you need me to take you down sooner than planned, hold up three fingers and I'll land us as soon as we can."

I went through the checks and climbed in myself. The mechanic spun the propeller for me and soon we took off.

It was a lovely flight. I took us southeast, toward Atlantic City, and a little bit out over the ocean, before turning around and heading back.

I was proud of my landing, and when I'd parked, Mira turned to me beaming. "That was grand! I never realized how close we are to the ocean!"

She nattered on happily all the way back to the Drake about how marvelous it had been, and then to Margaret and her father, and I found myself warming to her. Yes, we might have different ideas about the particulars of faith, but as a person, she was very nice.

I still couldn't wrap my mind around the idea of thinking of her as a sister, though. I'd always been on my own.

Konstantin drove me to the airfield on Wednesday morning, after I said my goodbyes to Mother, Margaret, and Mira. He had to go work with his orchestra right afterwards.

He carried my suitcase for me over to Asterope and for a moment we stood there, me the stubborn porcupine and him the gentle sweetheart who wanted to include me in his family.

"Louise," he said, "I know this has all been a bit difficult for you, and I'm sorry about that. As I said back in February, I won't force myself into any role you don't want me to fill, but I also want you to know I would be very pleased if you chose to consider me a father."

I looked into his kind eyes—darker than Mira's, but more golden than George's—and on impulse I pulled him into a tight hug. He returned it, and when I stepped back, I said, "Thanks. I… I do see how happy you and Mother are, and she deserves all the best. Be good to her, will you?"

He laughed. "I wouldn't dream of being anything else."

I latched my suitcase into the hatch. "Tell Mira I'll write to her." And we said goodbye, but he didn't leave until I'd finished my checks and had taken off. I saw him waiting by the car until I'd gotten into the air. He waved and watched until I couldn't see him anymore. I suppose then he got into his car and drove to his orchestra, to remind Blackstone the clarinetist not to play like an ancient donkey.

Oh. And I'd been right. Konstantin gave absolutely marvelous hugs.

GEORGE

SAN FERNANDO, CALIFORNIA: DECEMBER 1, 1935

*T*he morning after Thanksgiving I stole away for a while to the library for my weekly scouring of newspapers... and that was the day I found the item I'd been hoping to see for so long.

It was small, tucked into a corner on page seven, but it was there.

> *Louise Pearson, local aviatrix, has returned from her voyage east to collect her new wings. She is again accepting students at Plover Field, and also offers private transport or delivery arrangements with her plane, a Taylor J-2 Cub.*

So there it was. I had an airfield now. If only I could catch her at it.

On Sunday morning after church, I left you with Mrs. Hays, took Lindbergh along for moral support, and drove the van to the airfield.

The drive was nearly an hour, which gave me plenty of time for my anxious anticipation to ratchet its way up to painful levels. If this went well, we could spend Christmas together. If it did not... well, I didn't want to contemplate that.

I parked, scooped up Lindbergh, and walked toward the main building. On our way there we walked by several planes, and I whispered repeatedly to myself: *I love you, marry me.* But Lindbergh broke me out of my reverie by leaping out of my arms.

Before I could stop him, he'd torn across the ground toward a bright blue plane. My heart leapt to my throat as he jumped up against a certain pilot's legs and barked an overjoyed greeting.

He'd found her.

The pilot crouched to take his front paws in her hands and scanned the field with an anxious expression that didn't exactly signal welcome, but I walked over anyway.

"What are you doing here?" she said, getting to her feet and taking on her arms-crossed, just-try-me stance. She didn't look exactly angry, though. Or even surprised.

It was unnerving to see her, to be so close to her, I forgot all my thoroughly rehearsed words. What came out of my mouth instead was, "Who the hell is Carlo?"

She did look angry, then. "Who cares the hell about Carlo?"

"The way you cared about Velma Johnson," I snapped.

"How do you even know about Carlo?"

I threw my hat on the ground as hard as I could and took her by

296

her shoulders, shaking her a little. "Who is he? What is he to you?"

She wasn't going to be shaken and pushed me away. "Why should I tell you about Carlo?"

I huffed. This conversation was going all wrong. I seized her shoulders again and, still furious, said, "What I'm trying to tell you is I love you and I was wrong and I'm sorry for messing everything up and I want to marry you."

She laughed. She actually laughed at me.

I'd had enough. I kissed her, cutting off her laughter in a squeak. I said, in broken-up phrases against her mouth, "I'm here because you love me. Because I love you. Because I was an idiot and all I've ever really wanted is you."

Despite her struggling, she was returning my kisses, gripping me back, hands pulling at my hair as she wove her fingers in.

"Who," she hissed, "told you I was here, anyway?"

And she yanked herself free, giving my face a stinging slap before pushing me up against the fuselage of the plane and kissing me back, hard and unrelenting and desperate as a camel at an oasis, drinking me in with a fury that left me stunned. Where in the world had she learned to kiss like this?

My knees went weak, my mind flashing back to the entrapment of Velma's kisses, and just as my head began to do that weird panicky fritzing, the insane tussle ceased, our faces inches apart, and our eyes locked. Hers were wide and wet and snapping, daring me to come clean with her.

"She didn't give me a choice," I managed to whisper over the racing of my heart, my own eyes filling. "She put something in my tea and I didn't want what she did to me. It was only that one time. She—" I couldn't say it. "I couldn't talk about it. It made me panic remembering. I still don't want to talk about it, but you have to believe me! It wasn't my choice. I wanted to tell you, but it was too hard, and I realized how badly I muffed up with you—"

I'd stopped trying to hold back the tears. I leant my head back against the plane and looked at the sky, sniffling in an incredibly un-suave way.

She'd stepped back, eyeing me with an unreadable expression, arms folded again. At last, in a level voice, she said, "Carlo is a valued friend and my dance partner where I work. He's been a gentleman when I've tried to get more out of him than was proper. Since I wasn't getting anything out of anyone else."

It was calculated to sting, and it did. "Gosh darn it, Lou, I just didn't understand, okay? I do now. I want to make it up to you, however I can. I'm half a whole when we're apart. You have no idea how much I regret not realizing it sooner. How much time I've wasted, that we could have been together, making love and babies and you bossing me around and me being... well, whatever it is that I am."

"George—"

We were interrupted by a young man approaching. "Howdy, Miss Pearson," he said. "I don't mean to interrupt, but—"

She glanced at her watch. "Sorry, Jake. I lost track of time. We're using the Jenny today. Go do the checks and I'll be with you in a minute." He nodded and strode off. "George, I can't talk. I've got a student."

"Then come see me tonight. I'm living by River Chapel in San Fernando. Do you have a way to get there?"

"Yes."

"Five o'clock?"

"Six would be better. It'll take me almost an hour to get there."

"Six then. We'll be expecting you."

Her mouth quirked slightly. "We?"

"Well... Fizz—Hazel—and me."

"I heard you kept her. I still find that unbelievable."

"She's my child. Of course I kept her!"

"You never liked babies."

"I didn't, particularly. It's different if it's mine, I guess."

"Okay. I'll see you tonight." And she let out a long breath and walked away without another word.

LOUISE

I climbed into the Jenny behind Jake and gave him instructions, but my eyes were on George, who had picked up Lindbergh again. George was wearing that red and gold scarf I'd knitted him so many Christmases ago. He wasn't any taller, but he looked different somehow, and not just because of the moustache he'd acquired at some point since I left.

"Ma'am?" Jake prompted me, and I jerked back to reality.

"Take her up, Jake."

GEORGE

I leant my back against the bright blue plane and watched Louise as she strode over to her student. I couldn't make out their conversation, but her cool professionalism was palpable even at this distance. I envied the student, albeit not the going up in an airplane part.

Another fellow smirked at me as I walked back to my van. He'd probably seen everything, and belatedly it hit me how ridiculous the whole interaction had been, and my face flamed. What had I been *thinking?*

I found out what *he'd* been thinking, when, in the paper later I read:

> *Shouting Match At Airfield, Injuries Reported:*
> *There's no end of excitement at Plover Field. Local aviatrix Louise Pearson was accosted today by an as-yet unidentified young man. She is unhurt, but he got a slap on the kisser that will likely be a lesson to him. When questioned, she declined comment.*

When I arrived back home, Hannah pegged at once that I had news.

"Did you find her?"

"I found her." I couldn't hold back a smile, and she whooped and went to tell Reverend Hays.

I brought you inside to give you a bath, then took one myself whilst Hannah took over the drying and dressing of you and taming your unruly fluff into two tight, tiny plaits.

I was stepping outside to clean my van in anticipation of company, but Hannah took me by the collar and pulled me back inside. "Oh no you ain't," she said. "You ain't feeding that girl Campbell soup in the cold on my watch. I know you want to be alone with her, but you're gonna eat inside like civilized folk, and you can have the sitting room to yourselves afterwards."

"Yes, ma'am," I said. "Well, at least let me help."

"Nope," she said. "You take your baby and sit at Cosmo's a while and come back. He'll wanna hear your news, anyway."

I took you by the hand and we walked slowly along the sidewalk. "We're having company tonight, Fizz," I said. "A lady who flies planes. A very special lady."

"Okay."

I let myself into the Styleses' house and Della grinned a welcome at me. Cosmo, who was lounging on the couch, immediately knew something was up. "Hey, you lit up like a Christmas tree," he said. "You found her! You found her, didn't you?"

I nodded. You had wandered off to gather some books to take to Belinda to have read to her, and Cosmo made room for me to sit by him. "She's coming for dinner tonight."

"Denver! June! Nigel!" he hollered. "George found his girl!"

I heard distant cheers, and then everybody burst into the room, even Gramps.

I loved this family so much.

I had hardly gotten back to the Hayses' when I heard the sound of a motor, which rumbled right into the street in front of the house and stopped. I looked out the window to see Louise step off a motorbike, and rushed to the door, throwing it open.

She'd come straight from the airfield without bothering to make herself pretty first, but I didn't care. A sudden shyness seized me, intensified by the memory of how stupid I'd been earlier, and I stood frozen in place, my eyes locked with hers.

She took off the leather helmet and gloves and shook out her hair until it looked uncannily like it had when we were children, but the moment was shattered by small arms grabbing my legs from behind.

LOUISE

*T*he force of Hazel's impact shoved George off balance, but he caught himself, and scooped her up. I smiled at the braids sticking out comically on either side of her head.

"It's Lindbergh's scarf," I said, gesturing to the scarf around the little girl's neck. He looked confused, and I laughed. "Don't you remember? I made the small scarf for Lindbergh."

"Oh! Yes. Well, he doesn't use it much."

We continued to stare at one another, time seeming to stand still. Hazel squirmed down and trotted off, saying something about potatoes, and a Black woman appeared behind George with a stack of plates in her hands. She looked at me over George's shoulder.

"Lou-ise!" she said. "You're here! About time that boy finds you! He's been suffering for months!" She turned to George. "Get inside and let your girl in out of the cold, for goodness' sake!"

He grinned sheepishly, but held out his hand in a gesture of welcome, and I came inside. He closed the door, and I saw the woman through the kitchen door, bustling about and laying the table. "I'm always telling him," she called out to me, "he eats too much Campbell soup, and I ain't gonna stand by here and watch him try to woo his ladylove with Campbell soup, no ma'am. You gonna have REAL food."

"Thank you, Hannah," George said, weakly. "Louise, this is Hannah Hays, Reverend Hays' wife. They've been so kind to let us park our van here and make us come in when it's cold."

Hazel came out again and held up her cat to me. "Potato," she said.

"This... is Potato," George explained, indicating the cat. "Fizz, make sure she stays off the table."

"Kay."

I crouched to stroke the little striped cat, who squirmed out of her mistress' grasp and scampered off, just as we were all called to the table. Hannah had made roasted potatoes and gravy, fried chicken, and a tomato salad, with oranges and chocolate cookies for dessert.

Hannah leant out of the kitchen door a second time. "Or-VILLE!" she hollered. "Here, you two sit here on the bench. I'll find another chair for Hazel."

"She'll be fine here," George said. Hazel had climbed onto his lap and settled there.

Reverend Hays came in after a few minutes and beamed at me, leaning across the table to shake my hand and welcome me. After the blessing we all dug in, and at last I plucked up the courage to ask, "How did you end up here, George?"

"You mean here with us colored folks?" Reverend Hays said, grinning.

"Well... yes."

"I met one of the Hayses' parishioners coming here," George explained, "and the next thing I knew I'd been adopted in."

"This white boy is okay," Reverend Hays said. "We all love him."

"Does he ever preach at your church?" I asked.

"I'm a little staid for their tastes, I'm afraid," George said.

"You're learning," Hannah said. He shrugged a bit self-consciously.

She and the reverend soon finished eating and left us to go to the evening service at the church, and strictly instructed us we were not to wash up.

When they had gone, I promptly cleared the table and took everything to the sink to wash.

"This is so... different from where I expected to find you," I said as I began scrubbing plates and running them through rinse water. George took up a towel to dry them.

"Where might you have expected to find me?"

"Oh... I don't know. Some posh church with a big congregation you could charm, I suppose."

He was quiet a minute, then said, "I'm not the same person I was a few years ago, Lou."

"I can see that."

He stopped drying for a moment. "You see, when I picked up Cosmo and we started driving down here the rest of the way together, I realized there's a whole world of hurt out there. What we collectively experience being Jewish isn't acceptable, but generally speaking we're not being lynched and driven out of town, and most of us can escape detection if we want to. When you're not white, everyone knows it. When Cosmo brought me here, I felt like I belonged because I understand, if only on a small scale, but also because I want to learn. I want to learn what they face on a daily basis so I can do what I can to fight it. Jesus wouldn't stand for racism, and white Christians are often the quickest to be racist."

I glanced at him out of the corner of my eye. "I take it back. You haven't changed as much as I thought."

He laughed and went back to drying. "Anyway, I'm learning a lot about what it means to be truly Christian from these folks, and they accept me."

"You mean your Jewish proclivities?"

"They're not proclivities, they're part of who I am." He looked up, and I met his eyes, then looked away. I knew that.

"I'm sorry," I said.

GEORGE

*W*e were quiet after that, seeming to have run out of things suitable to chat about over a sinkful of dirty dishes with you darting in and out singing incomprehensible songs about popcorn, Jesus, and Potato. When we'd finished, we all went upstairs to the guest room we'd been using, to get Hazel ready for bed. After putting on your little nightcap, which I knew you'd lose in no time because I couldn't tie it on, I beckoned you to come listen to her bedtime story.

"No," you said, walking to Louise instead with your blanket and book in tow. "Plane lady read."

I stifled a smile, but I didn't object. It was the same book every night and had been for weeks. The reprieve was more than welcome. I watched Louise as, after tying the nightcap strings, you nestled into her lap. The soft light illuminated Louise's pale hair, and you looked as content as I'd ever seen you. When the story was finished, I helped you say your prayers and tucked you into the little bed we'd put in the corner for you, then Louise and I waited in the quiet dark for a while.

You sat up with a rustle and said, in Yiddish, "Plane lady stay?"

I translated. "She's asking if you're going to stay."

"For a little while," Louise said, soothingly.

You nestled back in. "Potato," she said.

"Potato's asleep downstairs, Fizz."

"Want Potato."

I sighed and went to fetch the cat, who trampled herself a bed on the pillow above your head and settled in. I kissed your cheek and said, "Sleep now, Fizz."

"Sing, Da."

I glanced at Louise, oddly self-conscious, then launched into a

William Blake lullaby with enough verses to last until you drifted off.

Your eyes had closed by the third verse, and by the sixth you'd loosened your grip on my hand. I lightly kissed your cheek and stood up. Louise followed me back to the vacant sitting room, where we settled onto the couch. She kicked her shoes off and rested her back against the armrest, drawing her knees to her chest, watching me. "Why do you call her Fizz?"

I looked up from slipping off my own shoes, taken aback. Louise had always intuitively understood so much about me, it had never occurred to me she didn't know I could taste words. So I explained it to her.

"You never told me that."

"I've never told anyone," I said. "I don't know, I guess it just seems ordinary to me, and yet maybe people would think I was crazy?"

Louise didn't laugh. "What does my name taste like?"

"Cool clear water on a hot summer day. No flavor, exactly, but life-sustaining."

She looked at me for a long time before drily pronouncing, "You really do know how to make a girl feel special, George."

It took me a moment to parse what she meant. I decided not to dig my own grave any deeper and kept my mouth shut.

There was another long silence, and Lindbergh trotted in, settling into the space on the couch between our feet.

Louise spoke at last. "Are we putting all our chips on the table, George?" she asked.

"We might as well get it over," I said. "Do you want me to go first?"

She nodded.

So I told her everything. About the months leading up to That Night, every word exchanged, everything Velma had made me do, the trickery she'd employed once she knew she couldn't get me to willingly give in. The guilt and shame I felt afterwards, the strange experience I had praying on my steps, the moment I realized Louise loved me and I loved her, but how I knew I'd have to tell her everything and I couldn't, so I didn't say anything.

There was a long silence when I finished. She looked past me, her chin resting on her knees. I looked at Lindbergh, scratching his head, waiting for her verdict.

"Wow," she said, after the silence had become uncomfortably long. "I... guess that's maybe what Uncle Jamie meant when he said I ought to be careful of jumping to conclusions. I suppose you must have told him."

"As much as I could bear telling. More than I told Dad or Mamma. Not as much as I just told you. But do you see why it was something I just didn't want to talk about?" My voice was pleading. "I was as shocked as anyone else by Hazel. I almost didn't keep her."

"Yeah." Her voice was quiet. "Actually... I wish I didn't understand so well."

Cold fingers of dread pinched my heart at the strange tone of voice.

"Because I didn't want to tell you everything about Sam."

My hand reached out to rest on hers, and her voice was flat as she explained. "He told me I was ugly so often I still believe it. I thought that must be why you couldn't love me, because I was unattractive."

"Oh no," I said. "Never that."

"That's not all." She took a deep breath, stood up and paced a few times, her hands clenched tensely together behind her back. "He... threatened to rape me the night he beat me back in Turner."

I didn't have to ask which night.

"That's the reason Mother sent me to you. Why I wore the long underwear all the time. After my body started changing... I felt so much shame, see. And even though he was dead, I was terribly afraid someone else might do that to me, and I wanted to make it as hard as possible—" She hid her face in her hands.

I got up and pulled her into my arms. At my touch she collapsed into me and began to cry.

"This," she choked out. "This is what I wanted, countless times, to be held. The only kind of touch I got from men after Daddy was the bad kind. Mother had her own reasons for being distant... and I had so many nightmares of watching Daddy die, and Sam, and I cried myself to sleep many times wishing I could climb into your bed and have you hold me. Nothing else, just hold me, like this."

I ran my fingers through her hair as her shoulders heaved with her muffled sobs. "I wish I'd known sooner," I said, and I framed her face with my hands and said, "You are not ugly, Louise. You're lovely. Truly."

She backed away enough to fish out a handkerchief and blow her nose inelegantly. "I'm not done," she said, stuffily. "All the chips on the table, remember? I haven't gotten to Carlo yet."

She went back to the couch and slumped onto it.

"At my hotel there are four professional dancers, and we have rotating schedules so we can all have nights off. Carlo was hired after me, and we hit it off right away. He dances like a dream—not as well as you, of course—and taught me Spanish, and asks me at least once a month to marry him. He's had a ring for ages, waiting for me to get over you and say yes. It's blue topaz and diamonds. It's pretty. I've been tempted to give in, I admit." She paused. "And I have kissed him. I was lonely, and he's very... Latin. Are you bothered by that?"

"I haven't got any right to be bothered," I said.

"You haven't told me yet how you knew about Carlo. Did Mother say something? Or was it in one of those letters Aunt Estelle snitched?"

"You know about that?"

"Uncle Jamie wrote me to beg my forgiveness. Wasn't his fault."

"Well, by the time he found out, I'd already read them."

Louise cringed, hiding her face with one hand. "Oh, gosh. I don't even want to ask which ones."

"Do you still want my hands all over you?"

She groaned. "Oh no. Not that one."

I scooted Lindbergh off the middle cushion to make room for her. "Come here," I said, holding out my hand. "I have a lot to make up for."

She scooted closer, flushed and a bit nervous.

"And also... this afternoon... I was... well, it was hardly an acceptable way to greet you."

"I found it acceptable."

"It was still wrong."

Our eyes locked and for a moment we communed silently, before I leant in and kissed her. Nothing like this afternoon, not going in for the kill, but soft and shy.

She kissed me back, tentative, experimenting. It wasn't about passion, this kiss. It was about mending and healing. Discovery. About proving to myself that, with Louise, this was safe, and I could like it the way I had before things went south with Velma.

But I found myself involuntarily shaking and couldn't make it

stop until I pulled back and forced myself to take some deep breaths.

"It's not you," I whispered. "I'm just... it is hard to separate the way I felt with her and the way I want to feel with you."

She laid a light hand against my cheek. Waiting until I'd collected myself and drew her back into my arms. "Do you think we're still compatible?" I whispered against her face. "To marry each other, I mean? You could have the easy way with Carlo. With me there can be no promise anything's ever going to be easy, what with racial issues I can't not speak up about."

"I know. I've always known that. I mean, you are Jewish."

I spoke again. "Have we changed too much?"

She didn't answer for a moment, her mouth warm on mine, her

closeness becoming comfortable instead of strange. "You've changed enough to not mind spit swapping with me," she said at last, her fingers woven into my hair. It felt lovely, and I laughed.

"I suppose, for you, I can put up with a little spit swapping."

"Coming from you, that's nothing short of steamy."

"I'm not my father."

"It's not your father I've been in love with for eight years, you weirdo."

"I want you," I whispered into her hair, "to marry me."

"Mmm," was all she said.

"I haven't got diamonds and blue topaz, but I have all the love and devotion in the world, and this—"

I fished the bracelet out of my shirt pocket and opened her hand to let the warm silver slide into her palm. "I fixed it for you."

She startled and her other hand went to her mouth. Then she closed her hand around the charm, buried her face in my neck, and said, "This is all I've ever needed or wanted."

"And will you marry me?" I asked. "Are we us again?"

"'Whither thou goest, I will go,'" she whispered. "I love you, George. So, so much." And she held out her wrist to let me fasten the bracelet back on. I didn't let go of her hand afterwards.

"Have I changed?" I asked.

"Are you fishing for compliments on the moustache?"

"Not particularly, but if you hate it, I'll shave it off."

She touched it with light fingertips. "It does give you rather a dash."

"You did say once you didn't know if girls would want to kiss me with one."

She burst out laughing. "When I said that, it was simply to put the idea of kissing into your head, not because *I* cared one way or the other."

I touched her cheek with the backs of my fingers. "You could have just asked me straight out."

She ignored that and kissed me again. "What made you decide to grow one, anyway?"

"Being mistaken for Fizz's big brother was rather the last straw."

She laughed softly. I said, "I think you have her approval."

"Well, I did hold her before you did. She probably remembers."

"I doubt that."

"By the way, does she speak anything but Yiddish? I saw you've written a Yiddish translation into her book."

He laughed. "Mamma did that, actually. No, she understands both. She doesn't talk much in English yet, though."

Louise kissed me again, which kept me occupied for a moment. "How," I managed at last, "are we going to tell Fizz—"

"Leave it to me, if you like," she said. Then she pulled away and ran her hands through her hair with a deep sigh. "I'd better go. I would like you to take every stitch of my clothes off and ravish me until I am senseless, but there are only so many times seminaries can dismiss you for illegitimate babies before you'll start to have a reputation."

For some reason that made me laugh.

"Stop blushing, George, we're both thinking it. We're not going to be babyless for long if I have anything to say about it."

I decided to change the subject rather than admit I was still terrified of taking her to bed. "Will you please dance once with me before you go?"

She held out her hand. I took it and went over to my gramophone and wound it up, dropping on *It's Only a Paper Moon*.

"I'm out of practice with adult-sized partners," I warned her.

The opening bars stopped her in her tracks. "This song! It always makes me cry!"

She fell back into step with me, and I said, "It made me cry the first time I heard it, too. It made me long for you."

I held her closer than I'd ever held her before when dancing with her, our steps smaller, and the entire thing more intimate. This wasn't for show. It was just for us. "I wanted desperately for you to have believed in me," I whispered.

"I wish I hadn't made assumptions," she said. "I had waited so long and I was tired of putting my life on hold indefinitely..."

"I understand. I was a dope."

"We both were. In different ways."

When the song ended, we stood still, foreheads together, not letting go.

"I did not know," Louise said, "that you had it in you to be so aggressive."

"Do you mean today at the airfield?"

"Yes."

"It wasn't how I wanted that to go at all."

She sniggered softly. "Well, it certainly got my attention." She held my face between her hands. "I cannot wait to be married to you. I'm going to pinch myself in the morning wondering if any of today really happened."

I lifted the hand with the bracelet. "This will remind you."

Hand in hand we walked outside to her motorbike.

"I don't want to let you go," I said, as she put on her helmet and gloves.

"Come to my place tomorrow. I'll show you two around and we can send those telegrams."

PART FOUR

I don't want sunbursts or marble halls, I just want you.

LUCY MAUD MONTGOMERY,
"ANNE OF GREEN GABLES"

THE THREE TELEGRAMS
SANTA MONICA, CALIFORNIA: DECEMBER 2, 1935

TO: MR. AND MRS. GEORGE GRAHAM,
SALEM, OREGON:
MISSION ACCOMPLISHED.
NO DATE YET.
GEORGE

TO: MRS. LYDIA ZAFIROV,
DRAKE HOTEL, PHILADELPHIA:
CAN'T HAVE HAZEL
WITHOUT GEORGE
SO HAVING BOTH.
LOUISE

TO: LORD AND LADY INVERLOCHY,
INVERLOCHY CASTLE, SCOTLAND:
PLEASE ACCEPT THIS NOTICE
OF FORTHCOMING
WEDDING INVITATION
UNTIL PROPER ONE
DISPATCHED.
GEORGE AND LOUISE.

Louise

After the telegrams had been sent, I got behind the wheel of George's van and took the two of them to an ice cream parlor to celebrate.

George seemed hilariously self-conscious. I suspected it might take him some getting used to, allowing himself to indulge in something as alien as Being Engaged. He couldn't seem to get a single coherent sentence out of his mouth.

I, however, felt effervescent. I'd never been so happy, and it was all I could do, keeping my hands off the man across the table from me. I decided to distract myself with a different task. I turned to Hazel.

"Fizz," I said. "May I call you Fizz, too?"

"Mm." Hazel was too occupied with her ice cream to care. (Chocolate. A girl after my own heart.)

"Do you know who I am, Fizz?"

Hazel said something around a mouthful.

"She says 'plane lady'," George interpreted.

"Yes, I'm that, but also I'm your mother."

"Kay," she said. Her hair was all frizzy from yesterday's braids and her face was liberally decorated with chocolate smudges.

George was studiously finishing his own ice cream, and when he'd finished, I suggested I show them around.

I first took them to the ballet school where I worked as

a choreographer several mornings each week.

"I think they'll forgive my lateness today when they see the brilliant dancer I'm dragging in."

I introduced George and Hazel to everyone, and George watched the lesson in progress with rapt attention for some time. At the end of the lesson I clapped my hands and said, "Kids, would you like to see something?"

They crowded close.

"This, kids, is George Graham, my first dance partner, and we used to win competitions."

"One competition," George murmured under his breath.

"Now he's going to show you what you can aspire to. Got a few minutes to watch?"

Of course they did, and they all lined up along the wall as I'd taught them to do when I was demonstrating anything.

"What are we doing?" George whispered at me, and I grinned.

"What are *you* doing, you mean," I said. "The solo from *Giselle*." He followed me to the piano and I shuffled through a stack of music until I found what I wanted, and handed it to the pianist. "It's what we've been working on choreographing, so you can inspire them."

"Cold and dressed like this?" he protested.

I laughed. "When has that ever stopped you before?"

He sighed, albeit with amusement, handed me Hazel, and did what he was told.

He was such a marvel of grace. I held Hazel, but my eyes were on the man who became weightless on a dance floor. He hadn't lost a bit of his skill, and I was inordinately pleased.

"Your father dances like a dream," I whispered in Hazel's ear. Her only response was to twitch as if the whisper had tickled it. I tried again. "Don't you think so?"

When she still didn't respond, I gave up for the moment and went back to watching.

I introduced him to the teachers, who both asked why in the world George wasn't actively trying to become a principal dancer and were visibly shocked when he told them he was going to be a minister. After visiting a while, and after several starstruck kids had gotten him to talk with them, we went back to the van and I drove us past the hotel where I danced several nights a week. "Sometime I'll see if I can sneak you in," I promised, and then went to the airfield where I parked and turned to Hazel.

"Fizz, see the blue plane? That's Asterope, my plane. Do you want to ride in my plane?"

George made a horrified noise, and I grinned, but tried to reassure him. "No *Hell Divers* stunts," I promised. "I will bring her safely back to you. Unless you want to come too?"

I could tell he was remembering his (single) flight and the protectiveness he obviously felt for Hazel warmed me all over. But, in the end, he let Hazel go with me, and I did bring her back—not only safe, but extremely pleased with herself.

Then we bought sandwiches from a drug store and sat in the back of the van to eat them. George, still seemingly incapable of adult conversation, didn't say much, so I set to charming his child. Our child, I reminded myself. Ours, now.

"I love this," I said, gesturing to the van. "Fizz, where will I sleep when I come live with you?"

Hazel pointed to her trundle mattress.

"Oh, you're giving me your bed? That's awfully sweet. Where will you sleep?"

"With Da."

George laughed. "You'll have to learn to share me, Fizz."

The last thing we did was go to my apartment, where I introduced George and Hazel to Shirley, then left her to entertain them for the moment while I got myself ready for a long night of dancing: bath, hair, makeup, dress, stockings, shoes.

I emerged from the bathroom some time later, striking a melodramatic pose in my golden evening dress. George goggled gratifyingly, and I held out my hand to him. He crossed the room to me and I said, "It's all right if you hold me. You weren't this nervous yesterday."

He ducked his head and let his hands rest at my waist. "I can't explain it," he said. "I've been full of butterflies all day. I guess it seemed easier when we were alone and it was night."

I laughed softly and pulled him in closer. "You are lovely," he whispered in my ear. "I'm afraid of mussing you, now that you're all done up."

"I don't object to being a little mussed," I whispered back. "Gosh, George, I've missed dancing with you."

"Likewise," he said. "Fizz as a partner is decidedly inferior. Too much giggling."

I threw my head back and laughed. Then I asked, "I was trying to say something to Fizz at the studio earlier and it was like she didn't hear. Does she often do that?"

"Depends which ear. She can't hear out of the right one, from the scarlet fever."

"Oh!"

"I guess I've gotten so used to it I forgot to mention it. It doesn't seem to bother her much." He met my eyes and I melted.

In my heeled shoes, I was taller than George, and it occurred to me that I hadn't had the Problem of Heels since having Carlo for a partner. I kicked them aside so our eyes were level and said, "Guess I need to get myself some flats again."

He contemplated that. "Strangely enough," he said at last, "I hadn't even thought about it until you mentioned it. I suppose I'm not bothered anymore. Lots worse things to fret over than whether one's fiancée is marginally taller than oneself."

"Well, I never dreamed I'd hear you say that," I said. I was about to kiss him again when a knock came at the door.

"Brace yourself, it's Carlo," I whispered to George, then called out, "Come in!"

George stepped away from me, still holding my hand, and faced the door as it opened to admit my suave, ridiculously good-looking partner. I watched as their eyes met, read in their faces the male urge to size one another up in preparation to fight like stags for the right to their chosen mate. It would have been funny if it was someone else, but I was too involved to laugh. I bit my lip and waited.

When neither man spoke, I did. "Carlo, it's George."

"So I gathered." Carlo's expression changed to something I'd never seen before. Not disdain. Was it defeat? He didn't offer his hand, but

322

neither did George, whose entire stance seemed poised as if ready to spring on an instant's notice. I decided I needed to talk to Carlo alone as quickly as possible, and kissed George quickly and pointedly on the lips. "I'll call you tomorrow," I whispered. "Goodnight." I turned to Hazel and held out my arms for a hug, which she reluctantly gave me.

"Mama will see you later," I said. "I love you, Fizz." Then I took the arm Carlo offered me and we left.

On the sidewalk below my window, Carlo stopped walking and gestured up to where I was sure George was looking down at us. "So it is no, for sure?"

"I'm sorry, Carlo. I am. You're a lovely man and you've been a wonderful friend. But my heart has always belonged to George. You and I would never have worked. We'd have fought all the time, I know it."

He sighed. "You are... lit up, and I am jealous."

"You'd forever be jealous of me. There are so many things I've always known would never pan out, but I kept thinking maybe I'd give in out of loneliness, but everything's different now. I have what I know I want. Let's go to work."

GEORGE

I watched Louise and Carlo discussing something animatedly on the sidewalk below—me, presumably—before, his shoulders slumping, they set off in the direction of the hotel.

I said goodbye to Shirley, and you and I drove back to the Hayses'. I found a telegram waiting for me from my father.

> *MAMMA SAYS COMING NEXT WEEK.*
> *WILL TELEGRAM DATE AND TIME.*
> *CONGRATULATIONS FROM US BOTH.*

That night I sat down for a serious discussion with Reverend Hays about my prospects for the future. I didn't know yet what Louise made from her three jobs, but I did know that, having just bought her airplane, she wouldn't have much in the way of savings at the minute. I wasn't able to save much from my own jobs, and most of my decent meals came from my visits to the Hayses and Styleses and others from church. I had nothing to offer Louise in the way of financial stability yet, and this tore at my heart, because I knew it meant we would have to postpone our marriage indefinitely.

"There's a seminary in San Francisco," Reverend Hays said. "I've only heard of it, never been there. That might be a place for you to finish your schooling, at least. You said you have a year left. If you decide to go there, get your old seminary to send your records there. I'll give you a good reference, and I'm sure your home minister would too. But you don't have to graduate from seminary to be a good minister. If God's called you, that's the only thing that counts."

"I just like to finish what I start out to do." I sat back in my chair, pondering. Assuming I could get in sometime next year, I'd be finished sometime in 1937, and I could be ordained and, I hoped, have a church of my own. It wouldn't be a lot to live on even then, but I knew we'd at least have a roof over our heads, and I suspected Louise wasn't going to stop her flying because she acquired a Mrs. in front of her name. There would be that income.

"My mother is coming sometime next week," I said. "When she's here, perhaps I can investigate in San Francisco and leave Fizz with her."

In the morning, Louise telephoned me and I asked her if she had time to come discuss financial matters.

"I'll come over right away. I have time now."

So we sat together at the dining room table, being fed coffee and cookies by Hannah whilst Louise very capably put our current finances on paper. I was hopeless with numbers; she was not, and it helped me greatly to have her figure this out for me. She worked for some time, pausing occasionally to ask me questions, and then sat back to give me her verdict.

"If we stay here, we could get by on what I make. But if we move to San Francisco, it will be starting from scratch for both of us. I think you're right to go ahead and see what the situation might look like there, and I can make enquiries about flying jobs. I could run air mail again, if it came to it. And you're teaching here, even if only as a substitute. Surely that experience will count for something. Tutor college students, or seminary students?"

I ate another cookie before replying. "I don't mind being poor, but the idea of bringing more children into the world when I have no prospects of providing for them seems foolhardy."

She came and helped herself to a seat on my knee. "The Lord will provide," she said. "You do know 'the Lord helps those who help themselves' isn't a Scripture text, I hope?"

I laughed. "I do. But it also says 'thou shalt not tempt the Lord thy God.'"

She grinned. "I'll concede that. But we don't have to set a date until we've sorted these things out, so let's not worry too much yet."

"Okay."

LOUISE

Mrs. Graham took over the care and feeding of Hazel while George took a train up to San Francisco to investigate. It was so good to see her again, even though it wasn't as often as I'd have liked. It was two hours out of my day getting to San Fernando and back, after all. Mother and Mira wrote to me, too. Mira was quite effusive, and it made me smile. Maybe I should ask Mira to be my bridesmaid. I wondered if the three of them would be able to come.

I knew Uncle Jamie would be there, no matter what it took. Once I'd asked him if he'd give me away whenever I got married, and he promised he would. I had to hope Konstantin understood that, no matter how nice he was, Uncle Jamie had been my surrogate father first.

I decided to work all the extra hours I could, while I still could, and soon had made arrangements with the hotel and my fellow-dancers.

I knew that, in marrying George, I would be consenting to live the way he did. I'd spent so many years around Mrs. Graham and George that Sabbathkeeping didn't seem strange. I didn't mind not eating bacon and shrimp or whatever else, either.

So I swapped my Friday and Saturday nights with Joyce and took her Wednesday and Thursday. I'd keep Sundays and add in a Monday.

Nothing changed at the dance school, but I became more aggressive about recruiting flight students and getting more delivery jobs. I'd known it would take time to build up a clientele, but now I splurged for an ad in the paper saying I would transport single passengers privately, any destination, times and prices negotiable, confidentiality assured, Sunday through Thursday.

That soon got me results, and once I'd ferried one film star safely to a destination and back, the word got out among her cohorts that I was dependable and kept my mouth shut, and I was soon very busy. Money was no object to them, either, so I felt no compunction charging them a price that brought me a profit.

George telephoned nightly for five minutes for a quick debriefing. It wasn't nearly enough time to say all we wanted to say, but it was better than nothing. He said he had gone ahead and applied to the seminary and written for his records to be transferred and for references from Reverend Hays and Dr. Birtchet. "I'm sure this is what God wants me to do. If I'm accepted, I'm going to trust him to provide."

GEORGE

I caught the next train back to San Fernando. Cosmo and Nigel met me in Nigel's beat-up jalopy, a new acquisition of which he was extremely proud, and bore me in mandolin-accompanied triumph back to their house, where Mamma and you were waiting for me.

Mamma had initially been unsure what to make of being a lone white person in a Black crowd, but it appeared she'd gotten used to it, or at least was making a good show of it. Exuberance didn't mesh well with her personality, and the Styles bunch was nothing but.

"How are you holding up?" I whispered, as I came to her.

"The sooner you can get me out of here, the happier I'll be," she said. "It's... so very loud."

I grinned. "Taking Mamma back to the Hayses'," I called out. "Thanks for the lift, Nigel!"

We walked back toward the Hayses', and Mamma said, "Louise won't be back until tomorrow. She's on one of her clandestine transport-a-film-star runs."

"What?" I asked.

"She won't say much about it. Confidential, I expect. But it pays well. How do you survive all this noise, George?"

I laughed. "I guess I don't notice it. You hide out in the bedroom for a while and I'll look after Fizz."

I barely had a chance to see Louise except when she came to spend Shabbat with me.

"I rearranged my schedule," she informed me. "If you're taking the day off, so will I."

"I could kiss you," I said.

"Anytime," she said, so I did.

Chastely.

Because people were watching.

She slept on the couch that night, and after lunch the next day we took you and two of your little friends from church to a park and sat on the grass to watch them play and chase ducks, and I told Louise my tentative plans. "They said, if I'm accepted, and they don't see why I won't be, I could start in the fall. That gives us time to save a little and find a place to live up there, and something I can work at when I'm not studying."

"You aren't going to make us wait to get married until after that, are you?"

I sighed. "I don't want to."

We were quiet a moment, and she took my hand and cocked her head contemplatively.

"I think," she said, "you should write to every minister in the San Francisco area and find out if they would accept your services as an assistant in exchange for a place to stay. You may not be ordained, but you are licensed to preach."

"That's a possibility," I agreed.

"Also, Mother wrote to me. She says Konstantin has been asked to bring her to the Hollywood Bowl in May. It might be the only opportunity we'd get both of them here at the same time. I would personally like to have the wedding then."

"I'll let you take that on," I said. "You pick a date. My parents won't be terribly particular with enough advance notice."

"Also, she says in February she's to play at Carnegie Hall and it's going to be broadcast live." She could barely contain her excitement at the idea. "George, she's finally getting somewhere."

"I'm glad," I said. "We should have a party and get everyone together to listen. Cosmo's neighbor Bernie next door has a wireless. I'll talk to him."

"It's to be the ninth of February. Seven o'clock her time, so it will be four for us."

"Perfect," I said.

For a while we sat, and then Louise asked, "What would you be doing now if I'd said no instead of yes?"

"What kind of question is that?"

"Did you have another plan to fall back on if I turned you down?"

I thought a minute. "I suppose there'd have been June. Not that she would have made my life any less complicated than it already is."

Her mouth dropped open. "You really considered her?"

I shrugged. "Why not? She's nice. She's got a crush on me and thinks I haven't noticed, but she's about as opaque as a freshly washed window, unlike some people I know. But you needn't worry. It was an abstract possibility, not something I spent any real time dwelling on. I came here for you."

She snuggled next to me. "I'm glad you came. It was worth the wait. I guess it wasn't a bad thing we had to learn to get along on our own first, don't you?"

"Yes."

Then you came running up and knocked me backwards into the grass with the force of your impact. I lifted you up and you kicked and giggled in the air while the other two little girls jumped into Louise's open arms.

LOUISE

SAN FERNANDO, CALIFORNIA: FEBRUARY 9, 1936

I sent Mother a congratulatory telegram in the morning. Perhaps it was presumptive, but I didn't care. I knew she would be marvelous.

We all gathered in Cosmo's neighbor's little living room: the Hayses, the Styleses, Shirley, George and Hazel and me, Joyce and Gordon, and even Carlo. Carlo and I had to dance later that evening, but Nigel had promised to ferry everyone home afterwards. He was so proud of that jalopy.

"Is that safe for you?" I'd asked, genuinely concerned, and he said he had a chauffeur's cap ready.

"Y'all white folks," he said. "Nobody minds if I'm driving white folks."

It was crowded, but jolly. Della and Hannah had come armed with enough snacks to feed an army, and Bernie fiddled with the tuning until he'd gotten the right station.

Right at four, a wave of orchestral music cascaded into the room, and an announcer's voice said, "This is Alexander Armstrong, coming to you live from Carnegie Hall. In just a moment, we will be hearing from one of the most recently discovered talents in America. With me right here is conductor Konstantin Zafirov, who will be leading the orchestra tonight. Mr. Zafirov, tell us what will be hearing."

Konstantin really did have a lovely voice, I thought, as he answered the question—warm and comfortable. "Thank you, Mr. Armstrong! We are privileged to be here. Tonight our listeners will be treated to Beethoven's fifth piano concerto, Emperor, which was the first piece I ever heard tonight's pianist perform, two years ago as of tomorrow."

"And how did you react to that performance, Mr. Zafirov?"

"Listeners, I married her."

There was laughter, and Konstantin continued. "After the concerto, my wife and I have a special surprise piece to play for you, so don't go away. Ladies and gentlemen, please welcome the beautiful and talented Lydia Zafirov."

There was a roar of applause, and I closed my eyes, reaching for George's hand. He squeezed mine, and I listened to a performance I could almost see, even though I wasn't there. I could envision Mother in the green velvet dress she'd worn the night I met Konstantin, with the peridot earrings catching the lights, as her pretty hands danced over the keys.

And he would be entranced. The magic of what they became when they worked together was so strong, I could feel it through the airwaves.

"This ain't really my kinda music," Denver complained in a stage whisper.

"Hush, boy," Della said.

"I like it," said Cosmo.

He, too, was shushed.

I looked at George, and he squeezed my hand again. "You can put your arm around me," I whispered, and he did, looking a bit embarrassed that I'd had to ask.

There was a roar of applause at the end of the concerto, and Alex Armstrong's voice came through again, giving a word from the sponsor, and letting us know my mother was receiving a standing ovation. "Now Mr. Zafirov has joined her with his cello. The two of them are currently working on recording a second record together. What you are about to hear was the first piece they recorded, in 1934: Rachmaninoff's *Elegy*."

It was definitely a piece in which Mother was accompaniment to the cello, which took the starring role, but it wouldn't have been the same without the piano. It brought tears to my eyes, and I wondered if, when they played it, they ever thought of their first marriages, and the husband and wife they had each lost in such tragic circumstances. My mother had once written an elegy for Daddy, after all.

When it ended, I joined in clapping as loud as I could, hoping she could hear me all the way across the country.

I will add one more anecdote here. Sometime toward the end of March, I came in to meet one of my film-star passengers to find her on the phone ranting at someone on the other end. Privately Vicky Fairchild was a favorite of mine, because she danced beautifully, but I had made it a point to never ask autographs from my passengers, or even ask questions, but she seemed so genuinely upset that day, I ventured to enquire what was the matter.

"We're supposed to start shooting Moonlight in Madrid in three days, and my co-star had to go and break his ankle doing stupid things on the polo field!" she said, and sank into a chair.

"How awful," I said, genuinely sympathetic. "Who's going to take his place?"

"That's just it, we'll have to cancel everything if we can't find someone by the end of the week, and everyone who might be good for the role is already busy elsewhere."

"Tell me about the part," I said, picking up her suitcase and beckoning her to follow me.

"Laurence Oswald was to play it," she replied. "Personally not my preference, he's got a leaden left foot, but I was willing to work with it. He was the closest to a modern Rudolph Valentino they could rustle up with the budget they have."

"Miss Fairchild," I said, turning to face her and folding my arms, "I'm a dancer myself. I happen to know a lot of dancers, and I know one in particular who would be an absolute delight for you to work with and for moviegoers to look at." I took out the little wallet in which I kept my pilot's license and all my photographs of friends, and handed her a small copy of one Carlo had done to try to get attention from Hollywood.

Vicky Fairchild peered at it and back at me. "What a *dish*," she said. "And he's good?"

"Very good indeed."

"Can he act?"

"He's brilliant at it, and I don't think I'm too prejudiced. He had a screen test once. I'm sure it's in some archive somewhere."

"Can I keep this?" she asked.

"You can, but here—" I took it back and flipped it over, scrawling a telephone number over the back. "He lives here. His name is Carlo Vallejos. Don't tell him I sent you. Get the manager at Casa Del Sol to recommend him or something, to keep me out of it."

We shared a conspiratorial grin, and I helped her into her seat, loaded her luggage, and the rest of the flight was rather boring, really.

It was an overnight hop, which meant I'd be taking her back the following day. She was staying at a considerably more lush hotel than I was, so I didn't see her until she was ready to go back, but was she ever beaming then.

"I called my director," she said. "He contacted your Mr. Vallejos for an audition and he's in."

I couldn't stop smiling all the way back to Santa Monica.

It was the least I could do for a man I couldn't marry.

GEORGE

SANTA MONICA, CALIFORNIA: APRIL 6, 1936

*I*t was very odd to be on my own for Passover, but many of my new friends were so curious that, with Mrs. Hays' permission, I invited them to her dining room to participate. They'd gotten used to our Friday night candles and prayers, and Mamma had been here during the first bit of Hanukkah, but this was a high holy day, and therefore quite different.

Mrs. Hays let me take over her kitchen for the day, which felt nice. I'd always liked to do proper cooking, but didn't exactly have the ability with a camp stove.

It was a lovely evening, and lively, and we were all up far too late for a Monday night, but it was worth it. Louise had taken a night off from her hotel to join us, which pleased me immensely. After you were in bed and everyone else had left, Louise and I sat on the porch step in the dark, listening to the sounds of the city around us.

"Just a few more weeks," she said. "Hold me, George."

I put my arms around her and she nestled into me. "It doesn't come naturally to you to touch me, does it?" she asked.

"I'm afraid not." I hesitated. "I should tell you something, Lou. I'm... I'm not like other men. I don't get turned on by how someone looks. I have to know them. I think that's why it took me so long to twig your feelings about me, because you were always there and I took it for granted you always would be. I don't know exactly what I thought. I never imagined a future without you, but also I couldn't imagine caring for kissing and lovemaking enough to make you happy. I loved your mind and all the connections we had in every other way and was content with that."

She listened, quietly, and I went on. "I like making you happy. It might not come naturally to me, but I can learn. I don't even know if I'm making sense."

She turned to look into my face. "I need to be touched," she said. "I starve inside without it. Carlo had no compunctions about constantly touching me, and it made me feel nice, even if I did sometimes have to remind him to rein himself in. He's so... Latin."

We both laughed, and some of the tension I'd felt cleared away. I lifted her hand to my lips and kissed it. "Being in your presence makes me complete," I whispered. "That's all I will ever need. But I'll do my best to make sure you get what you need, too, and we can tell each other if the balance is off, aye?"

"I am going to be doing a lot of telling," she said, and sat up, tugging me closer with a twitch of my tie. "Right now, I'm telling you I want you to kiss me goodnight, and don't be in a hurry about the goodnight part."

So I kissed her, and although she eventually did go home, we never did get to the saying goodnight bit.

LOUISE
SANTA MONICA, CALIFORNIA: APRIL 26, 1936

After church, George and Hazel and I went to the station to meet his parents, the first of our family to arrive in advance of the wedding.

I was surprised to see that, in addition to their own luggage, they'd also brought the cedar chest from my bedroom (my "hopeless chest") and a number of cardboard boxes.

"What's all this?" I asked, picking one up to carry to the van.

"We packed your room for you," Mrs. Graham said. "There's a buyer for the house, at last. The rest of the furniture will be auctioned off."

I stopped in my tracks. "The piano," I said.

She smiled. "Not to worry. I've had it brought to our house until you have a place of your own to put it in."

I could have hugged her, if we weren't both carrying boxes and she didn't object to hugs.

Mr. Graham had scooped up Hazel, who was a little skeptical of him, having forgotten him, but I didn't doubt that soon he'd have charmed her back into the old joyful camaraderie George said they'd shared.

"Did you bring the thing I asked you to?" I said to Mrs. Graham, softly.

"I did indeed."

So when we got back to the Hayses', I cornered George and said, "You are going to take me on a date tonight."

He opened his mouth, but I laid a finger on his lips and beckoned him to follow me outside. I raised the lid of my hopeless chest and lifted out the blue dress I'd worn to our competition, holding it up to myself. "You owe me one proper date, George Graham, and I worked an extra shift to pay for it, so you needn't argue that we can't afford it. Your parents will look after Fizz."

"I don't have anything suitable."

"I'm well aware." I carefully hung the dress from a hook on the ceiling and bent again to take out his "penguin suit". "That's why I asked your mother to bring this."

I saw from his eyes that an evening in a penguin suit was a worthwhile tradeoff for a chance to be carefree young things for once in our highly responsibly-conducted lives.

"I made reservations for seven," I said. "Let's take this stuff inside. I need to iron the dress, and that suit could use a brushing, too."

When it was time to get ready, we parted ways briefly before reuniting on the landing. I had his bow tie in hand, and took my sweet time tying it.

"How does it fit?" I asked.

"You fill it beautifully."

"Not me, goose. Your suit. But thank you, even if it is three years and a bit late in coming."

He laughed. "It's tighter than it was, but nothing I can't tolerate for one night. And look."

Out of the front pocket he pinched out a few bits of tissue paper. "Your snowflakes. I forgot you put them in here."

I took them, feeling all soft inside remembering. I smoothed them carefully on my palm and turned into his room to tuck them inside the front cover of his Bible before returning to him.

So that was how we had a night like nothing I'd ever imagined possible for us. Nigel drove us to the hotel and promised to be back at midnight to collect the pumpkins. George scanned the dance floor. "I don't see your Carlo fellow here," he said.

"He's not 'my Carlo'," I said. "Anyway, he got a lucky break. He's going to be a movie star. No more of this life for him, or so he's convinced."

"What?"

I shrugged. "A director called him, needing a leading man to replace one who broke his ankle."

"Well, that's good, I guess. It's what he wanted, isn't it? Is he coming to the wedding?"

"He said, and I quote, 'I would have to object when the minister asks if there is any reason these two should not be wed.'" I laughed. "He also said, 'There is no accounting for taste,' at which point I said he was no longer invited."

"I'm perfectly content to not have him there," George said.

"It's refreshing to see you exhibit a little possessiveness. Anyway, they told him his name was too hard for people to pronounce so they renamed him Carl Antonio. He says he's going to invite us to the premiere. I told him we aren't making a trip to Hollywood just for that, but promised we'll see the picture wherever we are at the time."

We had a lovely dinner, and danced for ourselves. Some of the regulars recognized me, of course, and Joyce and Gordon cleared the floor at one point and put us on the spot to do something for the guests.

So George asked the band to play *It's Only a Paper Moon*, and we improvised one of our old foxtrot routines. It wasn't bad, considering neither of us had the time we once did to practice for hours.

Afterwards we drifted out to the moonlit courtyard, where the music floated out to us, but we could dance mostly unobserved. There were a few other people around, but the atmosphere still felt intimate and romantic.

"I love seeing you happy," George said, holding me closer than was his habit. "Remember when you said we were not a machine?"

I laughed. "I had forgotten. But I do now. Why?"

"Because you are a machine. A flying one."

He lifted me, spinning me around making airplane noises until my laughter made him lose his grip, and we staggered backwards onto a convenient bench, giggling like idiots.

I snuggled into him and he sighed contentedly. "This is perfect," I said. "Thank you for indulging me."

"You paid for it," he said. "Oughtn't I to be thanking you?"

"Kiss me," I said, and he pulled me into his arms.

Kissing George was very different from kissing Carlo. There was

a hunger and a passion in the way Carlo kissed. With George, while I had no doubt in my mind that he was being incredibly intentional about it, he was gentle and sweet, always.

"Do you want me?" I asked. "In bed, I mean."

He considered a moment. "I think I do."

342

"Are you nervous about it?"

"Yes." No hesitation that time. "Am I making up for all your waiting, or do you want something more?"

I laughed. "What I want is to drag you to one of the unoccupied bedrooms."

I could see him blushing even in the dim light, and I hugged him closely. "Oh, I do love you, my silly, adorable boy. A week more isn't going to hurt me. Do put your hands on me, though, please?"

He let them come to rest at my waist. "Up a bit, goose," I said, nipping his ear, and he did as he was told, his thumbs barely brushing the sides of my breasts through the silk.

"You like that?" he asked, his voice catching.

"It's heavenly. Don't stop."

He was trembling, and I wondered if he was battling some demon.

"I wish I could think of something intellectual enough to say to make you let your guard down," I whispered.

George raised one hand to twist a strand of my hair around his finger. "Do you fancy discussing the ontological argument for the existence of God?" There was a smile in his voice.

"Maybe if I had the slightest clue what all those words meant."

"It's the thought that counts." And he leant in close and kissed my neck, holding me tightly. His moustache tickled, and I threw back my head, trusting he wouldn't let me fall.

GEORGE

*U*pon receipt of our official wedding invitation, Uncle Jamie and Aunt Estelle decided to use their approaching thirtieth anniversary as an excuse to take a prolonged trip together.

"It is hard enough to drag him away from home for any reason," Aunt Estelle had written. "Let alone *without all the children*. High time he takes me somewhere new! Just me!"

They arrived the day after Louise's and my date at the hotel, laden with presents and messages from the left-behind children. They took a taxi to the Porter Hotel first to settle in, and then arranged for a car, which Aunt Estelle drove to the Hayses' house.

She fairly glowed with excitement. Uncle Jamie looked a little shaken, and I stifled a giggle as we all assembled for dinner at Hannah's table.

"You *must* take me for a spin," Aunt Estelle said to Louise. "I've always wanted to go up in an aeroplane!"

Louise readily agreed. "And you, Uncle Jamie?"

"No for anything," he drawled with exaggerated Scottishness. "I've no got a death wish, woman."

Estelle snickered. "Just because you've one foot in the grave already doesn't mean the rest of you is going to follow it yet."

His lips twitched at her teasing. "Getting here alive with you behind the wheel, tearing along on the wrong side of the road, was enough of a miracle."

The last-minute preparations for the wedding seemed not to

involve me or my opinions in any shape, form, or manner. Hazel and I went on long walks with Dad and Uncle Jamie on Tuesday. On Wednesday, the Zafirov contingent of the family arrived. Louise had some flight lessons that afternoon, so I went with the van, because I knew we needed more space than Nigel's jalopy afforded.

Lydia was clearly exhausted from the long trip, but still radiant. She held Mira's chair still whilst Konstantin and another young woman helped his daughter step onto the platform so she could sit in it.

"So you're George!" she said, before she'd even settled herself. "Well, I can see why Louise is smitten with you. Will you dance with me after the wedding? I bet you're strong enough to keep me upright for at least a few minutes."

"Mira, Mira," her father murmured, but he was smiling, and I decided Mira must be teasing, but just in case, I answered her gravely.

"I would be honored to dedicate a dance to you."

She waved toward the other young woman. "This is Margaret, by the way. My nurse-companion."

We shook hands all round. Konstantin collected his cello case and handed Mira her viola, and Lydia took his free hand whilst Margaret pushed Mira along the platform, followed by several porters bearing suitcases.

"Where am I taking you?" I asked, getting behind the driver's seat.

"The womenfolk are all going to sit in the back, says Mira," Konstantin told me as he got in beside me in the front. "We've rooms at the Porter Hotel."

"So have my aunt and uncle," I said.

I spent the next hour with them, helping them get settled. Margaret and Mira had one room, with a communicating door to Lydia and Konstantin's. Mira fussed over setting up her little icons, with some help from Margaret. I watched with interest, and she was happy to explain to me all about them. "I only brought two," she said. "These are the ones Tato keeps in his room and takes on his travels with him. This is Christ, and this is the Theotokos. That means God-bearer, because she's the mother of God. But you've probably studied Greek, so maybe you already knew that."

346

I grinned. "I'm rusty on Greek. Hebrew is another story."

"I hear you've been living in a colored neighborhood. What's it like?"

"It's been very eye-opening. They're wonderful people and I'm going to miss them when we leave for San Francisco."

She finished fussing with the icons and, satisfied, turned to me. "And you're Jewish. Does that mean you're having a Jewish wedding? I've never been to one."

"No, Louise wouldn't hear of it," I said. "She said eating kosher and keeping Shabbat and holy days is one thing, but she drew the line at a Jewish wedding. Anyway, I don't know if any rabbi would bother with me."

"Why?"

"Because I believe in Jesus as Messiah. Jewish people are suspicious of me, if not openly hostile, and Christians are suspicious of me because I still consider myself Jewish. It's an interesting position to be in. No, we're using the Presbyterian service."

"When do we get to see Louise?" Mira asked next. "And I'm dying to meet your little girl."

Louise thrived on the chaos, as always, but Mamma found it a bit much, so I took her back to her room (also at the Porter Hotel) and we sat there a while, resting our minds.

After a long time, she spoke. "I'm sure you two are looking forward to being off on your own at last."

"Very much. I've barely seen Louise since Sunday night, let alone had a minute alone with her. I only wish I could take her somewhere special after the wedding, besides driving the van outside the city or something."

Mamma laughed. "You'll manage. You'll find you can have quite satisfactory sex in unexpectedly cramped quarters if you're clever about it. Stop blushing."

"Your eyes are closed," I said, wondering how she knew.

"And *you* are predictable as the sunrise. If you're interested, your father can tell you stories..."

"I'm not, thank you."

She laughed, turning to me. "You are so unlike him, George. Honestly, Louise should thank her stars."

The night before the wedding, Uncle Jamie and Aunt Estelle showed up at the parsonage unexpectedly, just as you and I were finishing our supper in the back of the van.

"We've had ours," Aunt Estelle said, cheerfully. (I must have looked alarmed.) "Jamie wants to talk to you and hasn't had a chance to get you alone yet. I'll look after Hazel."

You, like everyone else in the world, adored my aunt. You immediately lost interest in finishing your food and climbed onto her lap demanding a story, which was promised on condition that you finished her supper.

I smiled fondly at the two of them as Uncle Jamie and I turned to head down the sidewalk: you snuggled up to Estelle with Potato and a stack of Beatrix Potter books on your lap, solemn and sweet and unbothered that I was walking away from you. Lindbergh came along with us.

Uncle Jamie was slower than he used to be; he was gradually resigning himself to the unpleasant fact that his leg would always hurt, and it was beginning to wear him down. He looked tired and too old compared to Dad. I asked, "Are you well, Uncle Jamie? You don't look it."

He gave me a wry, mirthless smile. "I am very well, apart from this leg of mine," he said. "It has been a long journey, and although we have enjoyed every minute of it, Estelle's energy has always been three times my own. It is all I can do to keep up with her." He leant back against a tree trunk and studied me. "You and Louise are glowing. Or like starving, besotted puppies. Perhaps a bit of both."

I laughed, and he went on. "Estelle tells me you have no rings."

"Not yet," I admitted. "We thought it would be better to get them later, when we can spare the money. Maybe after I've finished seminary and get a church of my own."

"Wise of you. You won't be less married for not having one right away." He continued to study me, his fingers drumming lightly on the horse handle of his walking stick. Then, with a shyness I'd never seen in him before, he twisted something off the little finger of his right hand and held it out to me. "But I'd like for Louise to have this one, if you're willing she should."

I took the ring, eyes locked with his, questioning, before dropping my gaze to study the delicate gold band in the golden evening light, unsure what to say, but before I could decide, he'd launched into a story.

"In 1848, a man named Peter Davies bought that ring for his beloved intended, Clara, but on his way to give it to her, he got word she was dead of cholera. He never married, but wore the ring in her memory. Nearly fifty years later, he befriended a lonely, frightened young man who was starving for a father's love..."

He drifted off, and after a moment I prompted him. "You?"

"Aye, me," he said, coming back to the present. "I was with him when he died. I took that ring off his hand, put it on my own, and I've always worn it myself since—except during the war, when I wore my rings on a chain. Anyway, it has words engraved on the inside of the band, in Welsh. *Ti a fi am byth.* It means 'you and me forever'."

"And you want to part with it now?"

"I do," he said. "I was too selfish to give it to my own wife, back when we became engaged—" He shot me a crooked smile. "I needed it myself. All right, and also I was afraid it was bad luck. I was scared of her dying too if I was to let her have it. But of course that's ridiculous, and it's time to pass it on so it can belong to a much-loved lass, as it was meant to do."

"And Aunt Estelle doesn't want it?"

"I asked her. She says she only wants the ones I've given her and is very happy at the idea that Louise should have it."

"Thank you," I said, voice unsteady, and stepped up to him to hold him tightly. "Thank you isn't sufficient. She will be thrilled and honored." I took his hand, and slipped the ring back on, to settle into the groove nearly forty years of wearing it had created in his finger. "You keep it until it's needed, will you? We can surprise her. I'll just have to let Reverend Hays know we'll need that bit of the service after all."

GEORGE

SAN FERNANDO, CALIFORNIA: MAY 2, 1936

*T*he next morning at nine o'clock, my father and Uncle Jamie came to the parsonage. Hannah was busy with the other church ladies, decorating the church with all the flowers they could procure, so I let them in.

"Our women told us to make ourselves scarce," Dad said, following me up the stairs. "They'll be along later in the car. Estelle is driving, so I can't guarantee the cake will get here in one piece."

I laughed and tested your bathwater. "I'm no fashed about the cake," I said, "as long as my bride gets here in one piece. Fizz!" I called.

You were nowhere to be seen, and I stepped out into the hall and called again. Still no answer.

"She goes like a rabbit to ground if she knows she has to have a bath," I said, and I stepped into our room to hunt for the truant child.

You and one of the flower ladies' little girls were giggling, hiding under my bed. I dragged you out, tucked you under my arm like a naughty monkey, and hauled you back to the bathroom, followed by the other little girl whose name I couldn't remember.

I stripped you out of your nightie with difficulty, plunked you into the bath, and scrubbed you down, amid howls of protest. When you were clean and wrapped in a towel, glaring at me from the security of Gran-Da's arms, Uncle Jamie appeared with a parcel. "Your mother sent this over. It's what Hazel is to wear, she says."

"Oh, good," I said. "I'd forgotten it."

Dad laughed. "Hand it over, Jamie. I'll get her ready."

We crossed the hall to the bedroom and I tossed Dad your

stockings and underwear from a nearby drawer and soon you were submitting to his capable dressing.

"Where's Konstantin?"

"He's in the church with Mira and Lydia. They've got the music covered. What's to be done with her hair?" Dad gestured to your tangled head.

I groaned. "I have no idea. Just comb it, I guess." I took the comb from my pocket and he caught it deftly when I tossed it to him. "And then read her stories to keep her out of dirt and mischief, aye? And you—what's your name?"

"Sadie," said the little girl.

"Sadie, you stay and listen to the stories, too."

"Yes, sir."

I disappeared into the bathroom myself then, and when I came out, it was to see Uncle Jamie in the rocking chair with you on one knee and Sadie on the other, reading you *The Tale of Two Bad Mice*, which had surely never been performed quite so Scottishly before. I dressed with

shaking hands, hardly able to contain my nerves now that I no longer had your preparations to distract me.

Dad took pity on me and tied my tie for me, a new one also sent by Mamma.

Reverend Hays emerged from his office at ten-thirty and the women still hadn't appeared. I took him aside to speak to him about the ring. Belinda showed up looking for Sadie, with several other little girls whose mothers had shooed them out of the church, and you joined the group, a lone blonde head in a sea of black curls and braids. Dad followed, to be sure she stayed clean, and chatted amiably with any hapless person who came within speaking distance. I paced restlessly until Uncle Jamie, at the window, told me the car had arrived.

"Turn around," he said, making a spinning movement with his finger. "Let her come in and tell you when to look."

I obeyed, and stood rocking on my feet until I felt a hand on my shoulder and heard Louise tell me, "You can look now."

If I'd thought her ice-blue competition dress had been ravishing, this was even more so. It was made of (and I quote Louise here, because I would have called it "pink shiny stuff") rose-gold charmeuse, the same as Hazel's dress. It was drapey and elegant and, as I knew she intended it to be, reusable. She wore no veil, only a delicate circlet of silk flowers in her hair, and her mother's pearl earrings.

"Don't cry yet," she whispered impishly, touching my face and stroking away the errant, involuntary tear with her thumb. "Ceremony hasn't even started yet. Now go on into the church. You're supposed to be waiting for me in there!"

You, tired of being ignored by your favorite father, came and clung to my legs. "Hold you, Da," you demanded, so I scooped you up.

"Just for a minute," I said. "You'll have to sit with Gran and Gran-Da when the ceremony starts."

I pushed open the church's side door and went in. "What's cermony?" you asked.

"It's when your mama and I get married," I said.

"Oh."

"And afterwards we'll have cake and dance."

"Oh!"

I saw you had acquired a circlet of flowers of your own at some point since I last saw you, only it was knocked askew. I didn't fix it. It was far more like you to have it crooked, anyway.

Konstantin and Mira serenaded us all as the pews slowly filled. Della and her father and all five of the children. Cosmo, who'd agreed to be my best man, came to join me at the sidelines, where I continued holding Hazel until Reverend Hays indicated it was time to start. Reluctantly, you let go of me to sit between Aunt Estelle and Gran, and Cosmo and I went to stand and wait.

There was a pause in the music, and the two Zafirovs started into an arrangement of the Flower Duet from *Lakme*, and Uncle Jamie walked Louise up the aisle to me. Mira handed her companion her viola and wheeled herself over to Louise's side.

"Forasmuch!" began Reverend Hays, in a voice that could probably be heard for a square block, "as these two persons have come hither to be made one in this holy estate, if there be any here present who knows any just cause, why they may not lawfully be joined in marriage, I require him now to make it known, or ever after to hold his peace."

"Piece of cake?" you asked, hopefully, in the silence that followed, and suddenly everyone was laughing, which made you slouch angrily. Mamma leaned down, presumably to whisper an explanation, and Louise's eyes danced.

Reverend Hays grinned and waited for everyone to settle back down before continuing. "Who giveth this woman to be married to this man?"

"I do," said Uncle Jamie, with enthusiastic approval. He took her hand, Reverend Hays took mine, and joined them together. I was impressed with Louise's ability to hold herself so placidly together when I felt ready to burst into tears at any second.

I suppose every couple must have its stoic half.

Her voice, steady and familiar, comforted me. "I, Louise Pearson, take thee, George Graham, to be my wedded husband, to be thy loving and faithful wife, in plenty and in want, in joy and in sorrow, in sickness and in health, as long as we both shall live."

The first tiny crack in her composure appeared when Reverend Hays proceeded to ask for the ring. She glanced at me in alarm. I could hear her thinking, *Has he forgotten we haven't got rings?*

But Uncle Jamie had taken the promised band off his finger and handed it to me, and that's when she started to cry and didn't stop until everything was over.

"The Lord bless you and keep you: the Lord make His face to shine upon you and be gracious unto you: the Lord lift up His countenance upon you and give you peace: both now and in the life everlasting. Amen."

We were supposed to kiss, but I forgot until prompted, and even then I didn't realize what I was being prompted to do until Louise took the initiative to step forward and kiss me.

And just like that, I had completed my little family. You, as uninterested in adults being gooey as I had ever been, ran up to us and squished in between us, tugging at my sleeve and forcing us to stop soppily gazing at each other. "Cake now?" you demanded, not as loudly as your previous comment, but definitely loud enough to be heard.

Everyone cheered as I swept you up in one arm, took Louise's with the other, and the three of us went down the aisle together and out into the sunshine.

The parsonage and the entire area around the church and in the church buzzed with people then. Everyone had brought food, and you contentedly trailed about with Sadie and several others, helping yourself to more cake than any two-year-old should ever eat and getting away with it, showing off the tolerant Potato's pink neck ribbon to anyone who would stop long enough to look, losing your floral circlet, and becoming gradually grubbier. Louise and I were too busy being congratulated and chatted with to have a moment to ourselves, but I hardly let go of Louise's hand, afraid she might be spirited away and the entire day turn out to be a dream. She looked so lovely, flushed with excitement, the warmth of the day, and sheer joy. Eventually the crowd thinned until only the family, the Hayses, and the Styleses were left, scattered around the parsonage porch and the little front yard. Konstantin and Mira had brought their instruments outside and Uncle Jamie had pulled out his flute. Cosmo twanged along by ear on his ever-present mandolin. You fell asleep on me, surfeited with cake and attention. Your hair clung damply to your head, and your rosy mouth hung open ungracefully.

"Isn't she precious?" I said, an inexplicable wave of adoration rushing over me.

"I never dreamed I'd hear you say that about a child," Louise said. She leant against me, her chin on my shoulder, exuding happiness. Aunt Estelle regaled us with stories of her and Uncle Jamie's honeymoon in Paris and the particular weirdness they experienced as two people incredibly in love and yet also incredibly unused to spending time together.

"We were so chaperoned in those days, and had such a dreadfully long engagement," Aunt Estelle said. "My mother's doing, I found out later. She hoped I'd outgrow it and pick a man she liked better, but I did not." She laughed.

"She seems to have forgiven me for existing by now," Uncle Jamie said. Aunt Estelle lovingly punched him in the arm.

"Anyway, it was one thing to write endless letters and think you are on very intimate terms with someone and completely another to find yourself alone with him someplace and realizing you haven't a clue what they're actually like to be with."

Uncle Jamie beamed at her with the fondness only she inspired in him, and laid a hand on her knee. "It was rather a shock. Thirty years later, I'm still not over it."

She swatted at him, and he caught her hand and kissed it, then said, "George and Louise ought to have a dance, don't you think?"

There was a general assent, and he asked what Louise wanted him to play.

"*Beautiful Dreamer*," she replied without hesitation. "We can waltz to that."

I transferred you to Lydia's arms, and Louise took my hand, leading me a little distance away. "And be out of earshot," she added under her breath, lifting my hand to kiss it. "Still want them all over me."

"Soon," I promised. And we fell into step.

"It will be interesting," Louise said into my ear.

"What will?"

"Spending our wedding night with a clingy koala child, a dog, and the clingy koala child's voyeuristic cat." She said it so matter-of-factly I burst out laughing.

"We'll manage," I said. "Somehow. Although it's not exactly

shaping up to be the romantic evening worthy of you."

"I've been resigned to it." She snuggled into me. "I missed this so much. It was never the same with Carlo. Your arms are home. And I don't care where we spend tonight as long as I'm there, in your arms."

I brushed her cheek with my lips and lifted her off her feet, spinning her around several times.

"You make that look so easy," Aunt Estelle called out. "Dreamy, just dreamy."

After a few more songs and the promised dance with Mira, Uncle Jamie stood and said, "All right. In the car, you two."

As if they'd rehearsed it, he and Dad escorted us into the car, opening doors on either side for us, closing them, and Dad got behind the wheel and drove off.

"What are we doing?" I asked.

"You'll see," was all Dad would say. Louise shrugged, as confused as I was, although it was clear we were heading toward Santa Monica.

We pulled up in front of Louise's hotel, and Dad turned in his seat, dropping a key into Louise's lap. "All yours for the night," he said. "Now run along and make the most of it!"

I stared, speechless, but Louise understood immediately. "You got us a room, here?"

"You deserve at least one night all to yourselves," Dad said, winking, and Louise threw her arms around his neck from behind and nearly choked him in her enthusiasm, then pushed at my shoulder. "Well, what are you waiting for, George? Get out so I can get out!"

I stepped to the sidewalk, gave Louise my hand, and leant in to hug Dad (without choking him). "Thanks," I said, shyly.

"My son should have the best," he said softly, mussing my hair. "We'll be back here at noon tomorrow so we can all go out for lunch."

Then he was gone, leaving us alone on the sidewalk.

Louise fairly vibrated. She took my hand and walked off at a rapid clip into the sumptuous lobby. "How did Dad afford this?" I whistled softly. Louise had told me what the rooms cost the last time we were here.

"I suspect all of them pitched in together for it." She looked at the key for the room number. "We're on the fourth floor. Come on!"

We tried to act dignified as we took the elevator, but the giddiness we both felt put paid to that. We found the door and Louise handed me the key. "Do I carry you over the threshold?"

"I think that's supposed to be when we have a house," she said.

"Well, let's practice." I swept her up and through the door, kicking it shut behind me.

We both stared at the plush room. I let Louise slide down and put her feet on the floor.

They'd already been here, our mothers. There was a bottle of cider and two glasses and clothes to change into the next morning.

Louise pulled off her gloves and twirled with her arms out, flopping backwards onto the bed.

"I had the most instructive conversation yesterday afternoon," she said, mischief in her voice.

I sat on the edge of the bed, and she pulled me down so I lay beside her, lacing her fingers with mine. "Oh?" I said, wondering if my tightly wound tension was showing.

"Relax, George, you're like an oak slab or something. Aunt Estelle asked our mothers if I had been Talked To About My Wedding Night yet and was horrified to learn I had not. So she took it upon herself to do the honors. My mother was red as a beet the entire time, and yours was smirking into her hand and trying not to show it. I was trying hard to be the wide-eyed innocent to whom this was all shocking news, but I'm not sure I succeeded."

I turned my head to look at her. "How'd you find out all that stuff, then?"

She bit back a smile, trailing her fingertips up and down my hand. "Well, once upon a time your mother let drop the fact she'd given you a book about 'boy things', and I found it in your drawer and read it."

"You read—that?" I choked out, not sure if I was amused or horrified.

"Oh yes. The extra commentary by your father was the most enlightening of all."

"I shouldn't admit this, but I never opened that book until 1932. I didn't want to know and couldn't have possibly been less interested."

She howled with laughter. "Why am I not surprised? Then Aunt

Estelle asked if I had a fancy nightie to wear and I said I didn't want to take the time to change into something I was going to take off as quickly as possible anyway..."

She met my eyes, quite obviously waiting for me to suggest we get started taking things off.

I was enjoying looking at her in this delighted mood, feeling myself calming a bit, and after a moment she sat up and walked over to the table where the cider was, and I watched her appreciatively. I would undress her like she wanted. Just not quite yet.

She opened the bottle of cider and poured it out, and I joined her. We clinked our glasses together and drank, then I wandered over to the window with mine and looked out.

A crescent moon hung in the sky. Louise came and put her arms

around me from behind, resting her chin on my shoulder. I could feel her smiling.

"It's our moon," she said. I knew she meant our paper moon photograph.

"So it is," I said, and began singing softly.

> *It's only a paper moon*
> *Sailing over a cardboard sea,*
> *But it wouldn't be make-believe*
> *If you believed in me.*

Louise's arm reached for the cord of the curtains and with one swift yank shut them tight.

"Yes, George, I believe in you," she said. "Now take me to the moon."

Author's Note

First of all, the stickler for accuracy in me must apologize for taking liberties with the moon's actual phase on George and Louise's wedding night (a waxing gibbous, not a crescent). Please allow my taking this liberty for the sake of the story. It is, after all, fiction.

Now that's off my mind, let's talk about other things.

I first conceived of this book sometime in 2019, shortly after finishing the first version of *The Summer I Found Home*, and before *Shadows From the Sky* had even been suggested to my mind. It's been in the works for so long I can't even remember all the permutations it's been through to get to what you currently hold in your hand (also, it's been roughly a century since the beginning of the pandemic AMIRITE).

As with the previous two books, I heavily relied on local newspapers for creating a real-life framework to hang my plot on. The films George and Louise go to see were actually playing those days. Keith Smith was a real young man who died when his plane crashed in Roseburg. And the fire at the Capitol Building did, of course, happen.

I spent several afternoons up in Salem a while back walking the area George and Louise frequent, and pored over maps as well, to get my brain wrapped around the different orientation the previous Capitol Building had compared to the current one. (Incidentally, I think our current building is one of the ugliest capitols in the entire country, surpassed only by Florida, New Mexico, and North Dakota, but that's neither here nor there. My husband says I am being unnecessarily brutal and that the current capitol is "cool".) Reading over accounts of the fire, the thing that really stood out to me was the colorful flames people mentioned. This was caused, apparently, by the various kinds of metals that were in the dome.

Louise's Santa Monica airfield is inspired by Clover Field (https://cloverfield.org/), which operated from 1921-1939.

While the plot was up in the air for a long time, two things have always remained the same.

The first of these was Hazel. She popped into my head, named, as vividly and forcefully as Aveline Perrault's image did for *The War in Our Hearts*, and made it very clear that she was George's biological child but her mother was decidedly not Louise. It set off the domino run in my mind to figure out how that would come to pass, considering George is autistic and pretty clearly asexual.

The second of these was the migrant aspect. Originally I had toyed with the idea of George reliving his escapade of 1925 by train-hopping across country. Then I had him using a horse and surrey before settling on the repurposed delivery van. Where he was going and why were up in the air for a long time.

A late alteration to the manuscript was switching it to a dual POV. Originally the entire book was George narrating, but that put great limitations on how much real estate Louise got, page-wise, and much as I love George, he is pretty boring without the counterbalance of Louise, and one of my betas (understandably) wanted more Carlo Vallejos. So dual POV it became, and it was a good decision.

Despite not having any plans to write specifically about George and Louise's future lives, I do know that George will get deeply involved in the civil rights movement, and I needed to set him on that trajectory. I wasn't sure at first how to do it, until my newspaper perusals introduced me to *The California Eagle*, a Black newspaper based in San Fernando. So I knew where to take George when he got to California. But it wasn't enough for him to accidentally drift into the neighborhood; I wanted him to form a strong bond with a Black person before he ever got there. Enter Cosmo. The altercation with Uncle Boyd seemed like the perfect catalyst to bring them together, and I hope you loved the Styles bunch as much as I have come to!

Before saying *au revoir* to these characters for the foreseeable future, Lydia's arc needed some closure. Many of my readers really root for her, especially since the release of my novella *élégie*, and so I engaged in some fanfiction writing about my own characters. (I confess I frequently do this just to learn more about them.) This is how it started, in a message to a friend:

> *just stream-of-consciousness with me for a moment that lydia is playing in seattle at some point after louise runs off and the conductor of whatever she's part of, i would like to think beethoven's emperor concerto because i have A Thing™ for it, finds her incredibly interesting, turns out he's got his own tragic backstory because what is an eva seyler character if not defined by tragic backstory and a daughter a few years older than louise, la la la he has connections and a fast-developing crush, east coast concerts, what-would-you-say-to-touring-europe-with-me, who really needed oberlin when you're forking genius lydia pearson anyway, nobody at home has a clue about the probably-hot conductor's role in facilitating all of this because ofc why would she mention it to anyone, oops snogfest at the parthenon*

So Konstantin Zafirov came into existence, launching me into research on Orthodox Christianity and the Macedonian language, because rabbit holing is what I do best. Obviously my initial ideas did not all hold true to how the characters developed in the end, but I just know that there will be a snogfest at the Parthenon in their future, because OF COURSE THERE WILL BE.

I was limited in how much I could put into this book about Lydia and Konstantin, because the Zafirovs are the sidest of side characters, but I hope you have fun filling in blanks with your lively imaginations.

Thank you to Carol, Fayelle, Jen, Karen, Meggan, and Tara, who all helped this book along in some way.

A special thank you to Father Steve and Presbytera Katie of Holy Resurrection Greek Orthodox Church in Salem, as well as my long-time online friend Elizabeth, for patiently answering so many Orthodoxy questions.

The lyrics for *It's Only a Paper Moon* are by Yip Harburg and Billy Rose, first published in 1933.

The lyrics for *Make Believe* are from *Show Boat*, by Oscar Hammerstein II, first published in 1927.

The quote from *Quiet Hints to Growing Preachers in My Study* by Charles Edward Jefferson is from pages 179 and 180 of the 1901 edition.

The quote from *White Nights* at the beginning of Part 3 is from the Constance Garnett translation, 1918.

ABOUT THE AUTHOR

Eva was born in Jacksonville, Florida. She left that humidity pit at the age of three and spent the next twenty-one years in California, Idaho, Kentucky, and Washington before ending up in Oregon, where she now lives on a homestead in the western foothills with her husband and five children, two of whom are human.

ALSO BY EVA SEYLER

NOVELS:
The War in Our Hearts
This Great Wilderness
The Summer I Found Home
Shadows From the Sky

NOVELLAS:
Ripples
élégie

FIND EVA ON SOCIAL MEDIA

Bluesky: @theevaseyler
Instagram: @theevaseyler
Facebook: /authorevaseyler

To get book recs and news, consider subscribing to Eva's email newsletter here: https://www.evaseyler.com/index.php/contact-eva-seyler/subscribe-to-newsletter/